THE TEA PLANTER'S CLUB

ANN BENNETT

589076

Andaman Press

For Mary

1

EDITH

The Tea Planter's Club, Calcutta, 1980

EDITH MAYHEW STOOD on the hotel terrace amongst the potted geraniums, waving goodbye to the last guests as their rickshaw wobbled out through the wrought-iron gates and turned left onto Bunder Street, disappearing instantly into the crowds. With a deep sigh, she turned back into the empty lobby. Anesh, the receptionist, was behind the counter making his final entries in the ledgers.

'All finish, madam?' he asked, opening the till and starting to cash up.

'All finished, Anesh,' Edith said, forcing a smile, while a great feeling of emptiness washed over her. She looked around the deserted lobby; the cushions on the basket chairs still bore the indents from the last occupants; two half-finished cups on the coffee table, one with a lipstick stain, the only evidence of the recently departed guests. How many people had passed through here down the years since Edith had arrived on that fateful day back in 1938? For a moment, it was as if she could see faint shadows of them all converging on the lobby at once; arriving with their luggage, sipping welcome drinks on the basket chairs, leaning on the reception desk, returning hot and flustered from sight-seeing, rushing for a taxi. But now there was only silence. The old place was finally empty.

Edith wandered absently through the lobby, plumping cushions, straightening magazines, automatically running her fingers along sideboards and the backs of chairs on the lookout for dust, forgetting that today it didn't matter. She went into the dining room, with its linen tablecloths, potted aspidistras and framed prints of hunting scenes, where the two elderly "boys" dressed in starched aprons were clearing up from breakfast for the very last time. She watched their slow, stooping progress, as they loaded dirty dishes onto trays and removed the hotplates, as she had every day for the past forty years, only today she had tears in her eyes. She knew that neither of these faithful old gentlemen would ever find another job; that they'd given their lives to this place, asking for so little in return, and that tomorrow they would travel back to their villages in the hills for the very last time.

One of them, old Roshan, looked up, put his hands together.

'Namaste, madam,' he said, inclining his head, and she returned the greeting.

It all felt so final now, but it was what she'd been planning for some time. Trade had been dropping off for years and, a few months ago, she'd finally had to admit that the business could no longer make ends meet. There was so much competition now from the guesthouses and hostels along Bunder Street, attracting backpackers with their rock bottom prices, pool tables and cheap beers. No backpackers ever came to stay at the Tea Planter's Club, nor would Edith have welcomed them, with their bare feet and filthy T shirts. There was a dress code in all public parts of the hotel which had been rigidly maintained since the glory days of the Raj. But even the better-heeled travellers now tended to head for the big chain hotels on Chowringhee Road with their swimming pools and happy hours. No, no one seemed to want to partake of "gracious colonial living" anymore. The world had changed so much since Edith had come here as a young woman and she knew she hadn't moved with the times.

What would Gregory say if he was here, not lying six foot under in that war cemetery in Singapore? He would never have sanctioned her selling the place, but Edith normally got her way in the end.

She closed the doors to the dining room, leaving the boys to their final clear-up, wandered through the hallway and started climbing the wide, sweeping staircase. This was where Edith had hung framed portraits of interesting or famous guests; the faces of several tea planters stared down at her, from the days when the building really had been their club. They stood stiffly with their rifles next to their elephants or dead tigers. There were members of the British Raj peering solemnly from under their solar topees, a few lesser-known actors, a couple of Indian film stars.

The man from Clover Hotels, the multinational chain that was buying the place, had asked Edith to leave the pictures; 'So redolent of a past era, Mrs Mayhew. They add a certain olde-worlde charm,' he'd said. 'We're going to try to keep that if we can, whilst tastefully upgrading, of course.'

'Of course,' she'd echoed in a whisper, pleased that not everything she held dear would be ripped down or painted over.

But there was one photograph that she wouldn't be leaving behind. She peered at it now; it was of Edith and her sister, Betty, taken the week they had arrived at the hotel. Aged 26 and 24; fresh-faced, straight off the ship from England and bursting with enthusiasm for their Indian adventure. She could still see it shining in their eyes all these years later. The raw energy and sheer exuberance of youth.

She took the framed photograph off the wall and traced the line of her sister's jaw with her finger.

'How beautiful you were... you *are*, Betty,' she said, speaking directly to those dark, liquid eyes, the perfectly formed mouth she'd always envied.

'Why didn't you come back?'

Saying those words out loud now, made Edith experience another rush of nerves at the thought of leaving the place behind; the place where Betty knew to find her and where they'd last been together. It was 38 years since she'd received her last letter from Betty, telling Edith that Rangoon was falling to the Japanese and she was setting off for Calcutta, travelling on foot if needs be, that she would be with her as soon as she could. But the weeks had passed and Betty had never arrived. Weeks turned into months and months into years without any word. Edith had made enquiries of the authorities again and again, but had always drawn a blank.

During those first few terrible, empty years, Edith had often sat on the edge of the terrace, her eyes glued the gates. She expected Betty to stroll through them demanding a chota peg as cool as cucumber, but as the years had slipped by, she'd stopped watching quite so much. But she'd never quite given up hope. In fact, if she'd heard Betty's strident tones in the lobby now, she wouldn't have been at all surprised.

She knew that selling up and leaving the hotel would be severing that final link with her sister. It would amount to admitting that Betty was never going to stride across the terrace issuing orders. Butterflies besieged Edith at the thought of leaving all this behind. It was so much a part of her. How would she ever survive without it?

She looked again at Betty's smile, at her dancing eyes, and felt that familiar pang of guilt she always got when looking at that picture.

'I'm so sorry, Betty. I let you down. I know that and I regret it deeply,' she whispered, but no amount of apology could wipe away the guilt of decades, or the nagging feeling that perhaps the true reason Betty hadn't returned was because she'd known all along about Edith's betrayal.

Suppressing those thoughts, Edith put the picture down on the step beside her and let her mind wander back to the day the two of them had first arrived at the hotel. It was pure chance that they had stumbled upon this particular establishment. She'd often wondered how their lives would have panned out if they'd chanced upon somewhere different.

They'd come out to India after both their parents had died within a few months of each other. That might have been a blow to many people, but to Edith and Betty it had been a blessed release. Both parents were incurable alcoholics who'd drunk their way through the family money and incurred substantial debts on top. Edith and Betty had left home long before the final descent, to find jobs and to live together in a flat in Clapham. She remembers that time with warmth; they didn't have much money, but they'd tried to live just like any other young women, spending time with friends, going to the theatre and cinema on Saturday nights.

They'd been so close then, the two of them. But she shudders at the memory of the squalid apartment in Kensington where her parents had ended up, having sold successively smaller houses along the way. It was dark and smelly and crammed with heavy furniture. Every surface was covered in empty bottles, overflowing ashtrays and dirty glasses.

Edith and Betty had had to sell the flat to pay off the debts. An uncle had taken pity on them and had paid for tickets to India so they could both have a new start. Having spent his own youth in India in the army, his house in Hampshire was filled with memorabilia; animal skins, a tiger's head, a hollowed-out elephant's foot and a lot of heavy, teak furniture.

'Endless opportunities on the sub-continent for bright young women like you,' he'd told them. 'Head for Calcutta. Streets paved with gold. You can't go wrong there.'

He hadn't expanded on what those opportunities might be, but neither of them had bothered too much about that; they were just glad to get away and to leave London and its ugly memories far behind.

They'd been so excited at the thought of making a new life for themselves overseas. They boarded the British India Steam Navigation Company's *SS Dunera* full of hope for the future, and the voyage had shown them that their hopes were not misplaced. The generosity of their uncle meant that they travelled first class. On board were many young men returning from home leave, or travelling out to take up jobs in the Indian Civil Service; planters, officers, merchants, engineers, box-wallahs (as businessmen were known). There were a few other young women like themselves, but the women were far outnumbered by the men. They were never at a loss for a dancing partner, or someone to walk out onto the moonlit deck with to look at the stars.

During the voyage, Betty received no fewer than four proposals of marriage, but although she flirted mercilessly with all her suitors, to Edith's mind giving them false hope, she turned them all down.

'I'm not going to give up this adventure for life in some bungalow on some stuffy British station, playing cards in the club and complaining about the servants,' she'd said, as they lay awake side by side in their cabin one night, talking over the evening's events. Edith hadn't received any offers of marriage, but she took that in her stride. She was used to standing aside for her more attractive younger sister. It was just how life was back then.

When the ship docked at Kiddapore Docks in Calcutta, they took a rickshaw to Bunder Street where their uncle had told them they would be able to find a reasonably priced hotel. The rickshaw brought them all the way from the docks and the two of them had been entranced by the sights and sounds of the city; they passed exotic temples, where discordant bells chimed and incense and smoke wafted from archways, vibrant markets where exotic fruits were piled high on stalls and women in brightly coloured sarees squatted on the pavement gossiping, where the air was filled with the smell of cooking and spices mixed with open drains, and where whole families camped out under tarpaulins on the pavements. They passed Fort William, a massive, fortified structure on the banks of the river, then they crossed the maidan, a huge expanse of open grassland, where sprinklers pumped out precious water and lawn-mowers pulled by bullocks made perfect stripes in the lawn. In contrast to this show of colonial elegance, at every crossroads, ubiquitous beggars who lived in makeshift shelters beside the road, would emerge with hands held out and pleading eyes, desperate for a coin or two.

Bunder Street was a busy, crowded road off Chowringhee, the main thoroughfare that ran all down one side of the maidan. The rickshaw moved slowly along it. They passed a couple of hotels that looked promising; Queen's Lodge and Park Hotel, but had already agreed to go the length of the road before making any decisions.

They were just passing the gates of the Tea Planter's Club when there was a disturbance on the pavement beside them. A fight had broken out between two men, and others were joining in. Punches were being thrown in every direction, hate-filled faces loomed, shouts of anger filled the air. Suddenly the mob spilled off the pavement and onto the road in front of their rickshaw, forcing their rickshaw-wallah to stop dead. At that moment, to her horror, Edith saw the flash of a blade, a knife raised then plunged into soft flesh. One man fell to the ground yelling, clutching his stomach, and the mob surrounded him, but not before Edith had seen the blood gushing from his wound, spreading quickly over his white tunic.

She turned to Betty, but Betty's face had completely drained of colour and her eyes were flickering. Edith leaned forward to the rickshaw-wallah.

'She's going to faint. Can we go into this building?'

He turned into the gates of the Tea Planter's Club and drew up beside the entrance just as Betty collapsed into Edith's arms. Within seconds they were surrounded by uniformed staff. They quickly lifted Betty from the rickshaw, carried her gently under the covered portico and laid her out on one of the sofas in the reception area. A blanket was brought to cover her. Edith followed gratefully and when she looked back at the rickshaw, saw that their luggage had been unloaded and had been brought into the lobby.

A tall British man dressed casually in linens strolled towards her.

'I'm sorry,' began Edith. 'There must be some mistake. We're not guests here. It's just that there was a stabbing outside and my sister fainted.'

'I'm so sorry to hear that,' said the man mildly. 'The police will be along shortly to break up the mob. Things like that aren't uncommon around these parts, I'm afraid. There's quite a lot of feuding between factions. I hope my staff are looking after your sister.'

Edith glanced over at Betty. One of the uniformed bearers was kneeling beside her, fanning her face furiously, another was bringing a glass of water.

'They've been wonderful. So kind. It's just that... we can't stay here.'

'Of course you can. We have spare rooms.'

'But it's a club, isn't it? We're not members. Nor are we tea planters, I'm afraid.'

'Oh, that doesn't matter anymore. I've just kept the name. It started out as a club for tea planters and everyone knows it by that name. We've been letting rooms out to other people for quite a few years now. You have to pay a nominal fee to be a temporary member, that's all. It's just a formality.'

Edith heaved a sigh of relief. 'Well then, if you don't mind, we'll take a twin room if you have one.'

'Of course. We have a lovely suite upstairs. How long will you be staying?' he asked.

'I'm not sure. We've come to live in the city and we need to have a base until we've found somewhere permanent to stay.'

'That sounds perfect,' said the owner, smiling at her. She noticed the wrinkles around his eyes as he smiled and the fact that his skin was deeply tanned. 'Stay as long as you like,' he added.

And she had stayed. She'd stayed for forty-two years to be precise, and that first impression of Gregory had remained with her down the years. It had told her everything she needed to know about him; that he was an open, kind, generous-hearted and gentle man with no side to him.

Thinking back now, it struck her that the end of her extended stay was fast approaching. And that fact filled her with mixed emotions. She took the photograph, brought it down the stairs and laid it on one of the coffee tables in the lobby.

Taking a deep breath, she walked through the hotel to the back of the building, past the kitchen where the chefs were clearing up for the very last time, and into the back yard where the servants' rooms opened off a concrete courtyard. Tentatively, she approached the one at the far end. It was the best room; the biggest one, given to the most senior member of staff.

Outside, on the step, lay the stray dog whom Subash, the chief bearer, had loved and fed with scraps from the kitchen. The other servants still fed him, but he refused to leave Subash's doorway. As she approached, he looked up at Edith with soulful eyes. She patted the dog, then felt a little nervous as she turned the handle and pushed the door. She'd rarely ventured into the servants' quarters, and never into this particular room. Now she stepped inside and closed the door behind her.

'Oh, Subash,' she breathed, sitting down on the bed, her eyes filling with tears again. She pictured the old man coming in here to rest, to pray and to perform his puja, to wash and to change, every day of his working life, which had started well before Edith had moved here. This was his private, inner sanctum and even though he was dead, she felt as though she was stepping over some invisible boundary to be in here. He'd served her faithfully for decades, he knew everything about her, her likes and dislikes, her habits and foibles, and yet she knew so little about him. But looking around her, she realised that there was nothing to see anymore.

He'd died two months ago and it was partly his death that had prompted Edith to think seriously about selling up. It was the end of an era, the passing of such a stalwart figure. She hadn't been able to bear to come in here. Not until today. She'd felt his loss so keenly. The other servants had cleared his room, packing his meagre belongings into a trunk and shipping them off to his home in a village near Darjeeling. He'd always intended to retire there one day, but now he never would. Professional to the end, he'd served Edith her breakfast on the very last day and returned to his room to lie down for the last time.

Absently, she opened a drawer, partly checking to see if the boys had been thorough. There was only one thing inside and she stopped and stared at it. It was an envelope, addressed to *her* in spidery writing. Her heart beating fast, she snatched it up and stared at it. The postmark was Assam, and judging by the smudgy date, it was at least two years old. But why ever had Subash not given it to her when it arrived? It had already been opened by the receptionist, as all hotel post was. That wasn't a surprise. She fished inside and pulled out a single sheet. The address was at the top;

Dapha River Tea Plantation, Ledo, Assam

My Dear Mrs Mayhew,

I hope you don't mind me writing to you out of the blue. I was recently installed as manager at the Dapha River tea plantation in Assam after the death of the previous owner, Mrs Olive Perci-

val. My company, the Assam Tea Corp, bought the plantation from her estate. Whilst renovating, we found some documents including a diary that I believe may have belonged to your relative, Betty Furnivall. They date back to 1942. I have not looked at them in detail. If you would like me to send them to you, please let me know. I wanted to check I had the right address etc before putting them in the post.

Yours sincerely,

Richard Edwards.

Edith sank down on the bed, her heart thumping fit to burst.

'Why ever did you hide it from me, Subash,' she said into the emptiness.

2

EDITH

EDITH SAT THERE for a long time, holding the letter in her hands, a sob forming in her throat. She was trying to come to terms with the fact that Subash had purposely kept it from her; this letter that might have unlocked the mystery of what had happened to Betty during the war. But deep down she knew why he'd done that. Subash had been fiercely loyal to Edith in every way, but he had a deep and lasting disapproval of Betty, that must, in his declining years have trumped even his loyalty and professional pride. But even though she understood the reasons, she felt a stab of pain at the thought that her faithful old servant whom she counted as a friend, would have wanted to prevent her from receiving news of her sister. He must have known how much she'd pined for Betty's return. But Edith also knew that although she herself had been able to forgive Betty's actions back in 1938, Subash never had, and his disapproval and dislike had lasted as if freshly minted, all down the decades.

Now she left the room, locking the door behind her, narrowly missing tripping over the dog. She rushed through to reception. Anesh had already closed the till and left the desk. She heaved the heavy Calcutta telephone directory from under the counter and started to flick through it, looking for the number for the Assam Tea Corporation. It was a longshot, but perhaps Richard Edwards had kept the letters and diary, even though he'd not heard back from her in over two years. There was no entry in the Calcutta phone book, so she called the Post Office to try to track it down. After being passed from operator to operator, and hanging on the line for what felt like an age, she was finally given a number for the company in Assam. She scribbled it down and snatched up the phone again to call the company. But then she realised that the call would have to wait until the next day. It was a Sunday and the offices would be closed.

Struggling with her emotions, she went upstairs to her room which was at the back of the hotel. It was a pretty, light room with double doors opening out onto a balcony which she'd made into a little garden. How she would miss this once she'd left! She read the letter once again, then lay down on her bed, staring up at the revolving ceiling fan. She let her mind drift back to those early days when she and Betty had first arrived, musing on how the events of those days had shaped the rest of their lives.

Subash had been one of those servants, fussing over Betty as she lay there on the couch that first evening. As Edith hovered there, unsure what to do, she noticed another guest coming up the drive on a rickshaw. It was an Englishman, a few years older than herself. He swung out of the rickshaw and paid the rickshaw-wallah with an easy smile. He wore the usual pale linens and brogues of the colonial gentleman. He strolled into the reception area to collect his room-key, then seeing Betty, and all the commotion around her, he approached Edith, holding out his hand.

'Robert Furnivall,' he said as they shook hands. 'Is there anything I can do to help?'

'She fainted because there was a stabbing outside. She's going to be fine, thank you.'

'Let me get you a whisky,' he said. 'You look pretty shocked yourself. I just passed the scene myself. The police have just arrived, and an ambulance. Dreadful business,' he said, shaking his head. Without waiting for an answer, he strode off to the bar and returned balancing three whiskies in his hands.

'I got one for your friend too,' he said. 'She might need it when she comes round.'

'She's actually my sister,' Edith corrected him, used to people not making that connection immediately. At that moment, Betty opened her eyes, sat bolt upright and took in her new surroundings.

'Where are we, Edith?'

'You fainted, so we came into this hotel. They have rooms, so I thought we could stay here. Look, this kind man's bought you a whisky.'

'Oh, thank you,' said Betty, her eyes flicking towards the newcomer and immediately flicking away again. Edith knew that look. Betty had a habit of appraising someone within seconds and making a snap judgment. From the way her eyes had skated over him, Edith could tell that she'd already dismissed this man as a bore, or at least not worth bothering with. Edith felt her own cheeks burning, sure that the kind stranger had also picked up on the look and realised that he'd been summarily dismissed. But if he had, he hadn't shown it. He just stood there, sipping his whisky, a benign smile on his face. Betty took the whisky and gulped it down in one.

'Let's go to our room,' she said, pushing the blanket off

her, getting to her feet and stretching. The servants rushed around her, folding the blanket, removing the water. One of them came with a key and explained that their room was on the first floor, others picked up their suitcases.

'Thank you again,' Edith said to the man over her shoulder as she left. As she followed Betty upstairs with the entourage of servants, still holding her glass of whisky, she glanced back at him as he held up his glass and smiled to wish her well.

In the room, once the suitcases had been deposited, Betty threw herself down on the bed.

'Switch the fan on, Edie. It's boiling in here. I'm exhausted. I think I might have a nap.'

'Of course. It's because you've had a shock. You lie down and rest. Why don't I pop downstairs again and see about supper?'

When she arrived back in the lobby, the guest was still there.

'Why don't you join me for another whisky,' he said, when he saw her coming downstairs. 'Is your sister alright?'

'Oh, she'll be fine. She's a bit highly strung, that's all. She'll be better after she's rested.'

'Well, why don't you sit down here. I expect you had a shock too.'

She smiled gratefully. How perceptive of him to think of her feelings in the midst of everything that was happening.

'I saw you arrive with your suitcases. Where have you come from, if you don't mind my asking?'

'Not at all. We've come from England. London to be precise. Our ship docked this afternoon.'

'Really? What a dreadful impression you must have of the city. It's not always like that around here, you know.'

'Actually, until that point we thought it was fascinating.'

'That's one way to describe it,' the man said. 'It is fascinating in its own way, wild and chaotic too, but of course it has its civilised aspects.'

'And where do you come from?' she ventured, relaxing. This was a bold question for Edith to have asked. She wasn't used to male company. When she was out with Betty, the men always gravitated towards her sister, like bees around honey, so it was highly unusual for her to be alone like this, making conversation with a strange man.

'I live in Rangoon actually,' he said. 'I'm here on business. I have a few meetings in Calcutta.'

'Burma! How exotic. I'd love to go there one day.'

'And what are you doing in India, may I ask?'

So, she told him. She told him the whole sorry story about their parents dying and about their uncle paying their fare and encouraging them to have a new start in Calcutta. It wasn't normal for Edith to open up like this, she was usually shy and reticent in conversation, but there was something about this man; about his intelligent, friendly face that encouraged confidences and put her at ease.

'So, we're hoping to find jobs here,' she finished.

'What sort of thing?'

'Well, anything really. But we both worked as secretaries in London. Something along those lines.'

'You could try at the Writer's Building in Dalhousie Square. It's where the Indian Civil Service for West Bengal is housed. Hundreds of pen pushers. They're always looking for educated staff who speak English.'

He fished in his pocket and handed her a card. 'If you go there, ask for this man. Archibald Wainwright. He's a friend of mine. If you say Robert Furnivall sent you, he'll do his best to find you positions, I'm sure.'

'Well, thank you,' she said taking the card. 'Now I'm

afraid I must go and book a table for dinner,' she said, remembering the time. 'My sister will probably wake up soon, so I need to go and see how she is.'

'Oh, there'll definitely be a free table. The dining room is never full. That's what I love about this place. The personal service. I always stay here when I'm in Cal. You can't beat it for olde-worlde charm.'

'Are you a tea planter, then?' she asked. He shook his head.

'I'm a businessman. My company owns steamboats that ply the river Irawaddy in Burma,' he said. 'But I do know a lot of planters through my work. That's how I first came here. And now I know the owner, Gregory Mayhew. We've become good friends.'

He offered her another whisky, and forgetting all about Betty and the time passing, she accepted. She felt comfortable with this man, and it was nice to relax for once. Not to have to think about arrangements, or be the one in charge, the responsible one. They soon got on to talking about history and about books and discovered they shared a common interest in Charles Dickens. The time flew by and the sky grew darker outside. Candles and gas lamps were lit inside the hotel and lights were glowing in the street outside. They were still talking when an imperious voice rang out from the bottom of the stairs,

'Edie! I thought you'd just gone down to find out about dinner. I've been waiting for you.'

They both turned and looked. There was Betty, standing on the bottom step, arms folded, a sulky lip protruding.

'Oh, there's no problem about dinner,' said Robert smoothly. 'If you'll permit me, I'd like to treat you both as my guests. Won't you come and join us for a drink first?'

Betty shrugged, raising her eyebrows, and joined them

at their table. From then on the conversation became strained. Gone was the relaxed intimacy Edith had enjoyed with this man whilst they were alone. It was suddenly much more difficult to find common ground. Edith was acutely aware that Betty loathed talking about books or art or history. She liked gossip and trivia, so when Robert started to speak about *A Tale of Two Cities*, Betty gave a great sigh, rolled her eyes, picked up a magazine and began to flick through it.

Dinner was a stilted affair, with Betty hardly speaking and Robert trying to introduce subject after subject with little response. Edith felt her toes curl up with embarrassment. She loved her sister fiercely, but really couldn't forgive her this rudeness. As they got up to go back to their rooms, Robert said,

'I've got a free day tomorrow. I'd like to show you round some of the sights of the city, if you have time.'

'Oh, that would be...' began Edith eagerly. Then she saw Betty's face. Betty was looking at Edith with a thunderous frown, shaking her head.

'Um, we're not actually sure of our plans yet,' said Edith. 'Could we let you know in the morning?'

As soon as they were back in the room, Betty started on her.

'Why did you have to subject me to an evening of boring conversation with that man?' she demanded. 'It's our first evening in India. It would have been nice to be able to relax together.'

'I'm sorry, Betty. It would have been difficult to refuse in the circumstances. What excuse could we have made? It would have been very awkward to have sat at a separate table when he'd invited us to sit with him.'

'That's typical of you, Edie. You never stand up for yourself. There were a million excuses you could have thought up.'

'Well, I found him rather good company. I'm sorry you didn't like him.'

'Yes, he *was* the sort you like. Into books and history and stuff. Nothing makes me yawn more.'

'Well, you made that quite evident. Honestly, Betty. I was quite embarrassed by the way you behaved. I just hope Mr Furnivall didn't notice.'

'It's your fault, Edith. You should have known I wouldn't like it. And don't think I'm going to drag round with him on some boring tour of museums and monuments tomorrow. You'll have to find an excuse this time.'

But in the morning, Betty woke with a crucifying headache and refused to get out of bed. Edith hovered over her, slightly worried, wondering whether it was delayed shock from the fainting, or some tropical illness which everyone on the ship over had warned them about. Surely, she couldn't have succumbed already?

'Do you want me to stay with you?' she asked.

'No. I'll be fine. You go off and see the sights with your new friend.'

Edith hung at the door, hesitating to admit that that's exactly what she'd been thinking of. Betty had guessed what was in her mind, as she always did.

'If you're sure?' she said weakly, feeling a pang of guilt.

'Of course. Just close the curtains before you go, could you?'

Edith didn't need any encouragement. Robert was already at breakfast when she went down. He stood when she entered the dining room, politely enquired after her sister, then invited her to sit at his table. Once again, they lapsed into easy conversation and the time flew by as it had the previous evening.

Afterwards, Robert went out onto Bunder Street and flagged down a rickshaw.

'We'll go to the Victoria Memorial, take a walk around the maidan, and finish up at the museum – it's at the end of this road. Does that sound too much?'

Edith shook her head, delighted, 'It sounds wonderful,' she said, sliding in next to him on the slippery rickshaw seat, trying to keep herself from bumping up against him, which proved virtually impossible as the rickshaw set off, jolting through potholes and ruts. To Edith it seemed a perfect way to spend a day, but one she knew Betty would have loathed.

They headed out onto Bunder street. Edith was once again entranced by the sights and sounds of this vibrant, exotic city. Street sellers hawking their wares on the pavement, the smells of spices cooking in woks, every type of vehicle on the road, from plush motor cars carrying white men in solar topees, to bullock carts, to horse drawn tongas, bicycles and humble rickshaws. Each vied for space on the carriageway, narrowly missing several collisions at every turn. At the end of the road, they turned left down Chowringhee Road, a great, wide thoroughfare lined with graceful colonial buildings on one side and trees bordering the maidan on the other. Edith gazed about her, in wonder at the vibrant greenery. It was almost as if these beautiful, palatial buildings were looking out over the jungle, rather than a park in the middle of one of the biggest cities in Asia. Robert pointed out the sights on the way.

'That's the headquarters of P&O shipping line; that's a bank. Oh, and there's St Paul's cathedral.' Once again, Edith was stunned. There, between the tall buildings, stood a

church with a soaring spire, surrounded by a grassy cemetery. It could be a church in any English town, except for the
heat and the Indian beggars squatting along the railings
outside. She looked wistfully at the gravestones and a
shudder went through her. These were all graves of British
people who had died here, thousands of miles from home. It
brought home to her how vulnerable she and Betty were, so
far away from their roots, making a life alone in this strange,
alien city.

Soon the grand Victoria Memorial loomed on their right
and the rickshaw dropped them outside the gates. Edith
stood in awe, staring up at the great edifice in front of her.
Huge and startling white, with domes and grand arches, its
reflection shimmering in a great lake which surrounded it.

'It's the Brits' attempt at equalling the Taj Mahal,' said
Robert, guiding her through the gates and up a walkway
towards the building. Halfway along, they came across a
larger than life statue of Queen Victoria herself, seated on a
throne, looking down with a sour face at her Indian
subjects.

Inside the building, Robert guided Edith around paintings and artefacts, which told the history of the British
Empire in Calcutta from its inception. He seemed to have an
encyclopaedic knowledge for dates and historical facts.
Edith followed in his wake, listening to his eloquent and
amusing descriptions, hanging on his every word. He made
the whole thing come alive.

'You know such a lot about Indian history,' she remarked
as they left the memorial and strolled out onto the maidan.
'Have you studied it?'

'Well, I did study history, as a matter of fact, at
Cambridge.'

'And then you came out here?'

'Yes. Well, my parents already lived in Rangoon. It's home to me really. More so than England.'

She looked at him, amazed, that this very English of men, with perfect manners and impeccably British habits, was as foreign to her as any of the people in this park.

At that point, he went to take her arm, but she moved slightly to the side to avoid him slipping his arm through hers. She wasn't quite sure why she'd done that. It was something that she regretted for years afterwards. Analysing it later, she realised that it was probably something about the fact that she was new here, and that she had responsibility for both herself and Betty and she couldn't afford to get distracted by a man. Not quite so soon.

It was the same later, when, after a fascinating tour around the Indian Museum on Chowringhee, they went for a cup of tea in the museum tea rooms. As they talked, just as easily as they had the day before and at breakfast time, Robert slipped his hand over hers on the table. Once again, she pulled away, feeling a blush creep up from her throat to her forehead. She tried to hide her confusion by looking down at the table, and there was a short, awkward silence, but Robert soon recovered his composure, resuming the conversation with barely a second's pause. From his expression as he carried on talking, she gathered that he'd understood that although she liked and admired him, she wasn't looking for more, not at that moment anyway.

IN THE MORNING, Betty felt a little better.

'Why don't we go along to the Writer's Building and see if there are any jobs going? Robert knows someone who might help us,' said Edith.

'Robert, Robert...' mocked Betty, with teasing eyes. But she didn't disagree with the plan, and after breakfast they took a rickshaw to Dalhousie Square. It was an enormous quadrangle lined with monolithic government buildings, which wouldn't have looked out of place in any British city. The Writer's Building was the largest of them all. It was a vast, gothic structure, occupying one complete side of the square, built of red brick with four or five floors of arched windows, and a grand portico in the centre. They stood staring at it from the opposite pavement where the rickshaw had dropped them, and Edith felt butterflies in her stomach at the thought of entering it to ask for work. It looked so daunting and official.

'Come on, then,' said Betty, tucking her arm into Edith's and propelling her forward.

They crossed the lawns in the centre of the square and approached the giant building. As they got closer, they could see office workers coming and going from the front entrance; the British men dressed in linen suits and solar topees, and the Indians in stiff three-piece suits.

They mounted the marble steps and found themselves inside a vast, echoing entrance hall. The man on the desk studied the card Edith presented and asked them to wait. After a few minutes, an unsmiling middle-aged woman came to guide them to see Archibald Wainwright. They followed her up a marble staircase and along a maze of long corridors. Finally, she knocked on a door and pushed it open.

'Mr Wainwright. Two ladies to see you.'

The man sitting behind a large desk in the window wore pebble glasses and looked up from his work startled as they entered. Seeing Betty and Edith standing in the doorway, he got up hastily and held out his hand.

'Pleased to meet you. Whisky and soda?'

Edith and Betty exchanged a look. This seemed to be the compulsory drink of the Raj, at any time of the day or night.

'Please, do sit down,' he said, indicating two chairs and pouring them whiskies from a decanter on his desk.

'Now, what can I do for you ladies?'

Edith explained that they'd just arrived and that they were looking for work as secretaries or typists, that they both had good experience and excellent references.

'Mr Robert Furnivall said to mention his name,' she finished.

Archibald Wainwright's eyebrows shot up.

'Mr Furnivall! Well, well, well. If Mr Furnivall recommends you, then I'm sure we can accommodate you somewhere. I'll get onto it straight away.'

Betty leaned forward. 'Is Mr Furnivall known to you?' she asked sweetly.

'Oh yes. We do a lot of business with Mr Furnivall. His family company owns the Irawaddy Steamship Company in Rangoon. They own and operate all the river boats in Burma. Most lucrative concern...' then he frowned and peered at Betty. Betty's eyes had widened as he spoke.

'But surely you knew that already, my dear? Being friends of Mr Furnivall as you are?'

3

OLIVE

Dapha River Tea Plantation, Assam, India, 1941

OLIVE TURNED over lazily in bed and checked the time on her watch. It was five thirty in the morning and already chinks of piercing light were creeping in around the edge of the shutters. It was stiflingly hot in the room, despite the electric ceiling fan whizzing round above her. But, powerful as it was, it couldn't stir the air beneath the mosquito net. She threw back the covers, found a gap in the netting, slipped out of bed, and crossed the room to the window. She pushed open the shutters just in time to see the top of Henry's solar topee as it wobbled along beneath the window. It wasn't far below, as Henry was riding an elephant along the front path and, if she'd wanted to, Olive could have leaned out and lifted the hat off his head for a prank.

It was a long time since she'd done that. Not since the first days of their marriage, when life on the plantation had seemed exciting and fun, and she and Henry still had that playful side to their relationship. But that had long gone, alongside the novelty of living, just the two of them, in splendid isolation in an enormous house shaded by deep verandas and surrounded on every side by rolling hillsides covered in row after row of emerald green tea bushes.

'See you later,' she called out, and he turned and waved cheerily as he did every morning. She leant her elbows on the windowsill and watched as Hannibal the elephant walked slowly but majestically along the garden path, rocking from side to side, its tail swinging to and fro, down the gravel drive and out of the gates towards the plantation and the tea factory in the next valley. Hannibal was Henry's favourite elephant; the two of them had grown up together on the plantation and knew each other like brothers. Watching Henry now, heading off to his day's work, she knew he'd say he was the happiest man alive; that living here with her, working on the estate each day to produce tea for export to Britain and Europe was all he'd ever wanted in life.

She envied him that contentment. She'd never told him of her creeping disillusionment with life here on the plantation; of her boredom and discontent that sometimes threatened to overwhelm her and occasionally meant she couldn't make it out of bed of a morning. She couldn't do that to him, and in any case, he wouldn't understand. He was a very straightforward man who took pleasure in the simple things in life. But she'd often wondered if he suspected that she wasn't happy, despite all her efforts to hide it.

Crossing the room to get back into bed, she caught sight of their wedding photograph on the dressing table. It had been taken at the club in Dibrugarh. She and Henry, clad in their wedding finery, with marigold garlands around their necks, stood in the middle of a crowd of expats; the women wearing floral prints and the men white suits and solar topees. People were waving balloons and throwing streamers, or holding up champagne glasses. Looking at that crowd now, frozen in time, she caught a sense of how happy and crazy that day had been; how full of hope and expectation.

She'd met Henry in Calcutta where she'd been working as a governess to the family of a high-ranking official in the British Raj. She'd been there a year, originally travelling out to stay with an aunt, and later, having got used to the place, had found work herself. When she went along with a friend to a dance at the Great Eastern Hotel, she'd no intention of settling down or of giving up her work or her independence, but Henry had happened along and changed all that. Thinking back now, he'd been very persuasive. He'd made a beeline for her that evening, and he was an excellent dancer, sweeping her around the dance floor expertly, making her own clumsy moves feel and look polished. And under those sparkling chandeliers, and with the benefit of several glasses of champagne, he'd looked handsome and tanned, in his white dinner jacket and bow tie. After that first evening, he'd asked her out on five successive evenings.

Olive was unaccustomed to such attention. She was a timid creature at heart, petite and mousy, someone who would go unnoticed in a crowd. Men had never shown an interest in her until that day and she found Henry's attention almost overwhelming.

He'd taken her to eat in places off the beaten track. He knew all the back streets and hidden quarters of the city. India had frightened Olive at first; the strange noises and smells, the clamour and hubbub of the streets and the markets, the poverty of the people, and the thought that exotic and venomous wildlife lurked in the trees and drains, even in the city. It had taken her a long time to get used to it, but once she had, she warmed to it, even appreciated it, in a way that she knew would make it very hard to leave. She was surprised that Henry, an Englishman after all, knew all the nooks and crannies, odd corners and hidden quarters of Calcutta. When she'd asked him how, he said;

'I was educated here. So I got to know it then.'

'So, you grew up in India?'

'Yes. I was born on our family plantation in Assam. My parents didn't want to send me back to England to school, so they sent me to learn from a munshi in the backstreets of Calcutta. I lived with an Indian family and learned to speak the language and to cook their food. It wasn't a very conventional education, but it's served me very well.'

'How extraordinary,' she'd said, eyeing him with new respect, thinking that having learned everything he knew from an Indian, he must have a deep and intimate knowledge of the country, such that most Englishmen would never achieve.

Their courtship progressed quickly. Henry was in Calcutta for a fortnight, to sign some contracts for the export of his tea, so it was naturally compressed into that timescale. On his last evening, he took Olive to dinner at the Grand Hotel and asked her to marry him. By this time, she wasn't surprised, indeed she had almost expected it.

'But what about my work?' she'd asked. 'I'd have to give up my job.'

'You won't need to work on the plantation. You'd be a lady of leisure, doing exactly as you pleased.'

'But...' It had been hard to explain to him that she loved her work, that seeing the children's expressions light up when something had suddenly clicked with them was the best feeling in the world, and she relished the sense of achievement she got from watching their reading and writing improve day by day.

'Look,' he said, as if he could read her thoughts from the expression in her eyes; 'If you really love teaching so much, there's a school on the plantation. My father set it up for the children of workers. You could help out there. I'm sure the teachers would appreciate an extra pair of hands.'

'But... I can't speak the language.'

'That won't matter. You could help with the English lessons. It would be very good for them to learn from a native English speaker.'

And so it was settled. She handed in her notice and followed Henry to Assam on the next available train. They were married the following weekend.

She'd been very taken at first with the gracious beauty of the house, perched on a hillside deep in the jungled interior, above the Dapha River. She loved its high ceilings and spacious rooms, the long shady veranda where you could laze the hot afternoons away in a planter's chair, drinking cocktails, looking out at the lush, exotic garden and the charming symmetrical lines of the tea bushes on the planta-tion. There were numerous servants to cook, clean, look after her every need. There was really no need for her to do anything.

But companions were very thin on the ground, apart from one, whom Olive sometimes wished wasn't there at all; Henry's mother, Sylvia, lived in a small bungalow in the grounds. She'd moved out of the big house shortly before Olive and Henry were married. Sylvia usually kept herself to herself but had a disconcerting habit of appearing suddenly in the house at awkward moments; when Olive was changing, or having a long lie in, or lazing on the veranda with a book. The old lady was outwardly kind, but underneath could be subtly critical; 'When I was first married, I would normally have been in the kitchen at this time of day, giving instructions to cook for supper,' or 'I always found that the morning was the best time for a stroll around the plantation. It's really so refreshing to get up early.'

Sometimes Henry would take Olive to the club in Dibrugarh where all the local planters congregated, but most of the wives were a lot older than herself, and seemed content with bridge, gossip and endless chota pegs of whisky. Olive had always been shy, and she found it impossible to break into their well-established cliques. Each time she went, despite her best efforts, she found herself shrinking from any attention. She retreated more and more into her shell, feeling she had less to offer on each occasion, and her quietness seemed to put a distance between her and the other wives. She could tell they found her difficult and standoffish, but her shyness prevented her from overcoming that.

The early months slipped by and soon Olive was regretting her decision to throw up a job she loved and follow this man she hardly knew to the back of beyond. Part of the trouble, she knew, was that months had gone by and she hadn't conceived. It troubled her as she knew that having a baby would transform her life, give purpose to her days and was what she was secretly craving.

Henry must have sensed that she was discontented after a few weeks, because he again suggested that she should try helping out at the plantation school.

It was in the next valley, next to the tea pickers' "lines" or accommodation and in the shadow of the great wooden tea factory. The first time she went, she was very nervous. Her experience as a genteel governess tutoring the two docile children of an upper-class English family had not equipped her in any way for working in the noisy, ramshackle environment of the plantation school. The building was made of corrugated iron and consisted of two classrooms where the children sat cross-legged on the bare earth floor. The two young Indian teachers were very welcoming to Olive, but were so deferential and polite to her, she felt they would never accept her as one of them.

There were around thirty children in each class and they all stared at her round-eyed when she appeared and the teacher introduced her as Mrs Percival.

'Miss-is-Per-ci-val,' they chanted over and over again until the teacher held up a hand and they stopped immediately and burst into peals of laughter. Olive felt a flush of embarrassment creep into her cheeks and was forced to drop her gaze.

Her job was to teach them basic sentences in English; 'How do you do?' 'What is your name...' 'Where do you live...'. She would speak the words slowly, write them on the blackboard, then point to the letters with a cane as the class repeated what she'd said. It was easy enough, but Olive found it daunting to be in front of so many hostile pairs of eyes. She got none of the pleasure she'd experienced as a governess and it made her miss her old life even more.

The most terrifying thing about helping at the school was encountering the mothers at the end of each day. They were a raucous bunch, standing outside the school building gossiping and laughing in their colourful sarees of deep pink, vermillion, sapphire blue, their eyes dark with kohl, their skin burnt amber by the sun. With their nose rings and bare stomachs, they exuded a joy and a zest for living that Olive could only dream of. Many of them had broods of five or six children, carried a baby on their hip and displayed a distended belly showing that another was on the way. They managed all this childbirth and rearing effortlessly, whilst rising at dawn to spend eight hours picking the best tips from the bushes and living in a tin hut that was no more than a hovel.

Olive would watch them from the doorway of the classroom, fascinated by them, but too afraid to approach them or even show her face. The worst thing about them, as far as Olive was concerned, was their fertility. The fact that these poor, ill-educated workers could shell out babies year after year without any effort, or even any planning or thought, taunted her. To Olive each day was a cruel reminder of her failure to conceive.

So, after a couple of months, she ended up making excuses and only going to the school one day a week. And on those days, she was careful to arrive after all the children, and to leave before the mothers came to collect them. The rest of her time was spent idly at home, lazing on the veranda reading, wandering in the garden or around the estate, tending the pot plants she'd cultivated on the patio, or writing letters to her friend Amy in Calcutta.

This morning, although she tried, she couldn't get back to sleep. It was going to be a hot day, too hot to be under the mosquito net. She got up and went through to the bathroom where her ayah had already filled the metal bath with hot water. She bathed, dressed and went down to a solitary breakfast on the veranda. She loved that time of day, when morning mists were rising from the valley, giving the landscape a soft, ethereal appearance and she could hear the jungle birds and monkeys whooping in the surrounding trees.

The bearer had put the newspaper out for her to read as usual and she picked it up idly. It was *The Times of India*; it was difficult to get Western papers in this remote outpost of the empire. She expected to read how the Viceroy's visit to Bombay had gone, or about the price of rice and jute, or the outcome of a cricket tournament in Hyderabad, but the headline made her heart race.

"Japanese Troops Invade Malaya and Bomb Pearl Harbor." She scanned the article quickly, reading how the Japanese Airforce had taken the Pacific colony by surprise and destroyed many US warships and how the US was now officially in the war. At the same time bombing raids had been carried out on Singapore Island, and troops had landed on the north of the Malay Peninsula, at Kota Bharu taking the British by surprise.

She'd followed the war vaguely in the newspapers, but until this moment it had seemed too far away to touch her in a meaningful way. Europe was a world away, and although she worried for her parents back in England, they lived in a remote village in rural Sussex and were unlikely to be in danger.

But this was different. The war had finally come to the British Empire in the East. There had been rumblings before of Japanese aggression and the build up to a possible invasion, but no one had taken that very seriously. Olive was shocked. Malaya was a long way away from Assam, but it still meant that the empire was under threat. She wondered what that might mean for life here on the plantation. Remote as it was, it might not be completely immune. After all, tea was a valued commodity.

Olive stared at the headline again, and a sudden chill went through her. What might this mean for her and Henry, here on the plantation? She looked around her at the idyllic surroundings; the elegant house and garden, the beauty of the nearby hills with their lines of emerald green tea bushes melting into the jungle-covered hills beyond. It suddenly occurred to her that all this might be snatched away; this idyllic life and the business that provided a livelihood for so many. She frowned deeply. Bored and discontented as she had been, how on earth would she deal with that if it came down to it?

4

EDITH

Calcutta, 1980

EDITH ROSE EARLY the next morning. She'd had a restless night; the events of the distant past going round and round in her mind. The discovery of the letter from the Assam tea planter in Subash's room had brought all those long-buried memories of Betty rushing back. And with them the associated feelings of loss and guilt. She'd have loved to lie in bed and catch up on her sleep, but she had a busy day ahead of her; the executives from Clover International were due at 10 o'clock, but before that, she needed to get through to the Dapha River tea plantation on the telephone and see if she could speak to Richard Edwards.

She ate a solitary breakfast on her balcony, missing the usual bustle and noise of the hotel which she was so used to at this time of day. The balcony was above the kitchen, so she normally breakfasted to the clatter of pots and pans and the bickering of the cooks, but today was eerily silent from that direction, although the sounds of the city filled the space: the tooting of a million horns, the cries of street vendors, the high-pitched whine of motor rickshaws.

Edith had little appetite today, so dusting the crumbs off her lap, she hurried down to reception and dialled the number for the Assam Tea Corporation. It rang for a long time and she was about to hang up when someone answered. The woman's voice seemed detached and coming from a long way away, as if speaking from the other end of a long tube.

'I need the number for the Dapha tea plantation please,' Edith began.

'Dapha Tea Plantation? I can give you number, but estate is closed for few days.'

'Oh really? I need to speak to Mr Richard Edwards, the manager.'

'Mr Edwards is away on business. Back on Wednesday.'

'Is there any way I can contact him before that? It's very important.'

'Sorry, madam. Cannot contact. Try on Wednesday. Here is the number.'

Edith scribbled it down and rang off. Then she hovered there at the desk chewing the pencil, wondering what to do. Although it had been two years since Richard Edwards had written that letter, it had now become a matter of extreme urgency for Edith to speak to him. She needed to know if he'd kept Betty's things.

Suddenly she knew what to do.

Anesh was at the desk, working on spreadsheets.

'Have you still got the train timetables we had for guests, Anesh?'

He looked up, surprised. 'Yes, of course, madam.'

'Could you find the times of trains to Assam. Not sure

exactly where the Dapha Tea Plantation is, but I'll head for Dibrugarh and take it from there.'

'Of course. Right away, madam. When would you like to go?'

'Now. Today. Straight away. As soon as I can.'

'But, madam?' he asked slowly, a puzzled frown creeping over his features. 'What about the gentlemen from Clover International? They will be here soon to sign contracts with you.'

'Of course. Well, could you call them at their offices straight away, please? Say that I've been called away on urgent business and that we'll have to reschedule for next week.'

'If you're quite sure, madam?'

'Of course I'm sure,' she said impatiently. She rushed back to her room and threw a few things into an overnight bag.

Back at reception, Anesh told her that there was a train, the Saraighat Express, departing for Assam in about an hour from Howrah station.

'I have already called you a taxi, madam, and reserved you a ticket over the phone. You'll need to collect it at the ticket office at Howrah station.'

'Thank you, Anesh.'

'How long will you be gone?'

'I'm not sure. Three days maybe?'

His face was a picture of bemusement as she left him standing at the desk to hurry out to the taxi, and she felt a little guilty. Anesh had helped her set up the meeting with Clover and now he must be wondering whether she'd taken leave of her senses. Well, no matter, he didn't need to know why she was going. She wouldn't have been able to concentrate on the intricacies of the contracts today; not the way she was feeling and with this development on her mind. Finding out what had happened to Betty's papers was now the only thing she could think about.

AT THE TICKET OFFICE, she'd discovered that the train would take 17 hours and she would then need to change and get another one to Dibrugarh. She was used to train travel in India; Gregory and she had travelled the length and breadth of the sub-continent by train during their annual holidays from the hotel; they'd journeyed through every state, visited every city. He'd had such a love for the place, he'd wanted her to see it all. A night on a bunk in a first-class compartment and a thousand-mile journey didn't faze Edith in the slightest. Normally she would have spent the time looking out at the scenery, eating in the dining car and whiling the rest of the journey away with a good book. Although she'd brought a book with her for this trip, she didn't anticipate reading much of it; she had too much to think about; too many memories to recall.

She settled herself in the compartment and stared out of the window as the train rattled through the outskirts of Calcutta; she was used to the grinding poverty of the city she'd made her home, but it always shocked her afresh to see it at close quarters like this. The train rumbled past crumbling colonial buildings, now home to dozens of families with washing strewn from every opening; ramshackle slums built of plywood or corrugated iron, children playing in alleyways who stopped to wave at the train; stray dogs rooting in piles of rubbish and chickens pecking around in dusty backstreets.

But soon the city was behind them and she was looking

out over the fertile plain, at squares of emerald green rice paddies fringed with coconut and banana palms; at villages of wooden houses, where buffalos wallowed in swamps and bullock carts plodded between fields.

Her thoughts turned to Betty and the days and weeks after they'd arrived in Calcutta in 1938. She recalled now how that moment in Archibald Wainwright's office in the Writer's Building in Dalhousie Square had been a turning point in both their lives.

Mr Wainwright had offered them both jobs as secretaries in the Department of Trade, and asked them to report for work at nine o' clock the following Monday. That gave them a week in which to find accommodation and do some sightseeing.

As they left the building, Edith suggested they should walk around the square, see some of the great colonial buildings and find somewhere for lunch, but Betty had other plans.

'Why not just head straight back to the hotel? It would be nice to have our lunch there, don't you think?'

'If you're sure?' said Edith hesitantly. She was wondering what Betty was up to. There was a new sense of vigour and purpose in her tone. At that moment, Edith hadn't quite worked out what it was, but it wouldn't take long before the inevitable truth was revealed.

'Of course I'm sure. If we've got to move out of there this week, we might as well make the most of the place while we can,' Betty said, walking out into the road to hail a taxi.

Back at the hotel, Betty had made straight for Robert Furnivall's table in the restaurant, Edith trailing in her wake.

'Could we join you, Mr Furnivall? Oh, and I hope you don't mind me calling you Robert?' Betty said, putting on her most charming, attentive voice. Edith watched Robert's face. At first he registered surprise at the sudden attention from Betty, when she'd previously been so dismissive and rude, and then, as the meal progressed, he began to be flattered, basking in the attention being lavished by such attractive lips, being eyed from under those long eyelashes in that way. Edith herself squirmed with embarrassment. She could hardly bear to watch. She quickly realised what had prompted this change in attitude and it didn't take Betty long to introduce the subject.

'I was wondering, Robert, what exactly is your business in Rangoon?'

'Oh, didn't I tell you? Steamboats. My company owns most of the river boats in Burma, as a matter of fact. The Irrawaddy Steamship Company. You might have heard of it?'

'Indeed. And what is your position in the company, if I may ask?'

'I own the company, and I run it too. My father, and his father before him built it up from scratch. Just a couple of boats. They worked hard, bought out the competition and built several new boats too. We operate nearly all the routes in Burma now. It's quite a thriving concern,' he said, his eyes full of pride and pleasure.

'It sounds marvellous. You must be very proud.'

After lunch that day, Robert offered to take them to see the botanical gardens beside the Hooghly River and Betty leapt at the offer.

'We'd love to come, wouldn't we, Edie?' said Betty, her eyes shining with excitement.

'Actually, I'm feeling a bit off colour,' said Edith stiffly. 'If you don't mind, I'll stay here. You two go.'

Robert looked concerned, but didn't protest and she watched them get into a rickshaw together, setting off down Bunder Road, laughing and chatting, just as she and he had done the day before. She twisted her napkin tight in her hands and took a deep breath to suppress the pain. Then she went to their room and threw herself on her bed and sobbed into her pillow, until exhausted, she drifted off to sleep.

It was after dark by the time Betty came back. She breezed into the room, excitement radiating from her.

'You're not asleep are you, Edith?'

'Oh, I did drop off for a while.'

'What's wrong? Have you got a headache?'

'No, I'm fine thanks. Better now.'

'Well, why don't you get up and have a shower? Robert has offered to take us out this evening. To the Grand Hotel. How about that?'

Edith's heart sank. How could she bear an evening watching Betty simper and make eyes at Robert, when inside she would be shrinking with shame and her own heart breaking. But she'd never been able to deny her sister anything. Not since she was a tiny tot; pretty and bright and demanding. Betty had relied on Edith for everything, and Edith had taken it upon herself to be there for her, since their mother was so lax. And she wasn't about to deny Betty anything now. So, she swung her legs over the bed and stretched.

'Alright. That would be lovely,' she said. 'I'll get changed.'

So that evening, and for the next three evenings, Robert Furnivall treated the two of them to a sumptuous meal in one of the top hotels in the city. Edith found it almost impossible to bear, to watch the two of them flirt and tease each other. She would sit there on the other side of the table, frozen, with a fixed smile, feeling so alone and desperately miserable.

By day Robert took them to see the sights: Fort William, the Marble Palace, Kalighat, a temple on the river where the Goddess Khali was worshipped. To Edith it felt a wild, alien place. The chanting of the faithful and the blood splashed on the flagstones from the sacrifice of a baby goat chilled her to the core, but Betty was entranced.

'What a fascinating place, Robert. Thank you so much for taking us there!' she said. Edith suppressed the urge to remind her sister that she normally loathed sightseeing.

On the fourth day, Edith decided she could bear it no longer when Robert suggested a trip to another palace.

'I really think I need to stay behind today,' she said, 'I need to look at apartments for us. We've put it off long enough. We can't afford to stay in the hotel much longer.'

'Oh, I'm so sorry,' said Robert, his face instantly a picture of concern. 'I've been distracting you. How selfish of me. I'd completely forgotten that's what you should have been doing this week. Please allow me to pay for another week's stay at the hotel.'

'Oh, that's very kind, but I hardly think...'

'That would be wonderful,' gushed Betty. 'How very kind of you, Robert. We'd love to take you up on it, wouldn't we, Edie. That means you can come out to the palace today with us after all, doesn't it?'

Edith drew herself up. 'We really can't expect you to pay for us, Robert,' she said frostily. 'I insist on staying behind and looking for apartments today. I've seen a couple in the paper that are close by and look suitable.'

'Well, the offer's there. Let me know if you change your mind,' he said, turning to usher Betty out to the rickshaw. This time as Edith watched them go, she shuddered as she noticed Robert put his arm around Betty in the rickshaw and Betty lean in close to him. If they were prepared to do that in public, what had already passed between them in private? She couldn't bear to speculate.

Sighing heavily, she turned to go back into the lounge. As she did so, she caught sight of Gregory Mayhew, the hotel owner, leaning casually with his elbow on the front desk, watching her with a faint smile playing on his lips. She dropped her gaze and went back to the lounge, sat herself down in one of the basket chairs in the reception area and picked up a newspaper. She intended to go through the classified ads and take down the phone numbers for the apartments she'd already identified as being suitable. But as she sat there scanning the columns, she found her mind wandering and couldn't focus on the task. She couldn't help her imagination straying to what was happening between Betty and Robert.

She only had herself to blame; she knew that. And that was partly why she wouldn't say anything to Betty now. Robert had made it clear that he was interested in her on at least two occasions, but she'd given him the brush off. How she regretted that now! But there was no going back. Once Betty was set on a course of action, there was no dissuading her from it. And there was no denying her what she wanted. There never had been.

Edith tried to examine her own motives; she wanted to understand exactly why she'd rejected Robert when he'd moved to hug her in the rickshaw or tried to slip his arm through hers as they walked on the maidan. Was it fear of the unknown? It *was* partly that. She had so little experience with men, the thought of physical contact did frighten her a little, but she liked and trusted Robert and would have ultimately welcomed his embraces. No, she knew the real reason why she'd held back. Ironically, it was the thought that she needed to be around for Betty while they settled down in a new country. That if she encouraged closeness with Robert, Betty would have felt excluded. How badly that had backfired on her.

'Are you quite alright, Miss Davenport?' a voice broke into her thoughts. She looked up. Gregory Mayhew, the hotel owner was standing in front of her, a concerned expression on his face.

'Of course.'

'I thought you looked a little... well, a little bit lost if you don't mind my saying so. I wondered if you'd like some company?'

She blushed. Was it so obvious?

'Actually I'm looking for some accommodation for me and my sister in the newspaper. Perhaps I could use the hotel telephone to make some appointments?'

'Of course,' he said. 'I'll help you if you like. I can make the phone calls for you. Show me the addresses and I'll tell you what I can about the neighbourhoods. I've been here a long time. I know a lot about the city.'

So she let him help her, glad to let someone else share the burden, and as they went through the paper and he made some telephone calls on her behalf, she was glad of his help and support.

He made three appointments for that very afternoon, and when Betty hadn't returned from sightseeing in time to set off, Gregory offered to accompany her to view the apartments. It felt a little strange going to view one's possible home with a complete stranger. The agent who showed them around a property off Chowringhee mistook them for a married couple, much to Edith's embarrassment, but Gregory just took it in his stride and laughed it off. By the end of the day, Edith had decided upon a flat in a tall building on Clive Row. It wasn't far from the river or

Dalhousie Square, so she and Betty would be able to walk to work at the Writer's Building. It was on a quiet backstreet filled with plane trees, and the apartment was small but with two bedrooms and nicely furnished.

'Thank you for helping me,' she said to Gregory, as they jogged through the backstreets to the hotel in a rickshaw at the end of the afternoon.

'No problem at all. It was my pleasure,' he said. 'I'm surprised you didn't sign up straight away, though. That was a lovely flat.'

'Oh, I couldn't do that without Betty seeing the place,' Edith said, and noticed that Gregory suppressed a smile and raised his eyebrows.

In the end, Betty never did go to see the flat. When she and Robert got back to the Tea Planter's Club that evening, her face was flushed with excitement, her eyes shining, and Edith could tell that she'd been drinking. Edith was sitting in reception, flicking through magazines, when the rickshaw drew up outside, and Betty and Robert tumbled out, laughing.

Betty rushed up to Edith and flung her arms around her.

'You'll never guess what, Edie? Robert has asked me to marry him! Look what he bought me!' and she showed off a huge diamond ring that flashed and sparkled under the lights.

Edith felt tears of hurt and anger prick her eyes, but she swallowed hard to disguise them.

'How wonderful,' she found herself saying.

'Yes – he took me to the Great Eastern for cocktails and popped the question there.'

Edith looked up at Robert, who was brimming with pride himself, but he must have seen the pain in her eyes because he dropped his gaze. Did he know how hurt she was? How she regretted having rejected his advances herself?

'We thought we'd get married at St Paul's Cathedral before we go back to Rangoon next weekend. We can get a special licence, so we need only wait a week or so.'

'I'm so happy for you, darling,' Edith said, taking Betty's hand in her own and squeezing it tight. She felt lightheaded and detached, almost as if she was hovering above the scene, looking down on herself from a great height.

The next week passed in a blur. Betty turned down the job at the Writer's Building, and Edith asked to postpone her own start for a further week. She decided to stay at the hotel a little longer. She couldn't rent the apartment she'd chosen by herself, so would have to look for a different one. But there was no time for that in the immediate future. The week passed in frenetic activity; going to and from the tailors, having Betty fitted for a wedding dress at a shop in Hogarth Market. Edith also had a new dress run up for the occasion, a powder blue silk, stylish and subtle. Betty's dress was of the finest silk, trimmed with exquisite handmade lace. When she chose it, Edith said, 'It's very expensive silk, Betty. Are you quite sure?'

'Robert told me to spend what I like. He's a rich man, Edith. I'll never need to penny-pinch or worry about money ever again.'

There were only a few guests at the cathedral the following Saturday when Betty and Robert tied the knot. Gregory Mayhew accompanied Edith and stood beside her in the front pew. There were a few other guests from the hotel and some business associates of Robert's. Betty looked stunning in her ivory silk gown, with a huge bouquet dripping with cream and yellow flowers. Her blonde hair was done up in elaborate curls, but as she passed Edith on her way to the altar, Edith caught a glimpse of apprehension in her face, and, despite everything, her heart went out to her little sister, hoping she would be alright in that far off land with a man she barely knew.

They went back to the Tea Planter's Club for drinks after the ceremony. When Betty went upstairs to get changed into her going away outfit, Edith followed her. She felt awkward and tongue tied, as if she should say something to Betty about what was expected of her on her wedding night, not that she had any idea what to advise. But as soon as she entered the room, Betty turned on her.

'You don't need to say anything, Edie. I know all about it already. Please don't embarrass yourself.'

But Edith was embarrassed. Ashamed that she was of no use to her sister.

They were taking a ship that evening to Rangoon from the docks and Robert was anxious to get going. A silver Bentley was waiting for them on the forecourt of the hotel and their luggage was stowed in the boot. Betty emerged from the room dressed in a charming pale pink suit and hat. Edith went to hug her goodbye. Tears choked her throat and she could hardly speak. She held her sister tight and buried her face in Betty's hair.

'Goodbye my darling. Good luck. Write soon, please,' she whispered.

As she drew away, Betty mumbled something that she couldn't quite make out. She went over and over it in her mind afterwards and couldn't quite believe what she'd heard. It sounded very much like, 'I'm sorry. Please forgive me.' But surely it couldn't have been that, could it?

The car drew away and the guests wandered back to their rooms with their drinks or to the bar to get more. Edith turned back into the hotel, a feeling of emptiness such as she had never known in her life threatening to engulf her. As she turned round, tears standing in her eyes, there he was again leaning nonchalantly on the desk, his gentle eyes following her. Gregory Mayhew.

'Why don't you come along to the bar with me, Miss Davenport? I expect you need a drink.'

5

EDITH

Assam, India, 1980

IT WAS early evening and the Saraighat Express powered across the plain between Siliguri and Bihar. After returning from the dining car, where she'd eaten a three-course meal washed down with red wine while watching the setting sun streak the eastern horizon pink and orange, Edith waited as the steward made up her bunk with linen sheets. When he'd finished, he bowed deeply and left the compartment. Edith washed in the adjoining washroom with its old-fashioned sink and stiff white towels. It was still early, but already dark outside; there was nothing to see except pinpricks of light from far-flung villages. Edith decided to go to bed. She climbed up into her bunk, switched the overhead light on and settled down to read a chapter of *Smiley's People*.

But try as she might, she couldn't concentrate on the book. She needed to think about the past, about those days and weeks back in 1938 that had determined the course of the rest of her life. The memories kept crowding back, forcing out everything else, demanding her attention.

On the Monday after Betty's wedding, Edith dressed in her smartest skirt and blouse and took a rickshaw to the Writer's Building. There, she climbed the front steps and went in through the huge arched entrance with crowds of faceless civil servants. She was taken to an office on the fourth floor, given a typewriter and some written reports and asked to type them up. The work was undemanding and her desk was placed under a fan and beside an open window looking out over the treetops of the central gardens of Dalhousie Square. The other girls in the typing pool were either English or Eurasian, and were friendly and welcoming, including her in their gossip and taking her along to their favourite tea stalls at lunchtimes. She was shy at first, but it didn't take her long to settle down and become friends with her colleagues. To Edith, working at the Writer's Building, despite its limitations, was a welcome distraction after the traumas of the previous few weeks.

In the evenings, she went alone to view studios and one-bed apartments in the area, but many were either just out of her reach financially, or, if she could afford them, were cramped or unsuitable in some other way. So, she carried on living in the hotel, although she was aware that the money Uncle Jimmy had given her was running out quickly. She tried to save by eating at food stalls rather than in the hotel, but she became increasingly aware that she needed to find alternative accommodation quickly.

One evening, when she went to the desk to pay her monthly bill, and the Indian cashier was working out what she owed, Gregory Mayhew wandered up.

'I think we can give Miss Davenport a discount, Kasim,' he said, in his mild voice.

She looked up in surprise.

'Oh, surely not? I've been here a full month now. I wasn't aware that there were any discounts.'

'I insist, Miss Davenport. You've been put in quite a difficult position by your sister's marriage, I'm well aware of that. So please. You can have 50% off your bill and continue to stay here rent-free until you find somewhere suitable of your own. It would be my pleasure.'

She looked up at him, aware that a flush was creeping into her cheeks that she couldn't control, trying to work out whether to be grateful or humiliated. In the end she decided that gratitude was the most gracious position to adopt.

'That's extremely kind of you. I'll find somewhere else as quickly as I can, and when I'm settled, I'll make sure I pay back the debt.'

'It isn't a debt. This is my gift to you. If you'd like to do something in return, perhaps you'd kindly consent to dining with me occasionally in the hotel restaurant. It gets tedious always dining alone.'

'Well of course. I'd be glad to. Thank you, Mr Mayhew.'

'Please – call me Gregory.'

So, she dined with him that night and on several other nights, although she was careful not to abuse his hospitality and made sure that she bought her own food at least every other evening. On that first evening, she was a little nervous sitting down with him. He was a good twenty years older than her and at first he'd seemed rather intimidating, aloof company, but that soon proved to be a long way from the truth. He was charming and entertaining and a polite and thoughtful host.

He asked her all about how she and Betty had come to Calcutta and about their life in England. Edith hadn't wanted to go into detail about their parents, but she found herself talking about them, despite her reluctance. Gregory Mayhew didn't say much, just listened attentively, resting his quiet grey eyes on her face, and when she'd finished, said something that almost brought tears to her eyes with its devastating insight.

'It sounds as though you've had to bear the burden of responsibility for many, many years. That must have been very tough.'

'Oh, I don't know, it wasn't always so bad,' she said after a pause, looking down at the table, not wanting to invite his sympathy further in case she was unable to hold back the tears.

'And what brought *you* to India?' she asked, wanting to deflect attention from her own situation.

'Oh, I came out here to be a tea planter near Darjeeling after the Great War. Worked at it for fifteen years or more and put away quite a bit of money. I loved the life, but it's a young man's world really. I used to come down here to this club for some rest and recuperation. I loved the place. One day I came down and the Scottish owner said he was selling up and going back to Blighty. I had enough savings by then and thought, what the hell. So, I bought it from him, moved down here and have never looked back.'

'Would you ever go back to England yourself?' she asked.

He shook his head. 'All my family have passed away and this is my home now. I'm settled here. It would take a lot to tear me away from Calcutta. And I love running this place too. Especially now we take guests other than just planters. I get to meet new people every day. It's a real pleasure making them comfortable.'

Later that week, a letter from Betty arrived at the hotel. Edith took it up to her room and tore open the envelope impatiently.

My Dearest Edith,

We arrived at Rangoon yesterday, so today is the first opportunity I've had to write to you. The journey was wonderful. Robert ensured that we had the best first-class suite on the ship, of course, and everyone was very kind, treating us to drinks and meals given that we were newlyweds. On the first night we sat at the Captain's table and he made a little speech to welcome us and toasted us with champagne. The journey only took three days, which seemed very short after our trip from England, and the weather was beautiful, so during the morning we played deck games with other passengers and in the afternoons just lazed on deckchairs.

But I must tell you about Rangoon and about our house. I knew Robert was wealthy, but the house is beyond my wildest dreams. It is huge and beautiful, with white pillars and a portico at the front entrance and a long garden at the back which ends in untamed jungle. It has a circular drive with a fountain in the middle, behind wrought iron gates and is on the road which runs up to the Shwedagon Pagoda – the most stunning sight I have ever seen. It is a massive gold pagoda dominating a hill overlooking the city, surrounded by dozens of other mini pagodas. At night it is lit up and the light from it casts a golden glow over the whole area. Robert took me up there when we arrived to see the sunset. It was stunningly beautiful and very romantic.

But back to the house; it has a cavernous entrance hall, four huge reception rooms and six bedrooms upstairs. All the floors are tiled in black and white marble. There are at least ten servants, not counting the gardeners who keep up the grounds. Tomorrow I will be on my own so will have a chance to explore properly. Robert has to go to work at the company offices which are on Strand Road beside the river. I intend to get a rickshaw down into the centre and look around the town. Robert says he will take me to the Pegu Club in the city one evening and introduce me to everyone who is anyone.

I hope life in Calcutta isn't too dull without me. Have you started work in the Writer's Building yet? I'm sorry to have left you so suddenly Edith, but I had to seize this opportunity and I think you'll agree that Robert is a great catch and not to be missed. When I'm settled I hope you'll be able to come and stay with me in Rangoon. I'd love to show you the house.

Do write and tell me your news,

With Love, Betty.

Edith put the letter down, took a deep breath and closed her eyes, letting Betty's words sink in, trying to be as fair minded as she could about them. But then she read it again, and what shone through most to her was Betty's shameless gold-digging. It tore at Edith's heart that Betty regarded Robert, who was a good, kind and straightforward man, as no more than 'a good catch', and an 'opportunity' to be seized. She put the letter away in her drawer and tried not to dwell on it. In the recesses of her heart, she felt ashamed of her sister and deeply sorry for Robert.

The next day she wrote back, telling Betty of her own news, but leaving out that Gregory had let her stay at the hotel free of charge. She didn't want to mention her penniless state to her sister, or the fact that the job in the Writer's Building was poorly paid and rather boring.

More letters followed in the same vein; Betty described Rangoon, how Robert had taken her to see the sights and to expensive hotels for meals. He'd also lavished her with gifts, including a complete new, fashionable wardrobe. She told how she'd made friends at the club and spent her days playing bridge and gossiping with other wives. Edith shook her head when she read that, remembering how Betty had vowed not to do that very thing on the ship to Calcutta.

Eventually Edith found a bedsit near Dalhousie Square that suited her budget and moved out of the hotel. Gregory treated her to a meal on her final evening and helped her take her trunk by taxi to her new home. As he left he said,

'I hope you'll come back and visit me sometime, Edith. I shall really miss our chats and your company at dinner.'

She surprised herself by saying, 'I shall miss that too. Of course I'll come back and see you. Thank you so much for all your kindness.'

And when he'd gone, she sat down on her new bed amongst her luggage and wept. There was something so moving about Gregory's manner, about the quiet and intelligent way he spoke, about the way he watched her with his grey eyes without any element of judging, about his generosity and kindness that had touched her more deeply than she'd realised.

Over the following months she returned to the Tea Planter's Club for dinner two or three times a week. And although she didn't click with Gregory in quite the same way she had with Robert, she appreciated his constant friendship and his relaxing company. Visiting him was the high point of her otherwise rather boring and lonely existence. She tried to keep busy the rest of the time, to stop herself from brooding; she took long walks beside the river, explored the city, even venturing into some of the poorer quarters. She also tried to read a good deal and to learn the Bengali language. Anything to keep her mind off Betty and Robert and the pain she still felt.

She'd been in Calcutta for close to six months when

Gregory asked her to marry him. She'd gone to the hotel for her usual Wednesday evening meal with him and noticed that he'd made an effort to dress in a white dinner suit and the table was laid with flowers.

'What's the occasion, Gregory? You should have told me and I'd have dressed up.'

'You'll see. And you look lovely just how you are,' he said.

She noticed, as the bearer brought their soup, that Gregory seemed a little nervous, and that conversation didn't flow quite as well as it normally did, and by the end of the meal she had a shrewd idea of what he had planned.

Sure enough, as they sipped brandy at the end of the meal, he produced a tiny blue box. She noticed his hand was shaking as he laid it on the table and opened the lid to reveal a beautiful sapphire and diamond ring. But it was what he said that surprised her more than the request itself.

'I never thought I'd want to marry, Edith. I've been a confirmed bachelor for decades. But then you came into my life and I was struck by you the very first time you walked into the hotel. By your poise and elegance and the way you took it upon yourself to shoulder responsibility for everything. You're a beautiful, capable and intelligent woman.'

He took her hand on the table and she looked into his eyes.

'Now, I know you'll never feel about me the way you feel about Robert Furnivall. I watched the way you fell for him and the way you two got along those first couple of days. And I know the man, so I can see how much the two of you have in common. I watched the cruel way your sister took him away from you, and the way you just stood aside and let her, you were so used to putting her whims and desires before your own. But despite that, I hope you'll grow to love me in time, albeit differently, and that I'll make you a good husband.'

She dropped her gaze to the table, confused by his words.

'So, will you marry me, Edith Davenport?'

She looked up at him then and this time there were tears in her eyes.

'I will. And please, I think you have the wrong impression about me and Robert. There was never anything between us.'

She didn't know why she was lying to him. Was it to convince herself, or to save Betty from blame, or to put Gregory's mind at rest?

'You're not being honest with yourself or with me,' said Gregory. 'But let's not speak of it anymore. It's all in the past.'

And with that he slipped the ring onto her finger.

'It was my mother's and her mother's before her,' he said.

They decided to have a long engagement. There was no real hurry, and she had a horror of rushing into marriage in the unseemly way that Betty had. She gave notice on her studio, and moved back into the hotel, staying in a room on the other side of the hotel from Gregory's as propriety demanded. She gave up her job at the Writer's Building, and began to work in the hotel alongside Gregory as well as taking time to prepare for the wedding. She found that she enjoyed talking to guests, making them feel welcome and anticipating their needs. Having cared for a capricious and demanding younger sister all those years made her eminently qualified for the role.

War had just broken out when the wedding day finally came round. Betty and Robert arrived from Rangoon laden with parcels and luggage. Edith was desperate to see Betty and had impatiently counted down the days to her arrival. But the Betty who arrived in the limousine that day, although perfectly made up and coiffed and expensively dressed, didn't seem quite the same Betty who had left in a flurry of excitement almost a year before. She seemed more serious, a little careworn, certainly less frivolous.

Edith was keen to find out what was behind this change, so after dinner that first evening, when Gregory and Robert had settled down to smoke cigars, they went up to Edith's room with their brandies.

'So, tell me all about life in Rangoon, then. Is it a whirlwind of parties and dinners?'

Betty lit a cigarette, drew deeply on it and flicked the ash carelessly into the ash tray.

'Oh, I'm fed up with all that. I hardly go to the club anymore. It's all so superficial,' she said.

'Oh really? I thought you loved the life. At least that's what you say in your letters.'

'Not anymore.'

'So, how do you spend your time when Robert's at work?'

Betty eyed her carefully before saying. 'I've started helping out at a clinic for the poor.'

'Betty! How wonderful! That doesn't sound like your cup of tea though. Do you enjoy it?'

Betty shrugged. 'I hated it at first. But all that's changed now...' Then she looked away. 'Anyway, enough of me. What about you? How have you been? Tell me all about you and Gregory.'

Edith frowned, puzzled. Why the change of subject? She couldn't help feeling that Betty was holding something back, although she had no idea what that might be and she couldn't get it out of her, no matter how she tried. Betty had certainly seemed tense and preoccupied throughout her stay.

Now, lying on her first-class bunk, as the train powered across the Indian plain in darkness, more than thirty years later, Edith still had no idea what secrets Betty might have been hiding that day. And she hoped against hope that this trip to Assam might give her some clues.

6

OLIVE

Dapha River Tea Plantation, Assam, January 1942

DESPITE THE ONSET OF WAR, Olive's days on the plantation continued much as before. She felt as if she and Henry were buried here, with Sylvia and the tea workers, deep in the jungled hills between India and Burma. It felt to Olive that now, even more than before, they were completely beyond the reach of the rest of the world. At least she hoped that was the case.

Most days now, as she sipped tea on her veranda looking out over the majestic landscape, she read and re-read the *The Times of India* from cover to cover, gathering as much information about the war in the East as she could. She had followed it obsessively, battle by battle; the sinking of the great British warships HMS Repulse and HMS Prince of Wales off Singapore, the relentless march of Japanese troops down the Malay peninsula, how they had won battle after battle against the Allied forces as they pushed south, with their superior air power and training in jungle warfare. Now British and Allied troops had retreated to Singapore, that linchpin of the British Empire, previously considered a fortress, and were bracing for the final battle. Olive read these accounts breathlessly, almost as if they came from the pages of an adventure story. She'd been so used to discussion at the club, and everywhere else amongst the British expat community, of the superiority of British troops and inadequacies of the Japanese, that Japanese success in these battles seemed almost unbelievable.

Her heart beat faster when she read of how the Japanese Fifteenth army had launched an attack from occupied Thailand through the Tenasserim Hills into southern Burma. They had now taken by force and occupied the port of Moulmein and the Salween River, and were steadily marching north on Rangoon. They would be there in a matter of days.

This knowledge sent shivers down Olive's spine. Here, in the hills above the Dapha River valley, they were only a hundred miles or so from the Burmese border. Although it felt remote and protected by those high mountains at the moment, what if Japan decided to invade India? Would they be so protected then? If the Japs were marching north, perhaps India was their ultimate prize. She knew from the reports how territorial the Japanese were; how they wanted to take over the whole of the British Empire in the East and liberate it from British control. She knew it was only a matter of time before Rangoon fell, and then the Japs would surely start looking to the north.

Suddenly she felt differently about this place; about her beautiful, gracious home in its glorious surroundings, where she could sit on the veranda with a cocktail and watch the sun turn the distant mountains red and gold before it sank beneath the jungle each evening. She began to value this leisurely life Henry had brought her here to enjoy; waking to the gentle padding of the elephant across the garden in the half-light of early morning; the wisps of mist on the neat rows of tea bushes in the valley, the sound of jungle creatures from the encroaching forests. It had all become a part of her she realised, over these past five years, and she didn't want to let it go.

Even the plantation school held a new fascination for her, now this very existence was under threat. She began to look differently at the children, no longer seeing their gaze as hostile, now, reappraising it objectively, she realised it was merely inquisitive. How lucky she was to have this opportunity to educate them. How ungrateful she'd been for everything she'd been given.

So, she asked if she could come back and help in the school every morning. The young teacher beamed at her, showing a row of beautiful white teeth.

'We'd love you to, Mrs. Percival. The children so look forward to your lessons and it's very valuable for them to learn English.'

Olive's life entered a new, more purposeful phase. She got up early each morning, just after she'd watched Henry depart for his rounds of the estate on Hannibal. She washed and dressed and walked down to the school before lessons began. She started to devise new lessons for the children, not just content to point to the blackboard with the cane and get them to repeat words. She thought up games and exercises, got them drawing and writing and even singing. She began to feel the same thrill of pleasure she'd got from teaching the English pupils, when one of the children looked up at her with shining eyes because they'd understood something new.

It was ironic, she thought, sitting on the veranda one afternoon in January 1942, reading the newspaper, that it was the news of dreadful, violent events, of impending doom that had given her a new direction in life.

Even Henry noticed her change of mood. 'You look happy today,' he'd say, slipping into the chair beside her with a cocktail to watch the sunset after a busy day on the plantation.

That night they made love for the first time in months, and afterwards they lay awake, watching the moonlit shadows dance on the ceiling.

'You seem different, these last few weeks,' Henry said, leaning on one elbow and stroking her hair. 'What's changed?'

'It's something to do with the war,' she said, unable to articulate her feelings properly. 'I can't explain. It's just... it's just made me appreciate everything a bit more, that's all.'

He pulled her close to him. 'The war's not going to come here, so you mustn't worry,' he said.

'But what if it does? What if the Japs take over the estate and send us all to internment camps? It's happened in Malaya.'

'They won't make it over these mountains Olive. We're safe here. You'll see.'

With that, he drifted off to sleep, but Olive lay awake worrying, watching the dancing shadows on the ceiling, listening to the crack of every branch, the cry of every creature, until finally sleep overtook her too.

Despite their renewed closeness, still Olive didn't conceive, and the sight of her monthly bleeding at the beginning of February sapped her mood for a couple of days. But that didn't last long. She soon threw herself back into her work at the school, and normal life on the plantation.

Within a few weeks though, the news in the papers

began to really trouble her. Rangoon was being bombarded from the air on a regular basis and had been since December 1941. The papers contained graphic pictures of devastated streets and bombed out buildings; houses destroyed and families fleeing for their lives. An exodus had begun from southern to northern Burma, and the British were starting to evacuate civilians from Myitkyina, a town in the north, to British India. Others were taken by boat from Rangoon, back to Calcutta, Chittagong and other Indian ports. Olive pored over photographs of desperate families, many of them Indian, trudging north with all their worldly goods on their backs or in hand carts. Some of them were frail, some carrying children.

It troubled Olive that the fallout from the war was moving north in the shape of desperate people, trying to escape the bombing and the inevitable Japanese invasion of Rangoon. Her heart went out to those poor people, driven from their homes in the most terrifying of circumstances, escaping violence and death, but suffering hunger and exhaustion in their place, and the anxiety of not knowing what the coming days would bring.

One day, a few days into February, Henry came in from the plantation later than usual. He looked troubled.

Olive brought him a drink and sat down beside him on the veranda.

'What's the matter, Henry? Has something happened?'

He buried his face in his hands for a few minutes, then looked into her eyes.

'People have started coming through the jungle from the Chaukan Pass. Refugees from Burma, trying to walk through the mountains to India. I saw several groups today. They were walking along through the jungle beside the river, looking for a place to cross.'

Olive's hand flew to her mouth.

'How dreadful. I've read about refugees in the paper, but I didn't realise they would come through here. What do they look like?'

'Shockingly thin a lot of them. They've been on the road for weeks. They're carrying their belongings on their backs. There are women and children amongst them. They all look dead beat.'

'Did you help them?'

'I tried to. I went down to the river on Hannibal and took them some water. They were really grateful. Close up, they looked thinner and more pitiful than ever.'

Olive stared at him, trying to imagine the plight of these people, forced to walk for hundreds of miles, forced to climb mountains and navigate through untamed jungle.

'But we must do more. Surely there's something we can do for them,' she said. 'Perhaps we could take some food down to them tomorrow.'

'Yes, I suppose we could. It's not really the food that's worrying me, though.'

'What is it?'

'It's the river. They can cross it at the moment a bit lower down. There's a natural crossing place with stones. It's not that hard. But when the monsoon comes it will be impossible. They won't be able to cross at all. They'll be stranded here.'

'Do you think there will be many more of them?'

'Well, according to the paper there are thousands trying to get back from Burma. I thought they were being airlifted but that must have stopped.'

'There must be something we could do to help,' said Olive, twisting her hands.

'I've got an idea, but I'll need to get some of the other

planters involved. I'll give the Planter's Association a call tomorrow.'

'And in the meantime, let's take some food and tea down to those crossing at the moment.'

'Alright. We could make a campfire down there, boil up some water and give them tea as they pass.'

'And I could get cook to make up some fried rice and take that down in containers too.'

'If you don't mind coming down on Hannibal?' he smiled.

They both laughed, recalling her early nervousness of the elephant and how, the first time she'd sat up on the howdah and the elephant had taken a few steps she'd gone pale with fear. She'd gained confidence since that day, but was still not completely relaxed riding on the elephant's back.

'I'm sure I can manage it for such a good cause,' she said.

So that evening, she went to the kitchen and spoke to the cook, and in the morning, she got up at the same time as Henry. The mahout brought the elephant round to the kitchen door, and they loaded the canteens of rice, a basket containing some metal plates and spoons, a huge tea pot and metal mugs onto Hannibal's howdah while the elephant knelt for them. Then, Henry helped Olive onto the howdah and scrambled up beside her. With a click of the mahout's tongue, the elephant rose to his feet gently. Olive felt Henry's arms steadying her as they lurched sideways for a second, but she flashed him a smile. This time she didn't feel any fear at all, knowing that she was doing this for a worthy cause.

They headed out across the misty garden and down through the trees towards the plantation. She soon relaxed into the gentle swaying motion of the elephant and looked around her at the beauty of the landscape, the morning mists rising over the grey green hills, the flocks of white birds bursting from the jungle.

They passed the tea factory and the school and headed down through the tea pickers lines on the dirt track that led towards the jungle. Olive could smell woodsmoke on the air as they passed huts where families cooked their breakfast over open fires, but soon they were clear of the houses and heading off the plantation. The jungle closed around them and the road became a single-track path. Massive ferns and long, dangling creepers brushed against her face, depositing morning dew. They pushed through clumps of bamboo as tall as houses and passed beneath soaring teak trees. It was dark in there; the jungle canopy blotting out the sun, but it was already hot and sticky. Olive felt sweat trickling down her neck and her shirt sticking to her. She'd never been so deep inside the jungle before and hadn't realised quite how dense it would be. And alive too; the whoops and cries of jungle creatures and the hum and clatter of insects was almost deafening.

They continued on the same narrow path for about half an hour. It wound down through the undergrowth towards the river in the bottom of the valley. In places it was steep and slippery, and Hannibal had to make his way down sideways, but he was surefooted and careful and Olive knew there was no danger of him slipping.

At last they could hear the murmur of the river ahead and the path emerged from the jungle onto a wide grassy bank. They moved along beside the river for a few yards, then Henry commanded the elephant to stop and to kneel down in a clearing. They unloaded the supplies, and Henry tied Hannibal to a tree near a clump of bamboo which he immediately began to rip down and devour hungrily.

They found a shady spot beneath a teak tree and set out their things. Henry made a fire, fetched some water from the river and boiled the kettle. Soon the refugees started to come. They approached in dribs and drabs. The first to arrive was a family. Mother and father, grandparents and two small children. They were all filthy, their clothes ragged and they looked half-starved. But it was the look in their eyes that shocked Olive the most as they came towards her along the riverbank. They had a look of exhaustion and defeat, as if it wouldn't take much for them to lie down beside the path and give up their struggle. As she went up to them to ask if they wanted tea and rice, she realised that at last, she was doing something that would make a real difference to somebody's life.

7

EDITH

Assam, India, 1980

IT WAS early morning as the Saraighat Express rattled on across the endless plain towards Assam through the mists of dawn. The steward brought Edith's breakfast to her compartment. She'd been woken at six-thirty as she needed to change trains at Guwahati and this train was due to stop there at eight o'clock. She sat at the little pull-up table by the window, ate boiled eggs and cold toast and drank a mug of sweet tea. The railway ran along beside the great Brahmaputra River for several miles, past stilted villages where smoke rose from a dozen fires and fishing boats were moored up on the riverbank. The river was so wide at this point that it was impossible to see the other side. All that could be seen on the massive stretch of water was the occasional fishing boat, or larger passenger crafts plying their trade between its banks. Sometimes Edith noticed an island in the middle of the river that looked like a floating raft of palm trees, breaking up the endless expanse of water.

As the train slowed and entered the outskirts of the little

town, Edith gathered her belongings and made her way to the end of the carriage. The train came to a juddering halt in a busy station and she got out onto the platform where she was surrounded by porters, hawkers and beggars, all clamouring for her attention, trying to persuade her to buy something at the tops of their voices. Refusing all offers, she made her way through the throng to the first-class waiting room. She had an hour or so to kill before the train to Dibrugarh was scheduled to arrive and had enough experience of travel in India to know where to go to be comfortable.

She settled herself at a table near the window that looked out over the station, so she could watch the colour and activity on the platform. She ordered a pot of coffee. How little travel in India had changed since she and Gregory had first journeyed there in 1939. The atmosphere at the stations was still the same; families waiting for connections with all their worldly goods packed up in cardboard boxes, accompanied by cages of chickens and tethered goats. There were stalls selling every imaginable type of snack; the chai-wallah, who paraded up and down selling sweet brown liquid direct from a huge kettle, wandering minstrels playing sitars and warbling Indian folk music, and the ubiquitous sleepers, wrapped from head to toe in blankets, stretched out on benches or on the platform itself.

There was so much to see, but fascinating as it was, it couldn't displace the past that was still calling to Edith, demanding her attention. Now she was making this journey to see if Betty's papers had survived, it seemed all the more important that she should think it all through, remember what had happened back then and fix it in her mind.

It was amazing to think that the last time Edith had actually seen Betty in the flesh was at her own wedding.

Betty had been her bridesmaid, of course, and, dressed in a spotted blue silk dress, with her blonde hair piled up on her head, threatened to outshine Edith as she followed her down the aisle. St Paul's Cathedral was fuller for Edith's wedding than it had been for Betty's. Gregory knew a lot of people in Calcutta and even Edith had her own friends to invite by then; work colleagues from her time at the Writer's Building, and other friends she'd made since moving back to the hotel.

The ceremony was followed by a lavish buffet at the Tea Planter's Club, where there hadn't been much opportunity to speak to her sister. Edith and Gregory had left for the station at the end of the afternoon. They were travelling by train up to Darjeeling for a few days' honeymoon. Edith had held Betty tight as they'd parted.

'Do come and visit us in Rangoon, Edie,' Betty said. 'You'd love it there and I'm dying to show you around.'

'Of course. We'd love to come,' Edith replied, but it had never happened. The onset of war had meant that passenger services had been suspended shortly after Betty and Robert had sailed for Rangoon, and although Edith and Gregory could travel freely around India, it was much more difficult to go further afield. Edith and Betty had to content themselves with keeping in touch by letter.

Edith wrote assiduously every week with her own news, but Betty's replies were sporadic. It was difficult to read between the lines, but Edith sensed that the boredom Betty had expressed when she'd come over for the wedding had only increased on her return to Rangoon. Betty often wrote about her work at the clinic though, and Edith was gratified, if a little surprised that Betty appeared to have taken to it so well. Betty would describe the desperate women and children who they helped, and also her friendships with her fellow volunteers. Amongst them was a Burmese man, Ye Win, whose name began to crop up more and more frequently in Betty's letters.

He's such a unique and interesting person, Edith. I'm quite sure you'd like him. He was educated in England, at Oxford no less, and comes from one of the noblest of Burmese families. He confided in me that he's also a member of a secret movement, working towards independence for Burma, but he told me that I should keep that quiet.

Edith frowned, finding it hard to imagine the Betty she knew and loved finding such a person an interesting companion, and she wondered how suitable, or indeed how safe it was for Betty to be mixing with a member of the independence movement in Burma. She vaguely remembered having read of violent acts the movement had performed in the early thirties and she began to worry about Betty's judgment in counting him as a friend.

In another letter, Betty wrote: *I've learned so much about the real Burma through Ye Win. When he first came to the clinic, he took me into the poorer quarters of Rangoon, to show me how the natives live. He also took me to a Burmese tea shop. It's where the Burmese go to socialise and to talk politics. I'd never been anywhere like it in all the time I've been here. It was so nice to see something of the real Burma for once.*

When the war came to the East in the shape of the Japanese invasion of Malaya and the bombardment of Rangoon, Betty's letters all but stopped. Edith was terrified for her, living as she did in the heart of downtown Rangoon which was the target of the Japanese bombings, but some letters got through, reassuring Edith that Betty was fine and that the house was still intact. She also told Edith the news that Robert had signed up to fight with the Indian Army. He was already training for the battle against the Japanese when the invasion of Rangoon finally came.

I'm so proud of Robert for signing up. He could so easily have got out of it, on the grounds that the steamship company is an essential business and that he's needed to run it, but he has left it in the hands of experienced managers. So now I'm on my own in the house, apart from the servants, of course. I don't mind because I feel safe here, knowing that the British Army is going to defend the city when the Japs arrive. And I have my work in the clinic to occupy me, even though sometimes getting there can be a bit hazardous.

At around that time, Gregory signed up for the army too. Edith had tried her best to dissuade him.

'You don't have to go. You're not so young anymore, Gregory,' she'd said.

'I know that, but I'm not totally decrepit yet, my love, and if others are going, I want to do my bit.'

'But you're needed here at the hotel. Whatever am I going to do without you?'

Gregory drew her to him then and held her close. 'You're more than capable. You know that. I wouldn't go if I didn't think you could cope.'

They'd recently received an official letter to tell them that the hotel would be taken over by the RAF for the duration of the war, and that they must cease to take bookings; officers would be moving in at the end of the month.

And so Gregory had gone, signed up to India III Corps and shipped off to Malaya where troops were massing against an expected Japanese invasion of the peninsula.

Edith went along to the docks to see him off on that final day. She was terrified for him when she saw the other soldiers gathering there; most of them young and bursting with health and energy. Gregory seemed so gangly and thin in comparison, and a lot older than the majority. She clung to him, weeping, before he left.

'You don't have to go, you know,' she said, terrified to the core that she might never see him again. He laughed. 'I think I do now, my love. Now I've signed up and got the uniform and everything. There's no going back. Please don't worry about me, Edith, I'm made of pretty tough stuff, you know.'

She kissed him one last time and he turned away and joined the queues of solders crowding round the gangplank ready to board the ship. He quickly melded into the throng and she couldn't make him out on the crowded deck, but still she stood at the quayside with the other wives as the ship drew away, and waved and waved until her arm ached and the ship was just a tiny speck on the horizon.

He wrote to her from Kuala Lumpur, where he was billeted in a five-star hotel and was sent out training every day in artillery and combat warfare. Edith was reassured that he sounded content and optimistic but she was still concerned about the inevitable action he would face.

Two weeks later, the Tea Planter's Club filled up with RAF officers, who brought their Indian bearers with them to serve them. The main difficulty was finding accommodation for all these servants. Edith's own staff occupied all the staff quarters in the hotel, so she asked around and eventually found the newcomers beds in a local hostel. This didn't go down well with the officers because it meant that their bearers wouldn't be on hand 24 hours a day, but she wasn't prepared to turn her own staff out of their homes. Despite her efforts there was a certain amount of hostility amongst her staff about the interlopers, and Subash went round during those early days of the war with a long face, often coming to Edith to express his discontent.

But apart from that, the arrival of the officers meant less work for Edith. She had no need to be at Reception to greet guests, to supervise the staff to ensure rooms were made-up, be around at mealtimes to ensure things ran smoothly and to make guests feel welcome. Although the hotel staff still ordered in the food and prepared the meals, the officers' servants served them up in the dining room, answered calls for room service and cleaned the bedrooms. Edith found she was becoming a little bored, although some of the officers were friendly enough so she wasn't short of company.

She found herself brooding about what was happening in Rangoon and in Malaya. Newspaper reports from both places were grim. When she read in the paper that Japanese troops had advanced to just north of Kuala Lumpur and that the city was being bombed, she was terrified for Gregory and spent many sleepless nights worrying about him. It was difficult to glean any information about casualties from the newspaper reports. Edith was sure they were censored, but it was clear that the situation was extremely serious for the British and Allied troops.

There were bombing raids on Kuala Lumpur on the days leading up to Christmas and on Christmas Day itself. Edith didn't feel like celebrating. The RAF officers invited her to their meal and she sat there wearing a paper crown and pulling crackers as if in a dream, while the men drank and ate excessively and celebrated around her. She couldn't join in; her heart wasn't in it. All she could think of was the Christmas she and Gregory had spent in that very room the year before with a few guests. It had been a wonderful, uplifting day, celebrated in typically quiet style by Gregory. He'd given her a beautiful amber necklace that she'd put on that day to remember. She fingered it absently while watching the raucous celebrations going on all around her.

January 1942 arrived without any news from Gregory. Reports of bombings in Kuala Lumpur continued to appear in the papers and finally, on January 10th it was reported that the Japanese had taken the city. Edith sat there staring at the headlines, her heart sinking. What had happened to the British troops? Had they withdrawn? Were there casualties?

Two days later her worst fears were confirmed. A telegram arrived from Gregory's regiment to say that he'd died in the final battle for the city, but that he'd fought bravely to the end. Edith read the telegram over and over again. At first she felt numb. It took time for the full impact to make itself felt. The first sign was that her hands started trembling. That began slowly, but finally they were shaking so much that she could no longer hold the paper. She dragged herself up to her room, not wanting to face anyone. There, she locked the door and drew the curtains and gave in to her grief. In the depths of those moments, she realised that she'd never fully appreciated Gregory. That his quiet and supportive love over the last couple of years had become essential to her, but that she'd never quite recovered from the way Betty had treated her over Robert and it had cast a long shadow over their marriage.

'I'm so sorry, Gregory,' she sobbed into her pillow. 'I should have loved you more.' But it was too late now. She'd never look into those kind, grey eyes again, or feel his arms around her. She'd wasted her opportunities with him, she knew that now, and there was no way to repair that. Not now he was gone.

She thought back to what he'd said to her when he'd asked her to marry: 'Now, I know you'll never feel about me the way you feel about Robert ... But despite that, I hope you'll grow to love me in time, albeit differently, and that I'll make you a good husband...'

How perceptive he was. And how she'd appreciated that honesty. But still, she felt she'd betrayed him. She hadn't loved him enough or been a good enough wife and companion to him through the short time they had together. How bitterly she regretted that now.

She went through the days that followed in a dream. The officers occupying the hotel all got to know of her loss and went about quietly and respectfully. Their commanding officer, Squadron Leader Thompson, came to pay his respects and present condolences on behalf of the squadron. Edith was now glad of the fact that they were there and there was little for her to do. She would have found it hard to cope with the running of the hotel the way she felt. Every day she awoke and it struck her afresh with renewed force. In those first few days she felt she would never climb out of the dark state she was in.

She'd thought that she'd sunk to the depths of despair during that time, but a month or so later, just as she was beginning to emerge from the worst of her grief, she was to be dealt a fresh blow.

There was a phone call from Betty's neighbour in Rangoon. He was a doctor and Betty had mentioned that he and his wife had been very kind to her during her early days there.

'Mrs Mayhew?' his voice sounded subdued, respectful. 'Doctor Summers here. From Rangoon. A friend of Betty and Robert's. She gave me your number in case of emergencies.'

Fear and dread washed through Edith.

'What's happened?' she asked, a sick feeling in the pit of her stomach.

'I'm so sorry to tell you this, but the house was bombed last night.'

'And?' she asked hopefully. That didn't mean the worst had happened.

'I'm so sorry to say it was razed to the ground. Just a pile of rubble.'

Edith's mouth went dry. How could this be?

'I'm afraid there were no survivors. Impossible to find any bodies, in those conditions. It would have been very quick. Instantaneous. I'm so sorry.'

Edith sank to the floor, the telephone dangling from its string. She couldn't reply. She could hear the doctor at the other end of the line, 'Hello? Hello?' 'Mrs Mayhew?' but she had no voice.

After a few minutes she felt gentle arms around her. Subash was gathering her up and pulling her to her feet. He took the telephone from her grasp and replaced the receiver. Then, slowly and gently, without any words, he helped her upstairs, across the hall and into her bedroom. There, he pulled the curtains across and helped her onto the bed. Then he poured her a brandy and left it on her bedside table, backing out of the room and closing the door without a sound.

8

EDITH

Assam, India, 1980

THE BRAHMAPUTRA MAIL, from Guwahati to Dibrugarh, was an hour or so late into Guwahati. That was normal in India, even quite an acceptable level of delay. When the train ground into the station, with much hooting of the horn and squealing of brakes, the whole place came alive. The hawkers and sellers started shouting again, waiting passengers got up from their seats, gathered their belongings and pushed forwards through the crowd towards the train. Even the sleepers stirred themselves.

Edith found her compartment and installed herself beside the window. The journey would be many hours long and she always liked to look out at the scenery. The train pulled slowly out of the station before gathering speed beside the river. The landscape was flat, dotted with villages and smallholdings. In places the line ran along beside rice paddies bordered by mud banks, sometimes through tea gardens. It ran alongside a highway for several miles, passing bullock carts, motor rickshaws and highly decorated lorries, through towns and villages of ramshackle one-storey buildings that straddled the highway.

Her thoughts drifted back to those early days of 1942 when she'd been devastated by the deaths of the two people she loved most in the world. She clenched her fists thinking about it now. What she'd done during those dark days had to be faced up to. There were no more excuses. She'd been in denial for many years, pushing it to the deepest recesses of her mind, letting it fester there. But now she knew she had to think about those events, examine her actions and accept what had happened. Whatever news of Betty was waiting for her at the Dapha tea plantation, now was the time to face up to what she'd done.

She'd lain in bed, barely moving, staring at the ceiling, for four days and four nights. Subash brought her meals but she hardly touched a thing. He hovered over her with a worried frown on his face. She'd been thin before, but now she could feel her ribs beneath her skin and her hip bones protruded. She didn't change her clothes or take a bath or shower. It seemed pointless. Everything in the world seemed pointless, including her existence and her life to date. She couldn't contemplate a future without Gregory and Betty in the world.

On the fifth day, Subash came to her at lunchtime with a bowl of chicken soup and said,

'Madam, all hotel staff are asking about you. They are wondering where you are. They are asking if you are ill.'

She sat up in bed and took the bowl from him. 'I'm not ill, Subash. I'm just very, very sad.'

'We are sad too, madam,' he said, hanging his head, tears brimming in his eyes. 'Mr Gregory was our master. We all knew him very well and liked him.'

'Yes, I know,' she said, but it made her think, and realise

that perhaps she was being a little selfish taking to her bed when she needed to set an example to the staff. They were already disgruntled because of being displaced by the officers' bearers, and Gregory's death must have hit them hard. Many of them had known him for ten years or more. Subash's words had made her realise that they must be grieving too.

After Subash had left, she forced herself out of bed and into the bathroom. She stood under the shower for a long time, then dried herself and dressed in one of her smart dresses. Then she sat at her dressing table and applied makeup. When she looked in the mirror she was shocked by her sunken cheeks and the dark rings under her eyes, but with some foundation and blusher, and plenty of eyeshadow and lipstick, she quickly transformed her face into looking something approaching normal.

Taking a deep breath she went downstairs. She passed two of the RAF officers coming up, who bowed and gave her sympathetic looks, but she turned her broadest smile on them and bid them good morning. She went through the breakfast room and into the kitchen, where the three cooks suddenly stopped what they were doing and bowed their heads, avoiding her eyes.

'Please carry on,' she said in the brightest tone she could manage. 'I've been unwell for a few days but I'm better now. I want everyone to know that, and that things are going to carry on here in the Tea Planter's Club as normal. It's what my husband would have wanted.'

And from that day onwards, she was strict with herself. She didn't let her guard slip for as long as she was going about her work in the hotel. When she returned to her room in the evenings, she allowed herself to crumple, but she found that if she kept busy during the daytime, she could keep that at bay too.

About a month after the news of Betty's death, Edith came downstairs after lunch to a surprise guest. At first she didn't recognise him, he'd lost so much weight, and his face looked haggard and careworn. There were even streaks of grey in his hair, but there was no mistaking that voice.

'Robert!' she said. He looked up and as soon as her eyes met his, his eyes filled with tears. She went to him and they clung to each other.

'You heard the news then,' he said, 'About Betty?' he could hardly utter her name.

Edith nodded. 'I can't believe it. It's so dreadful.'

They went to sit in the lounge and Edith ordered some brandies.

'And I heard about Greg too,' said Robert. 'I'm so sorry, Edith. He was the best of men.'

'Thank you,' she said, unable to say more.

'What are you doing here?' she asked after a long silence.

'I was in the battle, when Rangoon fell to the Japs,' he said. 'We were in retreat, then I had the telegram about Betty. My commanding officer ordered me to take some time off. There was a naval vessel coming to Calcutta so I hitched a ride. I couldn't think where else to go.'

'Did you go back to your house while you were in Rangoon?' asked Edith tentatively. Robert shook his head.

'It wasn't possible. By that time it was behind enemy lines. And the city was in total chaos. I don't know if I'd have wanted to anyway.'

'Poor Betty,' Edith said. 'I hope she didn't suffer.'

They were silent for a while, then Robert asked if there was room for him to stay at the hotel for a few days.

'There are a lot of RAF officers here at the moment, but I'm sure there'll be a spare room,' she said.

Later they ate a desultory meal together in the dining room. It was difficult to find a subject that didn't bring to mind either Betty or Gregory, and neither of them was ready to speak about them at that moment. Edith couldn't help remembering their first few days together, before Betty had set her cap at Robert, and how she and Robert had found so much to talk about. How long ago that seemed now, but in reality it was less than four years.

Edith found Robert a room. It wasn't one of the best in the hotel, and was in a separate building at the back, but he was grateful for it. She left him sitting on the bed, his shoulders slumped in defeat and misery. Her heart went out to him. She knew exactly what he was going through.

In the evening they dined together, but once again it was difficult to find anything to discuss that didn't make either or both of them well up with tears. So, scouting around for a suitable subject, she asked him about the fall of Rangoon.

'It was chaos. Absolute chaos,' he said. 'We were so poorly prepared and the Japs so well trained. We'd fought and lost to them at the Sittang Bridge and at Pegu and by then it was clear that we'd completely underestimated the enemy. By the time we got to Rangoon, most of the population had evacuated. The Jap armies were already on the outskirts bombarding the city. When we entered Rangoon it was full of smoke. The last thing the British authorities did before leaving was to destroy the oil refineries to the south of the city. They were still on fire, filling the city with acrid black smoke. The city itself was virtually devastated by the bombings which had been going on since December. So many houses destroyed, streets completely flattened. It's the city I grew up in and it broke my heart to see it like that.'

Edith watched his face as he spoke. It was full of pain, remembering those days, the loss of life and the pointless destruction of the city he loved.

'Were you involved in the battle?' she asked.

He shook his head. 'There wasn't a battle as such. We were ordered to evacuate the city before the Japs arrived. High Command didn't think we had enough men to defend the place. They were cutting their losses. But I would have liked to have had a chance to fight. At least we'd have gone down fighting then. Given Rangoon a chance.'

He hung his head. The dining room was filling up with officers, ordering cocktails and starters. It was getting noisy and Edith could see from the way Robert's eyes flicked around the room that this made him nervous.

'Why don't we get Subash to bring us some brandies up to my balcony. It's peaceful there overlooking the garden. We can carry on talking.'

He agreed, and she showed him up the sweeping staircase, through the upstairs hallways to her room. There, she took him through to the balcony that was full of greenery and bright blossom: tumbling bougainvillea, bright red geraniums, and a flowering vine covered the back wall.

Subash brought them a decanter of brandy and two glasses. Robert poured them both large measures and he took a swig. They both sat down in the basket chairs and Robert fixed Edith with his gaze and said,

'She never loved me, you know. Betty. She wouldn't admit it, but I knew it from the start. I was just kidding myself. I so wanted it to work.'

'Oh, Robert. That's not true, surely. She was bowled over by you, don't you remember?'

'If I'm honest, I remember that she was pretty hostile at

first. She didn't like me. It was you and I who got on well. She changed her tune after a couple of days, though.'

Edith looked down at her hands in her lap. It was true. She couldn't deny it.

'Things were never easy between us when we went back to Rangoon either,' Robert went on, passing his hand over his face, 'Not once reality had kicked in. At first she loved the house. Who wouldn't have done? It is... *was* a beautiful house. And I was able to give her the life of luxury she so clearly craved. At first, she seemed to love all the trappings of wealth that I could provide. The trips to the tailor's for new clothes, the parties, the afternoons at the club. She lapped it all up at first.'

'So, what happened?' Edith asked quietly.

He shrugged and took another swig from his glass.

'She got bored, I suppose. Bored and restless. She started being difficult; cruel to me and foul to the servants. There was no explanation for it.'

Edith shook her head. 'She was always a little bit like that I'm afraid. Spoiled. It was my fault. I spoiled her myself but I knew no better. I was only a couple of years older than her. I had no idea how to treat her and in no position to bring up a child.'

'It wasn't your fault, Edith. Please don't blame yourself. You know, I loved her so much, but I had no idea what to do for the best. I knew she didn't love me, that she was bored to death by my company, that after the novelty had worn off she hated Rangoon and the expat community. She found it hard to make any friends amongst the wives.'

Edith shook her head. 'She was always the same. People were put off by her manner.'

'So then, someone suggested that she should start helping out at a clinic for the Burmese poor. She went along one day and, as I'd expected, she hated it. But she kept going and after a few sessions, she seemed to take to it. I was so relieved, but then she couldn't keep away from the place. She was going virtually every day. And when she wasn't there, she was out with the people she'd met there. I never got to meet any of them, but I guessed some of them were subversives, from a couple of things she said.'

Edith kept quiet. She didn't want to mention Ye Win. It wouldn't do Robert any good to hear about him, she was quite sure.

'I felt so alone, Edith. It was part of the reason I signed up. I couldn't see a way out of it. I loved her, but she didn't love me back. I tried so hard to please her, but she rejected me. It was never right between us, and now she's gone and I can do nothing to change that.'

Suddenly, he fell silent. His head dropped and his shoulders hunched and Edith realised he was sobbing. A wave of pity washed over her and she rushed over to him and put her arms around his shoulders. The sobs didn't subside, but he took her hand and held it tight. She stroked his hair and his shoulders to try to calm him and as she did that, he lifted her other hand to his lips and kissed it. Then he looked into her eyes and, instinctively, without considering the consequences for a second, she kissed him on the mouth. Before she knew what was happening, he was kissing her back, kisses of pain and grief and of long suppressed passion.

Still kissing, they moved back into the bedroom, closed the doors and fell down on the bed together. He was running his hands all over her body, caressing her, holding her close, still kissing her hungrily, and she was doing the same, pulling him close to her, wanting to heal his hurt and to heal her own. When they finally made love it was an act of longing; of desperate and painful searching, borne out of their mutual grief. But there was something else there too; beneath the rawness of the pain they were both feeling, Edith sensed that they were reclaiming something too; it was the chance that had been denied them when Betty had staked her claim to Robert.

FOR THE NEXT three nights they stayed together, cementing their bond, helping each other to recover from their pain and sadness. After making love, Robert would always go back to his room. During the daytime they would go out together; they strolled on the maidan, just as they had the first day they'd met. They walked in the botanical gardens, visited mosques and Hindu temples. They were as relaxed and comfortable in each others' company as if they'd been together since the day they'd met.

Edith was keen that the servants shouldn't know about their liaison. She knew they would be shocked, especially so soon after Gregory's death. Looking at herself in the mirror one morning, she noticed that there was colour in her cheeks again, and her eyes shone with a deep but magnificent secret. She glanced at Gregory's picture on her dressing table. Examining her feelings, she realised she didn't feel remotely guilty for what had happened between her and Robert. It had nothing to do with her love for Gregory, or Robert's unrequited love for Betty. She thought of all these things as existing on separate planes and having no effect on one another. Her love for Gregory was still as complete and intact as it ever was, as was her love for her sister. All she was doing with Robert, was reconnecting, as if an electric wire had been severed but was now repaired, allowing the current to flow freely.

But on the fourth day everything changed. Subash solemnly brought Edith her post on a silver tray at breakfast. There were several letters addressed to her; some obviously bills. Robert had just left the table to go to his room to get ready for their daily outing. He had to leave that evening to return to his regiment, so it was his last day. There was one letter that stood out from the others. Edith stared at the letter and shock coursed through her. The writing on the envelope was familiar. It was Betty's. Had she written it before the explosion?

Edith took up the letter and ripped open the envelope. Holding it between trembling fingers she read;

Dear Edith,

I've left Rangoon and have come north to Myitkyina. They are doing airlifts of civilians from here, so I may be able to fly out to India. If not I will get to you somehow, even if I have to walk across the mountains.

There have been a lot of bombing raids over the past few weeks. Our house was completely destroyed, but luckily I wasn't there. I'd had to go to see my ayah in the Burmese quarter at the time.

I've been writing to Robert, but he hasn't replied to my last letter so I've no idea if my letter got to him. If you happen to see him, tell him I'm safe and that I'm making my way to India as best I can.

There is something I need to tell you, Edith. I need to tell you in person, but it is a secret that I've been keeping for several months. I will save it until I arrive with you. You will be surprised, I'm sure.

Your ever loving,
Betty.

9

OLIVE

Dapha River Tea Plantation, Assam, 1942

IT BEGAN to rain as the people started to arrive. Olive watched them as they picked their way along the riverbank towards her; women and children, mothers and fathers, grandparents, babies. They came with all their belongings strapped to their backs, slung over shoulders, or pulled along in makeshift carts. Some carried babies, children, and even old people on their backs. Many were very thin, dressed in filthy rags, their bodies and clothes matted with dirt. To her surprise, some of them were dressed in finery. Dinner jackets and evening gowns, now torn and streaked with mud.

As they advanced along beside the river and drew level with Olive, she stepped out and offered them a cup of tea and some rice. Most nodded gratefully, heaved their belongings off their backs and sat down on the logs Henry had assembled around the fire with the help of Hannibal. Many of them were too exhausted or too dejected to speak, but some of them told her of their journey so far.

'We've been walking for a fortnight,' said one man. 'The way is slippery and dangerous. Sometimes at night we've managed to find shelter, at other times we've had to sleep out in the open. When we do that, my children are terrified that we might be attacked by jungle creatures.'

He had three young children with him, but he told her that his wife and their baby son had died during the first week of their march from Burma. They'd contracted typhoid and his wife had become so weak that she simply couldn't go on.

'The baby died first, and after that she lost the will to carry on,' said the man, staring into the fire. 'She just lay down beside the path and closed her eyes. There was nothing I could do to rouse her. In the end, I just had to leave her body there to sink into the mud, or to be eaten by tigers.'

Olive's heart broke for him. Her eyes filled with tears at his words. And she watched him, sitting on those logs beside his three young children, and realised that he had no idea of what the next day would bring, or whether he'd be able to make it through the hills to safety or not. How brave he was to try. How brave they all were.

She heard many stories like that. People came struggling along the Dapha River valley from mid-morning until mid-afternoon. Then the stream of refugees stopped. They had a certain number of miles to cover each day and they had to have got across the Dapha River by around three o' clock or they wouldn't make it to the next camp by nightfall.

Olive was especially struck by the plight of the children. Some were simply babies, riding on their parents' backs, others were toddlers, struggling to walk in the mud and to keep up with the others. Nearly all of them looked pitifully thin, their cheeks hollow and their eyes desperate. They had little energy even to walk, and no wish to play once they sat down.

'It's so awful to see what these people are going through,' she said to Henry. 'How can the government have let this happen?'

'I know, it is, truly dreadful,' he replied. 'I think they tried to evacuate as many people as they could, but the airfield at Myitkyina was bombed by the Japs and eventually taken over. People were told to walk to India.'

Some of the refugees carried flimsy maps with them. These looked as if they'd been issued by British officials in Burma. They showed a walking route between Langtao in Burma to Margherita in Assam. It was hundreds of miles, and the thin dotted line on the map, that traced the route of rivers, crossed mountain ranges and forded deep valleys, showed nothing of the monumental difficulties of the route. Or the fact that a lot of it was through untamed jungle, along swollen river valleys, battling monsoon, hunger, mud and disease.

'I wish there were more we could do to help them,' she said to Henry.

'We're doing what we can,' he replied. 'But when the monsoon comes, they'll need more help.'

Each day, for the next three weeks or so, Olive and Henry carried on with the same routine. They got up early, packed their supplies onto Hannibal's back and rode him down through the jungle to the water's edge. Henry would make a fire and boil up water for tea and they would sit beside the roaring river and wait for the first walkers to appear on the slippery path.

The monsoon came early that year. The days grew gradually hotter and the heat more oppressive. One morning Olive awoke to the sound of rain drumming on the bedroom roof, cascading down the house and splashing on the path outside. It was thunderous, deafening. In previous years she'd welcomed the onset of the monsoon. She'd watched and waited for it for weeks. It normally meant an end to the sticky, stifling days and unbearable nights, but this year she thought of the refugees, spending the night in flimsy camps or makeshift shelters, then walking through the daytime in these conditions. Their ordeal, already terrible, had just got many times worse.

She turned to Henry, who was stirring awake.

'Listen to the rain!' she said. 'What about the refugees? How will they cope in this?'

'It will be awful for them,' he said, sitting up and looking at the rain pouring down the windows. 'They won't be able to cross the river on foot anymore. That's where the elephants will come in. I'll phone round the other local plantations before we set off. I'm hoping we'll be able to get several elephants down by the bank to take the refugees over. I'll get the mahouts to take all ours from the plantation down there too for this afternoon.'

They put their waterproofs on before they set off. The journey on Hannibal's back, down through the dripping jungle, felt more hazardous than on previous days. The elephant had to proceed more slowly than before, and a couple of times on the slippery downhill sections, he slipped slightly on the mud and had to right himself. On one occasion, he lifted his trunk and trumpeted loudly, showing his displeasure at the task he was being asked to perform, but Henry encouraged him on with gentle words and the pressure of his heels behind Hannibal's ears.

The river had already risen at least a foot by the time they got down to their usual spot along the bank. Henry had built a wooden shelter to store the kettle and sticks overnight, but it was still difficult to get the fire to light. When they arrived, he set about making something stronger and more permanent, so that people could sit and rest out of the rain.

By the time he'd finished, the first refugees were already coming towards them along the slippery bank, their heads bowed against the relentless rain. This time it was an Indian family consisting of mother, father, grandmother and two young children. Seeing Olive offering tea, they stopped and sat on the logs while she handed out tea and rice. They took it gratefully and sat in silence while they ate and drank. Olive sensed that they were too exhausted to speak.

Henry spoke to them, telling them that they needed to cross the Dapha River to continue on their route, but that it was now too swollen for them to do so on foot. As he said this, the father's shoulders drooped.

'Don't worry. We can help you,' Henry said. 'My elephant can cross the river and you can ride on his back.'

The man lifted his eyes to Henry's. They were filled with gratitude and hope. Henry fetched Hannibal who knelt down on the riverbank whilst the whole family climbed onto his back, followed by Henry who straddled his neck. The elephant got to his feet carefully, while the children shrieked with delight. Olive smiled herself, seeing their faces light up for the first time.

'Be careful Henry, please,' she said, having to shout to make herself heard above the roar of the river. She was suddenly afraid for her husband. Was this sensible? Was he sure Hannibal would be able to cross?

'Don't worry,' he mouthed, and they set off along the riverbank towards the crossing point. Olive followed on foot, putting up her hood against the pelting rain, knowing that she should really wait in case more people came, but she needed to watch this first crossing. She walked behind the elephant, who swished his tail to and fro. He walked carefully and steadily on the slippery path, and although Olive herself lost her footing and slipped a couple of times, Hannibal didn't put a foot wrong.

It was half a mile or so to the crossing point and as they neared it Olive gasped when she caught sight of the river. The day before there had been stepping stones across a shallow section, just before the river narrowed and plunged into a deep gorge, but today the water roared past, swollen and frothing, a couple of feet above its normal level. The stepping stones had disappeared. No human would have been able to cross the raging torrent at that point.

Henry turned the elephant to face the river and urged him forwards. At that point there was a little beach at the water's edge, so it was easier for Hannibal to get into the river. Without hesitating, the elephant strode forward into the torrent and was quickly up to his belly in the water. Olive held her breath, hoping that the current wasn't too strong for him, but she knew that his instinct would have prevented him from entering the water if he'd feared he couldn't cross. She watched anxiously as the elephant progressed towards the opposite bank. The family clung to the howdah, crouching down, either through fear or because they thought it might assist progress. The current was so strong that with every step the elephant was nudged down a little closer to the gorge, where the current was even stronger. As he reached the middle point of the river, the water was halfway up his belly, frothing and eddying around his legs. He lifted his trunk in the air majestically and trumpeted loudly. That frightened Olive momentarily, remembering how he'd done the same when he'd been afraid on the way down through the jungle, but this time he was trumpeting in triumph. He was over the worst and making for the opposite bank. She held her breath as he forced forwards through the current for the final few steps, then hauled himself out on the other side, trumpeting again with the achievement of having made it across.

Olive started clapping as Hannibal sunk to his knees and his passengers climbed off. They were thanking Henry with handshakes, bows and 'namaste' gestures. Then they turned and waved to Olive on the opposite bank. She waved back, smiling, swelling with pride and relief that they'd reached the other side safely. She watched them gather their belongings and set off on the path which led them along the opposite bank of the Dapha River.

Henry returned across the river on Hannibal's back, and as he got closer, Olive could see the broad grin spreading across his lips. When he saw her returning his smile, he punched the air with his fist. Arriving beside her on the bank, he jumped down from the elephant, took her in his arms and spun her round in a circle.

'Thank you, Mrs Percival,' he said. 'I couldn't have done that without you.'

Later that day, the rest of the elephants arrived from the estate, accompanied by five others from neighbouring plantations, all with their mahouts on board. By this time there was a crowd of people waiting on the bank to be carried across. Olive helped Henry to organise them into groups of four or five and help them onto the backs of the kneeling elephants. This time, they went across in convoy, with the older and most experienced elephants going first side by side, followed by pairs of others. Some of the younger ones were reluctant to go at first, but the older ones encouraged them with their trunks.

As on previous days people kept on arriving at the

crossing point until mid-afternoon and the convoys of elephants kept on carrying them across the swollen river. Every couple of hours they had to take a break to allow the elephants to rest, drink water and eat some bamboo on the edge of the forest, but then they were ready to resume. The expressions on the faces of the refugees said it all for Olive; at last there was someone willing to help them on their impossible journey and for that they were incredibly grateful.

This routine carried on day after day. The refugees kept coming and the elephants were ready to take them across. As the elephants became more experienced, they went across more quickly and were able to transport more people across each hour than on the first day.

Olive kept a tally of how many people had crossed and soon it was almost two hundred. The numbers had started dwindling by the fourth day, but still they kept coming. Now, Olive noticed that the walkers consisted of those who had taken longer than the others to get to that point from Burma; those weakened by illness or starvation; the old, or those encumbered by very small children.

One of the last to arrive was a single woman with a tiny baby. She stood out from the others as she was alone, and she was obviously British, whereas the majority of refugees were Indian. As the woman drew closer, Olive noticed that her hair was matted with mud, but that it could have been blonde underneath. She was dressed in a blue cotton dress that was also streaked and filthy. She carried the baby on her back, tied on with a shawl. As she approached, Olive could see that she was stick thin and could barely walk. She looked as though she was sleepwalking, stumbling and staggering, wandering along the path without direction. As she drew closer to the shelter, it was obvious to Olive that the woman was very ill. Her face was deathly pale and streaming with sweat, her eyes flickering with delirium.

As Olive rushed out to help her, the woman staggered and fell forwards, landing face down in the mud. The baby started screaming. Olive knelt down in the mud beside her, Henry arrived at the same time.

'She looks really ill,' Olive said, as she went to release the baby from the shawl.

'Malaria probably,' answered Henry. 'Lots of the refugees have got it, but she looks to be really bad.'

'Let's carry her into the shelter,' said Olive. 'At least she'll be out of the rain then.'

'Yes. We can make her comfortable there, and when we go back to the house we can take her with us,' said Henry, as he bent forward to turn the woman over and haul her up out of the mud.

Olive cradled the tiny baby in her arms and as she looked into its beady black eyes, it stopped crying and smiled, a smile that melted her heart.

10

EDITH

Calcutta, March 1942

As EDITH SAT at the breakfast table staring down at the letter, she felt the blood drain from her face. Betty was alive, something she'd hoped and prayed for fervently for weeks, but the implications of this news also crushed her inside. She was seized with the most dreadful guilt at what she and Robert had been doing for the past few days. What had she been thinking? What had they both been thinking? It was as if she'd woken from a dream to harsh reality with an enormous jolt. Instantly she knew she had to face the consequences of what they'd done.

She took a few gulps of water, composed herself as best she could and went upstairs and through the hotel to Robert's room at the back. She could hear him humming as she approached. The door was open and she stood for a minute in the doorway watching him. He had his back to her and was packing his things into a holdall, getting ready for the return to his regiment. There was a lightness in his step and his manner that had been lacking when he'd arrived at the hotel a few days ago. Edith took a deep breath and steeled herself. She knew this was the end for the two of them, and despite her guilt at having betrayed Betty, there was a deep sadness inside her too, that the two of them could never be together again.

She knocked gently on the door, 'Robert,' she said weakly. He turned and smiled at her, deep love in his eyes.

'What is it, my darling,' then as he noticed the look on her face he said, 'Good God, you look as if you've seen a ghost.'

'You'd better read this,' she said, handing him the letter.

As soon as he saw the handwriting he blanched. 'My God,' he said, sitting down heavily on the bed. Edith held her breath as he read the letter. When he'd finished he looked up and said, 'She's alive. Betty's alive. I can hardly believe it.'

'What have we done, Robert?' Edith said, coming to sit on the bed beside him, burying her face in her hands, fighting back the tears.

They both sat there for a long time, side by side, not touching, contemplating what had happened between them, and what Betty's news meant for them. Edith couldn't bear to think about how she'd betrayed her own sister. How could she have done what she'd done?

Finally, Robert broke the silence.

'We must never speak of what's happened between us, Edith,' he said quietly.

'I agree,' said Edith.

'And it must never happen again.'

'Of course not,' she turned to look at him, her face wet with tears. 'I'm so sorry, Robert. I mean... I'm not sorry that Betty's alive, just sorry for the way things have turned out.'

'Me too,' he muttered, not meeting her eye.

Then he grasped her hand, lifted it to his lips and kissed it.

'Now,' he said, getting up from the bed, 'I'm going to get my things together and leave the hotel in the next hour. Once I'm gone, as far as we're both concerned, these few days never happened. And we must never mention it again, whatever the future may hold.'

AS THE TRAIN clattered on towards Dibrugarh, Edith thought back to that time with tears in her eyes. The few days she and Robert had spent as lovers counted as one of her sweetest memories, but at the same time, to think about it filled her with anguish. So much so that for years she'd banished it from her thoughts completely. Perhaps that's why it was so painful to revisit those days.

Robert had left the Tea Planter's Club that day and gone back to his regiment. She'd stood beside the reception desk and said goodbye, her heart breaking as he went. Neither of them could look the other in the eye.

She had no idea what had happened to him during the war; which battles he'd fought in, whether he'd been at the famous Allied victories of Imphal and Kohima, or even whether he'd been captured and sent to prison camp. She did know that he was still alive though; she'd read an article in *The Times of India* about the Irrawaddy Steamship Company. It had been nationalised, of course, when the generals took over Burma in 1962, but several old employees had been kept on, the paper reported, amongst them, Robert Charles Furnivall. Since reading that, she'd often wondered how it must have been for Robert, seeing his family's pride and joy that he'd worked a lifetime to build, taken from him and turned over to the state like that. She'd often wondered too if he'd ever remarried. Had he ever gone back to rebuild the house he'd shared with Betty, that had been razed during the bombings?

She stared out at the stretch of untamed jungle that the train was now racing through, thinking back to that time. Even though Betty had not turned up in Calcutta, Edith had never given up hope that she might have survived. And for that reason, she knew she could never see Robert again. While there was any lingering hope that Betty was alive, it wouldn't have been right.

The train drew in to Dibrugarh station and Edith got down stiffly, knowing that there were two further legs to the journey to come. Having asked the guard on the train, who was a local man, she'd found out the whereabouts of the Dapha River Tea Plantation.

'It's beyond Ledo,' he said. 'Maybe one hundred kilometres by road from there.'

'Ledo?'

'Yes, madam. A little town in the Noa Dihing River valley. It is the end of the railway line. The train will take around two hours from Dibrugarh to Ledo and then you might be able to find a bus or taxi to take you the rest of the way.'

Edith wasn't fazed by this journey into the unknown. She'd started out with only a vague idea of the whereabouts of the plantation, but she knew she would get there somehow. There was always a way in India, you just had to be patient. She knew the language and was used to the whims and vagaries of the train network and of Indian transportation generally.

The train to Ledo was already waiting in the station when Edith's train drew in. It was a diesel train, very basic, although it did have a first-class compartment. Edith bought some samosas and some bottled water from a hawker on the station. It felt a long time since breakfast.

The journey to Ledo was less than three hours long and once again the landscape was flat, although leaning out of the window Edith could make out the grey smudge of distant mountains on the horizon. A thrill went through her at the sight of them. That was where she was bound for; the Dapha Plantation lay somewhere up in those hills. Now the mountains were actually in sight she couldn't wait to get there. She might have waited almost forty years, but she was getting impatient now for answers about Betty.

The landscape the train was crossing was flat and featureless. So she turned to her book again, only looking up as the train rattled across the metal bridge that crossed the wide brown Noa Dihing River as it entered the little town of Margherita.

A couple of hours later, at Ledo, Edith got down from the train. She glanced at the sky. It was darkening rapidly, the huge red sun sinking behind the shabby buildings beyond the station. She hadn't wanted to, but she now realised that she needed to find somewhere to stay in the town. She was never going to find a taxi to take her into the hills at this time, and in any case, there would probably be no one at the plantation when she arrived.

A taxi took her to a flea-bitten hotel on the main street of the small town. It seemed to be the only one in town. Her room was stuffy and noisy, directly above the road. The puny ceiling fan made little impression on the stifling air. There was a mosquito net over the bed which had some obvious rips in it, but Edith was so tired she was past caring. She lay down on the bed and closed her eyes.

Even though she was exhausted, sleep wouldn't come. She was plagued with memories; those few precious, forbidden days with Robert, Betty's mysterious secret in her final letter, the knowledge that Betty must have set off on foot into the nearby hills but had never emerged. Edith felt keenly that she was on the brink of some discovery on this journey. That knowledge had kept her awake until the small hours.

In the morning, the taxi that had brought her to the hotel, returned to collect her just after dawn. It was an ancient, battered Toyota and Edith had her doubts that it was capable of travelling one hundred kilometres, especially into the mountains, but all the others in town looked equally decrepit. At least the driver was friendly and seemed to know the way to Dapha.

Edith was tired from her restless night but couldn't suppress the excitement she felt thinking about what the day may bring. It was Wednesday now. The day that Richard Edwards was due back on the plantation. She hoped against hope that he would have kept Betty's papers, but even if he hadn't, she needed to go into those hills and to the place Betty must have walked through on her long trek from Burma.

Soon they left the little town behind and took the road towards the hills. It was potholed and, in some places, just a dirt track. The driver hardly slowed down, despite the road surface. In the back, Edith was bounced around mercilessly. A few miles outside Ledo, the hills began to rise on either side of the road. Here the road was lined with trees. It crossed rivers and ran through straggly villages of one-storey huts. Cattle and goats grazed beside the road, buffalo wallowed in muddy pools and looked up to stare as the car passed. The hills gradually grew steeper and closed in either side of the road. The forest was thicker here and the road climbed higher and higher beside a gorge; on one side a precipice plunged down to the river below.

As they progressed, the tarmac eventually stopped altogether and they were bumping along on a single lane track through the jungle. It was incredibly steep in places, up and down hills, over river valleys. Edith began to wonder if the driver had come the right way. Was it possible that anyone actually lived and worked in such a remote location?

Eventually though, the road joined another, wider road that came in from the left and soon they saw a gate up ahead. "Dapha River Tea Plantation" said a sign above it. The driver flashed a toothy smile over his shoulder as if to say, 'I told you I knew where it was,' and swept on through the gates. On either side of the road now were tea gardens, stretching as far as the eye could see, covering all the nearby hills with row upon uniform row of neatly clipped bushes. Half a mile or so on, the road widened and ran between some buildings; a huge wooden tea factory, flanked on either side by rows of small dwellings. The driver stopped the car and Edith got out.

'You want me to wait?' he asked.

'If you don't mind. But I'm not sure how long I'm going to be.' She wondered how else she was going to get away from here.

He shrugged and took up a newspaper from the passenger seat. 'Let me know what you want,' he said.

There seemed to be no one about and Edith suddenly felt nervous. What if she'd travelled for two and a half days for nothing? She approached what looked like an office, pushed the glass door open and went inside. An

Indian woman behind the desk looked up from a typewriter and Edith enquired after Mr Edwards. The woman told her he was up at the house as it was lunchtime. Edith could wait for him to come back or go on up to the house herself.

'Won't he mind?'

'Of course not. Go on up. But you might want to take the car. It's quite a long way – up that road.'

Thanking the woman, Edith got back into the taxi. It was over half a mile further on from the buildings, up a winding road that ran through a patch of trees and beside some tea gardens. The house appeared before them round a bend and the sight of it took Edith's breath away. It was a square, white, two-storey building with a deep veranda wrapped around each side on both floors. In front was a beautiful garden with an immaculate lawn and filled with flowering rose bushes. There was something elegant and pleasing about the place.

As they drew up at the front door, a man emerged and came down the front steps. He looked to be in his early thirties; tanned and energetic.

'Can I help you?' he asked, speaking through the open window of the taxi.

'Are you Mr Edwards? Mr Richard Edwards?' asked Edith.

'Yes. What can I do for you?'

Edith got out of the taxi and shook hands with him.

'My name is Edith Mayhew. You might not remember this, but you wrote to me a couple of years ago when you first came to the estate. The letter never got to me, but I found it recently. It was about my sister's papers. Betty Furnivall. Do you happen to have kept them?'

'Mrs Mayhew. So pleased to meet you after all this time.

Why don't you come in and have a drink on the veranda. You must have had a long journey.'

Then he leaned into the taxi and spoke in rapid Assamese to the driver. Edith couldn't understand everything, but understood that Richard Edwards was telling the taxi driver to drive round to the back of the house where someone would give him refreshment.

The veranda was long and shady, with ceiling fans whirring at regular intervals to keep the place cool. Edwards asked her to sit down at a cane table, and brought a jug of lemonade and a plate of sandwiches. Once he'd given her a glass, he said,

'Please. You must be hungry after your journey. Eat as much as you like. And the answer to your question is yes, I have kept your sister's papers. They looked far too important to throw away.'

Edith's heart missed a beat. This vindicated her decision to come on this wild expedition.

'She was trying to get to Calcutta during the war,' she said. 'Perhaps she stopped off here?'

The man took a sip of his drink and fixed Edith with a steady gaze. 'According to the servants, Mr and Mrs Percival who lived here at the time, helped a lot of refugees fleeing from Burma to India. They had several elephants for transporting tea down the mountains to the railway. They used the elephants to help the refugees cross the river during the monsoon of 1942. Perhaps that's how her papers came to be here.'

'Probably. Betty never arrived in Calcutta, although she'd written to say she was coming. I've never found out what happened to her, and I've never found her name on any records of those who were reported dead. Where did you find the papers, if I may ask?'

'Funnily enough they were found at the back of a drawer in a bungalow on the estate. Apparently, Mr Percival's mother occupied the bungalow, but she died at some point in 1942. The bungalow was left empty after that. It had been neglected and was in a bit of a state when we bought the place.'

Edith bit into an egg sandwich and took a sip of lemonade, glad of the food and drink and the chance to sit down in a cool place, but she was anxious for answers.

'Could I see the papers please?'

'Of course. Apologies for keeping you waiting. They're under lock and key in my office. I'm afraid they're not in a very good state, but you'll see that in a moment.'

He leapt up and disappeared into the house. Edith felt herself tensing up. This was the moment she'd been waiting nearly forty years for. It felt overwhelming that now, at long last, she might be going to get some answers.

Richard Edwards returned within minutes, carrying a large brown envelope. He handed it to Edith and she took it with trembling hands.

The envelope was unmarked. 'I kept them in there for safekeeping,' he explained. 'Everything we found to do with your sister is inside.'

She put her hand inside the envelope and pulled out the contents. It was a leather-bound book with a blue cover, a sealed envelope, together with a wartime identity card. She stared at the envelope and was stunned to see her own address written on it in Betty's handwriting. The envelope was damaged almost beyond repair. The edges were singed black and yellow as if it had been in a fire. The ID card and the book were the same. The cover of the book was burned and destroyed all around the edges, and when she opened it, the edges of the pages had been singed away.

She stared down at the front page and read: "Betty's Journal. Rangoon, 1938."

Seeing Betty's handwriting, her ID card with her address in Rangoon and her signature suddenly brought it all home to Edith. Finally, she had a link to Betty after all these years. She found her eyes filling up with tears. Edwards leaned forward.

'I'm so sorry, Mrs Mayhew. It must be an emotional moment for you. Would you like me to leave you alone? I should be getting back to work soon anyway.'

Edith wiped her tears away. 'Don't worry. I'll be fine shortly.'

'Look, I've just had a thought,' he went on. 'I mentioned the bungalow in the grounds. The company did it up to let it out to tourists. There's no one in it at the moment. Perhaps you'd like to stay there tonight? It's a very long way back to Calcutta.'

She paused, considering his offer. The plantation was a beautiful place, and it would feel right to read Betty's words in a place where she herself had once been.

'That's very kind, but what about the taxi?'

'Well, the driver could either stay here – we have quarters for drivers when tourists stay, or he could go back home and one of our drivers could take you down to Ledo tomorrow, or whenever you're ready to leave.'

'I hope you don't mind my asking, but how much might it cost to stay the night?' she asked.

'Please, Mrs Mayhew. I'm asking you to stay as a guest of the plantation. You've had an extraordinary journey and it must be a momentous occasion to see your sister's things. It would be an honour to have you stay, and if you do, I hope you'll dine with me here this evening?'

'Well... that's very kind of you indeed. I would love to stay, but... I'll need to make a couple of calls if that's OK?'

LATER, Edith sat on the terrace of the bungalow, looking out over the gentle hills covered in lines of emerald green tea bushes. She'd telephoned Anesh and asked him to put off the Clover International people for another couple of days. Richard Edwards had then shown her to the bungalow, a short walk from the main house nestled out of sight behind some trees at the edge of the estate. Inside it was beautifully restored, light and airy, with pale furnishings and white gauze curtains at the windows. The views over the mountains were stunning.

Once he'd left her alone, she felt ready to start looking at Betty's papers. She took a deep breath and ripped open the envelope addressed to her. There was a just single sheet of paper inside, the edges singed, but the writing was still legible. She unfolded it and read;

My Dearest Edith,

I hope this letter reaches you eventually and finds you well. I've no idea where I'll get a chance to post it, but I'm writing it in readiness for that moment. The walk from Burma into India has been the hardest thing I've ever done in my life. It has tested me to the limit. You'll find me a very changed person from the frivolous girl you used to know.

I'm writing this because I haven't been honest with you Edith. There are secrets I've kept from you these past few years. I want to change all that. I could wait until we are together, but it will be very hard to tell you everything and to make sure I tell it properly and don't forget any of the details. So, I've thought of a way of doing it which will mean you will know everything before I arrive with you. I'm going to send you my journal. I started it when I arrived in Rangoon and I've kept it ever since. It explains everything, Edith, so once you've read it, you'll know, and I hope, understand. Please don't judge me too harshly when I finally arrive.

Your ever loving,
Betty

11

BETTY'S JOURNAL

Rangoon, 1938

November 15th

ROBERT and I arrived here in Rangoon a week ago today. I've been meaning to start a journal, so I can look back and remember everything about this time, but I've only just got round to it. Yesterday, I went down to the department store, Whiteway and Laidlaw on Merchant Street in the centre of the city. It is a beautiful shop, far more sumptuous than anything at home, with uniformed doormen to greet you and a luxurious interior. Robert was at work at the office, so he couldn't come with me, but I took the car and driver and just went. I found the stationery department easily and they had just what I wanted. This beautiful blue leather-bound book complete with a pencil on a ribbon.

The day after we arrived from the boat, Robert took me on a tour around the sights of the city centre. What a beautiful, majestic city it is, with huge colonial buildings lining the long, straight roads near the river. They wouldn't look out of place in London, with their pillars and arches, but the difference here is that there are rows of palm trees in front of them, and Burmese men in long sarongs, which they call longyis, going in and out of the entrances.

Robert took me for a cocktail in the bar of the Strand Hotel, and we bumped into a couple of his business associates. Two men with whom he has contracts to transport teak and jute from up-country. They seemed very friendly, but quite surprised that Robert had brought a new wife home with him from Calcutta. As we left, they both said that it would be nice to meet up at the club, and that their wives would be delighted to meet me.

We haven't got to the club yet though. Robert has been very busy at work since we returned and has just wanted to dine quietly at home in the evenings. I must say, I was expecting to go out a bit more to celebrate our arrival, and for Robert to show me off to his friends, but I can't complain about staying at home, since the house is just about the most beautiful home I've ever seen.

When we came here from Rangoon docks on the first day, we drove up Shwedagon Pagoda road and already I could see that I was going to be living in the smartest district of Rangoon. All the houses, on either side of the road, looked like mansions. They are built in all different styles – some look Chinese, with elaborate, pagoda-style roofs, others are traditional English homes, with Tudor-style timber frontage, others are more imposing; white stuccoed walls with pillared porticoes. All are set in huge grounds, behind double gates and have long driveways lined with coconut palms. Robert looked as proud as punch as we turned into the driveway and scrunched along the gravel to the front of the house. He could see how impressed and excited I was.

He showed me inside and all the servants lined up at the front door and bowed low when we entered. There were so many that I couldn't count them all, but at the top of the line was an exquisitely beautiful Burmese girl, whom Robert introduced as Daw Ma. She is to be my maid, or ayah as it's known in the East. It is difficult to imagine her looking after me; she is so petite and beautiful she looks of noble birth, but Robert assured me that she is an experienced maid and that if I look around, all Burmese women are as delicate and poised as she is.

Then Robert showed me around the house, pride brimming in his eyes. And no wonder he's proud. It is like a palace; black and white tiled hallway with a cavernous ceiling and a sweeping staircase. The reception rooms are panelled and beautifully furnished, and upstairs, our bedroom suite, overlooking the garden with a wrought iron balcony, is equally magnificent. There is a four-poster bed with silk hangings, a carved dressing table and a velvet upholstered chaise longue beside the window. I knew Robert was rich, but I hadn't appreciated quite how well he lived here in Rangoon!

I must write to Edith and tell her all about it. It's been worrying me that she did look a little downhearted as I left after the wedding. I know she will miss me desperately, as I will her, but it seemed to be more than that. I must admit that it has troubled me a little that she and Robert were getting on so well before he and I got close. But I don't think there could have possibly been anything romantic in their friendship. I mean, how could there have been? Edith is so plain and she's never been popular with men. I admit she does have a certain understated style, but I don't believe Robert could have fallen for her. And there is no reason why they can't go on being friends, is there? After all, they are family now.

The day after we arrived, Robert took me on a tour of all the sights as I mentioned. Rangoon is an extraordinary city, bustling with colour and life and noise. In many ways it reminds me of Calcutta; the cries of street hawkers, the smell of spices on the air, the teeming crowds and the beautiful architecture. But the people are different. Here they are petite and neat and seem a little less curious than in India. They appear to be very self-contained, going about their business quietly, almost shying away from contact with Europeans, and I get a distinct feeling of hostility from the way people look at me, although they instantly look away if they see me looking back.

The highlight of our tour was the magnificent Shwedagon Pagoda. It is built on a hill and dominates the skyline of the city wherever you are, especially from our road which is so close. The Pagoda, a great shimmering spire, gives out a sort of golden glow that is so bright when the sun shines directly on it that you have to look away. We went there just before sunset and had to climb many flights of steps to get to the main platform. We walked up between stalls selling artefacts, and items for the faithful to offer when they worship at the temple; lotus buds, marigolds, candles and incense. There were many monks climbing beside us up to the temple, with shaved heads, bare feet and clad in maroon robes. The beauty of the twilight, the smoke from incense and candles, and the chanting and discordant sound of gongs from the temple up above, made the whole experience spiritual somehow. I gripped Robert's hand and said, 'Thank you for bringing me here. It's a magical place. I know I'm going to love Rangoon.'

The temple itself took my breath away when we finally reached its base. This enormous gold structure, rearing up in front of us with its perfect symmetry, surrounded on every side by dozens of other, smaller stupas, all elaborately carved and decorated, like filigree jewellery, was like nothing I've ever seen before. We walked all the way round the platform at the base of the pagoda, where thousands of flickering candles lit the way. Buddhists knelt to worship or sat meditating in front of shrines. We walked round slowly, just absorbing the atmosphere. The sun was poised above the city at that point. We went and stood at the railings at the edge of the platform and from there we could see the whole of Rangoon stretched out beneath us, the lines of streetlights sparkling like something from a fairytale. As the sun went down, the sky was streaked all the colours of the rainbow, and the temple seemed to glow even brighter than before, its golden light intensifying as the day faded.

In the morning, Robert rose early and went off to work. He kissed me before he left and said,

'I'm so sorry to leave you alone on your first day, my love, but the business needs me. I'll take you to the club soon and introduce you to everyone so you won't be lonely.'

I didn't mind at all being alone in that glorious house. My day started with a scented bath, following which Daw Ma helped me to get dressed in one of the new floral print dresses that I'd had made in Calcutta. Then I breakfasted alone in the dining room, waited upon by two bearers, following which I went outside on the terrace to read and write letters. In the afternoon I asked the syce, or chauffeur, to take me down to Strand Road to see the centre of the city and to look at the Rangoon River. It felt wonderful to be swept along in that comfortable, luxurious motor car, between those great buildings, past rickshaws and bullock carts, pony traps and bicycles. The pavements were crowded; hawkers peddling their wares, locals in their longyis and conical hats shopping at street markets, eating at food stalls, all turning to stare as we passed.

I asked the syce to stop the car beside the river on Strand Road. Go-downs, or warehouses, stretched along the river in either direction. I got out on the dockside to watch the activity; boats being loaded and unloaded on the quayside, multitudes of coolies at work lugging boxes and crates of supplies, other boats plying to and fro on the great, wide river. Amongst them I saw at least two paddle steamers with the words "Irrawaddy Steamship Company" emblazoned on their side. This made me swell with pride just to see them there and to know that after all the years of scrimping and saving in London, I was now part of something magnificent like that.

November 17th

Yesterday evening, as soon as he got back from the office, Robert took me down to the Pegu Club for the first time. We drew up on the sweeping drive just before sunset. It is a beautiful building; two-storied with wooden balconies running round each floor and louvred blinds covering the windows. It is all made of Burmese teak, Robert tells me, and built that way specially to catch the evening breeze. Inside it is equally imposing; marble floors, high ceilings and lit by chandeliers. All the staff know Robert personally and he shook their hands and greeted them in their own language when we arrived.

We went straight through to the bar which was already

buzzing with people. The hubbub of conversation stopped as Robert and I entered, everyone looking round to stare at me. Of course, I'd been in Rangoon a week already, and Robert had warned me that news travels like wildfire amongst the ex-pat community. All the women in particular craned their necks to take a look at me, one old lady even holding her pince-nez up to her eyes to peer. I didn't mind the attention at all and smiled broadly at everyone. I was proud to be on Robert's arm, dressed in one of my best silk cocktail dresses, my hair piled up on my head. We went up to the bar and Robert asked the barman for two Pegu cocktails.

Many people came up to us to be introduced; business associates of Robert's, civil servants, barristers and judges, army officers. All came to introduce their wives to me and to welcome me to their world. After a while, I lost track of the names and my jaw ached from smiling. It seems that all social activity of the British community centres around this club. There's a library, a games room, a billiard room and outside are some beautifully mown tennis courts. One of the wives asked me if I play tennis and I said, 'Badly, I'm afraid,' but she still invited me to play one morning next week. Another asked me to a coffee morning at her house, which isn't very far from our own. I accepted gladly, wanting to meet people and to fit in, but as I did that, I couldn't help remembering what I'd said to Edith on the ship out to Calcutta, about not becoming one of those wives content to spend their lives playing cards at the club and living on gossip. For the time being, I'm happy to do it though. I need to make friends and find my feet here, after all.

There was one woman who wasn't introduced to me though, and didn't come up to the bar to say hello. She was sitting alone, smoking a cigarette in a long holder and playing solitaire at a table in the corner. She had chic short dark hair and wore a simple black cocktail dress. She gave me a long, scrutinising look and an absent sort of smile. I asked Robert who she was.

'Oh, that's Florence Anderson. Her husband is a teak dealer. He spends quite a bit of time upcountry supervising work in the teak forests so she's alone a fair bit. But she has her own career here in Rangoon. She's a journalist. I have to warn you, she can be a bit frosty.'

I wondered why he didn't introduce me to her, but by the time I got round to asking him that, she'd left the club. I made a mental note to speak to her if I saw her again. Out of all the women I'd seen in the club, she looked by far the most interesting.

December 15th

I've been here over a month now and life has fallen into a familiar routine. Robert is always up early and out of the house by eight o' clock. He works long hours, so I've had to find ways of entertaining myself. There are three or four women I met at the club on that first evening, who have gone out of their way to welcome me into their circle, invite me to their houses and take me out whenever there's an opportunity. I've become quite friendly with Mary Curtis, the wife of a civil servant who lives just around the corner. It is her house I went to for my first coffee morning, three weeks ago now.

Last week she took me downtown to an Indian tailor's shop. 'He's the best man in town,' Mary said. 'He can run up anything overnight, and copy any garment you want.'

Although I had several dresses made in Calcutta before the wedding, I was happy to order more to the same pattern.

The cloth is exquisite here and, as Mary had promised, the tailor amazingly skillful. It was lovely to spend an afternoon in the shop gossiping with Mary, marvelling at skeins of silk, choosing the best colour for our skin, being measured up for dresses. It was the sort of female company I've been missing since I left Calcutta, although Edith was never as enthusiastic about clothes as me.

I went back two days later to collect the dresses I'd ordered. They were beautiful, I must say and I took them home and tried them each on, one after the other, admiring the results in the mirror.

So, there are coffee mornings, cards or tennis at the club, after which a group of us sits on the veranda and gossips. The time passes quickly like that, especially with a couple of cocktails to drink. Now I know as much about the private lives of all the ex-pats in Rangoon as anyone does; who is sleeping with who, who is "in" and who is "out", whose career is on the up and who's about to be put out to grass. I know it all.

Florence Anderson is never at these meetings. I once asked about her during one of these gossipy sessions and there was an awkward pause and I noticed looks being exchanged. Then, Alice Boswell said, 'Oh, she's not really one of us.'

'Why is that?' I asked.

'She's a career woman for a start. She's busy during the daytime and never comes to the club apart from during the evenings.'

'And she's a bit superior,' added Jean Philipps. 'She thinks she's too good for the likes of us.'

'Really?' I found that hard to believe.

'We've tried to invite her to things; tennis tournaments,

whist drives, things like that, but she doesn't seem interested. She's never accepted.'

I shrugged and the conversation moved on quickly, but I made a mental note to speak to Florence Anderson if I saw her in the club. She's so different from the others and so elusive, and the way she looked at me on that first day was very strange. She's started to intrigue me.

12

BETTY'S JOURNAL

Rangoon, 1939

January 20th

A COUPLE of months have passed since I arrived in Rangoon. Christmas has come and gone with very little in the way of celebration.

Christmas was very different here. It was simply too hot to really bother about it and we spent the day at the club where there were decorations hung from the beams and a Christmas tree in the dining room. They served roast chicken with all the trimmings and plum pudding for dessert. I knew it wouldn't be the same as at home, but I did find myself missing a good old traditional Christmas with cold weather and a log fire.

It was slightly overshadowed by some riots that disrupted life in Rangoon for a few days. Robert told me that members of the Burmese Independence Movement had marched on the British Secretariat in Rangoon after a strike by workers at the Burma Oil Company. Robert was very worried about it for a few days, going round with a preoccupied frown, not really listening to what I had to say. He told me he was concerned that the strike would spread to the Steamship Company. He's also a member of Rangoon City Council, involved in deciding how to respond to the demonstrations. Apparently, there's been a growing protest movement amongst the Burmese, especially students, against British rule and this is the third year in a row that there have been riots at Christmas.

Once, on my way to the club in the car, we passed the end of the road that leads up to the Secretariat. I was shocked to see crowds of protesters with banners, running down the road shouting and yelling. Mounted police were trying to break up the crowd, charging at them and beating them with sticks.

'Don't look, madam,' said the syce, putting his foot down and speeding past. I tried not to, but in those few fleeting seconds as we passed the end of the road, I'd already seen several protesters fall to the ground, their heads or faces bloodied. It made me feel quite queasy and I had to have a stiff brandy when I arrived at the club.

Edith writes to me every week. She seems happier now. She's started her job in the Writer's Building (thank God I was spared that!) and although it sounds a bit boring, she's made quite a few friends there. Also, reading between the lines, she's started seeing a lot of Gregory Mayhew. I never rated him. Too aloof for me and far too old to be remotely attractive, but if Edith has a new man in her life I can only heave a sigh of relief, to know that she's not holding a torch for Robert after all. That niggling worry has been the one slight blemish on an otherwise flawless horizon. That, and the fact that I hate to have to admit this, and I only will in my journal, but I am starting to get bored with life in Rangoon.

I am beginning to tire of endless trips to the club, coffee mornings at the same old houses, seeing the same familiar faces time after time. The gossip is getting tiresome too. There is never anything new to discuss. I'm even getting fed up with lounging around at home, despite the fact that it is such a beautiful house. I wish Robert wasn't out quite so much, although I guess he needs to be working at the company to make it the success it so undoubtably is.

However, and here is another admission that won't go beyond these pages: sometimes Robert himself has a tendency to bore me. There, I've written it down! He is a little highbrow and intellectual for my taste if I'm absolutely honest. I think I'd prefer a man who was a bit more interested in sport and more manly pursuits. Robert hasn't the least interest in that sort of thing. He won't play tennis at the club, or go on a shooting party into the jungle with the other men. He'd prefer to stay at home in his study with a history book, or potter about tending the roses in the garden.

All these things have compounded lately to make me get a bit short tempered with Robert on occasion. I shouted at him the other day for not wanting to go to a cocktail party at the Strand Hotel.

'I'm tired,' he said. 'I've only just got back from work.'

'You never think of me, do you? Stuck at home all day or forced to spend time with the same old crowd while you're out at work. Honestly, Robert, sometimes I think you don't care about me at all, you're so self-centred!'

He looked shocked at my words, but he didn't retaliate. I went stomping up to my bedroom and there was Daw Ma standing stock still in the doorway with a sheepish look on her face. I even stormed at her then.

'What are you staring at? You have no right to judge me!'

She frowned, looking wounded and humiliated, and slunk off downstairs. I immediately regretted my words to both of them. Neither deserved what I'd said. It was just the result of my boredom and dissatisfaction and I didn't really mean what I'd said to either of them. I flung myself on the bed, weeping tears of frustration, both at my situation and at the way I had behaved. Soon, though I felt Robert's hand on my arm. He was leaning in to kiss my wet cheeks.

'I'm so sorry you're bored my darling,' he said. 'Why don't you get dressed in one of your lovely dresses and we'll go down to the Strand after all this evening. And I was going to suggest something else. I need to go up to Pagan on business in a couple of days. I was planning to take the train. Why don't you come with me? Pagan is an amazing place. You can take a look at the temples while I have my meetings.'

So, tomorrow we're setting off for Pagan on the early train. I can't wait. It will be wonderful to get out of Rangoon and to see something of the country.

January 22nd

So here we are on the steam train, heading north to Pagan. The syce drove us to the station very early this morning and the train left promptly at seven o'clock. I detest having to get up early, but when I stepped inside our carriage, I knew it was worth it. It is beautifully laid out, with picture windows, a living room, a double sleeping compartment and a little bathroom. I sat myself down on the sofa and watched the countryside roll by as we left the straggling outskirts of Rangoon behind and trundled across the great brown plain northwards. If only we could have gone by steamboat up the river, but when I asked Robert he laughed and pointed out that Pagan is on the Irrawaddy whereas Rangoon is on the Rangoon River and the two don't connect. He promised that one day he will take me from Pagan to Mandalay by paddle steamer though, when he has a few days off.

The landscape was flat and quite featureless, with an occasional outcrop of rock covered in trees and topped by a temple with its many white and golden stupas pointing to the sky. We passed dusty villages surrounded by fields of brown grass, fringed by coconut palms. Sometimes groups of children would stop their play and wave to passengers on the train, or we would pass monks in their maroon robes walking in pairs, their heads bowed. The train plunged through cuttings of red earth, past dirt tracks winding their way across the flat terrain. More than once I saw a pair of white bullocks ploughing a field. Further on, a distant mountain range hove into view and the track ran parallel to it for several miles.

There was a writing desk in our carriage where Robert sat working for the first part of the journey, but after an hour or so he looked up and said, 'Shall we go along to the dining car for a spot of breakfast?'

The dining car was as ornate and luxurious as our compartment, and we were shown to a table covered by a linen cloth and set with silver cutlery. A uniformed bearer in a turban came to take our order. As we waited for our breakfast to arrive, I scanned our fellow first-class passengers, looking for familiar faces. There was no one I recognised, until my eyes alighted on the occupant of the table in the far corner. It was a woman dining alone, and there was something about her manner that was vaguely familiar. She was dressed very differently from the night I'd seen her in the club, which is why I hadn't recognised her straight away.

Now she was wearing a smart linen business suit, but there was the tell-tale cigarette holder she held between two fingers as she scanned a magazine.

'Hey, Robert,' I whispered, leaning forward. 'Don't turn round now, but when you get a chance, look at who's over there in the corner.'

He smiled. 'You'll have to tell me, if I can't look. Unless you're going to keep me in suspense.'

'It's that strange woman, Florence Anderson. I've been meaning to say hello to her at the club, but she hasn't been back since the night we arrived. Perhaps I'll get a chance to meet her now. I must say, she does sound rather interesting.'

I noticed his face cloud over for a second or two before he recovered his composure and smiled again.

'Of course. I'll introduce you if you like. I know her a little. But I have to warn you, please don't go telling her any secrets if you do speak to her.'

'Secrets? Whatever do you mean? I don't know any secrets for one thing.'

'Well, what I mean is, be discreet. Don't tell her anything you wouldn't want appearing on the front pages of the local paper.'

'Really? Has that happened then?'

'She's a journalist, Betty. And an unscrupulous one at that. She'll stop at nothing to get a story.'

'How mysterious,' I said, smiling into his eyes. I didn't ask more, but I was sure there was something he was holding back.

When we were halfway through our breakfast, the woman got up, folded her magazine, picked up her handbag and moved away from her table. As she squeezed past ours, she stopped.

'Robert?' she said. 'I didn't notice you there. Long time no see. How are you?'

Robert stood up politely and shook the woman's hand. Close up she looked a little older than I'd first thought. Late thirties probably. Her face was heavily powdered and she wore a lot of dark eye makeup and strikingly red lipstick. She must have been more than ten years older than me.

'Florence. What a pleasure,' said Robert. 'Allow me to introduce you to my wife, Betty.'

'I heard you'd married. How do you do?' she asked taking my hand. Didn't she remember that night at the club when everyone had been coming up to congratulate us and she just sat there staring?

I shook her hand and felt her intelligent eyes appraising my face.

'And what are you planning on doing in Pagan, Robert?' Florence asked.

'Oh, just business. And Betty's coming with me to see the sights.'

'Are you new to Burma?' Florence asked. I nodded and she went on, 'Well, you'll find Pagan incredibly beautiful. So much so it feels almost unreal to the first-time visitor.'

'And what takes you to Pagan, Florence, if I may ask?' Robert said.

'Well, under all its beauty and charm there is a seamier side,' she said, leaning forward and lowering her voice. 'Insurgents, Robert. Communists. It's a hotbed of them. Didn't you know?'

Robert looked flustered suddenly. 'Well, no, actually. It always seems such a peaceful place. So, what are your plans for these insurgents?'

'Oh, I plan to interview their leader, if I can get hold of him.'

'And your paper will publish that?' Robert asked looking sceptical.

'Not my paper, no. This is a freelance piece I'm doing for a left-wing American magazine. I cast my net wide, you know.'

'Clearly.'

'Well, I'll leave you to it. But Betty,' she said, turning her gaze on me, 'I'm bound to have some free time tomorrow morning. Would you like me to take you around to see some of the temples? It would be nice to have some company.'

'I'd love that,' I said, before I'd noticed Robert's frown of disapproval.

'Alright. I'll be in touch tomorrow morning after breakfast. I take it you'll be staying at the Government Rest House?'

Robert nodded and she left the carriage.

'I'm sorry, did I do something wrong?' I asked.

'No. It's not your fault. You couldn't refuse her invitation, I realise that. But it's best not to get too close to her, that's all. She has a habit of insinuating herself. You need to be careful.'

'She seemed perfectly charming to me,' I protested. He didn't reply but I could tell by the stiff set of his shoulders that something was bothering him.

January 23rd

This morning, we sat on the terrace of the Government Rest House, eating breakfast overlooking the fast-flowing Irrawaddy River that ran past the bottom of the grounds. I'd already realised that Pagan was a unique place, with temples and stupas everywhere you looked and I was looking forward to exploring the surrounding countryside.

Robert got up to leave. He bent to kiss me.

'Have a lovely day, my darling. I'll be back around six. And remember what I said about Florence. Don't let her fool you into betraying confidences.'

'Oh Robert, stop worrying, please,' I said, laughing.

After he'd left, I finished my coffee and strolled across the lawn to the chalet where we were staying. I put my hand on the handle to open the door when a low voice behind me said,

'Are you ready then? I waited until Robert had gone. Why don't we make an early start?'

'Of course,' I said, startled. I turned round. Florence Anderson was standing there right behind me, but I hadn't heard her approach.

She'd hired a tonga – a small cart with a pony – and asked the driver to take us out onto the surrounding plains to get the best views of the pagodas. As we jogged through the streets of the little town, she leaned over to me and said,

'You know, I almost envy you, seeing all this for the first time. It makes such an impression upon one.'

'Well, thank you for taking me,' I said.

'Oh, it's my pleasure. And I'd love to get to know you, now we've met. I'm so curious about who Robert's finally married.'

I frowned. Was this what Robert had been warning me about? I thought it was a slightly tactless statement so decided to ignore it.

The cart carried on along the dusty road until we were clear of the town and the strip of jungle surrounding it.

'Look ahead of you,' Florence said. She motioned to the driver to stop for a moment. 'Stand up and you'll see better,' she said.

I stood up, wobbling slightly in the cart, shaded my eyes and gasped at what I saw. The parched brown plain that was spread out in front of us was dotted with pagodas and stupas as far as the eye could see. Some glinted with gold leaf, others were built of terracotta brick or painted white. The sun was so hot that the landscape glittered in the heat, and the thousands of temple buildings took on a sort of ethereal quality. Far away, on the horizon, the misty plain melted into the shimmering sky.

'It's quite magical, isn't it?' asked Florence. She was smiling with genuine pleasure at my reaction.

'It's stunning. I'm lost for words.'

She asked the driver to take us to some of the main temples. We spent the next couple of hours being ferried from pagoda to pagoda, climbing up flights of steep steps to reach the top of some and stare at the amazing view, others were crumbling with age and neglect, or overgrown so we couldn't get close for fear of snakes. It was exhausting because of the extreme heat and quite soon I was covered in sweat and my face red and perspiring. I didn't mind because it was so fascinating to see these relics of an exotic, bygone age, and Florence was an excellent guide. She knew a lot about the temples and told me a potted history of each as we approached.

After a couple of hours, she asked the driver to take us back to the town.

'Let's go back now. I expect you'd like to get a drink. This is thirsty work,' she said, lying back on the cushions. 'You've done well for a beginner, I must say.'

'Well, thank you for taking me,' I said, lying back myself and closing my eyes. All I could see, once I'd closed them was the colour red burning my eyelids, as the sun beat down on my face.

After we'd gone half a mile or so, Florence said, 'How did you and Robert meet, if you don't mind my asking?'

The warning bells rang in my head, but it was a natural enough question.

'We were staying in the same hotel in Calcutta. My sister and I had just arrived from England,' I answered, hoping that Robert wouldn't think I was giving away too much information.

'I see,' she answered, pausing. Then she said, 'You're not his usual type, I must say.'

I snapped my eyes open at that, shocked that she would say such a thing.

'So, what is his usual type?' I asked.

She laughed long and hard and after a while I propped myself up on my elbow and said,

'Why is that so funny?'

'Well, because it's me!' she answered. 'I'm his usual type.'

My face must have dropped. I could feel the blood rush to my cheeks at the shock of her words. Her smile faded and she peered at me.

'You mean you didn't know?' she asked. I shook my head.

'He didn't tell you?' Again, I shook my head, feeling very foolish and at a severe disadvantage. Was this what he'd been hinting at all along, why he wasn't keen on me spending time with Florence?

Still amused, Florence fished in her bag and pulled out a cigarette and her long tortoise shell holder. She lit it with a silver lighter.

'Do you want one?' she asked, and again I shook my head.

'Well, yes,' she said after a long pause. 'We had a little thing going on. Lasted a couple of years.'

I sat up straight then. 'But... but...'

'But, I'm married? Is that what you're trying to say?'

'Yes, I suppose so. I'm a bit surprised, that's all.'

'Oh, don't be so conventional. My husband turns a blind eye. He's hardly ever around himself so he can't complain.'

'Does he know?'

Florence drew long and hard on her cigarette. 'I'm not sure. He's certainly never mentioned it if he does.'

I was lost for words. There seemed nothing to say after that. Examining my reaction as I watched the countryside roll by, I realised I was more upset at being called conventional than I was by the knowledge that Florence and Robert had once been lovers.

Once we reached the Government Rest House, I got down from the cart. Florence got down after me. She took my hands in both of hers and looked me straight in the eye.

'Please don't judge me for what I told you earlier. It was over between us a long time ago, I can assure you. I think you and I could be good friends, though, don't you agree? It would be nice to see some more sights tomorrow morning if you have time?'

'Alright,' I said hesitantly, not sure how I felt about that but not being able to think of a reason to refuse.

'I have my interview with the rebel leader this afternoon. So, see you tomorrow at around nine o'clock.'

I wandered back to our chalet, had a long shower and threw myself down on the bed under the whizzing ceiling fan. I needed time to digest the news that Florence had divulged, to adapt to it before Robert came back.

I asked him about it as we sat down to dinner on the terrace that evening. I came straight to the point.

'Robert, you didn't tell me that you and Florence had been lovers,' I said. Robert put down his knife and fork.

'I thought she might tell you, but I was hoping she wouldn't.'

'Why?'

'Because it's not a memory I'm proud of. She was married, of course. I felt a bit manipulated to tell you the truth. It ended very badly.'

'Why was that?'

He cleared his throat and leaned forward to whisper. 'Because she was spying on me. That's why I warned you to be careful. When she was at the house she would go into my study and look through my papers. On the lookout for a story, of course. I caught her at it once and that was the end.'

My hand flew to my mouth. 'That's awful,' I said. Now I could understand why Robert had told me to be discreet. I wasn't surprised that he was wary of her.

Next morning, Florence collected me in the same cart and we set off to see yet more temples. She had a camera with her this time and took photographs of me posing in front of various different pagodas.

'I'll give them to you when we're back in Rangoon,' she said.

Back in the cart she asked me how I was finding life in Rangoon.

'Oh, it's very pleasant,' I said.

'The colonial lifestyle can pall after a bit,' she said, drawing on her cigarette and staring out at the horizon. 'I must say, I think I'd go mad without my career.'

'Yes, I must admit that one can get a little tired of coffee mornings and whist rounds at the club,' I replied.

'Why don't you look for something a bit more reward-ing?' she asked. 'I know just the thing. I volunteer at a clinic for the Burmese poor once a week. They're always looking for helpers. There's an interesting crowd of volunteers who go there. Quite different from your usual club crowd. I think you'd like it.'

'I don't have any medical training,' I said quickly. It didn't sound like something I would enjoy at all.

'Oh, there's no need to worry about that. Nor do I. You don't need any medical background. They're just glad of an extra pair of hands. Why don't you try it? At least come along once. You might actually enjoy it.'

I paused, leaning back on the cushions, closing my eyes and letting the light flicker across my eyelids. I thought back to how tiresome I was finding life; the endless rounds of coffee mornings and tennis parties; lonely and mind-numbingly bored in my luxurious house. Why not try something new? I snapped my eyes open and sat up.

'Alright. I will. Next time you go to the clinic, I'll come along too.'

13

EDITH

Dapha River Tea Plantation, Assam, 1980

EDITH PUT Betty's journal down and stared across from where she sat on the terrace of the bungalow at the rows of tea bushes. Now there were women picking the tea in the next field. She hadn't noticed them arrive but there were dozens of them, like a kaleidoscope of butterflies. They wore sarees in all the colours of the rainbow and carried baskets on their backs, into which they threw the leaf tips over their shoulders. They were so close she could even hear their shouted conversation and laughter as they worked.

She thought back over what she'd read in the journal. Betty's description of her boredom and behaviour rang true and she suspected there had been more tension than she'd described in those pages. There was nothing so far that surprised her too much, other than the introduction of Florence Anderson. Robert had never mentioned her, though why should he have done? Edith examined her reaction to this. She was surprised that Robert would have had an affair with a married woman. He was such an honest, upstanding person, it seemed an odd thing for him to have done. Perhaps that was the reason he hadn't mentioned it to Edith. It sounded from the journal as if Robert had been manipulated into it. Perhaps Florence had only got close to Robert in order to get information from him; though what information that might be, Edith could only speculate.

Glancing at her watch she saw that it was six o'clock. She went through to the bathroom, showered and changed into a crumpled skirt and blouse. She looked at her face in the mirror. Her nose was red from the sun. She wondered about putting on makeup but quickly decided against it. She'd never really been a one for that. Only when she needed to boost her morale after Gregory's death. And she was only dining with Richard Edwards. He was hardly likely to notice.

She walked through the gardens to the big house and waited on the veranda. Richard came out with a decanter and they sat and watched the sun go down over the jungle with their drinks.

'Did you read your sister's papers?' Richard asked gently.

'Some of it, yes. She left a really long journal. I've only got part of the way through. You know, it's still a mystery to me what happened to her. She was clearly here on this plantation, or her papers wouldn't have been here. But where did she go from here?'

'I'm wondering if Mrs Percival had any family who might know something about it. I believe she did have a son, but when we bought the estate we dealt with her executors, a firm of lawyers in Calcutta. I believe the son's lawyers were in Rangoon. I could give you their address.'

'Perhaps I could write to them and find out what they know.'

'They might put you in touch with the son, I suppose.

Although I'm not sure how old he is. He might have been too young during the war to remember anything.'

The bearer brought their meal out onto the veranda and Edith discovered she was ravenously hungry. She tucked into a delicious duck curry cooked with gourd, that Richard said was a speciality of the region.

'Maybe I should introduce Assamese food at the restaurant...' she began before remembering.

'Why not?' asked Richard.

'Because I'm about to sell the hotel. I'd more or less decided that I'm never going to make a living out of it, so I might as well move on and do something different.'

'You don't sound totally convinced,' he said.

'No, I'm not. You know, this journey has made me think about it a bit. It's good to get away. It gives you perspective. I've realised that the hotel means so much to me. It's my life. I'm not at all sure that I'm ready to give it up.'

Richard smiled. 'Well, if this trip has settled your mind about that, it must have been worth doing.'

'It's done a lot more than that,' she said. 'It's reunited me with my sister after almost forty years.'

Later, she went back to the bungalow and although she was yearning to lie down, close her eyes and sleep off the exhaustion of the day, she couldn't resist the pull of Betty's journal. So, she covered herself with mosquito repellent, sat outside on the terrace with a cup of tea and went back to where she'd left off earlier in the day.

Betty's Journal

March 10th

This morning, Florence picked me up in her car from the house and drove me to the clinic in the backstreets of Rangoon. She's the only woman I know in Rangoon who drives herself around. Most of us go about in limousines driven by Indian or Burmese syces. In fact, I've never thought to do otherwise, but Florence is different. She told me her car is a Buick roadster that came from America. 'Giles had it imported, but hardly ever uses it himself,' she said, navigating her way down Pansodan Street between the rickshaws and bullock carts.

'Is Giles your husband?'

'Yes,' she said, with a sideways look, but didn't elaborate.

She drove through the side streets a little too quickly, but with the skill of someone familiar with the city. As she drove, she chain smoked from her tortoise shell cigarette holder, flicking ash casually over the side of the car. Soon we had left the city centre way behind and were moving deep into the poverty-stricken suburbs; dusty streets lined with flimsy shacks. Some made of cardboard, some tarpaulin and others corrugated iron, where skinny children stopped and stared as we passed, and equally malnourished chickens pecked around on waste-ground while packs of pariah dogs scavenged in rubbish heaps.

'Welcome to Mingaladon township,' said Florence. 'This is one of the very poorest parts of Rangoon. Not many westerners venture here.'

I was shocked and a little sickened by what I saw. It was such a contrast to the British quarters of beautiful buildings set in spacious grounds. I'd had no idea that there was such poverty such a short distance away. We passed a shabby, four-storey building without windows, where destitute looking people sat outside on the front steps.

'That's a clothing factory,' Florence remarked. 'Churning out cheap goods for the British market. Those people outside are probably waiting for work.'

I stared out at the desperate faces as we flashed past, stunned yet again that this exploitation was happening right under our noses.

After a few more twists and turns, Florence stopped outside a single-storey brick-built building.

'This is it. I'll show you inside.'

Inside the front door was a crowded waiting room, where many people sat silently on a row of wooden benches waiting to be seen. She showed me through the waiting area and along a passage. There were four or five rooms opening off one side.

'These rooms are surgeries,' she said. 'There's one staff doctor here and one nurse. The others are volunteers. This is the only place for miles around. In fact it's the only free clinic this side of Rangoon. The people in this area are desperately poor. They either work in one of the factories for a tiny wage, or don't have any work. If it wasn't for this place, they wouldn't have access to medical care at all.'

She pushed open some double doors at the end of the passage and showed me through to a small ward with around ten beds arranged in rows. All were occupied with sick looking patients, most with their eyes closed; all looked very thin with sunken cheeks. Those who did look up stared at us with glazed eyes, without interest.

'Who pays for this?' I asked as we left the ward.

'Oh, it's a Christian charity. They built the clinic a few years back and pay for its upkeep and for two of the staff as I mentioned. The rest is reliant on donations and volunteers.'

I swallowed. These truths, and in fact everything about the place made me feel uncomfortable. Not just because of the stark reminder of my wealth and privilege, but also because the very smell of the rooms made me feel queasy. I was reminded suddenly of mother's final hours; she'd been rushed into Paddington hospital when her liver finally collapsed, her skin by then a waxy yellow through years of alcohol abuse, her eyes dull and she was drooling from the mouth. That smell of disinfectant brought it all back to me far too sharply.

I turned back to Florence.

'So, what do you want me to do?' I asked.

'Well, I'm going to help one of the doctors, and this morning you can sit in and watch, so that this afternoon you can do the same.'

Nerves besieged me at the thought of actually doing anything practical that brought me into direct contact with the patients, but I smiled and nodded.

'Don't look so nervous, Betty,' said Florence. 'It's really not that hard.'

She opened one of the doors and a doctor looked up from behind his desk. I was surprised to see that the doctor himself was Burmese. There was a patient lying on the couch, his clothes filthy, his arm twisted and bloody.

Florence introduced me to the doctor; Aung Myint, who nodded politely and asked Florence to clean and bandage the wound while he got on and saw another patient. I watched as Florence did just that. She filled a bowl from the sink, cleaned out the wound with lint, dabbed on bromide and finally dressed and bound the injured arm. The patient winced as the bromide went into his open wound. As she worked, Florence spoke to him in fluent Burmese.

'He works in the clothing factory round the corner,' she

explained. 'His arm was crushed in an unguarded machine this morning.'

'That's dreadful,' I said, taking deep breaths, still trying not to faint at the sight of the wound. I hate the sight of blood at the best of times, but the knowledge that soon I would have to dress wounds myself was making it worse.

For the next couple of hours, I watched as Florence skilfully cleaned and bandaged wounds, dispensed painkillers, took temperatures and blood pressures and generally supported Doctor Myint in his work.

At lunch time we went outside to a tiny terrace with a table and someone brought rice and curry from a nearby food stall. Some of the other volunteers were European women. One was a colleague of Florence's at the newspaper, another the wife of one of the doctors. There were also three Burmese volunteers; two women and a young man, who Florence explained were medical students getting some extra experience.

Doctor Aung Myint sat next to me and asked me why I was here. I told him that Florence had persuaded me to come.

'It is very good of you. We don't get many ex-pat wives here. They seldom look outside their own community. Thank you for giving your time.'

I smiled, not saying that it was against my better judgement to come, that I was only here because I was at my wits' end with boredom, and that Florence was very persuasive, not for any noble motives at all.

'I'm worried that I don't have any skills or experience,' I faltered.

'Please don't worry, my dear,' he said kindly. 'You can assist me this afternoon and I will help you to learn.'

So, in the afternoon, I took Florence's place beside

Doctor Myint in the surgery while she went back to work at the newspaper.

'I'll be back to collect you at five,' she said as she left.

I spent all afternoon trying to help the doctor while he patiently instructed and supervised me in everything that I did. I felt so clumsy, trying to take a blood sample for the first time, wrestling with the blood pressure machine and unable to read the thermometer properly. All the time I was fighting back nausea and revulsion at the sight of sick and wounded people. By five o'clock I was exhausted, waiting impatiently in the doorway for Florence to return. When I got into the passenger seat she said,

'My God you look as white as a sheet. Did something happen?'

'No, it's just that I don't think I'm cut out for that sort of work.'

'Nonsense,' she said as she accelerated away down the narrow street. 'I was just the same at the beginning. It's just a question of toughing it out. You'll get used to it in time.'

When I got home I took a long bath and changed my clothes. By the time Robert came home I'd completely recovered. But I'd more or less determined to tell Florence I couldn't return to the clinic.

April 10th

Despite my early misgivings, I've been back to the clinic several times now. After the first time, Florence persuaded me to return at least once to give it a chance. I continue to find the work repellent and unrewarding but the doctor always thanks me profusely before I leave.

'You are so kind to come, Mrs Furnivall,' he always says

with a deep bow which embarrasses me. 'You have a real gift for this work.'

I know it's not true, but is his way of trying to get me to return. Now, as time has gone on, I haven't got the heart to tell him, or Florence that I'm not going back. Even so I dread spending time there; the smells, the sight of blood, the cries and groans of the sick.

On the way home today, Florence said to me; 'Tomorrow we're expecting one of our most devoted volunteers to return to the clinic. He's been working away for a time. I'm sure you'll find him fascinating company.'

She must have sensed that I was about to say I couldn't go to the clinic again, but what she said piqued my interest. I decided then that I will go back tomorrow. I like all the volunteers, finding them an interesting contrast to the people at the club. It is good to mix with different people and I'm intrigued as to who this might be.

April 12th

So, I went to the clinic again this morning; Florence collecting me from the house at eight thirty. She dropped me at the clinic and then went on to work. I always tell her that I could get my syce to drive me, but she won't hear of it. I think she secretly believes that I won't go at all if she doesn't take me. As she dropped me off, she said,

'Give my regards to Ye Win.' Then she roared off.

'Who's Ye Win?' I said into emptiness then turned to go into the clinic and bumped right into a tall Burmese man making for the door himself. He smiled conspiratorially.

'I am. I am Ye Win,' he said. 'Who is asking?'

I must have blushed bright red at this strange turn of

events. I couldn't meet his eye, so I looked down at my shoes and told him my name.

'Oh...' he said thoughtfully as he pulled open the door and stood aside for me to enter. 'Florence has told me all about you.'

I felt chills running down my spine at his words. Had she already spoken to him about me? How and when had that happened?

'Oh, Florence and I had a drink together yesterday evening,' he said as if reading my mind. 'She mentioned that a new young woman had started at the clinic.'

I wondered why she hadn't mentioned that in the car, but Florence is still full of mysteries to me, so I wasn't surprised.

Ye Win and I went our separate ways once we were through the front door, but he was sitting on the terrace at lunchtime when I came out for my usual meal of fried rice. He motioned for me to come and sit beside him. Glancing at him for the first time properly, I took in his perfect features, flawless skin and perceptive brown eyes. A thrill of something I didn't understand went through me as I sat down next to him. I noticed the fine hairs on his strong forearm as he doled out the rice.

'So, I understand your husband is a businessman,' he began, his eyes searching my face so I had to look down.

I nodded. 'He runs the Steamship Company,' I said.

'Ah. I'm pleased to hear it. One of our better employers in Rangoon. Not as exploitative as most,' he said, smiling a quizzical smile. 'But exploitative all the same.'

I asked him why he would say such a thing.

He leaned back in his chair. 'Oh, it's the nature of the relationship, isn't it? Employer/employee. It can't be anything else.'

I shrugged, 'I've never thought of it like that, but I suppose there's something in what you say,' I said.

'It only takes a moment's thought to come to that conclusion,' he said, a smile playing on his lips, leaning in to look at me in the eyes. Was he mocking me? I felt colour rising to my cheeks again but refused to let it bother me.

'And what is it that *you* do?' I asked, changing the subject.

He laughed. 'Oh, didn't Florence tell you? I don't have a job as such. I work for the Thakin movement, sometimes called the Thirty Comrades. It's a Burmese Independence movement, working to free our country from British rule. But I'm a lawyer originally, by trade and still take the odd case.'

'Oh,' I said weakly, not knowing how to respond.

When we went back inside, he held the door open again gallantly and smiled at me. There was something knowing in his smile and a private amusement that I had no idea how to react to.

May 15th

How time has flown over the past few weeks! I've been back to the clinic in Mingaladon township three or four times a week since my last entry and each time Ye Win has also been there. We've always sat together at lunchtimes, and bit by bit he's told me about his movement and how passionate they are about gaining independence for their people. It feels slightly odd, him telling me this, because I'm one of those he's trying to expel from his country, but he never alludes to that. He treats me as an equal and seems to assume that I naturally share his views. I don't tell him that I know what he says is sedition, and if I was known to be friendly with him I could well be arrested.

Of course, I haven't told Robert about Ye Win's presence at the clinic. He would be appalled I'm sure that I'm friendly with a member of the Burmese independence movement. And if he knew how good looking Ye Win is, and how his eyes rest on my face and linger on my body when we're speaking, he would certainly be jealous.

I've gradually overcome my aversion to blood and have learned a lot about caring for the sick. For example, I am now adept at taking blood in a syringe, giving vaccinations, taking blood pressure and temperatures. I can clean and dress wounds and bandage respectably. I've even started enjoying the work, but I have to admit to myself, the work isn't the reason I keep going back.

Once, when the clinic was very busy, Ye Win and I worked together. Ye Win stood in as a doctor and I assisted him. I watched him as he worked and interacted with the patients. His dark eyes, so often blazing with passion when he speaks at lunchtimes, were filled with compassion as he spoke to the patients. His strong hands were gentle as he examined them, felt their stomachs or foreheads for fever. It was amazing to see this new side to him; this gentle, caring side that he'd never shown me before, but I understood as I watched him, that this is why he comes to the clinic.

One day we got talking about the poverty that surrounds us as we work.

'I don't suppose you've ever seen it properly, have you? You just sweep in through those streets in Florence's car, trying to ignore the ugliness and squalor that you're passing.'

I hung my head. It was true. Sometimes I had to grit my teeth at the sights I saw on the way there, the appalling stench coming from open sewers, the heart-breaking looks the children gave me from their huge brown eyes.

'I'll take you on a tour after we've finished,' he said.

'Oh, but Florence will be coming for me at five. She doesn't like waiting.'

'She can come too. She won't mind, I'm sure,' he said.

I'd never been able to work out the exact nature of Florence and Ye Win's relationship. They seemed to understand each other and I sense that they go back a long way, like old friends. I often catch them exchanging looks, which disconcerts me and makes me feel excluded from their world.

'Alright,' I said. 'If she doesn't mind, I'm happy to go.'

When Florence arrived and she saw Ye Win standing beside me at the door, she smiled and motioned with her head for us to both jump into the car. Ye Win vaulted into the back seat, and I climbed in the front. As I did so, I got the feeling that this had been prearranged. Otherwise, how did Florence know that we'd decided to do this? But I told myself to stop worrying.

'We've decided to take a tour around the neighbourhood,' he explained and I relaxed a little. Didn't that prove that Florence knew nothing about the plan?

I settled back in the seat and Florence drove us around the local streets. As we went, Ye Win gave a running commentary about who lived in the local houses, their occupations, how much or how little they earned, how many children they had and the number of rooms in their houses. It was a sobering litany. These people were desperately poor and lived in cramped conditions with no running water or proper drainage. Sewage ran along an open drain at the side of the road, right next to where children played in the dirt, chickens and pigs rooted around. The children themselves were filthy, skin and bone and dressed in rags. And as usual, as we passed, they stopped playing and stared at us with mournful eyes.

When we'd been driving for a while, Ye Win asked Florence to pull over beside a wooden shack. A man dressed in a stained longyi leaned in the doorway and his face lit up as he recognised Ye Win in the back of the car. Ye Win got out of the car and shook hands with the man. Then he turned and beckoned Florence and myself to follow him.

We went inside the little house, stooping as we passed through the low doorway. Once inside, my eyes started to smart and water. There was a fire in the corner, with a hole in the ceiling above it, but the smoke was escaping and billowing out into the room. A woman, dressed in a colourful longyi was crouched by the fire, stirring a pot with a stick. She looked up and smiled with blackened teeth.

The man gestured for us to sit down on some low benches around the edge of the room. He then took up a large kettle and poured some liquid into clay cups and passed them around. I stared down into my cup, balking at the idea of drinking anything in this place, but knew it was unavoidable. But when I put the cup to my lips and took a sip, I realised that the tea was aromatic and delicious. Putting my fears aside I drank it down. But then the woman started handing around bowls of rice. Once again, it was impossible to refuse, and I stared down at my bowl. I couldn't help wondering how long the rice had been sitting around, and what other ingredients had gone into it. I knew though that these thoughts were prejudiced and uncharitable, so once again, swallowed my doubts and ate what was offered.

On the way back in the car, I was silent, thinking about the poor family we'd visited, happy to share their meagre meal with rich foreign guests without question. It made me feel guilty about the thoughts I'd had about the food and also about how we live up in our enormous house, with every luxury laid on. I felt especially guilty that I was often bored and ungrateful for what I had. I vowed to think differently from that moment on.

As we made our way back towards the centre, Ye Win leaned forward, putting one arm around my shoulder and the other around Florence's.

'Why don't we go to a tea house in the city centre?' he said. 'We can show Betty where the Burmese go to talk politics. I bet you've never been in one before, have you Betty?'

I shook my head, unable to turn to face him. I knew my face was flushed with pleasure and surprise at the touch of his hand on my shoulder. Apart from shaking my hand on that first day we met, it was the first time he'd ever touched me and it sent chills down my spine.

'I could drop you at one of the tea houses near the High Court, but I'm afraid I'll have to head back to the office. I've got some copy to finish,' Florence said.

'Would you be happy with that, Betty?' Ye Win asked, leaning forward.

'Of course,' I answered. I could think of nothing better than to spend some time alone with Ye Win. My only concern was that if it was close to the High Court, some of the lawyers from the club might see me going into a tea house alone with a Burmese man. But I was willing to take that risk.

Florence dropped us in the city centre near the Sule Pagoda. We crossed the gardens opposite and ducked into a tea house under the shadow of the gothic looking Supreme Court building. It was filled with Burmese men, sitting at low tables on tiny chairs, sipping from chipped cups and chatting earnestly. A young boy with bare feet showed us to a table in the window and brought some snacks. Ye Win ordered tea and we sat down. I felt self-conscious but I need not have worried. No one seemed to be bothered that a white woman was in their midst. They were too engrossed in their conversations.

'What do you think?' Ye Win asked, leaning forward so I could hear him above the hubbub.

'It's a fascinating place. I've never been anywhere quite like this before.'

'It's where all politics is discussed and conducted in Rangoon. We Burmese are passionately political, you may have noticed,' he said with a smile.

'I've noticed that you are,' I replied.

'Not just me. If you scratch the surface, you'll find that most Burmese have strong views. I bet if you ask your servants, although they may look docile and obedient, they will be passionate about independence underneath.'

'Perhaps,' I said, thinking about Daw Ma and her sweet temperament, our kindly bearers who went out of their way to make life comfortable and the syce who seemed so loyal to Robert. It hardly seemed credible that they were fierce radicals underneath.

'It's a shame you don't speak the language, but I'm sure you get the gist of the place,' he said, sipping his tea and nodding at the nearby tables.

I looked around. All the groups of men looked so animated in their conversations, some red-faced, others gesticulating wildly to make a point.

'I think so,' I agreed.

Then Ye Win changed the subject. He asked me about London and my home life there, about what I felt as a young wife coming to Rangoon for the first time. It was awkward at first. I didn't want to tell him much about Mother and Father, but found myself telling him more than I wanted to. Having his beautiful deep brown eyes fixed on my face as I spoke was addictive and I would have spoken about anything to keep them there.

After half an hour or so, I told him that I should be getting home.

'Robert will be back soon,' I said.

'Steamship Man,' he said with a broad smile. 'Are you going to tell him about our little trip out today?'

'I don't think so,' I replied instantly and he held my gaze for a little longer than necessary. I realised instantly that I'd made him complicit in deceiving my husband, however small a lie that might be, and the significance of that was not lost on him.

We went outside and he hailed me a taxi. He opened the door and as I got in, he leaned in and said,

'My apartment is just round the corner. Perhaps one day, you will do me the honour of visiting me there?'

'I'd love that,' I replied instantly. He closed the door and waved goodbye and, as I looked at his slim body retreating into the crowd, I realised that I was falling under his spell, and that I was doing so like a sleepwalker, making no attempt to stop what was happening.

14

BETTY'S JOURNAL

Rangoon, 1939

June 15th

TONIGHT, after the clinic, I went to Ye Win's apartment in Shwe Bon Thar Road near the Sule Pagoda. He's asked me on several occasions since mentioning it that first time after our outing to the tea house, but I've always resisted, although we've been back to the tea house together on two or three further occasions.

I resisted for a reason. To go to his home feels taboo; a step too far. It's one thing going out in public with a known enemy of the regime, in itself risky, but explicable all the same. Explicable to Robert, I mean. If he were ever to ask, I could quite honestly tell him that I was having tea with a fellow volunteer. Not that he ever does ask where I've been. He trusts me implicitly, I'm aware of that, which is why my actions and even my thoughts feel wrong somehow. To look at Robert's open, contented smile over supper, feel his arms around me at night and to know that my thoughts are with another, more exciting, far more dangerous man, I know is disloyal and ungrateful. Robert doesn't deserve this treatment. It is squaring all this in my mind that has prevented me from accepting Ye Win's invitation until today.

Florence has been encouraging me.

'He really likes you, you know,' she said once as she drove, flicking her ash away. She was trying to keep her voice casual, but I know her well enough by now to pick up that any reply from me seemed to matter to her. I felt my cheeks colouring and was glad that she had to keep her eyes on the road.

'I don't know what you mean,' I said finally.

'Oh, I think you do. Ye Win is an attractive, desirable man. He can have any woman he wants, but he's chosen you. You don't know how lucky you are.'

'You are forgetting something, Florence,' I retaliated, although her words thrilled me to the core. 'I'm a married woman.'

'Oh, that,' she said dismissively with another flick of ash. 'I've never let that stop me, and you shouldn't either. This isn't a chance that comes round every day. You should seize it while you have the opportunity. That opportunity could easily pass.'

I thought about her words and once again my mind went back to poor Robert. And in that moment something clicked inside. I suddenly realised that I didn't love Robert, that I've never really loved him. I pursued him through greed and ambition, attracted by his wealth and position. He bores me to death really, especially in comparison to Ye Win. I should have left him to Edith. I know now how unfair I was back then. I behaved like the selfish, foolish girl that I was.

So today I thought, what the hell. Why not take him up

on his offer? So, when we sat down to lunch together and he leaned forward and fixed me with his mesmerising gaze and said in his teasing tone,

'When are you going to accept my offer to visit my home, Betty?' I finally gave in.

'How about today?' I asked lightly. He looked surprised for a moment, but quickly recovered his composure.

We went separately to his home at the end of the afternoon. Ye Win had set off a little early in a taxi and I followed in Florence's car. She looked pleased when I told her where I was going.

'You won't regret it,' she said.

She dropped me off in front of Ye Win's building. It was in a pleasant, tree-lined street just back from Mahabandoola Road. I stared up at the tall terraced house, overcome with nerves all of a sudden. I hesitated in front of the door. Now was my last chance to walk away. I could easily do that and make up an excuse when I saw him again. But as I was hovering there, I heard an upstairs window squeak open and Ye Win's voice calling down to me.

'Betty! I'm so happy you're here. Push the front door and I'll come down.'

I did as he said and found myself standing in an empty hallway with doors to apartments leading off it and a bare wooden staircase winding up in front of me. I heard Ye Win's footsteps on the stairs.

'Welcome to my home,' he said, taking my hand and holding it to his lips. I followed him upstairs to the second floor and he showed me inside. The apartment was small, but beautifully furnished with Burmese teak tables and chests, shelves displaying antique ornaments, a low settee strewn with silk cushions and Burmese art on the walls.

'This is beautiful,' I said, looking around admiringly.

'Do sit down,' he motioned for me to sit on the settee and I saw that snacks were laid out on the low table in front of me.

'Oh, you shouldn't have gone to any trouble,' I said.

'No trouble at all,' he assured me. 'Would you like whisky, or brandy?'

'I thought you Buddhists didn't drink,' I said, laughing. 'But whisky if you're offering.'

'Oh, it's a bad habit I picked up in England.'

'England?'

'Yes. Didn't I tell you? I studied law at Oxford. Many years ago now. But old habits die hard.'

'Gosh,' I said, impressed.

'Yes. That's where I met many of the people I know now. Since coming back to Burma, we formed our independence movement. It's called The Thirty Comrades.'

He poured us both a generous measure of whisky and handed me a glass.

'So, what inspired you to do that?' I asked.

'I suppose it was my father,' he said, after pausing for thought. 'He was a lawyer himself and he fought against injustice his whole life. But the British laws in this country mean that we Burmese can never gain justice for ourselves. We are second class citizens in our own country.'

I looked at his face. His expression was one I'd seen so many times, serious and earnest, full of passion for his cause.

'There were some riots and demonstrations in Rangoon in the early thirties. Many people were arrested and my father represented some of them in court. They were never going to get a fair trial. The odds were stacked against them, many of the British judges were biased. Lots of people ended up being convicted and some were executed.

That left my father bitter. He used to say to me that we Burmese could never rest while Burma was ruled by the British.'

'I see,' I said, digesting his words as I sipped my whisky. I had been brought up to believe that the British justice system was the fairest in the world. Could all this be true?

He leaned back in his chair and smiled.

'But enough of that. I didn't ask you here to indoctrinate you into the cause. I wanted to show you my home. I'm glad you like it.'

'Oh yes. It's beautiful, as I said.'

'Not a patch on your home though,' he said and I saw in his gaze that teasing, quizzical look he often gave me when he'd said something controversial or pushed something a bit too far whilst we were talking at lunchtimes. I smiled back, not rising to the bait.

'I'm very lucky,' I said.

'You married well. Your husband is one of the richest men in Rangoon. Probably only eclipsed by some of the Chinese merchants who've settled here.'

'I wouldn't know about that,' I said.

'And he has a social conscience too,' he went on. 'He treats his workers well and pays above the average wage.'

'Robert is a good man,' I said, dropping my gaze, pricked with guilt that here I was in another man's home, speaking about Robert as if he was just a common acquaintance, not my husband.

'And he sits on the city council too, doesn't he?' he asked and I noted there was a studied casualness in his tone as he asked that. I looked up, surprised.

'Yes, he does. But what of it?'

'Oh, I was just remarking that he cares about his community, as well as about his workers.'

'He does care about Rangoon, yes. He's lived here his whole life. It's his home, more than England even.'

I was getting more and more uncomfortable about discussing Robert, and Ye Win must have sensed that because he simply replied, 'I was just remarking that your husband is a model citizen,' and dropped the subject.

We chatted about inconsequential things for the next hour or so while I ate the delicious Burmese nibbles laid out on the table. Ye Win let slip that he'd cooked them himself in the tiny adjoining kitchen and once again I was impressed that he had hidden skills.

We'd been chatting for so long that I had lost track of time, but as I was halfway through my third whisky, I noticed that the sky was darkening outside so it must be nearing seven o' clock. Robert would be home soon. I stood up suddenly, flustered.

'I need to go,' I said.

'Must you? I've so enjoyed our chat,' he said standing up and coming towards me.

'Yes. I'm sorry but I must.'

'I hope you'll come again,' he said.

'I'd love to,' I replied without even thinking about it. I drained my glass and turned towards the door, feeling light-headed. As I reached it, I felt his hands on my shoulders and I turned around. He was facing me now, standing very close, looking deep into my eyes.

'I'd like to kiss you goodbye,' he said and then his lips were on mine and he was kissing me hard, and I kissed him back, moving my body close to his, feeling his desire pressing against me. I broke away.

'I must go,' I said, opening the door and rushing down the stairs. He was right behind me.

'I'm sorry. Betty. Did I do something wrong?'

'No. Not at all. I need to go that's all, it's getting late.' What I didn't tell him was that I didn't trust myself to resist him if the kiss had carried on. His allure was so potent that I found it almost overwhelming.

He let me out of the front door and came out on the street to hail a taxi. I got inside and he leaned in through the open window.

'Thank you for coming. See you at the clinic,' he said. The taxi moved off and I glanced over my shoulder. He was standing there, staring at me intently as I drew away, and I could still feel the heat of his kiss on my lips and the urgent press of his body against mine.

Edith
Dapha River Tea Plantation, Assam, 1980

Edith put the journal down, rubbing her eyes. It was well past midnight and she couldn't read any more, her eyes were too tired. She was disturbed by what she'd read about Betty and Ye Win and about what Betty had admitted regarding her feelings for Robert. Betty had been as selfish as ever, even though she was making a show of helping the sick, the real reason she was there was to pursue this illicit relationship with a Burmese insurgent. How could she have done that?

Edith thought back too, to how she'd given up Robert the instant she'd known that Betty was alive. It had been the honourable thing to do, and it had torn her heart out. Not a day passed without Edith thinking of Robert, working away in Rangoon, and what might have been between them. They'd kept their vow to stay away from each other for Betty's sake, even though she could well have perished on the long walk from Burma.

'Was it all worth it, Robert?' she murmured to the silent garden now. They'd sacrificed their love and a lifetime of happiness for someone who'd admitted to not loving him; who'd been pursuing another man within a few months of marriage.

Edith threw the journal aside and got ready for bed. But when she finally closed her eyes, sleep wouldn't come. Betty's words danced in her mind, taunting her. It was only now that she was finding out the truth and it was making her realise that the sacrifices she'd made were all for nothing.

15

BETTY'S JOURNAL

Rangoon, 1939

July 15th

TODAY THE INEVITABLE HAPPENED. It has been building since my last entry when I went to Ye Win's apartment for the first time. I've been back twice since then and each visit followed the same routine as the first. We chatted, drank whisky, ate Burmese delicacies and finished with a passionate kiss. Nothing more.

I've become obsessed with Ye Win. He occupies my every thought, day and night. So much so that even Robert has noticed my preoccupation.

'You seem distracted, my love,' he said one evening after our meal. 'Is something the matter? You don't seem your usual self at all.'

I shook my head, told him I was fine.

'I worry about you spending so much time down at that clinic that Florence has got you into. It shouldn't become a chore for you. If you're finding it stressful, you should give it up, or at least take a break for a week or two.'

'No. It isn't that,' I said a little too fiercely. He looked at me, frowning.

'You never seem to go to the club anymore, my darling.'

'The club bores me now. I told you that.'

'Even so, it's good to get out and let your hair down sometimes. You've grown very serious lately. It isn't like you.'

I knew it wasn't like me, but he doesn't understand that I have changed since I first came to Rangoon. That empty-headed, self-centred young bride has vanished. I'm no longer that person.

'Why don't we go down to the club tomorrow evening? We haven't been out together for an age. It will do us both the world of good.'

'Alright,' I agreed reluctantly. I could hardly refuse. Poor Robert. He's no idea what's going on, but his instinct is right. I am preoccupied and I am more serious. I'm no longer interested in clothes and cocktail parties and gossip. My mind is full of Ye Win and his views and the discussions we have together. They mean everything to me.

Ye Win is genuinely interested to hear my ideas and he takes what I have to say seriously. Nothing is off-limits in our conversations. He tells me all about his comrades, his organisation, their plans for rebellion against British rule and for a future free Burma. He talks of the injustices and cruelty that the Burmese have suffered at British hands. And the way he speaks is so persuasive, I am beginning to believe in the cause myself. Alongside that, how can club trivia compare?

But looking at Robert's puzzled face I felt a little guilty and that I owed it to him to spend an evening out with him, so I went along to the club with him last night. We sat at a table in the bar, overlooking the sumptuous tennis courts, and drinks were brought to us by a liveried bearer who bowed when he set them down on the table.

Familiar faces were all around and many people came up to our table to wish us good evening.

'We haven't seen you here for ages, Betty,' said Mary who came with her husband, Reginald, to say hello.

'Oh, I'm sorry. I've been busy lately. Volunteering at a clinic in Mingaladon township. Florence Anderson introduced me to the place,' I said.

Mary flushed and tried to change the subject. I realised it must be because of Robert's affair with Florence. Perhaps Mary thought it was dangerous territory, or that I didn't know about it.

But Reginald piped up, 'I hear that place is a hotbed of insurgency. I should be careful.'

'Really?' Robert asked, frowning suddenly, then turning to me, he said, 'You haven't mentioned anything about that.'

I shrugged, trying to damp down my panic, 'I haven't experienced it. That's why,' I said, feigning ignorance.

Mary's husband stroked his moustache absently and said, 'Oh. Must be somewhere else, then. Places like that are sometimes recruiting grounds for some of these independence groups, that's all.'

'All the volunteers seem perfectly above board,' I answered, looking him straight in the eye, willing him not to mention Ye Win.

'Perhaps I should have a chat with Dr Myint,' said Robert, still frowning. Dread rushed through me. I cursed Mary and Reginald for mentioning this, and myself for introducing the subject of the clinic.

'That won't be necessary, Robert,' I said. 'Like I said,

there's absolutely no cause for concern. Ask Florence if you don't believe me.'

'Well, we must be tootling on,' said Mary, again looking flustered. 'Lovely to see you, Betty. Do give me a bell and we must go on one of our shopping trips again.'

'Yes let's,' I said absently, but all the time my mind was going over the dreadful possibility of Robert speaking to Dr Myint and finding out about Ye Win, wondering why I'd never mentioned his presence at the clinic at home, and eventually putting two and two together.

'Let's go home, shall we?' I said as soon as Mary and Reginald had moved away. 'I'm tired.'

'Oh, I thought we could eat here. We haven't done that for a long time.'

He put his hand on mine and looked into my eyes. 'Come on, Betty, for me?'

I shrugged. 'Of course,' I said. Anything to take his mind off the clinic and what Reginald had said. But I didn't enjoy my evening at the club. It just served to remind me of how shallow and complacent everyone is in our narrow, privileged little community, and how dull compared to the times I'd spent with Ye Win.

So, this morning, I was doubly anxious to get off to the clinic. I got up early and tiptoed around getting ready while Robert was still asleep. I didn't want to make a fuss or for him to suddenly remember the conversation with Reginald. But he woke up well before I was ready and propped himself up on one elbow.

'I'm afraid I'm going to be a bit late home this evening, darling,' he said. 'Are you all right to have dinner alone?'

'Of course. Where are you going?'

'Council meeting. It's likely to go on a bit. We're organising a parade for next month. The Secretary of State for

Burma is visiting from Britain. That's a bit hush-hush though at the moment. So, please don't mention it to anyone.'

'Of course not. See you later then,' I said, pecking his cheek as I left the room.

Ye Win wasn't at the clinic this morning. My heart sank when I discovered he hadn't turned up. He normally comes in on a Wednesday. I asked around, but none of the other volunteers knew why he wasn't there. They just shrugged when I asked. The work is voluntary after all, they must have been thinking.

I spent a tense day doing my usual routine of bandaging, taking temperatures and dispensing medicines alongside the doctors. At lunch time I sat alone, missing Ye Win's presence, his flirtatious teasing and his lively conversation. My mind worked overtime and I was racked with worry. Had he been arrested? Had someone mentioned the clinic to the authorities? Had that stopped him coming here today? I thought back to what Reginald had said. Reginald was a senior member of the British Security Service. He obviously was aware of this clinic and the fact that it attracted radicals. He probably even knew about Ye Win. Had my mentioning it sparked some sort of action on his part?

By the end of the day I'd worked myself up into a state of high anxiety. I was convinced that Ye Win had been arrested on his way to the clinic this morning and that I was partly to blame. When five o'clock came round and I went outside to Florence who was sitting in her motor car filing her nails, I had made up my mind what to do.

'Could you take me to Ye Win's place?' I asked her. She looked amused.

'Has he finally broken your resistance down?' she asked, lighting up a cigarette and starting the engine.

'No. I'm just a bit anxious about him. He wasn't at the clinic today,' I replied.

'Oh, he's a free spirit. I shouldn't worry about him,' she said, her voice unconcerned.

'All the same. He's normally very reliable. I can't help worrying a bit.'

'He won't like that,' she warned. 'He doesn't like clingy women.'

I fell silent, but after a while she said, 'Why are you so worked up? You seem very tense today.'

So, I told her about the trip to the club and what Reginald Curtis had said about the clinic. Florence snorted.

'What does he know?' she asked.

'Well, he is someone high up in security,' I said.

'Even so. They don't have good intelligence on the Movement,' she assured me. I wondered how she knew so much but didn't want to prolong the discussion.

She dropped me outside Ye Win's house. The front door to the building was ajar so I pushed it open and ran upstairs. I knocked on the door to his apartment and waited. There was no reply, but I thought I could hear the rumble of voices inside. I put my ear to the door and sure enough, there was the rise and fall of male voices speaking low. I knocked again. After a couple of minutes Ye Win opened it and as he did so, I couldn't help gasping at the way he looked. His face looked alien to me; as I'd never seen it before. Hard and cold. Almost unrecognisable from the friendly, teasing, adoring looks I was accustomed to from him. I took a step back.

'Betty!' he said, and his face softened instantly. It was almost as if that other face hadn't existed.

'I have some friends here, but they are just leaving. Gentlemen?'

He held the door aside and four young Burmese men filed out of the room. As they passed me they nodded politely. They were well-dressed and looked educated, much like Ye Win himself. I watched them go downstairs and then I turned to him:

'I was worried about you,' I said, my voice wobbling. I hadn't realised how desperate I'd been, how near to tears. To see him safe was such a relief.

'Why? Come on in. Tell me all about it.'

I went inside and as soon as he'd shut the door he took me in his arms, enfolding me, holding me close. My face was next to his chest and I could smell the spicy cologne he wore, wild and exotic. I took a deep breath of it and looked up into his face.

'I thought you'd been arrested.'

He laughed. 'Arrested? Why would you think that?'

So, just as I had told Florence a few minutes before, I told him what Reginald had said and how my mind had been working overtime all day when he hadn't turned up at the clinic.

'I don't know why you were so worried,' he said, stroking my hair. 'The authorities have nothing on me. As far as they're concerned I'm a jobbing lawyer, occasionally out of work, helping my fellow citizens by volunteering to help the sick sometimes.'

'Is that so? How can you be so sure? Reginald seemed to know all about the clinic.'

'It's pure speculation. There was another clinic on the other side of town where volunteers were recruited to the Independence Movement in the early thirties. Perhaps that's what he's thinking of.'

He held me at arm's length. 'You look worn out. Would you like a drink? Why don't you sit down?'

I sank down gratefully on the silk cushions and allowed him to pour me a stiff whisky.

'So,' I said, watching him, 'What were you doing today? You normally come in on a Wednesday.'

'I had a meeting. A small sub-group of the comrades. You saw them leaving just now. It was all arranged at pretty short notice. Otherwise I'd have told you.'

I took a gulp of the whisky he offered me and closed my eyes, savouring the feeling of the alcohol seeping into my veins, slowing my pulse, calming me down.

'What was it about?' I asked as he came to sit down beside me. I was making conversation rather than really wanting to know.

'An important visitor to Rangoon is expected in the coming weeks. That's all the intelligence we have. We were discussing tactics. We're trying to find out who and when, so we can take action on the day.'

I felt my scalp tingle, recalling what Robert had said to me this morning about the Secretary of State's visit. It must be what they'd heard about. I tried to keep my face blank, I didn't want to give anything away.

'How are you feeling now?' he asked, moving closer. My heart started beating faster, feeling his thigh brush against mine.

'A little better, thanks,' I said, looking down, not wanting him to see the colour in my cheeks, the confusion in my eyes at the effect that simply sitting beside him was having on me, but I couldn't help the fact that my breathing was quick and uneven.

Without warning, he ran his hand along my thigh, sending shivers right through me, then taking my face in one hand, turned it towards him and kissed me hard on the lips. I yielded immediately, kissing him back, knowing that this wasn't just a goodbye kiss, that this time it meant more, and I also knew that I wanted more too. Then he was shifting my body round, and moving on top of me, pushing me down onto the cushions. I was only too willing to do what he wanted, desperate for him to carry on. I was sliding my arms around his back, pulling him towards me, into me, until we were moving together, quickly and hungrily, and it was then that I understood what I'd been yearning for all these weeks since I'd become obsessed with this man.

Afterwards, he showered me with kisses. 'Are you alright, Betty?' he asked, looking deep into my eyes.

'Of course.'

'It was what you wanted, wasn't it?'

'Yes,' I whispered, not wanting to speak, not wanting to disturb the magic of the moment. We lay there, side-by-side on his silk cushions, listening to the traffic outside, the horns and bells, the chirping of birds in the trees outside the window.

Finally, he got to his feet, padded through to the kitchen and made us some jasmine tea.

'Don't you have to go soon? It's getting dark,' he said.

'Oh no, I can stay a bit longer this evening. Robert's got a council meeting.'

I realised, as soon as the words were out of my mouth that I shouldn't have said that. That Robert had told me it was all hush-hush. I saw Ye Win's eyes light up with interest as he came and sat down beside me.

'Council meeting, you say,' he said. 'Any idea what they might be discussing this evening?'

I shook my head.

'Something to do with the visit no doubt,' he said, half to himself. Then he turned to me and took my hand.

'Betty, do you ever have access to the council minutes or papers?'

I drew my hand away.

'No. Of course not. It's Robert's business. It's nothing to do with me.'

'But, if you wanted to, do you think you could find them?'

I looked away from him. What was this? I was head over heels in love with Ye Win, but that didn't mean I was prepared to betray my country for him. Was that the bargain I'd struck?

'I don't know. I don't think so,' I said, confused. 'Look, Ye Win, I think I'd better leave now after all. I thought you cared for me. I don't think you should ask me something like that.'

'I do care for you, Betty,' he said quietly, gripping my hand. 'Haven't I just shown you that? I love you. Please forget what I asked. It was wrong of me to try to get you involved. Please forgive me.'

His eyes were so full of remorse that I couldn't be annoyed with him for long. I kissed him then, but got up to leave anyway. I needed to be home and changed before Robert got back.

'Will you visit again soon?' he asked before we stepped out onto the pavement.

'Of course,' I said, turning to kiss him one last time.

Outside, he hailed me a taxi and as always stood watching as I got in and the taxi pulled away. But gone was the yearning look of hunger. Tonight there was something different in his eyes. A certain satisfaction and a gleam of possessive pride.

16

EDITH

Dapha River Tea Plantation, Assam, 1980

EDITH HAD BEEN READING Betty's journal on and off since breakfast time. She'd been unable to put it down, astonished and appalled by her sister's behaviour; the thoughtless way she'd treated Robert and the obvious lack of regard she had for him. Edith was ashamed of her and desperately sorry for Robert. It brought it home to her again how misplaced his loyalty had been back in 1942.

Earlier, as the morning sun burned the dew off the moist garden and clouds of steamy air rose from the surrounding hills, she'd breakfasted with Richard on the veranda of the plantation house.

'I should leave today,' she'd said as she finished breakfast.

'You can stay as long as you like. We don't have any bookings for the bungalow. It's nice to have a bit of company.'

'That's very kind of you, but I should be getting back to the hotel. I've left things in such a state of limbo,' she said.

'Well, the offer's there. Your taxi driver decided to go home yesterday evening by the way, so just let me know when you'd like one of our drivers to take you down to Ledo.'

'Thank you. You've been so kind,' she said.

When she'd got back to the bungalow one of the maids was cleaning the floor. Edith put her hands together in a greeting. The woman was at least her own age, if not older. She returned the greeting, nodded politely and continued with her cleaning.

Edith took up the journal and went to sit in one of the chairs on the terrace to carry on reading. After Richard's invitation, she'd decided that she might as well stay on the plantation and finish the journal. As she did so, she noticed the woman leaning on her broom and watching her for a few seconds, then when she noticed Edith looking her way she carried on sweeping.

Edith put it down to the woman being curious about a new visitor and turned back to the journal without thinking much about it. She was keen to find out more about Betty and Ye Win's liaison.

Betty's Journal

September 1st

Life has gone on much as before since my last entry. I've been so busy that I haven't opened this journal for months. The reason being I now have a new joy in my life. A secret pleasure. One that I can't speak of to anyone, not even to Florence, but from the sideways looks she gives me from under her false lashes, I'm quite sure that she knows.

I'm also sure that Daw Ma knows. On the evening that I

returned from Ye Win's apartment after making love with him for the first time, I bathed and got changed quickly. Daw Ma went into the bedroom and picked up my discarded clothes. When I emerged from the bathroom in my towel, she gave me a long, searching look, as if she'd guessed exactly where I'd been and what I'd been doing that evening. She knows me so well and she has a kind of sixth sense which sometimes sends chills right through me.

I still go to the clinic in Mingaladon township three times a week, but my principal reason for going there is, of course, to be close to Ye Win. Even if we are working in separate rooms, the knowledge that he's there in the building thrills me and fills me with a feeling of peace and wellbeing. We always eat our lunch together and after the clinic has closed, usually get a taxi to his apartment to make love. Florence has given up coming to the clinic to collect me in the evenings now.

The Secretary of State's visit came and went. Ye Win didn't ask me to look for Robert's papers again, but I could tell that he wanted to. Robert was very busy on the reception committee prior to the visit, often working in the evenings. He would apologise to me, but I would just smile and say it was fine. Little did he know that those long council meetings gave me more opportunity to be with Ye Win.

I knew Ye Win and his comrades were planning something for the day of the visit, but I could take comfort from the fact that I hadn't supplied them with any information or betrayed any confidences.

On the day of the visit, I had to join Robert on the reception committee and meet the Secretary of State, Lord Dundas and his wife as they landed from their ship in the harbour. The Governor of Burma and his wife greeted the couple as they came down the companion-way, they then passed down the line of VIPs to shake hands. I had to curtsey to Lady Dundas who gave me an icy smile as I did so.

We followed in a limousine as they drove from the docks on Strand Road to Government House. Halfway up Pyay Road, we had to wait in a traffic jam. The Governor's car carrying the visitors was up ahead, moving very slowly. Crowds of Burmese citizens lined the route, waving flags and cheering. Robert had told me that they were there under sufferance and had not come along voluntarily. I peered at their faces as we passed. Although they were cheering, no one looked happy, in fact their expressions said it all; they looked crushed and humiliated.

As we waited for the traffic ahead to move on, I glanced out of the window at a side street. Indian soldiers on horseback blocked the entrance, and behind the line of horses I could see crowds of protesters carrying placards, shaking their fists and yelling. As I watched, some of the mounted police started lunging at the protesters, hitting them with batons, charging at them with their horses. Many protesters fell to the ground, heads or faces bloodied.

'Look at that, Robert!' I said. 'The police are attacking those innocent people.'

'I know. It's far too heavy-handed. But last year there were dreadful strikes and riots throughout Rangoon for months. Many lives were lost and it did great damage to morale and to the economy. It's these independence protesters stirring everything up. I suppose the Governor doesn't want a repeat of last year.'

'Even so,' I said, shocked, realising that Ye Win and his cronies must be behind this demonstration. Had they known that their followers would be greeted with violence?

The visitors were given a formal lunch at Government

House and I had to sit beside Lady Dundas and make polite conversation. I found it the dullest and most difficult of occasions. She was very starchy and proper and it was impossible to get a conversation going. And all the time I was longing to be sitting outside at the clinic at that bare wooden table, eating fried rice from a food stall, looking out over the slums of the township and chatting freely to Ye Win.

I've been going to the club once a week with Robert since Lord Dundas's visit. It is my way of holding off Robert's suspicions about the clinic. On those evenings I drink my chota pegs, chat with the other women and give every appearance of embracing club life just like a proper memsahib. I know it makes Robert happy to see me there, and to go along himself, play a round of bridge and chat with his friends. It gives him the feeling that we are just another normal couple, not slipping away from each other and growing more distant on a daily basis, which is in fact the reality of the situation.

Conversation at the club often turns to war. Things are building up in Europe, with Hitler and his aggressive expansion of Germany, and the Japanese on our doorstep waging war in China.

'The Japs are building up to invading Malaya,' said Cedric Brown, one of the club bores who props up the bar most evenings. 'And once they've done that, it'll be us next, you mark my words.'

'Nonsense Cedric,' someone else chimed in. 'Have another whisky and forget all about it. The Japs don't have the manpower or the skills to take on the British Empire.'

'I think you'll find that all the Jap civilians here in Rangoon are watching us. Spying on us in fact, sending information back to Tokyo ahead of an invasion.'

That was met with derisive laughter. I must admit that the war in Europe feels so far away, it's difficult to imagine how it could ever reach these shores. And people have been worrying about the Japs here forever. I can't get too concerned about it myself. I have other things on my mind.

Another thing I've done though, to try to keep things as normal as possible and to deflect attention from myself and Ye Win, is to visit Mary Curtis now and again. I went to one of her insufferable coffee mornings a few days ago. It was all I could do to stop myself from yawning. Things were just the same. Endless gossip and speculation about affairs, husbands' career prospects, who might be going home to England, who might be coming out to Rangoon. Sometimes they ask me about the clinic and I try to deflect their interest, by emphasising how awful and mundane the work is. The last thing I want is for one of them to ask to come along.

'It can't be that bad, surely Betty,' said Mary. 'You've been going there for months now. Three times a week isn't it? There must be something good about it to keep you going back for more.'

I met her curious gaze with a level look and just said, 'I suppose it's just my way of giving something back to the community. After all, I'm so lucky, and the people we help there are so poor. It's the least I can do.'

She gave me a sceptical look, but seemed to accept what I said, and changed the subject.

Apart from those tiresome interludes, my life has revolved around Ye Win. He still speaks passionately about his cause, and since the brutality of the British I witnessed first-hand from the cavalcade, I have more and more sympathy with what they stand for. I agree with him now, that we British are only here to exploit the country, its resources and its people and not for any higher purpose.

But I suppose I'm so obsessed with Ye Win, that I'm bound to identify with his views. I think about him night and day and live for the moments we're together. I truly believe that my life would be meaningless without him.

October 1939

Since Lord and Lady Dundas visited, Robert has been involved in planning something else with the city council. From the hints he's dropped, I realise that it could well be the Viceroy of India who is coming this time. It is many months away yet, but it certainly won't be anyone from Britain. The war in Europe, that started in September, has stopped all travel to and from Britain to India and Burma.

Ye Win has again been asking me for minutes of the council meetings, the route the Viceroy will take, anything I can lay my hands on. He's been quite brazen about it this time. I suppose he thinks our relationship is on stronger ground now, that he has a right to ask me to help him, and that after what I witnessed on Pyay Road the day of the last visit, I'm more sympathetic to his cause.

We were lying on Ye Win's bed in his tiny bedroom when he last asked me. It was hot in there, the ceiling fan hardly stirring the air. Both our bodies were covered in droplets of sweat.

'How can you ask me that?' I said, looking into his eyes.

'Easily. I know you're with us now, Betty. You'd be helping something you believe in. Why wouldn't I ask you?'

I stared at the ceiling, mulling over his words.

'Supposing I *could* get hold of the papers, Robert would know they'd gone. He would be suspicious then. He might even find out about us.'

'Does he ever leave the papers at home during the day?' he asked.

'Probably. They must be in his study. I don't suppose he would take them to work with him.'

'Well, all you need to do, is to get them to me in the morning. I can arrange for them to be copied in a matter of hours, so you can return them before he comes home in the evening.'

My stomach was filled with butterflies at the prospect of doing this. What if someone saw me? What if the papers were damaged while they were being copied? And besides, I would be betraying my country, not just my husband.

'I thought you said you'd do anything for me,' said Ye Win. 'I thought you loved me, Betty, as I love you.'

'I do love you,' I said instantly, not even trying to keep the desperation from my tone. 'You know that. More than anything in the world. It's just...'

'You wouldn't want to lose me, would you?'

There was an edge to his voice and those words hit me like a physical blow. What was he threatening? How could he blackmail me like this? But I was weak, completely in his power.

'I'd hate to lose you,' I answered, looking earnestly into his eyes. 'You know that. Look, if it means that much to you, I'll get you the papers. If it takes that to prove my love for you. Of course, I'll do it.'

So, this morning, once Robert had left for work, I crept into his study. One of the bearers saw me going in there and frowned. I felt the need to justify myself, but I shouldn't have done. It is my house after all, but I was worried that he might mention it to Robert.

'I'm just looking for some writing paper,' I told Ali who was watching me as he dusted in the hallway.

I rushed into the study and shut and locked the door behind me. my nerves scattering all over the place. I rummaged quickly through Robert's desk looking for anything I could find to do with the city council. There didn't seem to be anything there, but then I noticed a leather briefcase beside the desk. I remembered then that I'd seen Robert taking it when he went to council meetings. Inside were several folders and when I took them out and flicked through them I knew I had found what I was looking for. They were minutes of Rangoon city council dating back weeks and months, as well as memos, plans and maps of the city.

There were too many to sneak out easily, so I picked the latest folder, slipped it inside a big brown envelope, took it out of the room and rushed up to my bedroom. Luckily there was no one in the hallway, Ali must have finished his dusting, but my heart was beating fit to burst in case any of the servants appeared. I shoved the papers into a shopping bag, found a hat and sunglasses and left the house through the front door. Ali was polishing the door knocker as I left and he looked at me with curiosity.

'Would you like me to call the syce to bring the motor car, madam?' he asked.

'No,' I said, nerves making my voice sharp. 'I'm going for a walk.'

'Very good, madam,' he said, but I could feel his eyes on my back as I walked along the gravel drive to the road. This was such unusual behaviour, no wonder he was suspicious.

Once through the gates I turned left and started up the hill towards the Shwedagon Pagoda. Ye Win had said he would meet me at the bottom of the steps at ten o'clock. It was further than I'd thought. I'd only ever travelled there by car, so I had to hurry, and by the time I got there, my hair was plastered to my head and sweat was running down my face.

I noticed him before he saw me. He was scanning the crowd, shading his eyes with one hand. His eyes had that hard, aggressive look, the one I'd only seen once before. It made me stop in my tracks, but then he saw me and his expression changed.

'Betty! Did you get them?' he asked, drawing me behind a food stall selling roasted cashew nuts. I nodded, handing him the envelope.

'Go up to the pagoda, walk once round the platform and then come back down the steps. That will take around an hour. By that time I will be back here and can return the papers to you.'

'Alright,' I said and watched him get into a waiting car and be swept away.

I walked up the many flights of steps towards the pagoda, ignoring the cries of stallholders, and the monkeys that sat on the steps waiting to snatch food from unwary visitors. I was hot and breathless by the time I reached the top and alighted onto the main platform. The stunning golden pagoda soared up above me and I started walking around the platform, stopping to admire some of the shrines and mini-pagodas as I went, trying to behave like a normal visitor. But I felt anything but normal. My mind was spinning, my stomach churning with nerves. What if Ye Win didn't get the papers back to me? What if he was stopped?

I couldn't help but compare this walk round the pagoda to the first visit I'd made with Robert on the day I arrived in Rangoon. How naïve and full of hope I'd been on that day, how astonished I'd been at the magnificence of the pagoda and at the views. And how different I felt today. It was as if I was another person; a nervy, cynical and duplicitous person at that.

Ye Win was waiting at the foot of the steps when I arrived back beside the cashew nut stall.

'All done,' he said handing me the envelope. 'There are some interesting things in those minutes and the maps will be very useful. It's given us what we need. Thank you, Betty.'

'I'll see you at the clinic tomorrow, then,' I said and walked away.

Back at home I slipped the papers back into Robert's briefcase and went upstairs to shower and change. It is done now. I have to square it with my conscience. I have already started to worry about how the Comrades will use the information I've given them. But I know it is useless to think like that, it is all out of my hands. I must come to terms with the fact that I have betrayed my husband and my country for the man I love. Was it worth it? Only time will tell.

17

EDITH

Dapha River Tea Plantation, Assam, 1980

SHAKING HER HEAD IN DISBELIEF, Edith put down the journal. She felt tears of shame and humiliation in her eyes. It was hard to believe that Betty would have done those things. It was one thing to be unfaithful to Robert. That was bad enough, but to betray her country on top of that... Betty was not the sort of person one would have expected to have been swayed by a cause like the Burmese Independence Movement. Edith had to admit it to herself; Betty had been far too shallow and self-centred. She must have changed a great deal after she met Ye Win.

Pondering what she'd read, Edith found herself softening a little. She was clear that the British had no right to be ruling Burma by force and against the will of the people, but did that justify the level of duplicity Betty had displayed? And in any case, Betty's betrayal was because of her need for Ye Win's continued love and attention, not because she had a deep belief in the cause.

Edith checked her watch and realised that two hours

had passed. The cleaning lady was still there, doing a thorough job of making the bungalow spotless. Now she was sweeping the terrace near to where Edith sat. Edith smiled at her as she came close.

'What is your name?' Edith asked.

'I am Simi,' replied the woman with a shy smile.

'I am Edith,' she replied. But at the same time she noticed that Simi's eyes were lingering on the journal lying in her lap.

'Do you know anything about this?' she asked holding it up.

Simi's smile disappeared suddenly, she shook her head quickly and backed away. Within moments, she had vanished up the path with her brooms and mops. Edith vowed to ask Richard about her at some point. Perhaps she did know something, but maybe her English wasn't good enough to explain.

There was another hour or so before lunch, so Edith turned back to the journal, gritting her teeth. What more unpalatable truths lay between these pages?

Betty's Journal

November 1939

I haven't written in here for a while because we've been away in Calcutta for Edith's wedding. To tell you the truth, I didn't really want to go, the way things are with Ye Win. I'm afraid that he's slipping away from me and that only regular reminders of what we have together will keep him close.

I'm so happy for Edith though, having found someone who suits her. Any guilt I might feel about having snatched Robert from under her nose has now completely vanished. I have more important things to worry about. Gregory certainly wouldn't be my choice, as I've mentioned before, he is a good twenty years older than Edith, but he seems to genuinely care for her and he is a kind man. The hotel, although fairly modest, brings in a good income and Edith told me that she enjoys working there.

The wedding was bigger than my own, but standing there in St Paul's Cathedral in Calcutta reminded me of the day I tied the knot with Robert and how happy and hopeful I was for the future. Things have turned out very differently from how I expected, but I can't say I regret marrying Robert. It is only through marrying him and going to Rangoon that I have met Ye Win.

I was dying to tell Edith about Ye Win. She saw that I was preoccupied and asked me what the matter was a few times. But how could I tell her the truth? She would be deeply shocked, not only that I'm being unfaithful to Robert, of whom she is still very fond (I can tell), but that I'm helping Ye Win and his cause by deceiving Robert further. So, I had to duck her questions and pretend that nothing was wrong.

Edith and Gregory looked so happy setting off for the station after the reception. I felt a pang of regret that the love I feel for Ye Win may only be acknowledged in private. How I'd love to shout it from the rooftops, but I know that will never happen.

January 1940

Tomorrow is the day of the Viceroy's visit and I'm aware that I haven't written in this journal for a couple of months. Life has gone on much as before, but I have seen a little less of Ye Win lately, which has saddened me.

Christmas came and went. Robert and I spent it at the club, just as we did last year, but I entered into the spirit even less this time. My mind was on Ye Win and I longed to be with him. It meant that I could hardly engage with Christmas, its meaningless traditions and rituals.

After I gave Ye Win the papers from the city council meetings, I didn't see him for a week or so. He didn't come to the clinic or try to contact me once. My mind went into over-drive, thinking that now I'd delivered what he wanted he no longer wanted to see me, but he turned up the following week and things were just the same as before between us. We went again by taxi to his apartment, as we had so many times and from the way he kissed me and took me in his arms that evening, I was reassured that his feelings were just the same.

However, he did ask me if there were any further papers in Robert's study and I had to tell him that the briefcase contained several more folders of minutes and that I'd picked the ones I thought would be of most use.

'I'd like to see them all,' he said.

'I thought you said you had what you needed,' I protested.

'We do, for the Viceroy's visit at least, but we'd like to see what decisions have been made over the past few months. What plans are afoot for the city. Please, Betty? You did such a wonderful job last time.'

I had no choice but to agree, so the next day followed the same routine as before. This time was a little easier. Ali wasn't hovering around outside Robert's office and I managed to slip out of the house without anyone seeing.

Having taken such risks for Ye Win, I thought he could have been a little more attentive, but I know he's been busy preparing a protest for the Viceroy's visit and that that has taken him away from the clinic and from me. I know how much the cause means to him; that I only take second place and I must accept that. My own love hasn't dimmed at all though, I remain obsessed and infatuated with him. He occupies my every waking thought and even my dreams at night. I'm hoping that once tomorrow is over, he will have more time for me once again.

February 1st

Today has passed in a blur and I'm still in shock from what happened this morning. What has added to the shock is the knowledge that I am partly responsible for what happened today. If I hadn't given Ye Win the papers from Robert's office he and his comrades wouldn't have known where to target and at what time.

At first, the Viceroy's visit started very much like Lord Dundas's last year. He arrived, alone except for some officials and servants, by ship at the docks on Strand Road and the Governor was there to meet him. Robert and I were in line for a handshake, then the whole party got into cars and went up to the place where the Viceroy was due to address the public. It was a wooden platform in the gardens opposite the Sule Pagoda. It had been constructed for a military parade the year before and never dismantled. Robert and I took our places on seats behind the Governor and Viceroy on the platform.

The Governor gave a welcome speech, then the Viceroy got up to say his bit. He'd only uttered a couple of sentences when suddenly there was an almighty bang and a crashing behind us, and half the platform was blown into the air in an instant. I turned to see boards, chairs, body parts flying through the air in the wake of the explosion in a haze of dust. Robert and I were luckily on part of the platform that was unharmed, as was the Viceroy, but all the rows behind us were obliterated. Behind our seats was a yawning gap, filled with splintered boards, bent metal and bloodied bodies.

The Viceroy and Governor were immediately surrounded by policemen and soldiers, bundled into a car and driven away at speed.

'Come on,' said Robert, his face deathly white, stumbling towards the steps, 'let's get out of here.'

'No,' I said, reeling from shock and from the knowledge that this was my doing, the lives lost were my responsibility. 'I need to stay and help. I've trained at the clinic,' I said.

'You're coming with me,' he said, taking my arm, but I wrenched it away. It was the least I could do. Not looking back, I scrambled down the scaffolding onto the grass where bodies were strewn about. Some obviously dead, others groaning and in need of attention. I found one woman bleeding from her stomach. I recognised her face. She was the wife of a member of the Burmese government. She was wearing a shawl, so I took it from her, ripped it into strips and bandaged her wound. As I finished, ambulances arrived, so I signalled for stretcher bearers to come and pick her up.

As I looked across at the stretcher bearers, I realised that Robert was amongst them. I stood up and wiped the sweat from my eyes, smiling at him.

I worked tirelessly for hours. I was able to help some people; others died before my eyes. I had no idea how many casualties there were. No doubt we will hear that tomorrow. When all the bodies had been removed, and workers were taking the splintered planks and broken scaffolding away on carts, I sat down on a bench and gave into the tears I'd been bottling up all morning.

It was the shock of the explosion, the exhaustion of all the frantic work I'd done that morning to help save survivors, but there was something else that was troubling me. It was only sitting down on that bench that I was able to articulate it to myself. It was the knowledge that Ye Win must have planned the bombing in the knowledge that Robert and I would be sitting on the platform a few rows back from the Viceroy. In fact they had no idea where we would be sitting, so Ye Win had gambled on my life. I thought back to the terrifying look I'd seen in his eyes on two occasions. Just thinking about it makes chills run through me. Was that the real Ye Win? Someone who would risk their lover's life if it meant advancing the cause they believed in? I shook my head, refusing to believe that of him. How many times had he told me he loved me?

Someone touched my shoulder and I looked up. It was Robert. His face was covered in dirt and there was blood on his forehead.

'I've just come back from the hospital,' he said. 'We've done what we can here. Shall we go home?'

I let him put his arm around my shoulders and guide me across the gardens to a waiting car.

August 1940

Some months have passed since the bombing in Mahabandoola Gardens. Life has gone on as before and I am still as much in love with Ye Win as I ever was. I was angry with him for a long time about the bombing, and challenged him many, many times, asking him why he wanted to kill innocent civilians, especially as many of those who died or were severely injured were Burmese citizens.

'This is a war, Betty. People will get killed.'

'If I'd known what you were planning, I'd never have given you those papers,' I said. I have been riddled with guilt at my part in what happened that day. Ten innocent people lost their lives.

'Face up to it Betty, stop deluding yourself,' he said, taking my face between his hands and looking deep into my eyes. 'You knew. Or even if you didn't know for sure, if you'd stopped to think for one moment you would have realised.'

'And what about me?' I asked him then, while he was looking straight at me. 'You knew I would be there. You were prepared to risk my life.'

He shrugged. 'I had no idea you would be there, my precious one,' he said, tracing the line of my jaw with his index finger. 'If I'd known, I would have warned you.'

'And what has it achieved, this act of terrorism? This waste of innocent lives? Tell me that?'

He laughed. 'Everything we do has a greater purpose,' he said. 'It will feed into the endgame. When we negotiate for our freedom. The British are shaken to the core by it. They are on the run now. They know we are not to be underestimated. It will serve us well in the end.'

Since that day, Ye Win has continued to ask me to give him papers from the council meetings and I'm so much under his spell that I have willingly gone and done it for him. Every week, the day after the typed minutes arrive through the post, I walk up to the Shwedagon Pagoda with them in my shopping bag, just as I did the first time. I haven't really squared my actions with my conscience, I'd prefer not to think about it that way, I just know that if I don't do this for him, there is a risk that he will stop seeing me. It's as simple as that. I want to keep his love and our evening trysts in his apartment.

I try not to look at the Rangoon newspapers too closely, not wanting to see news of an explosion or an attack on a member of the council, or other activities for which Ye Win and his comrades could be responsible. But Florence normally fills me in as she drives me to the clinic in the mornings.

'A council member's house was vandalised yesterday. Did you read the article in *The Post*?' she said, with a sideways look at me, no doubt assessing my reaction. 'How they knew his address is anyone's guess.'

Or another time; 'There was an independence march yesterday down Merchant Street. Just when the mounted police were having a parade. I wonder how they knew about that?'

I would shrug, look the other way and refuse to be drawn. But by now I'd read enough of Florence's writing to know that she herself was extremely sympathetic to the independence movement, if not an active part of it. She was in no position to judge my actions.

In the meantime, talk of the Japanese threat has continued to dominate our evenings at the club. People seem to take the possibility of a Japanese invasion more seriously now, and the papers are reporting that Singapore and Malaya are being fortified in advance of an invasion. Even Robert has become a convert to the theory that the Japs are building up to invade Malaya.

But to my confusion and dismay, Ye Win told me that he's looking on the possibility of a Japanese invasion of British territories with hope and pleasure.

'They will help us free ourselves from the tyranny of British rule,' he told me on more than one occasion. 'They are our fellow Asians after all. They are talking about an Asian Co-Prosperity Sphere, spanning all countries in Asia.'

'They may say that now, but once they're in power it could be a different story,' I said, echoing the sentiments I'd heard many express at the club, 'Just look how they've behaved towards the Chinese.'

'I know that, but they are our best hope,' he said. 'There's no point negotiating with the British. They're never going to give up their stranglehold. Just look at how they cling on in India.'

It troubles me that he should think like that and that he might consider siding with the Japanese against the British. I realise that I've already compromised myself in what I've done for him and his cronies, but going over to the Japanese seems a step too far. I'm not sure I could ever support him in that decision.

November 1940

I've been very remiss about writing in this journal for the past several months. It is probably because nothing much has changed. I continue to go to the clinic in Mingaladon township three times a week and afterwards take a taxi to Ye Win's apartment to see him. The visits follow the same routine every time. We drink whisky and then make love.

My love continues to burn as brightly as it ever did, but I worry about Ye Win's feelings and whether or not mine are reciprocated. I sometimes think if it wasn't for the regular supply of papers from the council meetings, he wouldn't bother with me at all. But I carry on bringing them to him. I have no choice; I'm a slave to my obsession.

It rankles with me sometimes that our love has no outlet. We cannot go out together, apart from occasionally to the tea houses, and we cannot acknowledge our relationship publicly. This doesn't seem to trouble Ye Win, but it troubles me. However, I suppose I should be thankful for what we have together, and not seek change. What we have is, in some senses, perfect.

February 1941

Life has gone on as before for the past few months. Christmas followed the same pattern as it did the previous two years, but I resented every moment of festivities that kept me away from Ye Win. My visits to Ye Win's apartment have continued although he has all but stopped coming to the clinic now. He says he is too busy with the cause and that the clinic must take second place to that. I am concerned that there is so much he doesn't tell me. He never tells me what he and his comrades do with the council papers I bring him and I am left to find out of their attacks and sabotage from Florence. Perhaps he's worried that if he tells me, I might decide not to give him the papers anymore. He knows how shocked I was about the bombing at the Viceroy's visit. However, I don't want to lose his love and I know, to some extent at least, that it is contingent upon me continuing to help his cause.

I'm concerned most about his views on the Japanese. We have had many arguments about that. He thinks a Japanese invasion of Burma would be a good thing, but I cannot understand why. I argue that the Japs would subjugate the Burmese just as they have done the Chinese population, but Ye Win cannot see that. He has hinted that he is already in discussion with some undercover Japanese agents offering them assistance ahead of the invasion. I cannot believe that is the case, and if it is, my love will be sorely tested.

March 1941

I have discovered something that brings equal portions of joy and despair. I am expecting a baby. From my dates I have worked out that it must have been conceived in late January. That means that it is unlikely that it is Robert's child and that it must be Ye Win's. One part of me is overjoyed that this has happened as a complete affirmation of our love, but another part of me is dreading the fallout from this news.

My first concern is that if this child is indeed Ye Win's, my secret will be out in the open. He or she will be half-Burmese and that will be impossible to disguise. I know from overhearing whispered conversations at the club that any child of mixed race here is regarded as an outcast by both communities, much as Anglo-Indians are regarded in British India. There are probably many of them, but they are never acknowledged by their British fathers. There was a tradition of British men taking Burmese mistresses and the products of those unions were generally packed away to boarding schools, outcasts from their families. How could I let that happen to a child of mine? But at the same time acknowledging this child would mean admitting to my affair. I have no idea how Robert would react to that. He would be hurt and angry, I'm sure, but would he abandon me?

Secondly, I have to face it, although it pains me to do so, I worry about breaking the news to Ye Win. How will he react? I live in fear of his face clouding over and that terrifying, alien expression appearing. That's the side of Ye Win he likes to keep carefully hidden. I know he professes his love for me, but in reality, if he's prepared to make that love contingent upon my helping him, I have to face the fact that his love doesn't run that deep. It is possible that he too would abandon me. Then I would be left alone to rear a child without help or support from either side.

My pregnancy can only be a few weeks advanced, but Daw Ma has already guessed my predicament. Although I've tried to hide it as best I can, I've been feeling nauseous and on occasions have been sick after breakfast. On one of those occasions, when I was lying down on my bed to recover, she came sidling up to me and said quietly,

'Are you in trouble, madam?'

'I don't know what you mean, Daw Ma,' I said, avoiding her gaze.

'In trouble, madam. With a baby.' She said it bluntly. Trouble was an apt way to describe it.

'No trouble Daw Ma, I'm just sick, that's all,' I said, and she shuffled away but I know she wasn't satisfied with the answer.

I haven't had the courage to tell Ye Win yet. I think I'll leave it until three months have gone by. It is possible that nature may take its course and that I may end up not having to tell him after all. Yes, I think that's the best thing to do.

April 1941

I have just come from Ye Win's apartment and I am in deep shock. I had to lie down when I got home just to let my heartbeat die down, but now I'm ready to write about what happened.

He looked different today when I arrived. He was clearly distracted and when we made love he wasn't as attentive as usual.

'What's the matter, my love?' I asked as we lay together on his bed. He propped himself up on his elbow and looked me in the eyes.

'I leave here tomorrow,' he said. 'This is the last time we'll be together.'

Shockwaves washed through me at his words. 'What on earth do you mean? Where are you going?'

Tears stung my eyes at the prospect of losing him. I blinked them away, but I couldn't look at him. Should I tell him about my pregnancy? Would that stop him going?

'You won't like this and I wasn't going to tell you, but I'm going to Japan.'

The words hit me like a hammer blow. I sat up.

'Japan? Whatever for? Why?'

'I'm going with the comrades for military training to help with the Japanese invasion when it happens.'

I was dumbfounded. I had no words with which to reply. I knew he was sympathetic to the Japanese but I hadn't realised that his negotiations with them had been about this. For things to have advanced this far, he must have been talking to them for weeks, months even. I found myself shaking all over. I was suddenly cold, covered in goose-bumps but pouring with sweat at the same time. I got up without speaking, pulled on my clothes.

'What are you doing?' he sounded surprised.

'I'm leaving. I can't believe what you've just told me. I don't want to be with you anymore.'

Then he was angry, his face clouded over and I saw that hideous mask I'd seen twice before, only then I realised that it wasn't a mask. This was his true face, the one he'd successfully hidden from me for almost two years. His eyes were slits of hatred, his whole expression exuded anger and hostility. He leapt out of bed and grabbed me by both arms.

'Don't leave like this. We still need you. Even if I'm gone, we need those papers. I will arrange for someone else to meet you at the pagoda.'

'No!' I spat at him. 'I've done enough. I've betrayed my country enough. I won't do it anymore.'

Then he pulled me close.

'Then know this,' he said quietly, his dark eyes narrowed, pure venom in his voice. 'I never loved you, Betty. Not for one minute. It has been an ordeal to be with you. I chose you and I worked on you until you were in my power. Just as Florence worked on your husband before. I just needed you for what you could do for the cause.'

'It's not true!' I said, horrified, but knew in my heart that it was. It was what I'd half suspected all along.

'Florence is my real lover. Ask her if you don't believe me. It was her who brought you to me. It wasn't a coincidence.'

He let me go then and I rushed out of the apartment and clattered down the stairs and out onto the street, banging the doors as I went. I doubled over on the pavement and vomited into the gutter, such was the shock of what had just happened.

18

EDITH

Dapha River Tea Plantation, Assam, 1980

IT WAS lunchtime now and Edith put the journal down sighing deeply. What she'd read in the latest section had shocked her even more deeply than the earlier entries. Betty's betrayal had caused the deaths of ten people. How could she have done that? And how could she have lived with herself afterwards?

The news of Betty's pregnancy also came as a shock to Edith. Why had Betty never told her in her letters? She remembered now that Betty had hinted at a great secret that she needed to tell her. This must be it. But what had happened to the baby? Had she miscarried? She didn't think Robert had found out. He would have surely told Edith when he came to the Tea Planter's Club later in 1942. Had Betty taken the baby on the walk through the mountains to India? Edith was itching to read the next instalment, but she'd promised Richard she would meet him for lunch at one. She put the journal aside, brushed her hair and walked briskly up to the house.

He was already sitting outside. When she stepped onto the veranda, he offered her some lemonade.

'How's the journal going?' he asked.

'Quite amazing,' Edith said. 'My sister was a dark horse. She had all sorts of secrets that I had no clue about. It's quite a revelation. I really had no idea...'

She fell silent as the bearer brought the meal. This time it was chicken korma and rice. It smelled delicious and Edith realised that she was ravenous.

'I can imagine it must have been difficult, not knowing what happened to her,' Richard said.

Edith nodded. 'I thought she'd come eventually. She had such a survivor's spirit, you know. For years I watched and waited for her. But she never did. I searched everywhere for news of her. The authorities held lists of casualties, but her name was never on them.'

'There's something I haven't told you,' he said, 'but there is a grave at the bottom of the garden. There is no name, and the inscription states it is a young woman who died during the trek out of Burma in 1942.'

His words hit Edith hard. She found her hands shaking uncontrollably. She had to put her fork down.

'I'm so sorry to have broken it to you like that, but I've been trying to find the right moment to let you know.'

'It must be Betty,' she said. 'It has to be. But if it is, why didn't they record her death and let me know? Her ID papers were right here all along.'

'Perhaps it isn't her,' he said with a shrug.

'Can you take me to it? After lunch? I'd like to see.'

'Of course.'

Later, they walked down the path, between rows of delicately scented rose bushes towards the end of the garden.

The path sloped gently downwards, and Edith realised that this end of the garden bordered the jungle, not the tea plantation. There was a spreading banyan tree in front of a high wooden fence and behind it the jungle began; tall teak trees formed a wall and underneath its high green canopy hung with creepers grew thickets of bamboo, huge alien ferns and palms, and as they got closer, Edith could hear the sounds of the jungle. The incessant buzz and clatter of insects, the whooping of exotic birds, the cries of monkeys. A shiver went through her. There was something eerily forlorn about this spot.

'It's here, under the banyan tree,' said Richard, stopping in the shade of the great, spreading branches. The grave was a mound covered in grass with a simple wooden cross on it. Edith read the inscription:

'Here lies the body of a young woman who died of malaria on April 16th 1942, on the long march from Burma into India. Her name is unknown, but her bravery will live on in our hearts. God Rest her Soul.'

Edith stared at it. This couldn't be Betty, she thought instantly. How would they not know her name, when it was written clearly on her papers and on the front of the journal for all to see.

She shook her head. 'I don't think this can be my sister,' she said, but looking deep into her heart, she couldn't be sure.

Betty's Journal

July 1941

It has taken me weeks to get over the blow that Ye Win dealt me that day back in April. I became a virtual recluse for a while and Robert was quite worried about me. When I got home the evening that Ye Win gave me the devastating news that he was going to Japan, that he'd never loved me and had been using me all along, I went straight upstairs to bed. I closed the curtains and sobbed into the pillow for what felt like hours. There was no disguising my distress and when Robert came home, he came upstairs and sat on the bed.

'Whatever's the matter, my love?' he asked, stroking my back. Of course, I couldn't tell him, I made up something about the heat tiring me out. It would have been a relief just to talk to someone about it, to unburden myself. But I had to hold it all inside; the guilt, the shame, and the feeling of humiliation at having been used. I couldn't get over Florence's betrayal either. I'd thought we were friends. The knowledge that all along she'd been sleeping with Ye Win almost destroyed me. They'd both been manipulating me, probably laughing about me behind my back. I screwed up my fists and beat the pillow in a furious rage.

The next morning, I heard Florence's car on the drive at 8.30 as usual. She'd come to take me to the clinic.

'Go down and tell Mrs Anderson that I'm unwell and that I won't be going to the clinic today,' I said to Daw Ma. 'In fact, I won't be going again this week.'

After a few minutes, I heard the car draw away and lay back on my pillows, relieved. Florence has never returned. Not the following week, not ever. Ye Win must have told her about our conversation and that he'd revealed the fact the two of them were lovers. I'm glad she's had the sense not to try to speak to me. I will never forgive her for her betrayal, no matter what excuses or explanations she might come up with.

Gradually though, as the days and weeks passed, I

started to recover from the blow that Ye Win had dealt me. I started to see a little more of my old friends at the club, and although I'd previously found them trivial and boring, now there was some comfort in the company of women who made no more demands on me than asking me to show up to coffee mornings and to display an interest in their idle gossip. None of them noticed that my belly was swelling. I've kept that hidden from everyone, including Robert, although Daw Ma has definitely noticed. I know from the way she looks at me, but she's never mentioned it again, not since that first time. It is an unspoken secret we keep between us.

After a couple of weeks' break from the clinic, I started going along again. I've carefully avoided being there on the day that Florence helps out. I have no wish to bump into her. Now I get our syce to take me there in the mornings and collect me in the afternoons. I have found that although the work is harrowing and demanding, the clinic helps me to feel a sense of purpose in life which would be lacking if I just focused on the club and coffee mornings with the other memsahibs.

Today Robert broke the news to me that he's signing up for the army.

'I feel it's the duty of every able-bodied British man in Burma,' he told me at breakfast time. 'A new division of the British Indian Army has been formed to defend the country. It's an infantry division that they're calling the British Burma Army. They're going to need every man they can find if the newspapers have got it right. The Japs are building up to invade Malaya and they'll definitely turn their attentions to Burma after that. They have their eyes on India, of course, and this is their best route in.'

Despite the fact that Robert could be putting himself in

harm's way, I felt a sense of relief steal over me at this news. If he were away, I would find it a lot easier to hide my pregnancy. It has been getting more and more difficult to conceal it from Robert and I have no idea what to do when it comes to the baby actually arriving. I felt I had to protest against him going to war though, for the sake of appearances.

'But what about the company, Robert?' I said. 'Surely that must be an essential business? You could insist on staying behind if you wanted to. There's no need to volunteer.'

'I've got two really trustworthy Burmese managers I can leave in charge of operations. I would have no qualms about their ability to cope. It's you I'm worried about, my darling.'

'Oh Robert, that's sweet of you, but I'll be fine on my own. After all, the servants are here to look after me.'

'I *shall* worry about you though. You've seemed so vulnerable lately. Not your normal self at all.'

'Please Robert. I'm fine. I was tired for a time but I feel better now and there's really no need to worry. I shall worry about you though, and I hope you'll write often.'

'Of course. As often as I can.'

So it is fixed. Robert will leave next week for infantry training. He is even busier at the office now, working long hours getting things sorted out in advance of his going. I'm proud of him for signing up to defend his country when he'd have the perfect excuse not to. It puts me and my treacherous actions to shame, however, and now I feel guiltier than ever.

September 1941

Robert has been gone for a couple of months now and I have adjusted to life without him. It is a relief not to have to be so careful about hiding my condition, although of course I need to conceal it from the servants.

Robert has written to me several times from his army base in Tangoo, over a hundred miles north of Rangoon. He has been promoted to the rank of Lieutenant and is now being trained in manning guns and commanding infantry soldiers. He can't tell me much in his letters, and some of what he has written has been blacked out by the censors, but I'm relieved to see that he appears to have taken to army life so well.

As for me, I'm still going regularly to help out at the clinic but having to take more and more elaborate steps to conceal my condition. I've taken to wearing loose smocks, but this can't go on much longer. Someone is bound to notice soon so I've decided to take a break from it and return once the baby is born.

On that subject I've had to take Daw Ma into my confidence. It was easy to do so as she clearly already knew what I was about to tell her. I spoke to her the other day as she was putting clothes away in the bedroom.

'Daw Ma, this is difficult, but I need to speak to someone in confidence,' I began. I was sitting on the bed and she turned and smiled at me, her sweet, open smile.

'You can speak to me, madam,' she said. 'I will not tell anyone.'

'As you probably know, I will be having a baby in a couple of months' time.'

'Yes, I know that, madam,' she said looking at me steadily.

'And... and well, this is very awkward, but the baby isn't my husband's. It will be half-Burmese, in fact.'

She came and sat down beside me on the bed.

'I know, madam,' she said quietly, but how she knew that

fact I've no idea. Was she aware of my liaison with Ye Win? And if she knew, how many others also knew? Did the rest of the servants? Would one of them tell Robert?

'I cannot hide it anymore,' I went on, 'I need to stay in my room from now on so the rest of the servants won't see me.'

She nodded gravely. 'I understand, madam,' she said. 'I will tell them you're ill and need to rest. I will bring you food from the kitchens.'

'Thank you. But there is something else, Daw Ma,' I said, looking into her gentle eyes. 'I am worried about giving birth. I haven't seen a doctor and I won't know what to do when the time comes.'

'Oh madam,' she said, looking earnestly at me. 'Please not to worry. I know a woman. She lives near my home. She can attend you for the birth.'

'I will pay her, of course,' I said, relief flooding through me at her words.

'She is not expensive.'

'And once the baby is born...' I broke down in tears then. I was so wrung out with anxiety about what to do once the baby arrives. I know that I won't be able to bear to part with it, but at the same time, if people were to see it they would instantly know of my infidelity.

'Madam, please do not worry. Do not cry,' she said, putting her arm around my shoulders. 'I can help you.'

I looked at her with my tear-stained face. 'How? How can you help me?'

'If you will permit me, madam, I will care for the baby in my home. You can come and see it whenever you want to, but we can pretend that it is the baby of a relative of mine who has died.'

'Would you really do that for me?' I said, looking at her through my tears.

She nodded. 'Of course, madam,' she said simply. 'You are my memsahib. I will help you. I wouldn't want to see you, or the baby suffer.'

Her kindness overwhelmed me and I was so choked with emotion I couldn't reply. I thought then of all the times I'd treated Daw Ma badly; spoken shortly to her, given her unreasonable tasks, been the self-centred person I sometimes am, and yet her loyalty was so strong. How I'd taken her for granted over the years, and how I'd worried about what to do, when all the time the answer was right here under my nose.

October 10th

This morning, just before dawn, my baby was born. I am exhausted but ecstatic at the same time. He is the most beautiful creature I have ever seen. A tiny little boy, with perfect honey-coloured skin and black, black eyes.

I won't dwell on the birth, suffice it to say it was the most pain I've ever suffered in my life. Daw Ma's midwife came late last night, when I felt the first pangs, and she stayed with me until after the birth. Her face was old and wizened, but there was deep wisdom in her gaze and when she laid her hands on my body I could feel the healing power in them. They were deft and soothing, she knew exactly when and where to massage me to soothe the pain and how best to help me.

She brought two herbal mixtures; one was an ointment which she rubbed onto my back and stomach and the other was to drink. Daw Ma brought boiling water and made a tea from it which I drunk down. It was bitter and foul-tasting

and I worried about what was in it, but as soon as I'd swallowed it the pain eased a little.

When the pangs got unendurable, the old woman put a
cotton rag between my teeth and told me to bite down. It
was to stop me screaming out as much as anything, because
Daw Ma had told her my circumstances.

On the final, excruciating push, when the baby came out
squealing, the old woman cleaned him, wrapped him in a
sheet and handed him to me to put to my breast. It was only
then that she smiled broadly, and I saw her blackened teeth.
I don't know her name, but without her I would have struggled so much more.

'Ananda,' she said.

'She likes to suggest names for the babies she delivers,'
Daw Ma explained. 'It brings them good luck. Ananda
means eternal bliss.'

'Ananda it is then,' I said. I hadn't given any thought to
naming the baby, 'It is perfect.'

The old midwife went away, as she'd arrived, by the back
stairway and rear entrance, and I was left to rest and to
marvel in the new being I'd brought into the world. I
thought about Ye Win, about his intoxicating charisma and
how I'd fallen for his charm. I tried to conjure up good
thoughts about him, but none would come. Even so, I could
clearly see his features etched on the face of my baby and I
was determined to love him whatever his provenance.

October 17th

Ananda is a week old now and I have just taken him to Daw
Ma's home and left him there. We'd agreed that a week was
long enough for me to nurse him and she will now give him
powdered milk from a bottle. I had to sneak him out of the

house when I knew the servants were eating breakfast. I'd ordered a taxi to wait out on the road, so I hurried up the drive concealing my bundle as best I could under a shawl.

Daw Ma's little house is a single-storey hut in one of the poorest Burmese townships to the south of the city. It is neat and clean, but tiny and very, very basic. Daw Ma uses a communal toilet in the street and there are open drains running in front of her home.

She told me that both her parents died recently so now she lives alone. I was touched to see that she'd already prepared an old orange crate for Ananda to lie in. She'd lined it with colourful material from the bazaar and put a woollen fleece in the bottom.

I laid him down on the fleece and as soon as I'd done that, he started to cry. It tore my heart out to listen to him, but Daw Ma picked him up and cradled and rocked him to and fro. He soon stopped crying and started gurgling contentedly.

When I left to come home, I couldn't stop crying. Daw Ma told me that I can go back there whenever I want to, and I intend to go every day, but even so, it was a huge wrench leaving Ananda there and walking away from him. It felt like losing a limb. The taxi had waited outside for me and drove me out of those poverty-stricken streets, through the centre of the city and back to my palatial home. I didn't say a word all the way back, but if the driver had looked in the mirror he'd have seen that my face was streaked with tears.

I will have to get used to life at home without Daw Ma. She told the other servants that she was leaving to take up another job. I won't get another maid; no one could replace her.

Next week I will return to my work at the clinic. I need to

get back to some sort of normality, and it will keep my mind from pining for Ananda.

December 10th

Life has fallen into a regular routine since Ananda was born. I take a taxi over to Daw Ma's township to see him every day. Each day there is a small change in him; in the last week or so he has started smiling and taking notice of his surroundings. He now knows my face and always greets me with a broad smile when I look into his cradle. Daw Ma is looking after him well. He looks healthy and strong and grows by the day. With the money I'm giving her, she is making small improvements to her little home as well, so it is now more comfortable than when I first went there. She has bought a chair for nursing, some cushions and cooking equipment for when Ananda starts on solid food.

On the days I go to the clinic, I visit Ananda straight after I've finished. It isn't far, in fact it is in the neighbouring township. I can't help remembering that I used to get a taxi in the opposite direction to visit Ye Win, all those months ago. There is a sort of odd symmetry in that, but I look forward to seeing Ananda with a pleasure that is untainted with anxiety and pain.

The papers are full of the news that the Japanese bombed Pearl Harbor three days ago and destroyed the US fleet there. America has entered the war now, but that war is moving ever closer to Burma. On the same night as they bombed Pearl Harbor, the Japanese invaded Malaya at Kota Bharu on the north coast and are making their way down the peninsula. They have already beaten away the British and Allied forces that tried to prevent them landing and are leaving havoc in their wake. At the same time they undertook a bombing raid on Singapore, destroying many buildings and causing many casualties.

After seeing Ananda yesterday, I dropped in at the club to see how people were reacting to the news. Cedric Brown was crowing that he's the only one who had warned of this. A lot of others looked worried, thinking that if Singapore falls, Rangoon will be next, but others were full of bravado.

'Singapore is a fortress,' said one man. 'Impregnable. Everyone knows that. And Churchill has sent two warships to defend it, just to make sure.'

Someone else piped up; 'The Japs are no match for British soldiers. They don't have the constitution for it for one thing. Look how short most of 'em are. And they're all short-sighted. We'll beat off this invasion and they'll go home with their tails between their legs soon enough.'

I found this attitude worrying in the extreme. If the Japanese are defeating the Allies in Malaya, they will rip through Burma like wildfire through a dry forest. Malaya was not properly defended, everyone knows that, but Burma has even fewer troops. I worry about Robert and his unit. He has been moved south now, in advance of an invasion through the Tenasserim Hills on the Thai border but I have no idea exactly where to. However will they fare when the inevitable battle comes?

I went home from the club and had a sleepless night, fretting about what will happen when the Japs turn their attentions to Burma.

December 23rd

This morning for the first time, the Japanese bombed Rangoon. I was at the clinic when it happened. Just before ten o'clock, I was stitching up a minor wound on an old lady, when I heard a faint droning noise in the distance. It grew louder and louder and within seconds it was obvious that it was the sound of aircraft. Then the air raid warning started up its wailing. They'd sounded on a few previous occasions, but those had been false alarms. I left the old lady and rushed outside, alongside other helpers, nurses and doctors. In the street people were running for cover, tripping over each other, upsetting stalls and trolleys in their haste. We stood outside and stared at the blinding bright sky.

I shaded my eyes to look up and what I saw chilled me to the core. Dozens of aircraft, flying in formation, from the south towards the city. They were not yet overhead, but there were so many, the cloudless sky seemed to darken at their approach. As they advanced, other aircraft, that looked heavier and less manoeuvrable, approached them from the opposite direction. I realised they must be British RAF planes, taking off from Mingaladon airfield, not far from where we stood.

As the RAF moved towards the enemy aircraft, the thump thump of guns sounded from the airbase; the anti-aircraft battery had sprung into action, but they sounded too late. Up in the sky, the lumbering allied aircraft started firing on the enemy aircraft. The ack-ack of machinegun-fire splintered the sky. One or two Japanese planes peeled off from the formation and fell towards the earth, streaming black smoke in their wake, but most persisted, dipping lower now as they approached the city. The swarm of planes was almost directly above and it was then they started releasing their bombs. I watched them drop, like dozens of huge black eggs, directly on the houses and shops of Mingaladon township and the neighbouring one, and as they hit the ground, the sickening boom and crash of each explosion, the splintering of wood and the screams of the people came from all around. Instantly, smoke, flames and dust rose from where the bombs had dropped. They were landing all around us. One only a couple of streets away. The aircraft moved on, dropping their sticks of lethal cargo all around, but mercifully the clinic was spared.

Within minutes, injured people started stumbling along the road towards the clinic. They came alone or in pairs, supporting each other, heads bleeding, limbs crushed, all of them white-faced and shaken, too deeply shocked to cry or even to speak. We went inside and started helping them. Dr Myint and the other doctors took those who looked the worst injured, while the nurses took the less serious-looking cases and we volunteers helped those with minor injuries.

All the time I worked dressing wounds, bandaging sprains, administering painkillers, I thought of Ananda and Daw Ma. I'd seen sticks of bombs landing in the direction of her home. My mind was working overtime, imagining the worst but I worked on. But after two or three hours I could bear it no longer. I went to Dr Myint and threw myself on his mercy.

He was trying to bandage a splintered thighbone.

'Dr Myint,' I began and the tears came before I could get the words out. 'I need to check on some relatives; they have a baby. Could I go for an hour to see if they are alright?'

He looked at me with curiosity then. Did he already know? At that point I simply didn't care, I was so frantic with worry for Ananda.

'Go home, Betty,' said Dr Myint kindly, 'You have done great work so far. You've helped many people. If your relatives are safe and you can come back, please do. If you can't, I'll understand.'

'Thank you, doctor,' I breathed.

I stumbled outside. In both directions the remains of

bombed out buildings blocked the street. There was no chance of any vehicles making it through. I realised that it would be far quicker to walk anyway. I set off in the direction of Daw Ma's house and before I'd got to the end of the road I'd passed many buildings that had been reduced to rubble by the bombings. Piles of shattered masonry blocked the way and I had to climb over many heaps of broken bricks and rubble. I walked through streets where shophouses had been destroyed, roofs blasted in, plate glass windows blown out, shattered glass covering the road. Little fires burned all around and rescue operations were underway.

Everywhere I passed there were bodies, some lying face down, often in pools of blood that seeped into the dust, with limbs blown off or half buried in masonry. I covered my face as the stench was horrifying, and stumbled on, through the shattered streets, past blown out vehicles, their occupants hanging out of doors or smashed against windscreens, past markets that had been hit, food scattered all around and packs of pi dogs feasting on the spoils. All the time my frantic thoughts pictured Ananda and Daw Ma struggling through the wreckage. Her house was in the densest part of the next township. I prayed fervently that they had been spared.

Finally, I reached the next street to hers, but one end of it had been blown away completely, the wooden houses obliterated, great craters in the ground where the bomb had struck. People sat on piles of broken belongings, too stunned to move, their eyes dull with fear.

I hurried on, finding a way around the heaps of rubble until I was standing at the end of Daw Ma's road.

'Thank God,' my heart stopped pumping quite so fast as her little wooden house hove into view at the other end of the road. It was still standing! As I got closer I started to run and when I was two or three houses away I began to shout.

'Daw Ma! Ananda! Daw Ma! Are you there?'

She came out of the door, clutching the baby to her breast, and I ran the last few paces to them, blinded by tears, and reaching them, enveloped them both in my arms.

19

EDITH

Dapha River Tea Plantation, Assam, 1980

IT WAS mid-afternoon and the heat on the bungalow terrace was stifling; the sun had moved round so there was no shade at all. Edith hadn't noticed before, but when she looked up from reading the journal, she realised that her arms were burning. In a lifetime in tropical countries, she'd hardly ever let that happen before. She quickly moved inside, anxious to continue reading, needing to know whether the journal held clues to what had happened to Betty.

She knew now that she had, or had had a nephew, Ananda. When she'd read about his birth, she'd paused, overcome with emotion. Betty had gone through all that without one word to Edith in any of her letters. Edith realised that it must have been difficult to tell her because of her need to conceal her affair with Ye Win. However, the fact that Betty had kept it to herself cut Edith to the quick, even at this distance in time.

But where was her nephew now? Had he survived the long march over the mountains into India? Or had he died in the bombings or somewhere on a remote jungle trail. She thought about the lonely grave of the young refugee under the banyan tree at the bottom of the garden. Yet again she wondered why, if it was Betty, her name hadn't been inscribed on the cross. Now another thought occurred to her; if Betty had been travelling with her baby, what had happened to him? That thought made Edith almost sure that it wasn't Betty's grave, but that of some other unfortunate traveller who'd stopped off at the plantation on her route through to India.

She turned back to the journal, anxious for answers. She was keen to finish it that day. She really must get back to Calcutta, speak to the Clover International people and make some proper decisions about the hotel. But she knew that she needed to be here to finish it. She needed to be in the place where Betty must have been and, she hoped, when she reached the end, she would know whether that grave belonged to her sister or not.

Betty's Journal. Rangoon 1942

January 1st

Since that first air raid on 23rd December, the Japanese have continued to bomb Rangoon on a regular basis. The centre of the city is all but destroyed. Many of the hotels, offices and shops are damaged beyond repair, their roofs are caved in and windows blown out. It is impossible to go there now, it has become quite lawless. Looters roam the streets, quite openly entering shops and storehouses and grabbing what they can. And the roads themselves are strewn with abandoned vehicles and dead bodies, the surfaces potholed with craters from the bombs.

Each time the Japanese bombers strike, many innocent people lose their lives. The raids follow the same pattern each time. The air raid warning goes up, people scramble for cover, we hear the anti-aircraft guns in the distance, then the hum of enemy aircraft as they approach in wave after wave. Mercifully they haven't struck our street yet, but it is only a matter of time. They even mounted a raid on Christmas day.

It happened, like the previous raid, in the morning, and in broad daylight, devastating more of the British government buildings in the centre of Rangoon and again some of the poorest southern suburbs near the Mingaladon airfield. Huge explosions came from the direction of the docks and fuel depots down on Strand Road, and the fires from the burning oil raged far into the night. A pall of pungent black smoke wafted inland from the river and hung over the town for days afterwards.

That air raid happened whilst I was visiting Daw Ma and Ananda, taking them Christmas gifts. When we heard the wail of the siren and the enemy aircraft passing overhead, we crawled under Daw Ma's table and stayed there until the bombs had stopped crashing down all around us and the "all clear" siren sounded. We came out stiff but unharmed, hugging each other with relief that by some miracle we'd escaped harm this time. But how many more raids like that will there be to follow?

After the air raid, I left Daw Ma's house and walked all the way into the centre of Rangoon, passing more devastated streets with their bombed-out houses and shops, wrecked vehicles and piles of rubble. I passed many dead bodies, some of which had been there since the first raid and were now bloated and heaving with flies.

I walked all the way to the club for the traditional

Christmas dinner. I didn't feel much like eating after what I'd seen, but I took comfort in the company of my friends and the other British people who'd gathered to mark the day. The bombing raids and the threat of invasion binds us closely together now. This Christmas too, for the first time in ages, I didn't wish I was spending it with Ye Win. How I wasted my time and energy pining for him back then. But that is over now, and apart from a slight regret that I could have spent more time with Ananda, I was fairly content to eat roast chicken and plum pudding at Mary and Reginald's table, and sing carols round the Christmas tree afterwards.

In the club there was a lot of talk of people leaving Rangoon. Many Indian workers and servants have already gone home to India, most of them evacuated by sea. It seems that everyone wants to get out while they can.

'Reginald and I are going north to Myitkyina in a few days,' said Mary Curtis. 'They're airlifting people out to India from the airfield there. Why don't you come with us, Betty?'

I hesitated. I would have jumped at the offer but for Ananda. But even in these desperate times, I couldn't bring myself to announce his presence to the world. Isn't that a shameful thing to admit? Denying the existence of your own son? But to have sat in the club that day and calmly accepted the offer of evacuation and said, 'Oh, by the way, will there be room for my son on the flight? Yes, he's two months old now. He's half-Burmese by the way. His father is a communist and insurgent who's now fighting with the Japanese.' I just couldn't do it.

So, I told Mary that I needed to stay in Rangoon a bit longer, that the clinic needed me.

'Well don't leave it too long, for goodness' sake, my dear,' she said. 'You don't want to be here when the Japs walk in.'

After the celebrations at the club were over on Christmas evening, I walked home. It's virtually impossible to drive anywhere in Rangoon now. I arrived just after nightfall. Normally the night watchman would have been sitting in his little booth by the gate and would have escorted me up the drive to the front door. But to my surprise the booth was empty. I shrugged and walked on alone towards the house. But as I drew closer, I realised there was something odd about it. There were hardly any lights on inside. Perhaps it was a power cut? There had been many of those since the raids.

I went inside and the house was eerily quiet. I called out in the darkness and footsteps came from the kitchen. It was Ali.

'Ali. What is going on? Where is everyone?' I asked.

He hung his head. 'They have all gone, madam,' he said.

'Gone?' I asked stupidly. He nodded.

'To India. They left for the docks this morning with their luggage. There are rumours of boats leaving for Calcutta and Cox's Bazaar. They just want to go back to their families.'

I sat down heavily on a chair. I couldn't blame them. Life was becoming untenable here in Rangoon, I just hadn't been ready to face up to it myself.

'What about you, Ali? Don't you want to go to your family in India too?' I asked.

'I stay for you, memsahib,' he said simply. 'Sahib Robert asked me to look after you. I couldn't let him down. I have been with his family for more than forty years.'

My heart swelled with gratitude towards this faithful old man.

'That's so kind of you, Ali, but please don't stay for me. You must go tomorrow. On the next boat.'

He shook his head. 'I no longer have family in India, madam. You and the sahib are my family now. I stay with you.'

'I'm very grateful to you,' I said, taking his hand and looking into his eyes. 'And my husband is too. But you need to think of yourself.'

Again he shook his head. 'My first thoughts are for you, madam.'

As I went upstairs I thought about the old man's words. He was my responsibility now, as were Ananda and Daw Ma. Everyone who could was leaving this town. To stay would be suicide. I shuddered as I thought about the news stories I'd read about the Japanese occupation of Nanking in China. How the conquering Japanese army had massacred and raped the civilian population. Hundreds of thousands had suffered. Could that happen here? Ye Win had assured me that the Japanese had no quarrel with the Burmese population. They just wanted to help liberate them from British rule, but how would they treat the British, and the Indians who had been brought here to work for the British? Some of the news reports from Malaya told of people being rounded up and taken to internment camps. I couldn't let that happen. If I was taken, who would be there to look after Ali, Daw Ma and Ananda?

February 16th

To my shame and frustration, six weeks after I last wrote in this journal, I'm still here in Rangoon. Yesterday came the chilling news that Singapore has fallen to the Japanese. The final surrender was on the 15th February and all 130,000 British and Allied troops were taken prisoner. I read the article with dread in my heart. Singapore was meant to be a fortress, but the two warships sent to defend it were sunk by the Japs soon after the invasion. They ripped down the Malay peninsula in two months flat, beating away all opposition on the way. So much for the great British Army, or the fact that the Japs are incompetent and short-sighted. They have outwitted and outflanked us at every turn. I laugh when I think of some of the conversations in the club, but shudder when I think of Gregory. Edith wrote to tell me that he'd signed up and been posted to Malaya. What will become of him as a prisoner of the Japs? They are known to fight to the death themselves, and treat all prisoners who've surrendered with contempt. But my biggest fears are now confirmed. If Singapore, with all its fortifications and an army of over 100,000 men has fallen, there is little hope of Rangoon holding out. I think of Robert, out there fighting somewhere and pray that he is safe and will survive this.

I've carried on going to the clinic most days. They need me there more than ever now. Many of the volunteers have stopped coming; some have been evacuated to India, others are too afraid to make the journey across the bombed-out city to the clinic each day. Until I finally leave Rangoon, I will continue to go there. Each day there are more sick and wounded people to attend to. The bombing raids take their toll. Broken bones, wounds sustained from being crushed under buildings or hit by falling glass or masonry; shrapnel wounds. There is a steady stream. On top of that, the lack of clean water has meant that disease is spreading; dysentery, diphtheria and typhoid are rife. We haven't seen cholera yet, but that will come, Dr Myint says.

I have been following reports of the fighting. I need to know how close the Japanese Army is to Rangoon, and I'm worried about Robert, out there in the thick of it. His letters have stopped coming altogether now and I have no way of knowing where he is other than by reading the newspapers. Even so, I'm not sure that we're being told the full story.

I know that the Japanese have been attacking southern Burma and have moved in across the border through Tenasserim, from Thailand. Somehow, they managed to advance through dense jungle and over the mountains to attack airfields in Tavoy and Mergui on the southern Burmese coast. Reports say that the Burmese National Army, led by the Thirty Comrades has joined them in these attacks. My blood ran cold when I read that. Ye Win is actively fighting against the British now. It fills me with shame to think of how I threw myself at that man; how obsessed I was with him for years and how blind I was to his true intentions.

So, the fighting continues, and from reading about how the Japanese are advancing, I don't hold out much hope for Rangoon.

Even Dr Myint told me I should be leaving.

'There are very few British left here in Rangoon, Betty,' he said. 'You should go to the docks and find a boat going to India.'

So, I did just that today. The docks were crowded, full of Indians carrying luggage on their heads, and children on their backs, pushing and jostling for position. It was hot and chaotic and tempers were running high. I witnessed at least two fights break out in the crowd as I tried to push through. There were two boats moored up on the quayside which people said were going to Calcutta. I fought my way through to the offices and found a British official. He told me the boats were full and that I should come back another day. I pleaded with him, telling him that I have a baby, but he just shook his head.

'Move on, lady. You need to try another day. These boats fill up very quickly.'

I went home discouraged and dispirited and lay on the bed staring up at the ceiling fan as it whirred round, wondering how on earth I will get us out of here. As time goes on, it appears to get harder and harder to find a way.

March 5th

After more than two weeks of trying, I finally have a way out of here. I've been sick with worry, wondering how to get the four of us safely out of Rangoon and away to India. The stories of fighting go on with more British and Allied defeats. The Japanese are getting closer to Rangoon by the day. Each morning I've walked down to the docks and been met with the same scene as greeted me on the first day. There is never any available space on the boats no matter how early I go or how hard I plead with those in charge.

Food has become very scarce lately too, and although Ali walks to the local bazaar each day, he's had less and less success in finding anything worth eating. We have taken to living on a diet of greens and rice. Sometimes he is able to get hold of a stringy chicken, which he plucks and guts himself and tries to make palatable with herbs and spices.

But this evening I had a stroke of luck; the means of escape came to me without any effort on my part at all. One of our neighbours, Doctor Summers, came to the door and presented me with two rail tickets from Rangoon to Myitkyina in the north of Burma and also two passes permitting passengers to board aircraft to Assam.

'Please take these, Betty. I was given them by the Health Department. They're evacuating people by air to India from Myitkyina. But I've decided to stay on in Rangoon. I'm needed here to tend the sick. There are so many people injured or suffering with disease. And while I'm needed, I can't even think of going.'

'But what about Mrs Summers?' I asked.

'I've tried to persuade her to go, but she won't leave my side,' he said. 'We're no longer young. If the Japanese kill us, we've had good, long lives. But you're young, Betty. You've got your whole life ahead of you. So please take these tickets. The train leaves at midnight tonight. You should be on it.'

I thanked him profusely and stared at the tickets after he'd gone. There were only two and I needed three. The baby would be able to travel free, but I needed to take both Ali and Daw Ma with me too. Finally I decided that I'd have to take my chances and try to talk my own way onto the train. I glanced at my watch. It was seven o'clock. Only a few hours in which to get everything ready. I rushed upstairs and found a knapsack that Robert had used when he went hiking. I packed a few essentials then went through to the kitchen to find Ali.

He was standing at a marble worktop chopping up one of his stringy chickens. His hands and apron were covered in blood.

'Ali there is no need to do that now.' I showed him the tickets. 'We leave by train this evening.'

'Oh, madam,' he said in a querulous voice, wiping his hands on his apron. He looked crestfallen, as if this was the last thing he wanted.

'Go and pack your things,' I said. 'I have to find Daw Ma. She will be travelling with us. And she's bringing a baby too. I will be back soon.'

I couldn't look at him as I said those words, but when I did manage to look up, I noticed that the expression in his eyes had changed from sorrow to bewilderment. But I had no time for explanations or recriminations. It would take me an hour to get to Daw Ma's house and an hour to get back and I needed to leave immediately.

I hurried through the devastated streets towards the townships. I knew my way instinctively now even though there were hardly any street lamps left to light the route; I knew where to climb over piles of rubble, to skirt around the edge of buildings in order avoid stepping on dead bodies, to take a diversion because a pack of wild dogs were always on a certain corner.

When I'd been walking for about half an hour, I heard the tell-tale hum of aircraft approaching from the south. The air raid warning started to wail at the same time as the thump-thump of anti-aircraft fire sounded from the airbase. All around me people were running for cover, dropping whatever they were carrying, abandoning stalls, tripping over each other in their haste, and within seconds the street was deserted. I hesitated, wondering whether to take cover too. But decided against it. I didn't have time if we were to make that train, so putting my head down I pressed on towards Daw Ma's house, breaking into a run to make up time.

I hadn't gone very far when the aircraft were upon me. As the sound of engines became deafening, I looked up. Chills of horror ran through me at the sight of them opening their bomb bays. The bombs rained down, landing all around with the sickening crash and thud of explosions. Wave after wave of aircraft came over this time, far more than in previous raids. I stood still and stared, shaking from head to toe at the sight; there were so many. When they'd passed over the townships they banked and turned north. I realised that they were heading towards central Rangoon to drop yet more bombs there.

As I turned into Daw Ma's street there was devastation all around. The street had been flattened and little fires had broken out everywhere. Stifling sobs of terror I made my way towards her house, picking through the chaos until I reached the spot. My heart lurched with shock at what was before me. The little wooden house was flattened; the walls had collapsed inwards and the corrugated iron roof lay bent and buckled to one side of it.

'No!' I screamed rushing towards it.

Without hesitating, I lifted one of the collapsed panels and crawled inside, groping my way in through the broken furniture, smashed pots and glass.

'Daw Ma!' I kept shouting, but there was no reply. All I could hear were the cries and screams of neighbours who'd been injured in the blast. I kept crawling forward, not knowing whereabouts in the house I was, bumping into obstacles, scraping my arms, banging my head as I went. My heart was in my mouth. Where was Ananda? Where was Daw Ma? Were they both dead? Then, after ten minutes or so, I brushed up against something soft. Feeling my way forward I realised it was Daw Ma's leg, covered by her longyi. She was there, lying prone on the bare earth, underneath her table that had collapsed under the weight of the falling roof.

'Daw Ma!' I kept yelling. 'Can you hear me?' I shook her body, but it was clear she would not respond and that the warmth was already draining from her. After trying to rouse her for several minutes I moved away, searching for Ananda. I groped around in the dark, feeling for any sign of him. Then I felt the side of something wooden. It was his orange crate. My heart leapt. I felt inside and there he was, moving around inside his box, perfectly safe. The strong sides of the crate had not collapsed under the wreckage and had protected him from harm.

I dragged him out and clutched him to me, sobbing tears of relief that he was safe, and sadness for the loss of Daw Ma.

There was no time to lose. Clutching Ananda to my chest with one arm, I crawled out through the collapsed building and stood up outside. I stared at the devastation all around, but there was no time to linger on the street. I made my way back through the fires and collapsed buildings and started my long walk home to fetch Ali.

Some of the streets that I'd walked down on the way here had been bombed during the latest raid, so on several occasions I had to find alternative routes. I walked more slowly on the return journey than I had on the way there. Ananda was heavy and wriggled in my arms and I was weighed down with grief for Daw Ma. I kept thinking of her kindness; her sweet smile, the way she'd stood by me through my pregnancy and how she'd looked after Ananda as if he were her own son. And now she was dead, lying under a pile of corrugated iron and wooden boards and I'd had no time to recover her body or give it the respect it deserved.

As I emerged from the townships into the British quarter, I could see clearly that here too the bombers had made their mark again. Yet more buildings were reduced to rubble, people were running about with buckets trying to douse flames, others sat grieving over the bodies of loved ones. Finally, I turned into the bottom of Shwedagon Pagoda Road where yet another devastating blow awaited me. The bombers had visited here too; two or three great houses that I passed had been reduced to dust, trees and shrubs flattened in their gardens, gates blown clean off their hinges. I neared our own house, my heart thumping, hoping against hope it had been spared, but as I reached the top of the drive my hopes were dashed. I stood there gaping, unable to process what was right there before my eyes. The house was no longer standing. Where it had been was a pile of rubble, bricks, slates and splintered wood. It could only have happened a few minutes before I arrived as clouds of dust still billowed from the wreckage.

I started to run down the drive, refusing to believe that I'd suffered a second loss that very evening; 'Ali!' I shouted, 'Ali, where are you?'

But when I got closer I realised that no one could have survived. The house was just a pile of rubble. It must have been hit by one of the bigger bombs. Maybe even two had been dropped here. The Japanese pilots must have picked out the largest houses in the district and targeted them, perhaps wanting to make an example of the British ruling classes.

I sank to my knees, clutching Ananda who started to cry. How could this have happened, to that wonderful old man? It made no sense and I started to sob, thinking of his mild-mannered kindnesses that, like Daw Ma, I'd always taken for granted.

My instinct was to turn away from the devastated house, but I knew I couldn't make my journey without trying to get back into whatever was left of Robert's study. I'd put the tickets in the desk drawer.

Cursing myself for not having taken them with me, I laid Ananda down on the floor of the gatekeeper's booth and, with faltering steps, approached the wreckage of the house. As soon as I'd left Ananda, he started to scream. Every fibre in my body told me to rush back and comfort him, but I knew I had no choice but to carry on. As I walked, I was enveloped in dust. It filled my mouth and nose and my eyes were soon smarting with it. There were a couple of little fires burning amongst the heaps of rubble and by their light I tried to work out where Robert's study would have been. I walked forward, picking my way over bricks and splintered beams, stumbling as I went. I bumped into part of the bannisters which had graced the wide staircase. Robert's study had been a few yards to the right of the stairs, so I clambered in that direction. At one point I fell and grazed my knee. Crying tears of pain and frustration, I sat back, nursing it for a moment, then I pushed on.

The first thing I found was Robert's wooden desk chair, lying on its back, its legs blown off. I hoped the desk wouldn't be far from it, so I felt all around it. Under the rubble I found the shelves of a bookcase, all the books spilled out, covered in dust and debris, then beside that, I gasped as I felt the smooth surface of the top of the desk. It had been separated from its drawers, and I spent several minutes throwing bricks and lumps of plaster aside until at last I found them. My heart soared when I felt them there under some broken floorboards from the room above. They were buckled and twisted, but with an effort of will I managed to pull the top drawer open. Tears of relief sprung to my eyes when I saw that what I needed was still there. My journal, and the tickets which I'd tucked inside the front cover. I grabbed it, and at the same time some blank airmail letters. Then I clambered back over the rubble and hurried back up the drive to where Ananda lay bawling. I picked him up and held him to me tight, rocking him back and forth until his tears subsided.

Then, I turned away from the wreck of my former home and, blinded by tears for both Ali and Daw Ma, retraced my steps up the drive and out onto the road. I had less than an hour to get to the station, buy provisions for the journey and a shawl for Ananda. I would have to do without clothes myself, but I couldn't focus on the practicalities. My heart was heavy with grief for the two kindest and most loyal people I'd ever known, lost to me in the space of an hour.

20

BETTY'S JOURNAL

Rangoon, 1942

March 7th

I WAS POURING with sweat and every muscle and bone in my body was aching by the time I reached Rangoon station that evening. I felt drained and in no state to battle my way through the crowds on the concourse. The place was thronging with people, mainly Indian and Burmese, all of them desperate to leave Rangoon. The noise of their chatter and the cries of hawkers was deafening, amplified by the echoing glass roof. Whole families had gathered there with their children and animals; goats tethered with lengths of string, chickens and ducks in baskets, cardboard boxes full of luggage bound with twine. They waited patiently for their trains, some sitting cross-legged in groups on the marble floor, some eating and drinking, while hawkers wound their way through the crowds, selling exotic fruit, chai or Burmese flat breads.

I pushed my way to the edge of the building where I

knew there had once been a small market catering to travellers. To my relief the stalls were still there, doing a roaring trade, and I was able to buy some snacks for the journey, a couple of muslin nappies, a Pashmina with which to carry Ananda on my back, and, miraculously, a glass bottle with a rubber teat, although there was no powdered milk to be found. I decided I would have to feed him chai, a sweet, sugary tea flavoured with cardamom. I'd have to trust that his stomach wouldn't rebel as it was the only thing available. I found a chai seller and got him to fill the glass bottle for a few annas, then carried on elbowing my way through the crowds towards the platform.

I finally found the right train. It was the Mandalay Express, and was already standing on the platform, the engine, far away at the front, was hissing out steam. As I stepped onto the first-class carriage, my heart sank. It was already full to bursting. Every seat was occupied and people were standing in the aisles with their voluminous luggage. As I pushed my way through to the two seats that were meant to be mine, the train jolted and jerked into motion, and everyone grabbed onto the nearest seat or luggage rack to steady themselves. Reaching my seats, I showed my ticket to the elderly British man and woman who were occupying them. The woman waved me away.

'There must be some mistake my dear,' she said. 'We've just bought these from the ticket office.'

'These were given to me by a doctor friend,' I said. 'They were issued by the government.'

The man shrugged. 'They've obviously double booked and I'm afraid we got here first. You look young and strong. It won't hurt you to stand.'

'But I have a baby,' I said and the woman raised her eyebrows.

'Not your *own* baby, surely!' she said in a loud voice and people turned to stare. After all the grief and heartbreak I'd suffered in the past few hours I found tears stinging the backs of my eyes. How could she be so cruel? I held Ananda tightly to me.

'Yes, he is my baby, actually,' I said, in a cracked voice, fighting back the tears.

Then I edged my way back to the other end of the carriage. It was clear that those miserable old people weren't going to give up the seats and I didn't want to be anywhere near them and their bigoted, spiteful attitude.

There was a tiny space in the lobby beside the door and I sank down into a squat, as many of the Indian women around me were doing. Ananda was crying now, so I introduced him to the bottle of chai. When he tasted the sweet, cloying liquid, his face registered surprise at first. But he immediately started sucking hard on the teat, so he must have liked the taste. When he'd finished, he fell asleep in my arms and I found myself growing drowsy from the rocking motion of the train.

The Indian lady squatting beside me said, 'Hand me your baby, madam. I will hold him while you sleep.'

The thought of giving him to a stranger filled me with anxiety, but when I looked into her kind, gentle eyes, I realised there was nothing to worry about. Gratefully, I handed him to her and watched her cradle him for a moment until sleep overcame me and I fell into a fitful, broken doze that lasted several hours.

I awoke before dawn, stood up and stretched my aching limbs. The woman passed Ananda back. I thanked her profusely, feeling a little guilty that I'd slept so long. I stood there rocking him, watching the dusty, flat countryside rolling by. I realised I'd grown to love it during my time in

Burma; the timeless rice paddies fringed with palm trees, pools where buffalo wallowed and winding tracks between clumps of bamboo where bullock carts plodded. On a distant rocky outcrop, I spotted a golden pagoda, surrounded by smaller stupas, glinting in the first rays of the morning sun.

It reminded me of my first trip by train in Burma, when Robert and I had travelled in style to Pagan. How naïve I'd been then, falling straight into Florence's trap. How much I'd changed from the selfish, materialistic girl who'd set out on that journey. And how my world had changed too. The war had torn it apart. I thought of Daw Ma and Ali, both of whom had shown me such selfless kindness, and both of whom had been mercilessly taken from me by a cruel act of war. I realised that everything was uncertain now, including where this journey would take me.

When the train squeaked and jerked to a halt in Mandalay station, everyone poured off and onto the platform; I was almost pushed over in the crush. I followed the crowd up the steps and over the bridge to another platform where the train for Myitkyina waited. This time I found a seat; on a wooden bench in a third-class carriage, crammed in between a grandmother and a woman with three chickens clucking away in a basket. But that didn't bother me, I was just glad to rest my weary body, and for much of the seemingly endless journey both Ananda and I dozed. I bought food from hawkers who walked through the carriage shouting for custom and more chai from a chai seller for Ananda's bottle.

All the people around me were Indian, workers from Rangoon, trying to get to Myitkyina and then on to India. As the journey went on, people overcame their shyness and started exchanging stories. But they all looked weary and like me; many of them slept for much of the long journey. This time I didn't pay as much attention to the countryside as on the previous train, I wasn't next to a window. For the first few hours I was dimly aware that we were travelling through the great, fertile Irrawaddy plain; emerald rice paddies dotted with lone coconut palms, then the landscape changed to dense jungle scrub, with the occasional village of thatched wooden huts nestling in amongst the vegetation. The train crossed rivers and waterfalls, and ran along deep valleys. Towards the end of the journey I noticed a great mountain range to the west which began as a smudge on the horizon, but as we drew closer the contours of the mountains became visible and I realised they were covered in jungle. I felt a tingle of nervous excitement at the sight of them. I knew that these were the Kumon mountains, that they lay on the edge of several other mountain ranges, and on the other side of them was Assam in India. It is there that we are heading.

It was dark by the time the train rolled into Myitkyina station. I got down with everyone else, stretching my aching bones, realising that I was exhausted and not ready to take on the next stage of the journey. There were a few Indian officials on the platform, herding people into covered lorries that were waiting outside.

'We will take you to where you can stay the night,' they said. 'Tomorrow there will be more flights to Assam.'

As we left the station, I noticed a couple of boards with newspaper headlines announcing: "Rangoon falls to Japanese; British troops withdraw." I stopped and stared, shockwaves running through me as the full impact of that dreadful news sunk in. I was thinking of Robert. Was that where he was? Had he been in Rangoon with his troops at the final surrender?

Still digesting the terrifying news about Rangoon, I clambered up onto the back of one of the lorries. It was already crowded with passengers. It lumbered through the little town and out onto a jungle road. I noticed that here the people milling about on the street were dressed in traditional, tribal dress of many varieties. This town felt truly like the final frontier; a melting pot of different tribes and different cultures.

A couple of miles up the bumpy dirt track, the lorry turned off and came to an abrupt halt. The driver, an Indian soldier, came round to the back and dropped the tailgate.

'This is your camp for tonight. Everybody out,' he yelled and we all scrambled down, wondering what awaited us in this remote spot. I got down and looked around. In the darkness it was difficult to see properly, but there were some gas lamps hanging from wooden poles and once my eyes adjusted, I could just about make out my surroundings. There were several rows of single-storey bamboo huts thatched with palm leaves, and a central covered shelter where people were cooking on portable stoves. Delicious smells of garlic and spices wafted over and already people were forming a queue for the food.

I joined the back of it. In front of me was an Englishwoman and her two young daughters. She smiled at me.

'Have you just arrived?' she asked.

I nodded. 'From Rangoon,' I said.

'We've been here a week already. Hoping to get airlifted tomorrow, but there are too many people arriving all the time and a couple of planes have been hit by the Japs on the way in.'

My heart sank. Throughout that uncomfortable and seemingly endless train journey, I'd been hoping that I wouldn't have to wait long to get out to India. But it seemed that things weren't going to be that straightforward.

'That's bad news,' I said, noticing that the woman was wearing a pink evening dress and high heels and her two little girls were dressed in party dresses trimmed with ribbons, all of which looked grubby and torn.

'Yes it is,' she said. 'We thought we were going to be flown out straight away. We only brought our most expensive clothes,' she explained, seeing my surprise. 'We're regretting that now, of course.'

'What are the sleeping quarters like?' I asked.

'Pretty grim. Just a bamboo platform. No bedding. But then in this heat, who needs sheets? The latrines are appalling, of course.'

When I reached the head of the queue, I was given a plate of vegetable curry and rice and a mug of tea. I found a place on the bare earth to sit down. I poured half the tea into Ananda's bottle and fed it to him, then laid him down on the shawl and ate the curry hungrily.

The woman was right. The sleeping quarters were simply a bare bamboo platform inside one of the thatched huts. I found myself a space near the door, and though I was drained and exhausted, when I laid down with Ananda snuggled beside me, sleep wouldn't come until the grey light of dawn appeared through gaps in the palm thatch. Despite my tiredness, it felt odd trying to sleep amongst so many strangers, listening to them tossing and turning in their sleep, coughing and snoring. But, thankfully, Ananda slept peacefully by my side all night, blissfully unaware of our difficult and dangerous predicament.

March 15th

We were forced to stay in that squalid camp for a week. Each morning, the lorry came to take more people to the airfield. When it arrived, everyone swarmed around the tailgate, pushing and shoving, trying to get a place. But people had to give their names before they were let on. The soldiers had a list of the order in which we had arrived in the camp and were strict about letting those who'd been here the longest onto the lorries.

Two days after we'd arrived at the camp, my friend in the pink evening dress managed to get a place on a lorry with her daughters. She came to tell me in the morning before she left.

'Oh, would you post a couple of letters for me, when you get to India?' I asked.

'If you're quick, the lorry's leaving soon.'

I found the two blank airmail letters in my bag and scribbled hasty letters to both Robert and Edith. I know Robert's is unlikely to arrive; I have no idea where he is and am sending it to his army HQ in Rangoon, but perhaps Edith's will. I'm worried that everyone will think I'm dead because our house was bombed to the ground. I want them to know that I'm doing my best to get back to Calcutta.

I scribbled the addresses on the letters and gave them to the woman. I never did ask her name.

'I'll post them as soon as we land,' she assured me.

'Thank you. And good luck,' I said, watching with envy as she and the two girls clambered onto the back of the lorry.

As it swung out of the camp onto the road, she waved at me from the back. She looked so happy, knowing that within hours she would be back in India and out of danger.

This last week has been one of the most uncomfortable I've ever spent in my life. As my friend warned me, the latrines are truly disgusting. They simply consist of a long trench behind a bamboo fence, full to the brim with faeces and heaving with maggots and flies. You have to squat in front of the trench and hang your backside over it. There is no privacy. The stench of putrefaction is unbelievable and the first time I went I found myself retching when the smell caught the back of my throat. Once a day, when the worst of the heat has subsided, some of the soldiers manning the camp bring shovels and dig earth over the waste. But that doesn't do much to dampen the smell. You can smell it all over the camp and everything seems to be impregnated with it. It even wafts into the sleeping huts at night.

The food is just rice and vegetables, but the army cooks do their best to make it appetising. I've spoken to some of the other families. Almost all of them Indian workers, trying to escape the war and get back to their homeland. Most of them accept the privations of the camp with resignation, focusing on the hope that any day they could be out of here and on their way.

Occasionally during the past week I've thought back to my cossetted existence in our luxurious house in Rangoon. It seems like another lifetime that I arrived there. My life back then was one long round of pleasure-seeking, particularly in the first few months. Parties and dinners, tennis and shopping. My every need was catered for and I didn't need to lift a finger.

It was a far cry from the situation I find myself in now. I only have the clothes I stand up in; one dirty blue-print summer frock and a pair of flat leather sandals, my hair is filthy and I'm constantly hungry. I've suffered the trauma of losing two people I held dear in the past week and I have no idea if I'll ever see my husband again. But there is one shining light in all of this; Ananda. Unaware of the miseries those around him are suffering, he is like a ray of sunshine, a constant reminder of my luck. He is always smiling, gurgling or laughing and he makes virtually no demands on me. He is the reason I get up each day and try my hardest to get us out of here. But for him I think I might have crawled to the edge of the camp, laid myself down and waited to die.

This morning, we got a place in the lorry. I said my name to the soldier with the clipboard as I reached the front of the queue and held my breath, hoping this time he would choose me. He looked at me, stony-faced, and waved me onto the lorry. I placed Ananda on the tailgate and climbed up, scooped him into my arms and found a place on the bench. I looked back at the squalid camp and breathed a sigh of relief that this stage of the journey was over.

The lorry was packed with people for that short trip along the jungle road to the airfield. Everyone was excited and nervous in equal measure about the coming flight. The trip over those mountains to India was known to be treacherous. The route was known as "the hump". We'd all heard stories of planes crashing into rocky peaks in fog, or losing their way and never arriving at their destination. The atmosphere in the lorry was electric with pent-up nervous energy. Everyone was laughing, shouting, singing, glad to finally be leaving that stinking camp.

There were several British people in the lorry, many wearing finery and jewellery, and many, many Indians, hoping that now their homeland was only a short flight away. Some had been injured in fighting or in bombing raids and on the floor in the middle of the truck, lay three people on stretchers, heavily bandaged.

It was only a mile or so to the airfield, and when we got

down from the lorry I was stunned at how small and insignificant the place looked. It was just an undulating grass strip with a small wooden hut on one side. It was completely surrounded by thick jungle, and the mountains loomed just behind it. Shading my eyes, I realised that any plane coming from India would have to fly over those peaks and make a sickeningly quick descent to land at the airfield.

We stood on the side of the airstrip, watched the sky and waited. We waited for over an hour until the sun was high in the sky and beating down mercilessly. There was no shade. By now my clothes were clinging to me and my body running with sweat. Even Ananda was getting fed up, wriggling around in my arms and grizzling.

Just when I thought I couldn't bear it any longer, I heard the drone of engines in the distance and two tiny planes appeared over the top of the mountain and descended into the shimmering heat haze that hovered above the jungle. A cheer went up from the crowd and everyone shaded their eyes, watching the two aircraft as they drew closer and descended sharply towards the airfield. The noise of the engines grew louder and louder and then we could see them clearly; two propeller planes flying towards us just above the jungle canopy, their undercarriages seeming to skim the tops of the trees. And as they got closer we could see that they weren't small at all; they were bulbous lumbering aircraft with a propeller on each wing, Douglas transport planes, both heading unsteadily towards us.

And then they were down, first one, then the second one, landing lopsidedly at the end of the airstrip and approaching us at speed. As they passed us they braked with a whoosh and roar of propellers, turned at the end of the runway and taxied back to where we were assembled.

The aircraft drew to a halt and both pilots jumped down.

They were clad in leathers, helmets and goggles. The crowd pressed forward surrounding them, shouting and waving in delight. At that moment, to we stranded evacuees, those two men looked like true heroes. Everyone clapped and cheered and the pilots waved in response.

The Indian soldiers started herding people onto the planes. Everyone surged forward. Of course I was at the back of the queue and watched anxiously as fifty or so people were allowed onto the first plane. They mounted the steps slowly and took their seats inside. Once seated, they waved out of the windows at the rest of us waiting patiently to be allowed to board the next plane.

The aeroplane doors were closed and we waited for the pilot to fire up the engines. But suddenly there was another sound from the direction of the mountains. It was the drone of more aircraft approaching. I shaded my eyes, expecting to see further rescue planes. But the aircraft that emerged from the heat haze above the jungle was different. It was slimmer and faster, and as it got closer, it was clear what it was. I knew the sound of those engines. I'd heard it so many times over Rangoon and shockwaves went through me when I realised what it was. A Japanese fighter plane flying low, heading for the airfield and directly where we were standing. Everyone started to panic.

'Run,' said one of the soldiers. 'Take cover.'

I didn't wait for further instructions; like the others I dashed into the jungle which came right up to the edge of the field. Ducking my head, and holding Ananda close, I pushed my way through dense shrubbery, snagging my clothes, tearing my skin on thorns. I found a huge teak tree with a thick trunk and sheltered behind it. I stood there, my legs shaking, my heart thumping, watching and listening to the sickening events unfold. The plane circled the field a

couple of times then flew back from where it had come.
There was a sudden, eerie silence. What did it mean? Had
the pilot decided not to attack after all, seeing women and
children on the field? But within seconds came the buzz of
more engines from the direction of the mountains, and
three more identical Japanese aircraft bore down on the
airfield.

This time they didn't hesitate. They dipped, circled, flew
past the two parked rescue planes and opened fire, strafing
both with machinegun fire, turning back and passing them
time and time again. I could hardly bear the sickening
sound of bullets pinging on metal, of breaking glass, the
shouts of the helpless passengers, trapped inside. They were
sitting targets, and cowering there, under the tree, I could
hear their chilling screams reverberating around the field.
In the final pass, the Japanese planes dropped three bombs
on the airstrip, each exploding with an ear-splitting crash.
Fountains of earth sprayed everywhere, and as the three
planes banked and headed back towards the hills, it was
clear that no more rescue planes would be taking off from
Myitkyina airstrip for a long time.

All was chaos around me. People were screaming and
crying, running everywhere. The soldiers were already
bringing the dead and injured off the Douglas and lying
them out on the grass. I went forward to help. Breathing
thanks that to God I hadn't been on that first plane, I laid
Ananda down on the shawl and started to help the
wounded. As the soldiers brought more wounded out of the
plane, I cleaned and bound wounds with whatever I could
lay my hands on; people's clothes, shawls, sheets.

An Indian soldier approached me. I'd noticed him
speaking to other people who'd emerged from the jungle,
handing them slips of paper. I looked up from where I was

kneeling, helping a woman who'd got a shred of metal from the fuselage of the plane lodged in her arm. She was squirming with pain on the ground.

'Thank you for your help,' he said leaning over, 'but you need to leave here as soon as you can.'

I looked up at him. 'Leave? But how? There's no transport out of here.'

'The Japanese army is on the edge of Myitkyina. You need to go into the jungle. There will be a battle for the town very soon.'

He handed me a slip of paper. 'This is a map of an evacuation route to India. It is via the Chaukan Pass and it should take three or four weeks to walk through to Ledo in Assam. It is the only way out now. There are other routes, but if you take this one, you might be able to get a lift for part of the way on a lorry. If you delay, the Japanese will be here. They will take you prisoner, or worse.'

'Walk?'

His words chilled me to the core and I stared down at the map, trying to understand what this meant for me with a small baby.

'What about food?' I asked him.

'There are camps on the way. The way is indicated by carvings marked on trees. At regular intervals there are food dumps and shelters to sleep in. It won't be easy, but it has been done.'

'But what about this lady? She's seriously wounded.'

'The army paramedics will help her. You've done enough. It's time for you to leave.'

I picked Ananda up and tied him to my back with the shawl.

'And by the way,' he added, 'you will see signs along the route warning that the Chaukan Pass isn't suitable for women and children. Take no notice of them. Any other route will take you south and you'd risk running into the Japanese.'

I stared at him, the full implication of his words beginning to sink in. He was seriously suggesting that I should walk to India in my thin cotton frock and sandals with my baby in my arms. Then I turned away from him, shaded my eyes and stared at the mountains that need to be crossed to get to India. There are hundreds of miles of them, covered in impenetrable jungle and uncharted rivers.

'I will try,' I said, taking the map.

'Good luck,' he said and I heard the sincerity in his tone. But I could tell from the expression in his eyes that, despite his assurances, he didn't think I was going to make it.

21

EDITH

Dapha River Tea Plantation, Assam, 1980

EDITH PUT DOWN THE JOURNAL, resting her eyes for a moment. It was tiring deciphering Betty's scrawling handwriting for hours on end. Sometimes the writing trailed away at the ends of words, sometimes the page was smudged and difficult to read. There were occasional doodles in the margin; overlapping squares or circles, and Edith was reminded of Betty as a schoolgirl, impossibly dreamy, always getting into trouble for doodling on her school books.

The Betty she was uncovering between these pages, was a very different woman from the sister she'd known. Betty was right. She *had* changed; changed dramatically from that self-centred young girl who had deliberately come between Edith and Robert, who'd always put herself first. She thought about Betty's love for fine clothes, for the latest hairstyles, for always looking her best. Edith could hardly imagine Betty with dirty, matted hair, filthy clothes, carrying a baby around in a shawl, putting the needs of others first.

Although Edith was shocked and ashamed by some of the things she'd read between the covers of the journal, there were many other things that heartened her. The events and hardships Betty had described, some of them self-inflicted, some of them the tragic consequence of circumstances, had combined to force Betty to grow up; to put others first, to be responsible, to be strong.

Staring out at the serried lines of tea bushes, where once again the pickers were out in force, laughing and chatting, brightening up the endless green with their colourful sarees, Edith felt a sudden pang of loss. It was different from those she normally experienced when thinking of her sister. This time she felt strongly that she would have liked to get to know that new, changed Betty. The regret Edith felt at never having met her, hit her hard.

Someone knocked on the door and Edith opened it to see Simi, the cleaning lady, on the threshold. She was carrying a basket of fruit and had come to replenish the basket on the table. Edith had only eaten a couple of apples, but she held the door open and waved Simi inside anyway, with gestures and smiles. The woman came inside the bungalow. As she approached the table she hesitated, her eyes on the journal, as they had been before. Edith had an idea. She rummaged in her handbag and took out a small photograph of Betty that she always carried with her. She held it up to show the woman, who frowned and peered at it. Then her eyes widened and she backed away.

'Do you know this lady?' she asked, but Simi was already at the door.

'Please... she was my sister. I'm trying to find out what happened to her.'

Simi stared at the photograph again and her face clouded over. Was that fear in her eyes?

'My English not good,' the woman muttered. Then she turned and wrenched open the door. It banged behind her and she was gone. Edith's heart was beating fast. She went to the back window and watched the woman running up the path towards the house, her saree flapping around her legs, she tripped in her haste. Edith was sure there had been recognition in Simi's eyes when she'd looked at the photograph. But why fear? And why react like that?

Edith was now more convinced than ever that the woman had known Betty. She remembered that she'd thought about asking Richard about her at lunch time, but it had vanished from her mind when Richard had mentioned the grave. She vowed again to ask Richard what he knew about Simi when she went up for supper.

Betty's Journal

March 20th

We have been on the road for a few days now, and it is only this evening that I am in a camp where there is enough light from a kerosene lamp to write about what has happened. But I sit here with my journal wondering what to write; the hardships that I and countless others have suffered so far on this route are hard to describe. Even so, I think it's important that I do. One day, when I've reached safety, I might want to look back on this time, to remember what we endured. And yet I get the feeling that far worse is yet to come.

Looking at the map the soldier gave me in Myitkyina, we seem to have hardly advanced any distance. He told me that the walk over the Chaukan Pass into Assam would take around a month. I can't help thinking that such an estimate would be for a strong man walking quickly with porters carrying proper supplies, plenty of food and sleep and no holdups; not a weak, ill-equipped woman, carrying a baby, who isn't eating enough or getting enough rest.

We have reached the little town of Langtao and are spending the night here. It is over one hundred miles from Myitkyina, but the road so far has been quite good, or at least passable for vehicles. It is only now that the map shows we have to take a path that winds through the mountains towards the infamous Chaukan Pass.

On that first day, I studied the map the solider had given me and headed north out of Myitkyina, following a long line of other people doing just the same. The road was crowded with desperate people who, like me, had been trying to get a flight out of the airfield. Whole families were walking together; some carrying children on their backs, some helping grandparents along, some with luggage balanced on their heads. Many were moving incredibly slowly, but all were headed in the same direction; north towards the Kumon hills. The road was just an earth track, very rutted in places, but wide enough for cars and trucks to pass. Often we passed abandoned vehicles that must have broken down or run out of fuel and had just been left to rust. Occasionally an army lorry would edge past us and I wondered why they were going north, when the Japanese were advancing from the south. One stopped beside me, after I'd been walking for three or four hours, and I had my answer.

A soldier leaned out of the window and asked me if I would like a lift.

'We're going north to get supplies from Suprabum. It's on this road, a few miles south of Langtao. You can ride in the back as far as Suprabum if you like.'

'Thank you,' I said gratefully and went round to the tailgate. The back of the covered truck was already crowded with refugees. Most were travelling with children, and I guessed the soldiers must have picked up those they thought looked most in need. I passed Ananda to a woman to hold while I hauled myself up, then climbed in quickly and wedged myself in at the end. The lorry rumbled into life again.

Progress was slow along that rutted track, but a lot quicker and less tiring than it would have been to walk. I looked around me at my fellow passengers crouched on the benches or sitting cross-legged on the floor. Most were Indian families, many like me had small children. Many were staring ahead, something nearing despair in their eyes. The man sitting next to me was travelling with two toddlers: a boy and a girl. He was hanging his head, not engaging with his surroundings. There were bags under his eyes and from the way he hunched his shoulders, I could see that he was already exhausted.

I introduced myself and Ananda to him and asked him his name.

'Rashid,' he said with a weak smile. 'This is Harish and this is Sophia,' he said, pulling his two children towards him.

'Where are you from?' I asked.

'We've come from Rangoon, but we are travelling to Madras in Southern India,' he said. 'That is our real home.'

Then, haltingly, he told me his story. He'd come to Burma to work in the rice fields and factories in Rangoon. He and his family had been unable to find a place on a train from Rangoon so they had taken buses and walked much of the way north to Myitkyina. His wife had died on the road.

'She became ill. Cholera I think,' he told me with tears in his eyes. 'She just wasted away overnight. We were sleeping in a shelter beside the road. In the morning she had gone from us.'

'I'm so sorry,' I said, a lump forming in my throat. The children, leaning against their father, looked at me with huge, sorrowful eyes.

'We had to leave her body where it was. There was no time or money for a funeral. So now it is just me and these two.'

I didn't know what to say to him, but now I understood why he exuded defeat and looked so utterly exhausted.

The truck bumped on along the uneven, rutted road. It was difficult to see out, as it was covered by a tarpaulin, and it was stiflingly hot, crowded in there with all those people.

At lunchtime we stopped at a village. There was a temporary cookhouse there, manned by soldiers, who were doling out rice and root vegetable soup with some black tea. I ate mine gratefully. Then I gave a few morsels to Ananda and fed him some tea from his bottle. I am beginning to get anxious for his wellbeing. Even over the past ten days or so, he has lost weight because he hasn't been having the right food. I've just fed him whatever I've been able to get hold of, but I know he can't be getting the vitamins and minerals he needs to grow. How ever will I do that when we get into the mountains? If he has lost weight already, what will happen to him there? I dread to think, but I must carry on doing the best I can for him.

For three whole days we travelled on the back of the lorry. The seats were hard and uncomfortable, but it was infinitely preferable to walking those hundred or so miles. Each night we stopped at villages and slept under tarpaulin shelters after another meal of rice and vegetable stew. It was uncomfortable lying on the bare ground and I got little sleep as Ananda kept waking.

When, on the fourth day, we reached the little town of Suprabum, a dusty outpost where there were a few wooden houses and some concrete army depots, the driver jumped down and came round to open the tailgate.

'That's as far as we're going,' he said. 'Now you need to follow this road up as far as Langtao, then take the path through the hills towards the Chaukan Pass. Your first stop on that route will be Hkamhu where there should be some sort of food and shelter organised by the army.'

Everyone scrambled down and thanked him. Then the lorry moved off in a cloud of dust and we all stood there in a huddle contemplating the road ahead. It seemed to stretch on endlessly towards the hills. I looked at Rashid who was kneeling down, lifting his daughter onto his back.

'We should walk together,' he said, looking up at me. 'We may be able to help each other.'

'Good idea,' I said, and we set off down the hot, dusty road, part of a long, straggling group of people taking their first steps on that long and treacherous road home.

March 21st

Today we walked from Langtao to Hkamhu, the first time we have branched off the road and onto the jungle path. I'm utterly exhausted, but determined to record the journey here before I rest. The going has been much heavier and we moved very slowly. Yesterday, the walk along the road from Suprabum to Langtao was long and tedious but not difficult. At Langtao there wan army shelter to sleep in and the usual meal of rice and vegetables.

This morning were up at six thirty and started walking at seven o'clock, before the sun got too high in the sky. Even so, we'd only gone a few yards by the time I was drenched in sweat.

The path was rough and narrow, and in places it was difficult to follow. Sometimes it almost petered out and we had to scout around to find which direction we should be going. There are crosses carved onto tree trunks at intervals we are meant to follow, but they are few and far between, so can't be relied on.

As soon as we were outside the little town of Langtao, the jungle closed in around us. At the start of the path was a warning sign which read: *This route to Assam via the Chaukan Pass is strenuous and should not be attempted by the weak or infirm or those with children*. I stared at it for a moment, remembering the soldier's words, then walked on. I didn't have a choice.

The path led through the undergrowth, winding between towering teak trees, with huge creepers like giant ropes hanging down from the high canopies. Sometimes we had to push our way through them, they felt like thick curtains. We passed massive clumps of bamboo, fifty feet tall, so thick that the path had to skirt around the edge of them; outsized ferns that brushed against your face and endless varieties of exotic bushes and shrubs growing on the jungle floor. The whole forest was teeming too. It vibrated with life; the chirruping of birds, chattering of monkeys and buzz of insects was incessant.

The path carried on like that all morning, sometimes on the flat, sometimes climbing, sometimes descending, and always through the dense, dark greenery and in the clammy, steamy heat that sapped my energy. Often the path was so narrow that we had to push our way through encroaching greenery. The canopy stopped daylight from penetrating and cast an eerie green light over everything on the jungle floor. It was oppressive and a little frightening too.

We moved slowly; Rashid could not carry both his children at the same time, so we walked at the pace of the slowest child. Other groups and families that had set off from the camp at Langtao at the same time as us, overtook us during the morning and left us far behind. It felt very lonely there on that remote jungle path, just the five of us, but I was glad that I at least had Rashid and his children for company and wasn't alone.

Towards the end of the morning we came across a horrific sight. A sight that I haven't been able to put out of my mind all day. The path dipped into a ravine and crossed a rocky stream, and as we approached it, I wondered whether it would be safe to top up my drinking water from the stream as I could hear that it was fast-running, but when we reached it I realised that was a foolish thought. Half in and half out of the water was the bloated and putrefying body of a woman. She was lying face down and must have crawled in there to drink and been so weak, either from hunger or disease, that she couldn't get back out. Her black hair floated to one side, constantly washed by the flow of the water and her dark blue saree was soaked through and clung to her wasted body. As we got close the stomach-churning smell was overwhelming. I had to hold the end of Ananda's shawl over my face as we crossed the stream.

Rashid held his hand over his daughter's eyes, but his son, riding on his back at that point, saw everything. As we moved away, he started to cry.

'Mama,' he kept saying. 'It's Mama.'

'No, my darling, it's not Mama,' said Rashid, but I could hear the shock in his voice. The sight of that unfortunate woman lying there in the stream must have brought back the darkest of memories for all of them. The boy kept on crying for the rest of the morning, a moaning, grizzling sort of cry and in it I heard the grief of a child for his mother and his fear for what the journey might bring.

At around noon we found a clearing and stopped for a rest. Other groups were already there, sitting around small fires, cooking up what little food they had between them. Rashid hunted around for firewood and lit a small fire. At the Langtao camp the soldiers had given us a supply of rice and salt to carry, saying that there wouldn't always be food available where we stopped in the jungle. They had also given us a tin to cook in. I carried some of it in my bag, but Rashid carried the bulk, in a small sack tied around his chest.

We cooked the rice over the fire with a little of our precious drinking water. The mood was gloomy, Rashid hardly spoke, just sat with hunched shoulders and I could tell from the look in his eyes that the bloated body of the woman in the stream had affected him deeply. Both Sophia and Harish cried constantly and refused to eat any of the plain rice that Rashid offered them.

In the afternoon we carried on. The path became steeper as we entered the mountains. Sometimes we were climbing for hours on end, at other times descending steep valleys, slipping and sliding as we went. Before we'd gone very far, I was exhausted; my legs were trembling as if they were about to give way. I wondered how I would cope in the higher mountains on the minimal rations available. We were often passed by other groups of walkers, trudging past silently, their clothes filthy, their faces set and grim. They rarely spoke a word to us, determined to press on and not to be burdened by the problems of others.

To my horror, we passed another two corpses next to the

path on the higher ground; a man and a woman lying side by side. Both bodies were bloated and crawling with maggots. The stench rising from them was sickening and I had to hold the shawl over my face again, but even so, once we'd passed, I found myself retching into the undergrowth. As well as deeply shocking in themselves, the dead bodies were a grim reminder of the treacherous nature of our journey, and that we might well end up that way ourselves. Neither Rashid nor I mentioned the bodies afterwards, preferring to put them to the backs of our minds. If we didn't give voice to our fears, perhaps they wouldn't materialise.

We reached Hkamhu as the light was fading fast. It was shown on the map as a village, but it was more a collection of deserted shacks. No other walkers were there and the place was silent. We wandered around, looking for any sign of habitation, but all inhabitants appeared to have fled. Perhaps they were worried about the Japanese army finding them. We went from hut to hut, peering inside, checking for people, but the place was eerily quiet. On the edge of the village was a newly built bamboo shelter in which some basic supplies including vegetables had been placed in a sack under the roof.

'It is for us,' said Rashid. 'Put there by the army for the refugees.'

Once again, he lit a fire, and with a knife I'd found in one of the huts I cut up some potatoes and greens and added them to the rice. The children sat around listlessly watching me with their huge, sad eyes. They had no energy to play or even to talk.

At least here there are some kerosene lamps and somewhere to sleep under shelter. But as we sat there eating, I must have been attacked by mosquitoes. My legs and arms are now covered in swelling bites which are driving me mad with their itching. As I finish writing this, I'm not sure that I'll be able to sleep; Ananda is getting restless. He is probably ravenously hungry. And the images of those poor souls who gave up the struggle and laid themselves down beside the path for the very last time haunt me still.

22

BETTY'S JOURNAL

Kumon Mountains, Burma, 1942

March 25th

THE LAST FEW days have passed in a blur. I write by the flickering light of the fire. It is hard for me to put into words what has unfolded since I last wrote, but I know I must. It's vital that it's not forgotten, that the truth is recorded here.

When we woke that morning at Hkamhu, both Sophia and Harish seemed very unwell. They were both crying and their faces were flushed with fever. We boiled up some hot water and made tea for breakfast, but both pushed away the cups that Rashid offered them, shaking their heads.

'They are ill,' he said. 'It looks like malaria.'

'Perhaps we should stay here and let them rest,' I suggested.

He shook his head. 'We need to keep moving every day,' he said firmly. 'The sooner we get to India, the better it will be for them. They can see a doctor there.'

I tried to reason with him but he wouldn't listen. He

hoisted Sophia on his back and pushed his son forward onto the jungle trail. 'Let's go,' he said.

But almost as soon as we'd started out, the skies darkened and it began to rain. Huge, globular raindrops that soaked straight through clothes and drenched everything around. The path was soon a muddy quagmire and where it had felt difficult to walk before, now it was almost impossible. My sandals, that were by now worn and ripped, slid about everywhere and stuck in the mud at each footstep. After half an hour of battling to keep them on my feet, I took them off and threw them into the undergrowth. Other refugees pushed past us, struggling in the mud themselves, their shoulders hunched under the weight of their belongings, their heads bowed against the rain.

The children cried constantly, including Ananda, who was soaked to the skin, but their cries were drowned out by the constant thunder of the raindrops on the jungle around us. At first I'd thought that the canopy above was thick and impenetrable, but the rain came straight through it regardless. We pressed on like that, making slow progress, at one point having to climb a very steep hill, slipping and sliding in the mud all the way. Little rivulets were forming everywhere, making the path into the bed of a stream and virtually impassable.

I watched Rashid ahead of me. All the time he was holding Sophia in place with one hand and pulling Harish with the other. Harish hung back, it was obviously a struggle for him. At the top of the hill we sheltered under a low tree and rested. There was no dry wood, and even though Rashid collected sticks and tried to start a fire it wouldn't light in those conditions. So, we had no lunch and no hot tea. My stomach was taut with hunger but already I'd learned to ignore it. It was more difficult to ignore Ananda's cries. I had nothing to give him but plain water and although he drank some down it didn't fool him, and he was soon crying again.

The other two children were too ill for tears by this time. Sophia, who'd ridden on Rashid's back all the way, appeared delirious, she lay on the sodden ground while he was looking for firewood, her eyes half closed, her pupils disappearing up under her eyelids. Her face was pallid and sweaty. All this terrified me. It was obvious she had a very high temperature. The boy looked hot and sweaty too, and lay curled up beside her, his eyes closed. He must have been exhausted. The climb would have sapped the energy of the fittest person, let alone a sick child running a fever.

'Why don't we rest here for a while?' I said again to Rashid. 'They don't look well.'

'We can't stop here,' he replied instantly. 'There's no shelter and no firewood. It would be better to press on to the next camp. It can't be too far.'

The walk down the hill on the other side was more slippery than ever. Without my sandals I had to contend with the soft mud squelching between my toes and occasionally stepping on a sharp stone or root. Harish couldn't walk straight, and kept stumbling and falling to the ground, he must have been delirious like his sister. Each time he fell, Rashid bent down, picked him up and pushed him gently forwards.

On that dismal, dank afternoon we passed several more bodies on the route. All of them were bloated and putrefying, some with bones exposed to the elements. We hurried past as quickly as we could, covering our faces, trying not to look or to breathe in for fear of disease. One body though was blocking the path on a precipitous section and to edge round it was impossible. It was a man, whose stomach was bloated by the rain, his whole body crawling with maggots. His skull gleamed white; part of his scalp must have been eaten away by jungle ants. We stood there in front of the body in the pouring rain, wondering how to get past without falling down the ravine. In the end we had to step over him. We did it gingerly; it felt like a breach of his dignity, but it would have been impossible to move on otherwise.

We'd been walking for hours and the rain was still pounding down mercilessly. The sky had been overcast and brooding all day, but now it began to darken quickly. There was still no sign of any shelter. We reached a small clearing.

'We must have missed it,' said Rashid peering at the map. 'We'll have to stop here. I'll build a shelter.'

I stared at him, wondering how he was going to do that, but I didn't protest; there was no real choice. We had no torches and it would have been dangerous to walk on in the dark. I sat down under a tree and cuddled Ananda to me, trying to soothe him. He was still crying, as he had been all day.

Harish and Sophia lay down beside me on the wet ground and it was obvious that they were now both seriously ill; their breathing was laboured, their faces pallid, sweat stood out on their brows. Rashid cut some lengths of bamboo with his penknife and constructed a rudimentary shelter, using a tree trunk with a low branch as one wall. He thatched it with huge ferns that were growing nearby, then he gathered some other sticks and tried to light a fire. It refused to light out in the open, so he brought the sticks under the shelter and eventually managed to light them there. Although the fire was very smoky and kept going out, we managed to boil water in the tin and to cook some rice and salt for our evening meal. We woke the children, sat them up and got them to take a few spoons of rice each, but neither seemed hungry, they just wanted to lie down and sleep.

Rashid and I hardly spoke during those tense few hours. After we'd eaten, I dampened the end of Ananda's shawl and mopped Sophia and Harish's brows, trying to bring down their fierce temperatures. I couldn't tell if I was doing any good. Both kept whimpering and twisting in their fevered sleep, trying to push the cloth away, but I persisted.

Rashid sat cross-legged and watched me, his eyes wretched, not leaving his children's faces.

'They are both going to die,' he said after a while. I looked up, horrified at his words.

'Don't talk like that. They will pull through,' I insisted. He shook his head.

'It is malaria, I can tell. We don't have quinine and they are both weak.'

'It may not be that,' I said, not wanting to acknowledge this possibility.

'I should have listened to you,' he said. 'We should have stayed in the last camp and let them rest. What does it matter when we get to India if they don't make it?'

Then he broke down, his heart-rending sobs ringing out through that dismal valley like the cries of a trapped animal.

That night when we lay down in the shelter, sleep wouldn't come. I listened to the cries of the jungle creatures, the hum of insects and I couldn't stop thinking of the bodies we'd passed on the path; bloated and grotesque. Each one of those poor souls had been like us once, setting out along the same path, thinking they were bound for India. Would that happen to us? I held Ananda close, praying that even if I were to perish, he would somehow make it through.

I woke as the first shafts of daylight penetrated the

thatch and it was immediately obvious that something dreadful had happened. Sitting up, I saw Rashid was on his knees outside the shelter, rocking back and forth silently. I scrambled across and looked at Sophia and Harish. Shock-waves went through me at what I saw. Harish's breathing was ragged and his face aflame with fever, but from the pallor on Sophia's waxy skin I could tell instantly that she was dead. I touched her little face, which was already going cold, put my ear to her chest and listened for her heartbeat, but could hear nothing. She had slipped away during the night.

Tears blurring my vision, I crept outside to Rashid and tried to put my arm around his shoulders but he shrugged me off.

'Rashid, I'm so, so sorry,' I said, but he didn't answer. He didn't even look up. I crept back into the shelter and waited. There was nothing I could do to comfort him. Nothing I could say to make things better.

After a time he turned to look at me. His face was blotchy and stained with tears.

'I sat up watching over her all night,' he said. 'I tried to cool her down but nothing would work. She just faded before my eyes.'

He broke down in tears and I went to him again. This time he didn't push me away and I held him tight until the tears subsided.

'I've let them down,' he sobbed. 'My wife and Sophia. I could have prevented both their deaths. If I hadn't been so hell bent on pushing on.'

'Don't think like that, there was nothing you could have done,' I said, doing my best to comfort him. After a time he drew a deep breath, and turning his grief ravaged face towards me said,

'You were right before. We need to let Harish rest or he will die too. We must give him the best chance to recover.'

I glanced around at the clearing. It had stopped raining a few hours before and a fine mist was rising from the jungle all around, giving it an eery, mystical feel. But there was nothing here to sustain us. Nowhere to collect water, no food other than the rice and salt we'd carried here ourselves and it was difficult to light a fire.

'I don't mean here,' he said, reading my thoughts. 'We will move on and find one of the shelters the army has built and dumped some food. If we find such a place we could rest there for a few days.'

'Yes, if we can find one,' I said, wondering why we'd missed the one we'd been looking for the day before. Had we strayed off the path?

'But first, I need to say prayers for Sophia, and bury her body,' he said. 'I don't want her left in the open like the poor unfortunates on the path.'

It took all day to dig the grave. Rashid found a spot under a tree where the soil was soft. We dug with sticks and a couple of flinty stones. It was tiring and slow going and we often had to break off to tend to Harish and Ananda. Harish's temperature still raged and he needed to be bathed with cold water regularly. Ananda was fretful still and I was terrified that he had whatever disease had carried Sophia away. We couldn't be sure it was malaria; it had acted so quickly, and normally malaria lingers for days.

It was growing dark by the time the grave was ready. Rashid was weeping when he brought Sophia's body out of the shelter and laid it on the ground. He washed her and placed a tikka mark on her forehead with some charcoal from the fire. Then he knelt and said prayers for her. I knelt beside him, and was moved by his voice, intoning his Hindu prayers in his own language. I thought of little Sophia, whom I'd only known for a few days. Her soulful brown eyes had always pulled at my heartstrings, knowing she'd just lost her mother, and the way she walked up hills when Rashid had had to carry Harish to give him a rest. She'd never once complained at the harsh conditions and until she was too sick to eat, had always been grateful for the food doled out to her at mealtimes, no matter how unpalatable.

It broke my heart watching Rashid lift his daughter into the grave. Tears were streaming down his face. We didn't speak as he laid her down and we shovelled the earth back over her fragile body. By now it was almost dark and we hadn't eaten for twenty-four hours. We lit the fire again and boiled some rice for our evening meal but I noticed that Rashid could hardly touch his food.

The water is getting very short now, but we cannot move on until the morning. In a moment I will lie down to sleep, my heart full of grief for that brave little girl, who, like so many others, lost the fight for life on this perilous walk through the jungle.

March 28th

Once again, it is hard for me to write this. Partly because I have to relive these terrible events when I write them down, which is not easy. But I feel I owe it to others to record what has happened, and to make sure I never forget.

We reached another abandoned village two days ago where some food had been dumped. Luckily there was still some left over from those already passing through. It was a long, hard climb from the previous camp; around eight hours strenuous walking, up and down steep inclines. We crossed a couple of deep river valleys on precarious wooden bridges, slung from trees at either end. Some of the slats were missing and we had to jump over the gap, the river raging over rocks fifty feet below. At one point we walked the length of a high ridge above the trees and could see the jungle covered hills stretching for miles around in both directions, with soft white clouds nestling in dips, and wisps of mist rising from river valleys. The mountains stretched as far as the eye could see dissolving into a purplish-blue haze and then melting into the clouds at the horizon. It would have been beautiful, but for the hardships of the march and the precarious situation we found ourselves in.

Rashid found it hard to leave the camp and say goodbye to his daughter, knowing he was unlikely to ever go there again. He spent a long time kneeling at the grave before he could finally wrench himself away. Then he visibly braced himself, knelt down to help Harish onto his back and begun the day's march. He didn't look back as we left the clearing.

'Her soul is not dead,' he said as we walked away. 'She lives on in our hearts.'

It started to rain as we left the place where Sophia was buried, and it carried on for most of the day. As soon as it started, Ananda began to cry. He'd been quiet up until that point, but he hates the rain. His crying always troubles me; I wonder if he's caught the fever and keep checking his brow, but so far, he's been lucky.

When we stopped to rest at midday, I looked down and to my shock saw that there were four or five slimy, black leeches stuck to my calves. I gasped and Rashid lit a match and burned them off, but more have stuck to me during the day.

'It is because of the wet weather,' he said. 'They drop off the trees, searching for blood. And you have nothing to cover your legs.'

So, as well as the swelling mosquito bites, I have to contend with leech sores. They are bloody and painful and I'm sure could go septic quickly if I don't keep them clean.

We saw the roofs of the village from the top of a hill and rushed the final few miles to reach them before dark. But when we got there it was the same story as before. All the villagers must have fled, fearing the Japanese. There were a couple of other groups of refugees who were camping out in two of the huts. They had already lit fires and were cooking when we arrived.

We looked inside all the other huts and each was empty, except for one in which there were four dead bodies. It was chilling to see them there, huddled together on a sleeping mat in the corner: a grandmother, a mother and father and a young boy. Had they died of disease? Starvation? Or had they killed themselves with poison perhaps, terrified of what the Japanese might do to them if they found them? Whatever the answer, we shut the bamboo screen in the doorway and kept well away from that hut.

We found an empty hut to sleep in and laid Harish down on the earth floor. He hadn't improved; his face was still flushed and sweaty, his body was heavy and clumsy, and all he wanted to do was to sleep. He seemed not to know what was going on. Rashid hadn't told him about Sophia and he hadn't asked where she was.

For the first time in several days, we were able to eat some protein. There was a tin of sardines left by the army. Although refugees passing through before and those already there that day had taken most of the stores, they had at least left that one tin of sardines. They tasted delicious and I fed a couple of morsels to Ananda, who chomped them down and gurgled with delight. With that and the rice, when I laid down to sleep, my stomach felt full for the first time since I left home. But poor Harish hadn't been able to take any food, he'd just turned away and closed his eyes when offered it.

The next day passed uneventfully. We spent it huddling inside the shelter to keep out of the rain which hammered down relentlessly. We watched as the other families packed up and left the clearing. The hours crawled by. At intervals we made tea and ate our meals, saving the remains of the sardines for the next day. Sometimes I laid down and slept, catching up for all the sleepless nights. Rashid and I took turns mopping Harish's brow, but he didn't improve and now it was hard to wake him up. He couldn't focus and seemed to have slipped into delirium.

Another dreadful blow awaited us the following morning. Poor Harish had finally given up the will to live. He had died in the night. Rashid was slumped beside him when I awoke. I went over to check on the boy and could tell as soon as I looked at him. His face had that same waxy appearance as Sophia's had and when I put my hand on his skin, it was cold and hard to the touch.

Rashid was as inconsolable as before. He' d been watching over Harish most of the night, but had dropped off to sleep sitting up. When he woke and saw what had happened he let out a roar of grief. Again, he spent a long time kneeling in prayer, tears streaming down his face, rocking back and forth in the agony of his loss. I couldn't think of the right words to say to him. What could I have said? "I'm sorry" doesn't seem anything like enough and although I said it and tried to comfort him, my words didn't seem to have any impact.

'We will bury him here,' he said and started wandering around the clearing looking for a suitable place to lay his son to rest. He walked like a beaten man; his shoulders drooped and he dragged his feet as if each step was an effort of will. As I watched him, I thought of how hard he'd tried to bring his family to safety and how much kindness and patience he'd shown me. It was heart-breaking to see him like this, his hopes and dreams cruelly dashed through no fault of his own.

In time he found a place to bury Harish. Like Sophia's grave, it was under a tall tree, where the soil was quite soft and easy to dig. He knelt down straight away and started digging with a stick. I'd noticed some spoons in one of the huts, so I fetched them and knelt down beside him, handing him one. We dug together and this time we were quicker. We worked in silence for several hours and the grave was finished by mid-afternoon. Just as he had the day before for his daughter, Rashid washed the body of his son, made a tikka mark on his forehead with ash from the fire, said prayers over him then laid him in the grave. Then we shovelled the earth back over him. There was a dreadful sense of déjà vu about what we were doing. I can't help thinking how lucky I am that Ananda remains well in the face of all this suffering and loss.

That evening we didn't feel like cooking, so we just boiled some water to make tea and ate the remains of the sardines. Rashid had no appetite, so after taking one bite, he handed his fish to me.

'Tomorrow, you must move on from here,' he said and I looked at him, alarmed.

'What about you?'

'I will stay. I cannot leave this jungle. There is nothing for me to return to India for now.'

'Rashid, don't think like that. You have your life to live. You must go back.'

He shook his head. 'I cannot,' he muttered. 'My life is

over. I belong here now. I need to watch over my children's graves.'

I tried to persuade him but he wouldn't listen. He was determined to stay in the forest with his dead children. I wondered how I would cope on the trail alone, but I didn't voice my concerns. I knew my own needs were nothing compared to the magnitude of his loss.

'You will be alright,' he said, reading my thoughts as he so often had. 'We are almost at the Chaukan Pass now. From there the way will be more clearly marked. You are stronger than you think. Just go slowly and carefully and follow the path.'

Later, we settled down to rest, but sleep wouldn't come. Ananda was restless and the sound of jungle creatures was oppressively loud. But even above that sound, I could hear Rashid sobbing quietly in his corner.

I must have drifted off eventually because when I woke with a start the sun was already shining through the slats of the hut. Ananda was stirring beside me. I looked across to Rashid's corner and was surprised to see he wasn't there. I got up and wandered around the deserted hamlet with a sinking feeling in the pit of my stomach. He was nowhere to be found. When I went back to our hut I realised that his pack and shoes had gone too, although he'd left a box of matches and some of his rice in a paper bag on the floor. I started to panic, running around the clearing shouting his name, but to no avail. There was no answer. My cries just rang out into the emptiness, unanswered.

23

EDITH

Dapha River Tea Plantation, Assam, 1980

EDITH PAUSED, and laid down the journal. It had been even harder to decipher the wavering pencilled words in this section, the pages were streaked with dirt and the letters sometimes distorted, as if Betty could not see what she was writing. The harrowing intensity of Betty's experience filled her with horror. Her heart went out to her sister, struggling through those mountains carrying a baby, all those years ago. How desperately sad that Betty had to go through that dreadful ordeal alone, without help or support from those she loved. And sad too that Edith herself had gone half a lifetime without knowing how Betty had suffered. Edith shuddered when she thought about the terrors of the jungle, the mud and the leeches, the dreadful sight of the bloated bodies by the side of the path and the harrowing pain of losing those two young children. How could Betty have possibly coped with all of that? Edith realised that in order to have survived that far, Betty must have grown strong, both mentally and physically during those last months in Rangoon and on the trek through the mountains.

With a sad smile, Edith thought back to how Betty had been as a child and young woman. She was a Londoner through and through, a committed townie who had no desire to go out into the countryside. She'd never wanted to walk anywhere, even in the town.

'Why not just get a cab, Edie?' she'd ask smiling, if Edith ever suggested it.

Once, when Edith had suggested taking the train out to the South Downs, she'd said incredulously,

'But there are beautiful parks in London. Why would we want to go out there? There's absolutely nothing to see.'

It was ironic, Edith thought, and it must have been such a rude shock to Betty, that she'd been forced to undertake the longest walk that anyone could imagine. She'd had to struggle through the most remote and inhospitable mountain range in the world, that only the hardiest explorers had ever attempted before.

But the fact that Betty had survived to write the journal, and that there were more pages yet to read was testament to her strength and her resilience.

Although it was growing late and she would shortly have to go up to the house for supper with Richard, Edith was keen to finish reading the journal. There were not many entries left, and she was desperate to find out whether those last few pages held the key to the mystery of Betty's disappearance.

Betty's Journal
Chaukan Pass, Assam, 1942

April 1st

I have been walking alone, barefoot and carrying Ananda on my back, for three days now. It has been so difficult to record all this here. On a practical level, it's been hard to find the time during the daylight hours, when I'm either walking, making a fire and cooking, or looking after Ananda. But I've forced myself to do it.

It took me a while to calm down from the shock of finding that Rashid had left me alone in that deserted clearing. When I first discovered that he'd disappeared I was in a state of blind panic, rushing around, crying out for him. I was angry with him for leaving me as he had, defenceless and alone, deep in this inhospitable jungle, hundreds of miles from civilisation. But I couldn't be angry for long; the man had lost his wife and both his children in the space of a couple of weeks and was not thinking clearly. I didn't want to contemplate it too closely, but I realised that it was even possible that he could have taken his own life.

When I was quite sure he wasn't going to reappear, I sat down in the shelter and wept tears of helplessness until I'd cried myself out. This place had felt lonely when I had Rashid and the children for company, now it felt terrifying. I thought of all the creatures that lurked in the forest; tigers, panthers, leopards, not to mention deadly snakes. We hadn't seen any predators so far, but perhaps that was because we'd been together. But I had heard the rustle of pythons slithering through the dead leaves on the forest floor though, many times.

When I finally calmed down and got my thoughts under control, I looked at my options. I could wait in the clearing for another party to catch me up. I knew that there must be more people setting out from Myitkyina all the time. It would only be a matter of hours before some others caught me up, surely. But would they help me? Everyone we'd seen so far had been keen to press on quickly, to secure their own survival. Perhaps, if I waited there in the clearing, Rashid might come back and I could try to persuade him to carry on with me. But the more I thought about that, the less appealing staying in that clearing was. I didn't want to sleep in the place where Harish had died, and so near to the hut where the four dead bodies lay. It felt a dismal, unlucky place. Also, I reasoned, if I waited too long, it was possible the Japanese army might appear through the jungle. Everyone knew their aim was to get to India. If they took Myitkyina, they could well try to get through this way.

So, I made a decision. I gathered my things: my sack of rice and salt, which I replenished from the paper bag Rashid had left in the shelter, and my can of water, which was running dangerously low.

I gave Ananda some water from his bottle, then tied him to my back and set off alone along the path that had been trodden by all those going before us. Now I was aware that I had to be very vigilant about following the route, whereas previously I'd let Rashid navigate and I'd simply followed his lead. As I went, I was constantly looking out for the markers that were carved into tree trunks. They were very crude; some in the form of an X, others just a squiggle and easy to miss. Sometimes the footprints I was following petered out, so I had to check out different possible routes, which wasted precious time and energy.

That first morning I was blessed with dry weather and made reasonable progress. I only passed two or three bloated bodies beside the path during those first few hours.

I've learned to hurry past them, holding the end of the shawl over my face, not stopping to look or to think.

The path climbed steadily upwards, winding through woods full of towering rhododendron trees in bloom, and on through the deepest, darkest part of the forest. Here, the atmosphere was so dank and the light so poor that the trees were covered in thick, dark moss. Fallen branches were rotting and covered in toxic-looking fungus; mushrooms with lethal red caps, huge, irregular shaped growths. Some of the trees were gnarled with age, giving the place the appearance of a fairy-tale grotto. It would have been enchanting but for my predicament. All the time I was listening out for predators, the crack of a branch or the low growl of a tiger. I'd even heard stories that tribes of head-hunters lived in the deepest parts of this forest, a thought that chilled me to the core.

I tried to keep my spirits up by singing. I sang all the nursery rhymes I could think of, then all the hymns and carols I'd learned at school. My voice sounded strange to me, ringing out there amongst those alien jungle sounds, but Ananda seemed to like it because he started crying every time I stopped.

By noon, I could sense that I was reaching the top of this particular mountain. The path flattened and the trees thinned out, so that I could see the mountains dropping away from me on all sides. I paused to take in the views, shading my eyes and turning round in a complete circle. I was at the highest point for miles around. Layer upon layer of hills, covered in dark green jungle, stretched away into the mist in every direction. The valleys and ravines were filled with clouds. Above, the sky was a deep clear blue and the sun high and blindingly bright. This must be the fabled Chaukan Pass. The point we'd been aiming for since we started out. Ahead of me lay India, stretching far, far into the distance, and behind me was Burma. I knew I should have felt elated at having made it to this milestone, but I felt nothing; just exhaustion and revulsion for everything I'd seen and suffered on the march so far. My heart was filled with dread, too, for what might lie ahead.

As I stood there at the highest point of all amongst those magnificent mountains, I heard a faint humming in the distance, coming from ahead of me, from the direction of India. I listened for a few seconds before realising what it was. It was a sound I'd heard many times before. One that instilled the deepest fear into my heart. It was the sound of aeroplanes approaching. That only meant one thing: bombs and machinegun fire. Panicking, I looked around for somewhere to take cover, but before I'd located a place, I realised that the planes must be British. They couldn't be Japanese, coming from that direction.

Now, more curious than afraid, I stayed where I was and watched them approach. There were two of them. Smaller than transport planes but bigger than fighters. They started to descend. I couldn't see where they might land in the jungle, but at a couple of hundred feet they flattened out and flew straight ahead. They were getting closer to me now. I wondered if they would make it over the pass, but then they started to turn in a great, sweeping curve and, as they did so, objects began to drop from their undercarriages. My hand flew to my mouth; I thought they were bombs, but as I peered closer, I saw that they were bags or sacks, strung together with great, trailing ribbons. And then I realised. The aircraft were dropping supplies on the camps for refugees like me making this dangerous trek over the mountains.

Tears sprung to my eyes as I watched those bags descend

into the jungle below me. It made me feel connected, as if I wasn't abandoned and alone here on the pass, that someone out there was thinking about me and wanting to help me. For the first time in days I dared to feel hope.

I descended from the ridge, walking as quickly as I could, trying to reach the place where the supplies had been dropped. But the path was steep and rocky, and I was hampered by having no shoes on my feet. I kept stepping on sharp stones and roots, and my feet and calves were already a mass of bites, sores and bruises. A family group passed me as I descended; mother, father and two teenaged children. They walked quickly and as they passed they didn't speak. I watched them disappear into the trees, envying them their companionship.

I didn't reach the sacks of supplies that day. By the time I'd descended from the ridge, the light was fading fast. I began to panic again, looking round for somewhere to sleep. There was nowhere obvious and I didn't have the skills or the tools to make a shelter. In the end I found a bush with overhanging branches and some soft grass underneath it. It was beside a fast-flowing stream. I lay Ananda down on the grass and scouted around for sticks to make a fire.

I wished I'd watched Rashid more closely. I had no idea how to build the fire properly so it would light and burn easily. It took me several failed attempts and wasted matches before I managed to get some flickering flames going. By this time Ananda was crying for food, but I had to leave him while I cooked some rice in a tin with water from the stream. When it was cooked I tried to feed him some, but he spat it out. The sardines had spoiled him, but I began to worry that the reason he had no appetite was because he had a fever.

Once the sky was completely dark, I laid down beside

him and cuddled him to sleep, but it took me a long time to drift off. My nerves were taut as I listened to the cacophony of jungle creatures, wondering what dangers were lurking out there.

I was woken just after dawn by a downpour. Ananda was soaked to the skin and screaming. I gathered him up and held him close, trying to shield him from the rain. There was no point trying to make a fire, so I just took a sip of water from my tin which I'd put out to catch raindrops, packed my things away and began walking.

I reached the food dump around noon. As I entered the clearing my heart lifted as I saw the sacks strewn all around, some hanging from trees, some lodged in a stream. Others had burst and were spilling rice and vegetables everywhere, providing a meal for millions of ants, but most had landed intact. I stood there, unable to move, overwhelmed by the sight of so much food, strewn about the clearing, after so many days of hunger and deprivation. Unable to resist, I ran crazily from sack to sack, touching potatoes in wonder, picking up cabbages, burying my face in their leaves, smelling their wonderful scent, pulling off a leaf to chew on while I went. Under my breath I whispered my thanks to God for this extraordinary windfall.

It had stopped raining now, so I gathered some sticks from under the trees and lit a small fire. I gathered potatoes and onions, sat down by the fire and peeled them with great care, lifting them to my face many times to revel in the delicious smell. I boiled up some potatoes, added onion for extra flavour, and when they were soft, I mashed them to a pulp with a rock. Then I added some salt to the mash and tasted it, as if I was a gourmet chef. To my deprived taste-buds the flavours were extraordinary.

Before I allowed myself the luxury of eating the meal

though, I fed some to Ananda. He wolfed it down, smacking his lips, gurgling with joy and waving his hands around for more, each time he'd finished a spoonful. When he could eat no more, I finished what was left. I ate it as slowly as I could, chewing each mouthful several times, conscious of the need to savour the tastes, to allow my stomach to adapt to the extra volume of food, all the time resisting the urge to gulp it down. After the days eating rice and salt, those onion flavoured mashed potatoes tasted better than any feast I'd experienced in London or Rangoon.

By the time I'd finished, Ananda was already asleep on his shawl. I laid down beside him, full for the first time in many days and a delicious drowsiness overcame me. I allowed myself an afternoon nap, enjoying, as I drifted off to sleep, that comfortable, sated feeling you only get after a good meal.

When I finally awoke, the sun had moved around and I realised I must have slept for an hour or so. I decided to set off again, although it would have been tempting to stay in the clearing where there was endless food. I knew I needed to make progress. I packed as much food into my little sack as I could carry, and found the path leading out of the clearing. One of the last sacks I passed on the way out had split on landing and the contents were strewn around it. I stared at it and smiled; it was such an unexpected sight. It was full of toys. Dolls, teddy bears and toy cars were tumbling out onto the grass. There was a small ginger teddy bear with a tartan ribbon round its neck that had fallen a little way from the others. I picked it up, dusted it down and put it in my bag. It would be ideal for Ananda. It would remind us in the coming years of what we'd both endured.

April 4th

It is so difficult for me to write this. I'm too tired and weary, wondering if we're going to make it through. But I tell myself to push on, to keep writing. As I said, it feels important. If I push myself to record our journey, then I will keep pushing myself to complete it.

The next two days were the worst I have ever had to endure in my life. I couldn't find shelter on either night and the path was steep and treacherous all the way. It rained incessantly and I slipped over in the mud many times. On one occasion I tripped on a root and sprained my ankle and after that each step was agony. But I gritted my teeth against the pain and kept battling on. Others passed me, in groups or in twos. I was tempted to ask if I could walk with them, but I knew I would slow them down. What right did I have to compromise their chance of survival?

Sometimes the path almost petered out and it was difficult to be sure I was going in the right direction. At other times it was a quagmire of footprints from those who'd gone before, difficult to walk through as my feet kept getting stuck, but it was comforting to know I was going the right way. I passed yet more bodies. Distressingly, a few of them were children; two tiny sisters had been laid beside the path on the steepest part of the route. I hurried past them, imagining their mother's heartbreak as she laid them there in the open jungle and was forced to leave them and walk on.

The food I'd gathered from the sacks at the food dump dwindled pretty quickly and soon I was back to rice, salt and water. Once, I sat down on a log to rest beside the path and could feel my hipbones digging into the wood, I'd grown so thin. I looked down at my legs. Legs that I'd once been proud of in more frivolous times. Now they looked like those of a skeleton and they were covered in bites and sores.

On the third morning after Rashid left me, we'd been sleeping out in the open again, in a clearing full of dry leaves. When I awoke and sat up, the trees spun around me. I tried standing up and taking a few steps, but could only stagger. I felt hot and my face and body were dripping with sweat. I realised with a sickening sense of dread that I had a fever. I sat down, contemplating this for a while. But there was nothing to contemplate really. I had no choice. I must push on, no matter how bad I feel, I need to get out of here and somehow back to civilisation.

I had no appetite for food and no energy to make a fire and cook, so I sipped a little water and gave some to Ananda, hoisted him onto my back and set off along the trail. It was tough but I pressed on all morning. I walked slowly; each step was a struggle but the trail was relatively easy to follow. It took me through dense forest, where I had to push my way through clumps of bamboo, giant ferns and dangling creepers. I scrambled down steep inclines, stepped over streams, and walked carefully along a narrow ridge high above a river valley.

Around noon, the trail emerged from the trees onto a grassy plateau. A group of people pushed past me, walking quickly, blocking the light from the trail momentarily, then disappearing over the horizon. I paused as I stepped out from the darkness of the forest into the sunlight, shielding my eyes. The light made my head hurt even more. From where I stood I had a view of the jungle-covered hills which spread out in every direction. But when I looked down at the ground the trail had petered out. This didn't concern me too much at first. It had happened to me before and it was usually possible to find it, so I set off in a straight line, expecting the path to reappear within a couple of hundred yards, but it was nowhere to be seen. Panicking, I returned to the edge of the forest and tried another direction. The noonday sun was fiercely hot out in that exposed place and my head was thumping with the fever.

I tried walking in four different directions and found no trace of the path in any of them. I retraced my steps to the place where the trail emerged from the forest, my heart hammering away with the panic of being alone and lost out here in this remote place. Suddenly, I was overwhelmed; the sadness of losing Rashid and his children, the hunger, the thirst, the exhaustion, the aches and pains of the fever and the sheer terror of what would happen to us both if I couldn't get us out of here. I sank down on my knees and let the tears fall. Before long I was sobbing my heart out.

When I finally looked up, a bolt of shock went through me. Four men stood stock still in a line a few yards in front of me. But they were not like any men I'd ever set eyes on before. They wore black fur headdresses; their faces were painted with white lines and circles; their chests were bare but for an embroidered sash and they wore loincloths. Each held a long spear upright in their right hand. They were all staring at me intently, without smiling.

I stood up and instinctively drew Ananda close to my chest, my heart hammering more than ever. The tallest man stepped forward, peered closely at me and addressed me in his language.

'I'm sorry...' I said. 'I don't understand.'

'We Naga people,' he said slowly, without changing his expression. I nodded and kept my eyes on his face, but I could feel my knees trembling. This was it. I was dead now.

The Naga tribes were the head-hunters I'd heard whispered stories about. They were ruthless to their enemies and they collected scalps as trophies from their battles. I didn't know what to say. I looked down at the grass. Would they kill me here, or would they take me to their homestead first?

'You England?' he asked after a long pause. I looked up, met his inscrutable gaze and nodded.

'You lost,' he announced then.

'Yes, I am,' I replied.

'I show you path,' he said. 'You have money?'

'Yes,' I said, in relief. If all they wanted was my money, I'd been very lucky. I fumbled in my shoulder bag. It was now full of rice, but my purse was at the bottom. I pulled it out and found a hundred rupee note. I handed it to him.

'Too much,' he said, holding his hand up. Then he smiled, displaying teeth heavily stained with red betel nut. I found some coins adding up to about thirty rupees and handed them to him. He nodded, took them and slipped them inside his loin cloth.

'I carry bag and baby,' he said, holding out his hand. I hesitated. Could I trust him? Would he run off with Ananda? Would I ever see my baby again?

I took off my shoulder bag and the sack of rice I also carried round my neck and handed them to him.

'I will carry the baby,' I said. He nodded briefly, then turned. 'We go,' he said and set off, striding across the ridge in a diagonal direction, one that I hadn't tried. The other three tribesmen melted away into the forest.

I followed at a distance, unable to keep up with him. My heartbeat subsided. This was working out better than I could have imagined even just a few minutes ago. I followed the man across the plateau and eventually, as we descended,

I noticed that we were on the path again. It then plunged into another jungle forest beneath the ridge.

All afternoon I walked behind him. He knew this trail well. He wore no shoes but he was surefooted, always finding the most solid ground to step on. I followed his footsteps and that way it was easy to make good progress. After a couple of hours we crossed a stream. He pointed to a rock and said, 'Sit.'

I did as I was told, released Ananda from my back and cradled him to me. I watched the tribesman gather sticks and make a fire. He did it expertly with a couple of flint stones he carried in a pack. Soon it was blazing away. From the pack he produced a tin, in which he boiled some water from the stream. He then made tea in a pottery mug which he handed to me.

It was jasmine tea which tasted fragrant and delicious, I was so used to plain water, or black tea made from a few stale leaves. I poured some into Ananda's bottle and fed it to him. I saw his eyes light up as he guzzled it down, delighting in the delicate flavour.

Before I'd finished, the tribesman handed me a tin with some rice and vegetables that he'd cooked up in a matter of minutes. I ate it gratefully, and as with the tea, the unaccustomed tastes exploded on my tongue, and I ate it hungrily. I fed some to Ananda and again, from the way he smacked his lips together at each mouthful and cried out for more, I could tell he loved the taste. I was anxious about him though, his cheeks looked pink after the meal. I put my hand on his brow for any sign of fever, but felt reassured that his brow was cool.

In the afternoon we walked on through the forest, crossing a ravine on a rickety suspension bridge and carrying on through thick jungle on the other side. Occa-

sionally, groups of other refugees passed us. They looked at
the tribesman with curiosity, but didn't stop or speak, just
pushed onwards, like all the others.

Where the undergrowth blocked the path, the
tribesman took out a lethal looking curved knife and hacked
it away so we could pass. When the light started to fade, he
found a suitable place beside a stream to stay the night.
Again, I sat on a rock while he cut bamboo and made a
shelter with sticks and palm leaves, far superior to anything
poor Rashid had put together. Inside, he spread out a shawl
he'd been carrying.

'For you sleep,' he said.

Later, we sat and once again he rustled up a meal at
astonishing speed. This time it was soup, made from
crushed leaves. It tasted faintly of aniseed or fennel, and as I
ate I prayed that it was safe to eat. When I offered the spoon
to Ananda though, he spat it out and at the next attempt
pushed the spoon away. It concerned me that he didn't want
food, and I checked his brow anxiously for fever, but once
again he seemed to be fine.

As I finished the meal I thanked the tribesman and
asked him his name.

'I am Konyak,' he said with a smile and I told him my
name, although he never once used it to address me.

We travelled like that for three days. On the second
day, I trusted Konyak enough to let him carry Ananda.
My fever waxed and waned. It usually reached its peak
during the morning, subsided in the afternoons and
returned in the evenings. I didn't mention it to Konyak,
worrying that he might leave me if he thought I was
carrying disease. I worried more about Ananda than
my own state of health, repeatedly checking him,
looking into his eyes for delirium, feeling his brow for

fever, but to my relief his health remained as robust as ever.

April 8th

I had worried that Konyak would leave me, having become so reliant on his guidance and skills, but this morning my fears came true and he did just that.

We got up as usual and trekked through the forest all morning. We stopped for lunch on a rocky outcrop and Konyak found some jungle plants to cook which were surprisingly aromatic. I worried that they might be poisonous, but the Nagas have lived in these jungles for generations and must know what is edible.

In the afternoon we carried on, but after an hour or so I became aware of a roaring, rushing sound ahead. In time it grew louder and I realised that it must be a river. A big one by the sound of it, and fast flowing. By mid-afternoon the sound was deafening when we emerged from the jungle onto the top of a ravine. I peered over the edge and saw that the river that ran below was a series of waterfalls, roaring over rocks and forming frothy whirlpools.

Konyak stood on the edge and pointed down.

'Noa Dihing River,' he announced. 'I no go further.'

Panic rose in me. How would I go on without him to guide me? I stared at him.

'Please,' I said. 'I need your help.'

He shook his head. 'I no go. No my country,' he waved his hand in the direction of the river. I realised that the river must form some sort of spiritual or mythical barrier, beyond which he couldn't pass.

He pointed to the path which carried on along the ridge beside the edge of the ravine.

'You go. Path to Dapha River. Two days from here,' he said.

I felt in my purse and handed him ten more rupees which he took with a smile. Then he untied my sack and Ananda from his back and handed them to me. With an incline of his head, he put his hands together as if to bless me, turned and stepped back into the forest.

24

BETTY'S JOURNAL

Assam, India, 1942

April 8th

I FELT bereft as Konyak disappeared back into the forest as suddenly as he'd appeared, leaving me alone yet again. I'd come to rely on him for everything; for food, shelter, for showing me the route. There had been no discussion of how long he would be with me, that would have been difficult anyway with the language barrier, but I hadn't expected him to leave so soon.

I straightened up, squared my shoulders, and walked along the top of the ridge in the direction he'd pointed. The way was sometimes muddy, sometimes taking me along the top of slippery rocks. Often there was only a narrow path carved into the cliff face high above the river. I was terrified of slipping, so went carefully, making very slow progress. I hadn't been going long when it started to rain. This meant that the trail became even more treacherous than before, but I pressed on. It had given me some sort of hope when

Konyak had said that the Dapha River crossing was only two days away. I'd heard that there was a camp there. Perhaps more supplies would have been dropped? There might even be some other people there.

I had only walked a couple of hours when the sky darkened. Night fall wasn't far off. Where could I sleep in this inhospitable, rocky valley? I wondered about leaving the path, scrambling up the rock face and finding some trees to shelter under for the night, but before long I noticed the opening of a cave in the cliff, half hidden behind some giant boulders.

Heaving a sigh of relief, I crept inside. Many others had been there before me, judging by the smell and the remains of fires dotted around. I lay Ananda out on the shawl and gave him some water. My head was thumping by this time and the fever was descending upon me. I had no energy to make a fire or to cook rice, so I just laid down on the bare earth and closed my eyes. It wasn't long before the drum of the rain and the voice of the great Noa Dihing river, rushing over the rocks down in the ravine, sent me into a deep sleep.

April 9th

It is not easy, finding a dry spot in my sparse shelter of fern leaves in order to write, and peering at the letters makes my head pound, but I'm determined to record my progress.

When I awoke, shafts of sunlight were shining in through the mouth of the cave. It had stopped raining and looked to be a beautiful day. But my fever had worsened. My head was pounding and when I sat up, the cave spun around as the trees had on the first day. I was drenched in sweat but Ananda was crying, so I hauled myself up and groped around for his water bottle. As I fed him, my eyes wandered around the cave. Now it was daylight I could see the source of the smell. Two bodies lay in the far corner of the cave, wedged under an overhanging rock. I couldn't tell if they were men or women; they were wrapped in coloured cloth, their faces covered. Perhaps it was all their relatives could do for them before having to move on. I didn't stop to find out, or to finish feeding Ananda.

Pulling the teat from his mouth, I gathered our things and got out of that cave as quickly as possible. Sobbing with shock, I started out along the rocky ridge, but it was even more slow going than before. I was so dizzy that I could hardly stand straight. I couldn't trust myself to go quickly and had to feel every inch of the way with my hands along the rocks. I needed to make frequent stops to rest, I was so weak.

All day I walked like that, not stopping to drink or cook rice. There were no other refugees on this path and I worried that I'd strayed off the main trail. Sometimes Ananda screamed with hunger, but I just gave him water and that pacified him for a time.

Several times the path descended right down to the raging river and I had to wade through the water, clinging onto the rocks for yards until the path reappeared and I could scramble out again. It was wonderful to feel the water on my legs, to bathe the open sores and septic bites that had been plaguing me since the beginning of the walk. I stood still for a moment when I first felt it, allowing it to soothe the pain. Then, although the current was fast, I couldn't resist the opportunity to wash my aching body and filthy clothes. I laid Ananda down on a rock and splashed water all over my body. Even here, deep in the jungle, I didn't feel comfortable enough to take off my dress, there could be tribesmen hidden in the trees, but I knelt down in the water, letting the skirt get wet, knowing in the steamy heat it wouldn't take too long to dry. Then I stripped off Ananda's clothes and dipped him in the water. His eyes widened as he felt the cold and he screwed his face up and roared, but I lifted him in and out and soon he was laughing with delight at the game. Wrapping him back up in the shawl, I quickly washed his dirty clothes, then tied them onto my belt so they would dry as I walked.

Although I yearned to sit beside the water and rest, I knew I had to move on, to find shelter before nightfall. The going was slippery and uneven and I stumbled several times, just managing to prevent myself and Ananda from going right under.

When it grew dark I sat down beside the trail. There was no cave this time, but there were a few woody bushes, so I managed to gather some sticks and make a small fire. I cooked some rice and salt. I could hardly force any down, I felt so nauseous, but Ananda ate hungrily.

The fever has not abated, but I am pinning my hopes on the Dapha River camp. Just one more day and perhaps I will find more supplies there and a shelter so I can rest for a while. If only I can hold out that long.

April 10th

Things have changed dramatically for me in the space of a day. I feel so dizzy I can hardly form the letters with the pencil, but I need to write about what has happened.

This morning I dragged myself up from the ground under the bushes where I'd slept and set off once again along the river trail. The way was similar to yesterday, along a treacherously slippery shelf carved out of the rock. If anything, my fever was worse and it was all I could do to drag myself along. Sometimes, when I couldn't stand up, I crawled a few paces. Many times the trail descended into the river and I had to walk along the slippery river bed, gripping onto the stones beside the bank to stop myself from being washed away by the current.

But at last I came to the end of the dark ravine that I'd been walking along for two days. The trail turned away from it, left the river behind and led back through the forest. It was easier walking here, following the muddy footsteps made by others, days or even just hours before me. This forest was dripping with moisture and after the relative cool of the river valley, I found the steamy heat oppressive.

But in a couple of hours the path emerged from the jungle again and onto another riverbank and as I did so, I caught sight of another group of refugees up ahead, trudging beside the river, their heads bowed. I realised then that I must have wandered off the main trail. Could it have been when Konyak was guiding me, or as I walked beside the Noa Dihing? Either way, I was comforted by the sight of others.

By this time it was raining. Huge, tropical raindrops which made it difficult to see clearly. Even so, I was sure that this was a different river. It was wide and shallow, fast flowing but the surface was smooth. My heart soared. This must be the Dapha River that I'd been walking towards for so long. I looked around expecting to see some signs of a camp. But there was no camp, no shelters and no packs of food anywhere to be seen.

Disappointed, head down against the pouring rain, I walked along the riverbank, following the muddy trail. It was easier walking here although slippery, but as I walked my fever descended on me even worse than before; my head felt as though swords were being driven through it and my vision became so blurred I could hardly see the trail ahead. I thought I might be descending into delirium, but I was sure of it when up ahead I saw a group of elephants wading across the river, each with several people on their back. On the bank waited a small group of people. I wondered now if they were real or just figments of my delirious mind. I staggered towards them through the downpour. I knew I had to reach them and if they were real they would help me, but before I could get to them I found myself falling forwards. Instantly there were two people running towards me, a man and a woman.

I felt their arms on mine, gently lifting me. One of them released Ananda from my back and lifted him up. I heard them speaking, but I couldn't say anything back.

'She looks really ill,' the woman said.

'Malaria probably,' answered the man. 'Lots of the refugees have got it, but she looks to be really bad.'

'Let's carry her into the shelter,' said the woman. 'At least she'll be out of the rain then.'

'Yes. We can make her comfortable there, and when we go back to the house we can take her with us.'

April 11th

It is more difficult than ever to write now, I cannot focus for any length of time. I have lost track of how long I've been lying in this bed in this darkened room with the fan whirring overhead and the shutters closed so the sunlight can't penetrate. When I collapsed on the path, I remember being taken to a shelter thatched with palm leaves beside the Dapha River and laid out on the bare earth there. Someone got a damp cloth and mopped my brow. That brought tears to my eyes as it reminded me of how I'd mopped Sophia and Harish's foreheads in their last hours. Their poor, sad little faces swam before my eyes and in my delirium I thought I saw the two of them holding hands and dancing around the clearing beside the river.

The next thing I was aware of was being lifted onto the back of an elephant. The beast was kneeling down on the grassy area beside the river and two men were lifting my body up.

'Where's my baby?' I managed to ask weakly as they laid me gently down on the howdah.

'He's being cared for. Please don't worry,' said a woman's voice.

As the elephant got to its feet, I was jolted and tipped to one side, but I must have been strapped in firmly as I didn't fall. Then we were on the move. The elephant's mahout was sitting in front of me, guiding the animal with his voice and heels. I was lying on my back and all I could see above me was the sky. I turned my head aside to avoid the rain falling directly into my eyes. Then we were moving under the trees and I could feel that we were climbing a steep path. Underneath me the elephant swayed gently and firmly. A couple of times I felt him slip backwards; the path must have been slippery underfoot, but he quickly recovered and plodded steadily on. The swaying motion made me sleepy, so I kept closing my eyes, but each time I opened them I was staring directly up at the trees above me; I could see right up into the jungle canopy, the leaves and branches making a pattern which danced against the colourless, rain-filled sky far above.

I don't know how long that journey up the hillside through the forest took. I had no notion of time, but it seemed a long, long way. Perhaps it was a couple of hours. Eventually we were out of the jungle and it had stopped raining. I was staring up at a clear, bright sky. When we finally stopped and the elephant knelt down, the mahout and the man I'd seen beside the Dapha River lifted me down from the howdah. There was another elephant there. The woman was standing beside it, cradling Ananda. I saw a house in front of me. A beautiful, graceful plantation house, gleaming white with verandas all around. The man carried me inside and up a long flight of stairs. He laid me on a bed and went to the windows and shut the shutters.

'I'll leave her and the baby to you, Olive. I must go back to the river and help now,' he said.

The woman stood over me. She was still holding Ananda, cuddling him to her. Another woman, an Indian, was also hovering beside the bed, watching me. I sensed her kind eyes on my face.

'You can leave now, Simi,' said the woman, sharply. The servant hurried away, then turning to me, the woman said, 'I will give the baby some water, then I'll come back and clean you up.'

I heard her leave the room. I wanted to ask her to leave him with me, but no words would come. Although it felt wonderful to be lying in a clean bed in a cool, dry house after so many weeks of sleeping rough, I had an uneasy feeling about Ananda being out of my sight.

The woman returned, as she'd promised, and cleaned and bathed my cuts and sores. She mopped my brow and gave me a drink of water. Then she left me alone. I would have liked to speak to her, but the fever was strong at that point and words eluded me.

I found myself thinking of Edith, and of Robert. The guilt of everything I'd done suddenly descended on me when they had hardly crossed my mind in all the weeks I'd been on the road. I managed to haul my shoulder bag onto the bed, found one of the airmail letters and and scribbled a few lines to Edith. I've decided to send her this journal. It will tell her everything she needs to know about what has happened to me the past few years. I'm not sure if I'd be able to tell her myself. I feel so ashamed of a lot of it.

The effort of writing brought the fever on with a vengeance and I had to lie back and rest afterwards. When I have enough strength, I'll ask the woman, Olive, to post the letter and journal to Edith. There is something about her that unnerves me, though. Can I trust her?

April 13th

I've been lying here for days and my fever has worsened. It descends at regular intervals and incapacitates me for hours. During that time I become delirious and dream the most extraordinarily vivid but disturbing dreams. Most involve walking along the jungle trail, passing body after bloated body, many of them with exposed bones or skulls, seething with maggots and flies. They terrify me and I cry out for it to stop.

I only have a few minutes of lucidity a day. When that happens I write a few words in here, but my writing is probably illegible.

I am sure it is malaria but Olive hasn't brought me any quinine. Doesn't she know I need it? I've tried to tell her, but am so weak I can hardly speak. Without quinine, I don't think I'm going to recover. I believe I will die here in this house, somewhere on a hilltop in Assam, high above the Dapha River. I did my best to get to India and to bring my baby to safety, but I failed.

I have not seen Ananda since I arrived here on the elephant. It tears my heart out that he isn't here lying beside me. I've asked for him many, many times. It is hard to form the words, but when I finally manage to blurt out his name, Olive just smiles and says, 'Baby is safe with me.'

Why have they taken him from me? I need to hold him to me, to see his little face wrinkle up into a smile when he looks up into my eyes. Without that I know I'm finished. I simply cannot go on.

EDITH LAID the journal down with tears in her eyes. She glanced at the clock. It was three in the morning. It had been more difficult than ever to read the wavering writing in the last section. At times, Betty had separated out the letters like a child, at others it had become a scrawl. Sometimes whole pages were left blank or streaked with dirt. Edith had been touched to notice some crude sketches in the margin; a sleeping baby's face, a teddy bear with a ribbon round its neck. She traced her fingers over them, thinking of Betty drawing them to brighten up her darkest hours.

She was appalled at what Betty had suffered on the walk out of Burma, the hardships of the trail, the hunger, the disease and the horrors of witnessing the dead bodies, the sadness of losing Rashid and his children. At the same time, she felt a surge of pride in how Betty had coped, at Betty's selflessness and strength, how she'd made it as far as Dapha in an attempt to bring her baby to safety.

But still the journal still didn't answer all Edith's questions. It was clear that Betty had been very ill, so why hadn't Olive called a doctor to see her, or at least given her some quinine to give her some sort of chance of getting better? She was almost sure now, that it was Betty's remains down in the lonely grave at the end of the garden. Poor Betty must have died up in the house, not down in this bungalow as Edith had originally thought. But whatever had happened to Ananda?

She thought of Simi, and of the look of fear in her eyes when she'd seen Edith reading the journal. Edith knew now that Simi had seen Betty, but she was also sure that Simi knew something else. Exhausted, she went through to the bedroom, undressed and got into bed. She started drifting off to sleep, the rush of the Noa Dihing River in her head, and the thrum of rain on the leaves of a makeshift shelter. Again her mind drifted to Simi. Tomorrow she would ask Richard to question Simi in her own language. That way she might finally get some answers.

25

OLIVE

Dapha River Tea Plantation, Assam, April 1942

OLIVE SAT beside the bed and waited patiently until the woman was asleep. Then, when she was quite sure her breathing was steady and even, she took the woman's bag from the end of the bed. She tiptoed to the other side of the room, sat on the chair in the corner and rifled through the contents. She wanted to find out the woman's name and where she was from. It puzzled Olive that the woman was travelling with a Burmese baby. Could he possibly be her own? Perhaps he was only half Burmese? His skin was very pale, but he had oriental features. His beady little eyes, framed in long lashes, were pitch black. They had lit up as he looked into Olive's eyes, and he had gripped her fingers and smiled. The most delightful, radiant smile she'd ever seen. It had put joy into her heart and made her remember what was missing in her life.

Now, Olive pulled from the bag what looked like a diary or a journal, with a pencil dangling from a ribbon, there was also an identity card. A flimsy blue airmail letter was tucked inside the diary. She scanned the ID card quickly. *Betty Furnivall, Irrawaddy House, Shwedagon Pagoda Road, Rangoon.* Olive stared at the address. She didn't know very much about Rangoon, but she did know that the woman must be rich if she lived on that road. So once again, why would she be walking alone through the jungle? Hadn't all the rich Europeans got airlifted from Myitkyina or taken boats from Rangoon to Calcutta? And again, why was she travelling with a Burmese baby?

She glanced at the address on the letter. *Mrs Edith Mayhew, The Tea Planter's Club, Bunder Street, Calcutta.* Olive frowned. She recognised that address. Thinking back, she was sure Henry had taken her there when they were court-ing. He'd known the owner. Gregory something. She remembered him now; a tall, amiable man, he'd been a tea planter himself once. He'd explained that he'd bought the place when it was a club for planters, but that he was in the process of turning it into a hotel and taking non-members as guests. Olive wondered who Edith Mayhew was. A sister perhaps? A friend? She slipped the letter back inside the diary. She stopped short of actually reading the letter, or the diary. That would have been to traverse an invisible barrier that even she wasn't prepared to cross at this moment.

Tiptoeing back across the room, she laid the journal on the bedside table, but she took the identity card and slipped it in her pocket. If the woman had her journal to occupy her when she awoke, perhaps she wouldn't miss the identity card. Olive wasn't quite sure what she was going to do with the ID card, but she wanted to hide it from Henry. The less he knew about this woman the better. She should remain a mystery.

Olive left the bedroom and went back into the other spare room, where she had laid the baby in a drawer on top of some soft blankets. Beside him was a grubby teddy bear she'd found in his shawl. He gurgled when he saw her and stretched out his arms to be picked up.

'You are quite adorable,' she said, gathering him up in her arms, cradling him to her, breathing in the sweet baby smell on his soft skin. She took him into her bathroom, filled the sink with warm water, removed the rags he was dressed in and bathed him. His whole body was filthy. The dust and mud floated out of every fold in his skin. It was clear that he hadn't been washed properly for days. But he loved the bath. Splashing and laughing his bubbly laugh, watching for her reaction with his observant black eyes. When she took him out and laid him down on a towel on the floor, the water in the sink was a deep, muddy brown.

She brought him some warm milk in his bottle, which she'd boiled in a saucepan because it had looked so filthy. Then she sat in an armchair in the corner of the spare room and fed him. He took it greedily, sucking hard on the teat of the bottle, gulping the milk down. It suddenly struck Olive as odd that a baby so young had been weaned onto a bottle already. Why wasn't the woman breastfeeding her own baby? Surely that must prove he wasn't hers, mustn't it?

Olive laid the baby down in the drawer again and knelt down beside him, rubbing his back and singing lullabies until he'd gone to sleep. Then, closing the door carefully, she left the room and stood on the landing for a moment, listening. Even from here, she could hear the woman, Betty, twisting and turning in her sleep, shouting out in her delirium.

'Ananda,' she kept saying over and over. 'Where is my baby? I need my baby.'

Olive went back into the bedroom and stared down at

Betty. She would have been pretty but for her sunken cheeks, matted hair and all the sores and bites on her face.

'Ananda!' Betty cried out suddenly, but her eyes were still closed.

Olive found the damp cloth which she'd left in a bowl beside the bed and mopped Betty's brow.

'Don't worry. Baby is sleeping,' she said. 'He's quite safe with me.'

As she was going downstairs, her heart sank as she saw an unwelcome sight through the open front door. Her mother-in-law, Sylvia, was making her way laboriously up the garden path, leaning heavily at each step on her walking stick. As she got closer, Olive was struck by how ill Sylvia looked. Her face was red and sweaty and she was clearly having trouble breathing. Olive rushed across the veranda, down the steps onto the drive and took Sylvia's arm.

'Ma, what are you doing out?' she asked. 'It's far too hot for you to walk this far. You haven't even got a hat on. I would have come down to see you if you'd sent one of the servants to let me know you wanted company.'

Sylvia allowed Olive to help her, but from the look on her face it clearly made her uncomfortable.

'I needed to come to see for myself,' Sylvia said between puffs, her voice wheezy.

'See what?'

'Simi told me you've brought a woman up here from the river trail. A refugee. And a baby, she said.'

Olive cursed Simi under her breath. News travelled like wildfire amongst the servants in this place.

'That's right,' she said, trying to keep her voice steady, 'But you won't be able to see them, I'm afraid. They're sleeping right now.'

'You'll need to get in touch with her family if you can,'

said Sylvia, leaning heavily on Olive's arm as she took a step. 'They will need to know where she is and that she's ill. They might even come and collect her.'

Olive felt a wave of irritation at Sylvia's words.

'All in good time, Ma,' she said. 'We don't know who her family are, and she's delirious at the moment. She hasn't even been able to tell us her own name.'

They'd reached the veranda now and once they were at the top of the steps, Sylvia flopped straight into one of the basket chairs, her stick clattering to the floor.

'Are you alright?' asked Olive, 'I'll get you some lemonade.'

How typical of Sylvia to poke her nose in where it wasn't wanted, Olive mused as she went through to the kitchen. But still, the old woman was lonely down in that bungalow and she did look extremely ill. Her lips were a purply blue colour and Olive had never seen her face looking quite as red before.

When Olive returned with the lemonade, Sylvia was drawing on her inhaler, squeezing the black rubber pump vigorously and taking great gulps.

'Are you alright? Is it an asthma attack?' Olive asked, alarmed. She'd witnessed Sylvia's attacks before, when she'd wheezed and struggled for breath, it had terrified Olive.

'Just a mild one,' said Sylvia, sipping the lemonade that Olive offered. Then she put the glass down decisively and said, 'I'm feeling a bit better now. I'd like to see your refugee and her baby.'

'Like I said, Ma. They are sleeping at the moment. It wouldn't be fair to disturb them. Perhaps later on?'

Sylvia huffed but didn't move.

'Have you found her address yet, so you can get in touch with her family?' she said after a pause.

Olive shook her head, not really understanding why she was doing it.

'I'm not sure she has any papers with her,' she said evasively, looking down at the floorboards, not wanting to meet her mother-in-law's eye. 'She looks as though she lost most of her belongings along the way. She only has what she stands up in. No shoes even.'

Part of the reason she'd lied, she told herself, was to put Sylvia off the scent. What business was it of hers anyway? Why did she have to interfere? But Olive knew there was something else in the back of her own mind that she wasn't yet ready to acknowledge.

They sat for a time in silence, watching the brightly coloured birds in the trees at the edge of the flowerbeds, a gardener watering the roses with a metal can, the pickers making their slow progress along the lines of tea bushes on the hill opposite. Then Sylvia said,

'I suppose I'd better start making my way back to the bungalow now, but I'd like to see her. When she wakes up.'

'Of course, Ma. But as I said, she was in a very bad way when we brought her up. I don't know how long it's going to take. Would you like me to help you down to the bungalow?'

Sylvia agreed, so Olive took her arm and they walked as slowly as it was humanly possible to walk, along the garden path and down the hill to the bottom of the garden where the bungalow stood behind a small spinney overlooking the tea gardens beyond.

'There's no need to come in,' said Sylvia stiffly as they reached the door. 'I can manage from here.'

Olive was glad that she didn't have to stay any longer than necessary, but when Sylvia opened her door to go inside she saw the reason she'd not been invited in. The room was in a state. Books piled everywhere, ashtrays overflowing on the coffee table, even an empty bottle of Scotch on its side on the floor.

'I thought you'd given up smoking,' she couldn't resist saying. 'It's so bad for your asthma.'

Sylvia turned round sharply then, her face redder than ever.

'I'd thank you to mind your own business, Olive Percival,' she snapped. 'My health is my own concern. And if the Lord sees fit to take me, that's *his* concern, not yours.'

With that she went inside and slammed the door. Olive stood smarting on the threshold.

'The hypocrisy of the woman!' she muttered to herself as she made her way back to the house.

When Henry returned from the river that evening, exhaustion etched on all his features, he sunk into a chair and told Olive that they'd transported another twenty-five refugees across the river on the elephants that afternoon.

'Some of them are so thin, Olive. It's hard to imagine what they must have been through to get to the river crossing.'

Then he asked after Betty, though of course he didn't know her name. He referred to her as 'our guest.'

'Oh, she hasn't really woken at all. She must be so tired after that ordeal.'

'But she has malaria too. Have you given her quinine? There's some in the bathroom cupboard.'

'Not yet,' replied Olive. 'She hasn't woken up, but I will tomorrow.'

'We might want to think about getting Doctor Stone out from Ledo if this carries on.'

'Oh, I don't think that will be necessary. It's only a touch of malaria, surely. We've all had it and survived.'

'Yes, but we hadn't just walked barefoot over mountains for three weeks, Olive. In her weakened state it could really take hold.'

'Well, let's give it a couple of days. Once she's rested she might feel better.'

That night, Olive brought the baby into the bedroom in his drawer to sleep beside the bed.

'Shouldn't he be with his mother?' Henry asked, looking up from his book.

'His mother's far too ill to look after him. It will only be for a couple of nights, darling. He's such a little dear. I couldn't leave him on his own in the spare room.'

'All right, but if he cries, you'll have to see to him.'

But he didn't cry. He slept peacefully all night and was still asleep when Henry got up in the morning.

'I need to drop in at the factory, then I'll take Hannibal down to the river again. There weren't so many people yesterday, I think it's almost over for now, but there might be one or two coming through that need help to cross the river. Are you going to come down with me?'

Olive shook her head. 'I can't. I need to look after our guests,' she said.

'Of course. Oh, and don't forget the quinine,' he said, kissing her as he headed outside to collect Hannibal.

Olive took the baby down to the kitchen, prepared a bottle and fed him his milk, sitting on the veranda looking out over the garden, watching the sun climb in the sky and burn off the morning mists. As she held him to her, a sense of peace and well-being stole over her. This was what she'd longed for the whole of her married life. And here it was suddenly, presented to her like a gift from heaven. It was almost as if fate had decreed that Betty and the baby should have come into her life as they had.

When the baby had finished his milk, she took him up to the bedroom to sleep, then looked in on his mother.

Betty was in a serious state. Her skin was so pale it was virtually translucent, sweat was pouring off her and she was twisting in the bed, muttering incomprehensible words to herself. A pang of guilt went through Olive and she rushed to the bathroom to fetch the quinine. She sat beside Betty, tried to sit her up and feed her the tablets, but each time she touched her, Betty pushed her away. In the end, Olive force the tablets into Betty's mouth and managed to get her to sip some water. Then she let her lie back on the pillows while she sponged her down. Once Betty had stopped thrashing around, Olive left her alone to rest.

The same pattern repeated itself for three days and three nights. Sometimes Olive managed to get Betty to take the quinine, at others, she couldn't force it between her teeth. On a couple of occasions, when Olive checked in on Betty later, she'd regurgitated the tablets, and they lay in a pool of saliva on the sheet.

Sylvia came up to the house again on the third day. 'Can I see your refugee now? Is she getting better?'

Olive shook her head. 'She's worse if anything. She's unconscious.'

'You should really get a doctor to her. Get Henry to call Doc Stone when he comes home.'

'Alright,' said Olive reluctantly. But thinking about Sylvia's words afterwards, she realised that she should do that, and that she regretted giving Betty the quinine far too late. Whatever her motives, did she really want the death of a young woman on her conscience? Her heart was twisting with guilt when she heard Hannibal's footfalls on the front path. She vowed to speak to Henry right away about calling Doctor Stone. Then she went up to check on Betty.

As soon as she entered the bedroom she knew something was very wrong. There was a deathly stillness about the room that hadn't been there before. Betty was lying motionless on the bed. Her mouth and eyes were open, and a line of saliva was dribbling from her mouth onto the pillow.

Olive felt Betty's forehead and drew back her hand in shock. It was cold to the touch. Gritting her teeth, she bent down and listened to Betty's chest. There was no sign of a heartbeat. Along with the shock, Olive felt tears of guilt and pity pricking her eyes, but she thought quickly. She picked up the journal and letter and rushed through to her bedroom. She pushed them under the lining of her underwear drawer then slammed it shut and hurried downstairs.

'Henry, Henry, come quickly,' she said, rushing out of the front door and across the veranda.

Henry was getting down from Hannibal, and the mahout was preparing to lead him away.

'It's the girl... the woman. I think she's...'

'Oh my God.'

Henry took the stairs two at a time and ran into the bedroom. He knelt beside the bed. Olive watched him feeling for Betty's pulse. He knew a bit of basic first aid in order to help the tea planters when there was no doctor available. He looked back up at Olive and shook his head.

THE NEXT DAY, after the worst of the heat had gone out of the sun, Henry and Olive stood side by side at the grave under the banyan tree in the corner of the garden. Two of the workers had dug it in the early morning. They'd carried the woman's body down from the bedroom wrapped in a sheet. Sylvia had wanted to come, but this morning her chest had been so bad she'd decided to stay in bed.

Henry had telephoned the district officer in Ledo and reported the death. He was unable to supply name, date of birth or any details. The man he dealt with didn't sound surprised.

'Many, many people have died walking over those mountains. Most of them have gone unreported. Many of them have lost their IDs, too. This isn't unusual at all.'

'She had a baby,' said Henry. 'My wife is looking after him at the moment. We don't know his name either I'm afraid.'

'Many, many poor children have been orphaned by this war,' said the man. 'You can take him to the nuns at Margherita. They are taking in orphans. That would be the best thing to do for him. There is no state provision for refugee orphans at present.'

'Can't we wait a bit? He is so thin, Henry,' said Olive when he told her what the man had said. 'He's doing so well here. I could look after him while he recovers from his ordeal, and we can take him down to the convent next time we go down to Margherita.'

Henry had been reluctant, but Olive had pleaded with him, and in the end, he'd agreed to the baby staying for a couple of weeks. Olive was hoping that in that time she could persuade Henry that the baby must stay longer, perhaps forever.

Now, standing by the graveside, Olive felt her cheeks wet with tears. She stared down at the body in the grave wrapped in a sheet as she listened to the prayers Henry was reading from the book of common prayer he kept in the house. She wondered again what had led Betty to walk over those mountains, and how she'd come to have a half-Burmese baby. She supposed she'd never know the answers to those questions. She tried to wipe her tears away, but still they kept on falling. Were they tears of guilt at the part she'd played in this poor woman's death, or were they tears of genuine sadness for the loss of a young life in such tragic circumstances. Olive tried her best to be honest with herself, but she really couldn't tell.

EDITH

Dapha River Tea Plantation, Assam, 1980

EDITH SAT opposite Richard Edwards at the table on the veranda overlooking the garden. The sun was at its height and the cloudless sky a startling bright blue. The fans whirred round above them, hardly making an impression on the stifling noonday heat. Also at the table was Simi, the cleaning lady. Edith had explained to Richard how Simi had reacted to the sight of Betty's journal and how she'd tried to ask her about it, but that the old lady appeared too frightened to speak. He'd agreed to invite Simi to lunch at the house and to see if he could set her at ease enough to speak about it in her own language.

But now Simi sat stiffly in the cane chair, her back ramrod straight, staring down at the table, hardly meeting anyone's eye. She'd put on a beautiful saree of magenta and scarlet, with a gold brocaded sash for the occasion, and lined her eyes with kohl. Edith felt decidedly under dressed in the old trousers and shirt she'd worn to travel to Assam.

'You've been at the plantation a long time, haven't you, Simi?' Richard began gently.

'Oh yes, sir. More than forty years. I came as a teenager.'

'So you knew Mr and Mrs Percival well?'

'Yes. Very well.'

'And their son?'

She paused. 'Their *adopted* son, yes. Alex. A very nice boy.'

'And old Mrs Percival, you knew her too?'

'Oh yes, sir. Mrs Sylvia. I was her ayah. I looked after her when she lived at the big house, and then when she moved down to the bungalow when young Mr Percival got married.'

'And you were close?'

She nodded. 'She was a kind lady,' she said. 'Although she sometimes had a bad temper.'

'You know that Mrs Mayhew here is the sister of the young lady who came here as a refugee and died on the plantation, don't you?'

She nodded, but kept her eyes cast downwards. She seemed afraid to look at Edith.

'She's been reading the journal we found in the bungalow when it was renovated.'

Simi visibly froze. She didn't reply or move a muscle. Richard didn't react to this. He simply went on smoothly in Assamese. After Simi had spoken, he translated for Edith.

'What do you know about that journal, Simi? Mrs Mayhew here has been desperate to know what happened to her sister for nearly forty years. The journal has told her a lot, but not quite everything. It would really help her if you could tell us what you know about what happened back then.'

There was a long pause while Simi looked down at her

lap, picking at a loose thread on her saree, then finally she looked up and spoke.

'She died up at the house, the refugee lady. Of malaria. She'd been here for several days. They buried her the morning after she died. Old Mrs Percival was very ill that day, so she couldn't go to the burial. That afternoon, I was sitting with her in the bungalow. She seemed to be getting worse. She was struggling to breathe. From her bedroom window you could just about see the compound where the gardeners kept their tools and had their bonfires. That day they had lit a small fire to burn some roots.

'Suddenly young Mrs Percival, memsahib Olive, came into the compound. It was a shock to see her. She'd never been in there before, but she was carrying something. Some papers. She looked around as if to check no one was watching, then she threw the papers onto the fire. It wasn't burning very quickly, and she was looking round for a stick to poke it with I think, but one of the gardeners came into the compound. She turned around and ran away.

'Old Mrs Percival got straight up out of bed. She grabbed her stick. She was heaving and puffing. She was very, very ill. I tried to stop her, but she pushed me away and wouldn't listen. She went straight out of the bungalow to where the fire was burning. She gathered up the things that young Mrs Percival had thrown on there and she brought them inside. They were singed by the flames. She shoved them into her bedroom cupboard and never said anything about them to me.

'Going outside in a hurry like that when she was ill must have been too much for her. That same evening she had a heart attack and died. Mr Percival shut the bungalow up when her body was taken up to the big house and I wasn't allowed to set foot in there again. I just assumed that Mr

Percival would have gone through her things and found the papers. In time, I forgot all about them. I didn't connect them with the refugee lady. It did not cross my mind that young Mrs Percival would have tried to hide that lady's identity. It was only when the bungalow was renovated and the papers were taken out of the cupboard that the truth came out. And it made sense then, how Mrs Percival held that child to her as if he was her own. I realised then that if I'd spoken to Mr Henry about those papers, I could have changed things for Mr Alexander. And for the poor lady's family. I feel so guilty I can hardly face this lady, Mrs Mayhew, now. It is all my fault.'

When Richard translated Simi's word to Edith, she leaned forward and put her hand on Simi's.

'Please don't worry, Simi,' she said, tears in her own eyes now. 'It's really not your fault. I don't blame you at all. I'm very grateful that you've spoken out now. I'm just relieved to have found out the truth.'

A MONTH LATER, Edith waited in the lobby of the Strand Hotel in Rangoon. She was a bundle of nerves and could hardly sit still. Dressed in her best clothes; a matching blue linen skirt and top, she'd even put makeup on for the occasion. She sat in one of the cane chairs to the side of the reception area. The hotel had seen better days, the paintwork was chipped, the walls a dull magnolia. There was a Formica counter in the reception area in front of which stood a restless queue of disgruntled European tourists. The whole place felt institutional and dull. Not quite the gracious colonial building she'd been expecting.

She was early for her appointment, but she wanted to

compose herself before he arrived. She was waiting to meet her nephew, Alexander Percival, for the first time and she had no idea what he looked like. Richard Edwards had given her the name of Alexander's lawyers in Rangoon. Once Edith had arrived back in Calcutta from her trip to Assam, she'd written to the Rangoon lawyers, explaining some of the highly unusual circumstances, saying that she thought she was Alexander's aunt and asking them to pass on her letter to him. Alexander had written back within days, expressing delight at finally being able to find out something about his birth mother. All he'd known was that his mother had been fleeing on foot from Burma to Assam and had died at the plantation. He'd tried many times to find more information about her but with no success.

They agreed that Edith would come to Rangoon and that they would meet at the Strand Hotel. It hadn't been easy for Edith to get a visa; travel in Burma was highly restricted. When she'd arrived she'd had to check in with Tourist Burma, the government run tourist board. She had to give details of where she would be during each of the seven days on her visa. She got the distinct impression that she'd be watched carefully throughout her stay.

Now, sitting in the lobby of The Strand, watching the revolving glass doors for any sign of Alexander, she let her mind wander back over the past few weeks. When she'd returned to the Tea Planter's Club after her trip to Assam, she'd reappraised her situation. The journey had given her the time and space to think about what she really wanted for the future. Through it, she'd gained a fresh perspective. Now she knew for certain that she didn't want to give up the hotel. It was her life; where all her memories had been made and where she was at her happiest. So, she'd arranged a meeting with Clover International and told them that she was withdrawing from the deal.

'That's very disappointing, Mrs Mayhew. We really thought we could turn this place around with some sensitive refurbishment,' the chief executive had told her.

'Well, perhaps I might be able to do that myself now,' she'd replied.

She'd walked around the old place, appreciating afresh the graceful lines of the building, the panelled walls, the sweeping staircase, the chandeliers, and the memorabilia from more leisurely times. The elegant decor of the bungalow at the plantation had given her some ideas as to how she might renovate the guest rooms. She wanted to give them the added luxury and comfort that modern guests expect whilst preserving the olde-worlde charm that the Clover people had been so taken with. She was brimming with ideas as to how to go about it and she'd already spoken to the bank about a loan. But she knew she wouldn't be able to settle to the task of refurbishing the hotel before she'd made the journey to Rangoon.

So, she'd flown there from Dum Dum airport in Calcutta, armed with two copies of Betty's journal and several photographs of Betty. She realised that the journal contained some revelations that might be difficult or embarrassing to read, but she felt that she owed the two people who would read them the truth after all these years of not knowing. One copy was for Alexander and the other for the person she'd carried in her heart for all those years, but had given up all hope of ever seeing again.

She'd written to Robert as soon as she'd got home to the Tea Planter's Club. She had no idea of his address now, but she guessed if she wrote to him c/o the Irrawaddy Steamship Company, the letter would get to him somehow.

It was a difficult letter to write, but she'd done it as tactfully as she could, explaining the circumstances of Betty's death and along the way that Betty had fallen in love with a Burmese dissident and had a baby by him. Once she'd committed it to the post she was on tenterhooks for days wondering how Robert would have taken the news, agonising over whether she'd been right to tell him what she had the very first time she'd been in touch. But Robert had written back straight away, putting her mind at rest.

My Dearest Edith,

It is hard to put into words the effect your letter has had on me. I was shocked by some of the things you told me, but it has released me from a dreadful burden I've mistakenly carried around with me for almost forty years. I've felt guilty all this time for what happened between the two of us when I visited in 1942. Guilty, and also sad that we had to give it all up and sacrifice our love through misplaced loyalty. Now I know that there was no need for that guilt. I feel as if a huge weight has been lifted from my shoulders.

I never married again, Edith. Not because of my loyalty to Betty, or because I thought she might come back one day, but because of you. I could never find anyone who matched up to you, or who suited me as well. It is wonderful to hear that you are coming to Rangoon. I would love to see you. And I would love to come to Calcutta to the Tea Planter's Club again if you will permit me. I have missed that old place along with everything and everyone else I lost during the war.

Let me know when you arrive and where you'll be staying,

Your ever loving,

Robert.

The letter had satisfied Edith that she was right to have told him news of Betty, but it had made her impatient to see Robert as soon as she could. Even though she'd waited almost four decades, she found the next few weeks while her travel arrangements were sorted out hard to bear. When she arrived in Rangoon, she was tempted to call Robert straight away, but she forced herself to hold back. She needed to see Alexander first.

As she sat musing over the amazing events that had brought her this far, she noticed a striking looking Burmese man enter the hotel. He was tall and slender, dressed in a navy checked longyi and white shirt, he moved gracefully across the lobby. Something about the way he carried himself told her instantly that this was Ye Win's son. She stood up and approached him. When he noticed her walking towards him he rushed forward and held out his hand; 'Mrs Mayhew? Edith?'

'Alexander?' she said tentatively, feeling a great lump in her throat as he shook her hand. They both stood there beaming into each other's eyes. His face was fine with chiselled cheekbones and dark eyes framed by long lashes. But there was something of Betty in him too; his fine mouth, and the way his eyes danced with pleasure.

'Let's go to the bar, shall we? We've got so much to talk about.'

'Yes, let's,' she replied, her nerves dissipating. She allowed him to usher her across the lobby and through the double doors into the bar, where liveried barmen served behind a polished mahogany counter. The room had a gloomy feel, panelled in dark wood and full of heavy furniture. Cigar smoke and alcohol fumes filled the air. Alexander found her a leather armchair in the window, behind some potted palms.

'What would you like? A Strand Sour?'

'That sounds perfect,' she smiled, not knowing what on earth was in it, but not caring either.

He brought the drinks and sat in the armchair opposite Edith and they spoke for a couple of hours. Edith hardly noticed the time flying by.

'It's difficult to describe what it meant to me when I read your letter,' he said. 'I've always wanted to find out about my parents. Over the years I've tried so hard, and suddenly the information came to me out of the blue. I can't thank you enough for getting in touch.'

'It's the least I could do. As soon as I found out about you, I wanted to meet you.'

He leaned forward and looked straight into her eyes. She noticed the intensity of his gaze, it was just as Betty had described Ye Win's eyes.

'One thing is troubling me though,' he said. 'How can I be sure that Betty was my mother?'

'Because you arrived at the plantation at Dapha with her,' said Edith. 'Is there any doubt about that?'

'I suppose not,' he said, taking a sip of his drink. 'It's just that I wish I had some proof. Something physical so I could be sure.'

Edith thought for a moment, sipping her own drink which tasted very alcoholic and very bitter. Then she remembered something from Betty's journal.

'Did you have a teddy bear when you were young?' she asked.

His face lit up in a dazzling smile. 'Yes. Yes. I called him Rusty. He was ginger and had a tartan ribbon around his neck. I took him everywhere.'

'So that's your proof then!' Edith answered, beaming back at him. 'Betty mentioned him in her journal. He'd been dropped on one of the camps on the path through the mountains by the RAF. They'd airlifted in a sack of toys along with the food parcels.'

'How amazing. I didn't realise he had such history,' said Alexander. 'He belongs to my son now.'

'You have a son? How marvellous. How old is he?'

'He's just three. I have a baby daughter too. I was married five years ago. My wife, Maya, is a teacher. If only I'd known you then, I could have invited you. You must come to my home and meet my family while you're here in Rangoon.'

'I'd love that. And you must all come and visit me in Calcutta. I have plenty of room.'

'That would be fantastic. If we can get permission to leave Burma. It might not be easy. You know I went to University in Calcutta, so I know it well.'

'Did you ever come to the Tea Planter's Club?' Edith asked. He shook his head.

'I don't recall going there. But I used to go to Bunder Street sometimes. There are some cheap restaurants there so it's popular with students.'

'What was it like, growing up on the plantation?' Edith asked after a pause.

'Good in some ways, not so good in others. My father, Henry, was a wonderful, patient man. He used to take me around the plantation on his elephant, Hannibal. Who wouldn't adore that sort of childhood? But Mother, Olive, she seemed to often struggle, even with the simpler things in life. Seemed to have no real idea how to bring up a child. She was a difficult woman in lots of ways, and I always got the feeling I wasn't quite what she wanted, that she would have preferred a white child. I think she was glad to pack me off to boarding school as soon as I was old enough.'

'How very sad,' said Edith.

'Yes,' he said, 'but a long time ago. Let me tell you, I was amazed to find out that my birth father was an indepen-

dence leader. One of the Thirty Comrades. I was fascinated
by the independence movement when I first came to Burma
in my twenties and read a lot about it. They made a dreadful
error aligning themselves with the Japanese, but at least
they saw the light and switched sides. Sadly, my father died
fighting the British before that happened.'

'It's an incredible story,' agreed Edith.

'You know, I've always had a passion for justice. Perhaps
I get it from him.'

'What do you do for a living?' she asked.

'I'm a lawyer,' he said. 'Just like him. I specialise in
human rights and often represent political prisoners and
protesters.'

'How interesting that you had that calling, even though
you had no idea that Ye Win was your father!' said Edith.
'What brought you to Burma though?'

'Curiosity, and wanting to know about my roots. I knew I
was half-Burmese and I was desperate to find out more
about the country.'

Then he asked if she had any photographs of Betty.
When Edith produced them, he stared at each one for a
long time, his eyes becoming moist with tears. She'd
brought several with her; a couple of Betty as a child, a
portrait of her on her wedding day, and one that
Alexander stared at for a long time. It was a photograph of
Betty standing in front of the Tea Planter's Club, with a
slightly haughty expression on her face. Her blonde hair
was beautifully coiffed and she was wearing a blue spotted
dress.

'I think that might have been on my own wedding day,'
said Edith. 'I seem to remember her wearing that dress.'

'She was very beautiful, wasn't she?'

'She was. Would you like to keep that photograph?'

'I would,' he said, rewarding Edith with one of his extraordinary smiles. 'How very kind of you.'

They talked on until the bar was filling up for the evening rush.

'I've brought a copy of my sister's journal for you,' said Edith, as Alexander prepared to leave. She dipped into her bag and, finding the copy, she handed it to him.

'As I said, some of it might be difficult to read, but I think you need to know the truth, warts and all. You'll see how strong she was walking over those mountains alone. She was determined to bring you to safety.'

He took it with tears in his eyes.

'Thank you, Edith. I can't tell you how much this means to me,' he said.

JUST BEFORE SUNSET, Edith took a taxi from the Strand Hotel to the base of the Shwedagon Pagoda. As she was driven up Shwedagon Pagoda Road, she looked out at the palatial houses, some of them neglected and shabby now, overtaken by the voracious jungle, and she wondered where Betty's house had stood. The taxi dropped her at the bottom of the covered staircase that led to the pagoda. She walked up between the stalls selling miniature pagodas, tiny Buddhas, postcards and other knickknacks for tourists. Higher up there were others selling lotus blossom and incense for the faithful to offer at the temple. The steps were crowded and noisy, many people were heading up to see the sunset, and she walked amongst the Burmese faithful, tourists and maroon-clad monks breathing in exotic smells of spices, candle smoke and incense.

As she walked, her whole body was tingling with a

mixture of nerves and excitement. She remembered how Betty had walked up these steps many times with papers from Robert's briefcase and she thought about Alexander too, and how amazing it was that that intelligent, handsome man was the result of such an intense but ill-fated love affair. And she thought about Robert, about the precious moments they had shared in Calcutta, before it was snatched away from them.

As she reached the top of the steps, she gasped as she looked up at the shining stupa, towering above her, lit up by the setting sun, casting a golden glow all around. The whole platform around its base was crowded with elaborately carved and decorated shrines, illuminated by an abundance of flickering candles. She stood for a moment, absorbing the magical atmosphere and watching the rapidly setting sun light up the sky with streaks of gold and purple. And as she stood there, she felt his hand touch her shoulder, and she turned and looked into his face. A face that, like her own, was lined and etched with the cares of a lifetime, but his smile and the look in those dark eyes was the just the same.

'Robert,' she said, smiling up into his eyes and taking his hand.

I HOPE you enjoyed reading *The Tea Planter's Club* as much as I loved writing it.

Would you like to read *A Daughter's Promise*? (a captivating story of love and loss set in World War 2 Burma).

Sign up to my newsletter on www.annbennettauthor.com for news, updates, giveaways and freebies. You can also follow me on Facebook for information and previews of future books.

Please turn over to read an excerpt from *A Daughter's Promise*.

EXCERPT FROM A DAUGHTER'S PROMISE

CHAPTER 1

Grace
Devon, July 2015

When Grace ripped open the parcel and glimpsed what was inside, she had to sit still for several minutes to recover from the shock. Finally, with trembling fingers she drew the three sheets of paper out of the huge cardboard envelope and laid them out side-by-side on the dining room table. Then she sat down in front of them, just staring at them, letting her mind flood with long suppressed memories.

She'd been humming along to a Beethoven concerto on the radio, chopping onions for supper, when the delivery driver had knocked. She'd rushed to the door wiping her hands on her apron. Now, as she sat staring at the artwork on the table in front of her, she forgot all about the frying pan simmering on the stove, about the half-peeled potatoes in the sink, the chicken defrosting on the worktop.

'Jack,' she murmured.

Jack's handiwork was visible in every brushstroke of the watercolour of the rose-covered cottage. It was there too in the pencil drawing of a busy street of shop-houses with Chinese roofs. The last piece puzzled her the most though; a roughly sketched map drawn in charcoal on grubby brown paper. From the way the paper was worn and creased she could tell it had been folded many times.

Grace groped for her reading glasses on the chain around her neck, and perching them on her nose, leaned forward and peered at the lines and shapes of the plan, trying to make out what they represented. As she looked closer she realised that some things were labelled in Jack's flowing hand in tiny letters: guardhouse: cookhouse: sleeping huts: cemetery. Beside a crudely drawn tree near the edge of the cemetery he'd marked a cross.

Dread washed over Grace as she made the connection. This must be something from Jack's time as a prisoner of war in Burma. It was a time she knew virtually nothing about, but that had hung over their marriage like a dark, silent cloud.

She opened the letter that had dropped out when she'd ripped the package open. She recognised the flamboyant writing instantly.

Dear Mrs Summers,

I hope you are keeping well. The gallery received these items belonging to your late husband from a Mr and Mrs Bell with whom he lodged in Oxfordshire for a few months in the early eighties. The Bells were clearing their attic with a view to selling their house and found these works in the back of a cupboard. They initially approached the gallery to have them valued, realising that some of Jack's paintings have recently changed hands for a considerable sum. However, we advised that these particular works had little value, so were asked to pass them on to you.

Do drop in and visit us next time you are up in London and if

you would like to discuss the sale of any more of your husband's
works we would be only too happy to help.

Yours ever,

Luke Chapman.

Closing her eyes, Grace tried to cast her mind back to the early eighties. Had she ever met a Mr and Mrs Bell? Had Jack ever mentioned them? She frowned with the effort of remembering. Jack had travelled around so much during those years. A few months here, a year or two there, working on and off, getting commissions to paint from time to time; houses, portraits, horses and pets. Grace sighed, remembering the hope in his voice on the phone when he used to call her with news.

'I've got a new job, Gracie. This one's going to last, I can feel it in my bones. I'll be able to send some money for you and Louise next month, I promise.'

She vaguely remembered him working as a caretaker at a school in Oxfordshire, and getting a commission to paint a big country house for Lord someone or other. But the details were scanty. She knew it hadn't lasted long and he'd moved on to... was it to somewhere in Wales? Shropshire? Grace sighed and shook her head. It was so hard to remember.

She frowned and peered at the map again. It must be a plan of one of the prison camps in Burma that Jack had been in. There was no name, and even if there had been, it wouldn't mean anything to her.

Then, laying the map aside, Grace turned back to the sketch of the oriental street scene. She picked it up and stared at it. It wasn't in Jack's usual style. It showed a row of shop-houses on a busy street. There were food stalls and vendors on the pavement, baskets of fruit and fish on display. People in conical hats going to and fro on bicycles and rickshaws, some pushing hand carts, others carrying baskets on poles across their shoulders.

Right in the centre of the picture, beside the front door of one of the shop-houses stood a young woman. She was the only still figure in a sea of movement. Long black hair framed her slender face and she was barefoot, dressed in a plain saree and short-sleeved blouse. She was looking directly out of the picture, with a solemn face and large, soulful eyes.

Grace turned the picture over. On the back was written: Marisa, Petaling Street, Kuala Lumpur, 1941. Puzzled, she looked at the drawing again. She knew Jack had been stationed in Kuala Lumpur before the Japanese invaded Malaya. Perhaps he'd drawn this then? But she quickly realised he couldn't possibly have done. The paper was smooth and well preserved. It didn't look like something Jack had carried with him through the battles of the Malaya campaign and for three and a half years moving from camp to camp as a prisoner of war. He must have held this scene in his memory and drawn the picture when he was living in Oxfordshire in the early 1980s.

Who was the girl with the beautiful eyes? Was her name Marisa? A prickle of something unsettling entered her mind. Was it jealousy? There was so much about Jack's past she had no idea about. And now she'd never know. Why should it matter to her now anyway?

Grace glanced across the room at the photographs on the windowsill. Her eyes skated over the one of Jack sitting on Brighton beach in a suit, smoking a cigarette, while Louise as a toddler with her shock of white hair played beside him with a bucket and spade. Beside it stood the photo taken on their wedding day. She hadn't looked at it, not properly at least, for a long time. There she was, grinning from ear to ear, dressed in her best suit and hat, clinging to Jack's arm, while Jack, smiling broadly too, looked urbane in a grey three-piece suit. Their joy and excitement radiated from the picture. Looking at it now she could still feel that buzz herself all these years later, despite everything that had followed.

She sat for a few minutes longer, musing about Jack. She usually stopped herself remembering, trying to avoid reliving the pain. But seeing these fresh, skilfully crafted pictures had brought the old Jack back with startling clarity. She allowed her mind to wander back in time as she hadn't for a long time. She thought about the Jack she'd first met in the hospital in 1945, a stick of a man with hollow cheeks from his years of starvation and sallow skin from exposure to the tropical sun. Grace hadn't seen those things about him though; it was the energy and intelligence in his dark brooding eyes that had first drawn her to him.

She went to the sideboard and took a small black box out of the top drawer. She opened it and took out the star-shaped medal inside. She ran the silk ribbon through her fingers and stared at the embossed crown and lettering on the medal itself. Jack's Burma Star. She'd kept it hidden away all these years and just looking at it brought back a flood of different emotions.

She was jolted from her reverie by the smell of burning. She put the medal back in the drawer, and leaving the pictures and the memories she dashed back into the kitchen.

'Sod it!'

The pan was smoking. She grabbed the handle with a tea towel and took it off the stove, plunging it into the sink.

She could hear Eve's voice in her head even as she did it, 'Gran, are you quite sure you can still cope on your own?

Perhaps you should think about getting some more help in the house?'

'Of course I can cope,' she muttered out loud to herself now as the pan hissed and sizzled in the washing up water. 'I'm just a bit forgetful sometimes. And it's not old age, I'll have you know. It's just me. I've always been like that.'

She checked the clock above the sink. Eve would be arriving on the train from London in less than two hours. Grace had said she would collect her in the car from the station in Totnes. She glanced around the chaotic kitchen in a mild panic. She needed to hurry up and get that pot roast in the oven before she set off.

Eve

As the intercity train sped west along the sea wall at Dawlish, Eve stared out at the breakers crashing against the stones leaving foam in their wake. The sun was going down over the shimmering horizon and the summer sky was gradually losing its light. Another half hour or so and the journey would be over.

The further Eve got away from London the more she relaxed, contentment seeping into her mind, replacing the tension of recent weeks. It had always been the same, that feeling of peace stealing over her, the blessed relief of homecoming, ever since she'd been at university and living with Grace in the holidays. Now she was looking forward to spending the coming weeks with her grandmother. And yet there was a niggling feeling preventing her from fully relishing the prospect.

What would Grace have to say about the bombshell she was about to deliver? Eve wondered if she should have broken the news on the phone. She'd thought about it each time she'd called, but in the end she hadn't had the courage. This was something she needed to tackle in person. Phone calls were always difficult with her grandmother anyway. Grace viewed the telephone as a means of transmitting essential information, not for catching up on gossip. Her voice always took on that impatient tone, indicating that she was keen to finish the call, if there was nothing important to say.

Staring out at the changing seascape, Eve couldn't help remembering the tension of the last few weeks; the mounting feeling that she was losing control of her life. She thought back to the daily battle she'd had trying to remain in control of the overcrowded classroom, the constant bullying, the rowdy behaviour, the name calling, objects thrown across the room. She'd found herself weeping in the staff loo on many occasions, having to will herself to go back in there and face up to the rest of the day.

The final conversation with the head teacher a fortnight ago played back in her mind as the train rumbled through the last tunnels cut through the red Dawlish cliffs and turned inland.

'I don't think I'm cut out for this,' she'd admitted. The final straw had been when one of the Year 6 boys had stuck chewing gum on her chair, ruining her best skirt.

'Oh, I've heard that from so many young teachers, Eve. I know it's tough. This is an inner-city school. It was never going to be easy. But you'll make it. I know you will.'

'But I'm not sure if I want to. I need to have some time away. This isn't what I came into teaching for.'

He'd done his best to persuade her to stay. All the time he was speaking, though, telling her how valuable the work was, how she'd be missing out if she left, she couldn't help thinking it was because it would be difficult for him to find a replacement. There was nothing he could say to persuade her. She'd already made up her mind.

In the end he gave up and said, 'We're really going to miss you, Eve. It might not feel like it at the moment, but you've got a real talent for this. You should seriously reconsider when you've had some time away to think about it.'

But she'd had no qualms about her decision as she'd walked away from the school on the last day of term with her plastic crate of belongings, her heart soaring with a new sense of freedom.

Now she stared out at the scenery as the train moved away from the coast and raced through a patchwork of emerald fields, dotted with white farmhouses and the odd spinney. It was partly the situation with Josh that had brought about this desire to shake up her life, she reflected. They'd stopped communicating properly years ago. Probably even before they moved to London together and rented a flat. It had seemed like a natural step at the time – they'd been dating since they met in fresher's week.

It was a sign of how distant they'd become, that when Josh announced he'd got a job in New York, Eve wasn't surprised. He hadn't even told her he was going for an interview. Neither of them discussed the future during the last month they were together. It was implicit between them that his departure would bring something that had become routine and unexciting to a natural end.

When she went to the airport to see him off, he didn't suggest she should visit him, and she didn't ask to. They kissed briefly, like old friends, and she stood and waved as he went through passport control. Walking back through the terminal to the tube station, she'd felt emotionless. She hadn't even cried, but getting back to the empty flat she'd suddenly felt that it was no longer her home; that she needed to move on.

They were rumbling through Newton Abbot now. Only a few more minutes and she'd be there. She got out her mirror and ran a comb through her glossy black hair.

As the train rattled over the river Dart and began to pull into Totnes station, Eve got down her rucksack and holdall from the shelf, picked up her small case and handbag and made her way to the end of the carriage. Peering out of the window, she scanned the platform for Grace as the train juddered to a halt. There was no sign of her grandmother.

Eve sighed, but smiled to herself all the same. Grace was almost always late for everything.

'It's because I'm an incurable optimist,' she'd once said. 'I always think things will take less far time than they do.'

Eve stood on the station forecourt and watched as other passengers were collected, got into waiting taxis or walked away from the station. It wasn't until the rush of activity produced by the train's arrival had long died down that Grace's battered Rover appeared at the entrance.

'I'm so sorry I'm late, Eve darling. Bad traffic, I'm afraid.'

Eve stowed her bags on the back seat of the car and slid in next to her grandmother in the front. When she leaned over to peck Grace on the cheek, she detected the smell of smoke, mingled with the aroma of onions.

'Have you been cooking, Gran?'

'Of course. Chicken hotpot.'

'My favourite,' said Eve, resisting the urge to ask if anything had been burnt in the process.

'Well let's get home and eat. I expect you're starving,' said Grace jamming the car into gear and accelerating away.

Grace's driving was erratic; it always had been, but each time Eve visited her it seemed to get worse. At almost ninety,

Grace's eyesight was deteriorating. Eve had to make a conscious effort not to grip the dashboard whenever her grandmother drove her anywhere. She clamped her jaw shut now as Grace roared up the station ramp and pulled abruptly out into the traffic, causing a van to brake and blast its horn.

On the train Eve had rehearsed the words she planned to say to Grace. She'd wanted to get them over and done with on the car journey, but now it felt safer to wait until they got home. Instead, as they crawled through the late rush hour traffic and up the hill out of the town, she chatted about anything she could think of; the weather, the train journey, Grace's neighbours. After a few minutes though, she realised Grace's answers were monosyllabic. She looked over at her grandmother who was peering at the road ahead.

'Are you alright Gran? You seem very quiet.'

'I'm fine thank you.'

'Sure?'

After a short silence, Grace said, 'Well, it's just that I had a bit of a surprise today. It's made me think.'

'Surprise?'

'Yes. The gallery in London sent me some old drawings and paintings your grandfather did. I've never seen them before. It brought back old memories.'

Eve turned to look at her. In the darkness she could see that the old lady's eyes were glistening with tears.

'Oh Gran,' she said, squeezing her arm. 'You must show me them when we get back. I'd love to see them.'

'I think you'll find they are a bit different from the usual.'

The reply was uncharacteristically tight-lipped and Eve shot a surprised look at her grandmother. She was on the point of asking more but held back sensing that this would be venturing into dangerous waters.

They carried on in silence as darkness gathered. Grace swung off the main road and they were soon speeding through narrow lanes, the headlights lighting up high grass banks on either side. Eve concentrated on the road ahead, her right foot twitching on an imaginary brake pedal. At least it was dark and Grace should be able to see any approaching headlights in enough time to stop.

It had started to rain as Grace pulled off the lane and onto the unmade road that led to her home. The old stone Devon farmhouse came into view in the headlights, long and low and nestled into a hill for shelter from the Westerlies.

'Wretched weather,' Grace muttered. 'I wanted it to be nice for your stay.'

'I don't mind, Gran,' said Eve. 'I love the rain here. It's part of what makes it home. Proper Devon weather.'

The house felt comfortingly warm to Eve as they went inside. It was filled with the old familiar smells she remembered; polish, woodsmoke and cooking.

'I'll take my bags straight up to the bedroom, Gran.'

As she passed the dining room door she noticed the big brown envelope on the table.

'Grandad's pictures? Is it OK if I have a look?'

'Let's wait 'til after supper. I'd like to show you them properly and the food will be spoiled if we don't eat it now.'

Later, as they sat at the kitchen table finishing their meal, Eve finally summoned her courage. She took a deep breath.

'I've decided to have a break from teaching, Gran.'

She watched her grandmother's face, waiting for her reaction. Grace put down her fork and stared at Eve.

'What do you mean? Have you left your job?'

Eve nodded. 'I had to, Gran. It was unbearable. It was making me ill.'

Grace shot her a sceptical look. Eve had known that giving up on a career would go against the grain with Grace; her strong work ethic, her own ruthless self-discipline.

'But you'd only been there a few months.'

'It was two years, Gran! It started out badly and it was just getting worse.'

Grace was silent, pursing her lips. Eve sensed she was making an effort not to blurt out exactly what she was thinking. Grace herself had never quit her nursing career from the age of eighteen until retirement and had never even had a break between jobs other than when she'd had Eve's mother.

'You know, all jobs can get tough at times,' Grace said at last. 'You should have talked to me. I'm surprised you didn't.'

'I'd made up my mind, Gran. There wasn't any point discussing it.'

'I'm very surprised, Eve. You've always been so ... so conscientious. So different from your mother.'

Eve stared down at her empty plate. She didn't want to get into that conversation. The criticisms of her mother, the barbed comments about Louise's lack of direction, her 'flightiness' as Grace often termed it.

When Eve didn't respond Grace asked, 'So what are you going to do?'

'I'm not sure yet. I've got some ideas...'

'Why don't you look for a job down here? A village school might be more your cup of tea.'

Eve took a deep breath. 'Actually Gran, I thought I'd

travel for a bit. South East Asia probably. I could start out in Singapore. Visit Mum and Dad for a few days.'

'Well it would be nice for you to spend some time with them of course,' said Grace, her tone careful. 'But where else would you plan to go?'

'Well I thought I'd travel up through Malaysia and on into Thailand.'

'Oh, Evie darling,' said Grace leaning over and squeezing her hand on the table. Grace's hand felt cold and bony to the touch. 'Why can't you leave it alone?'

Eve swallowed. 'Leave what alone?' she said in a feeble voice, but she knew exactly what Grace was referring to.

'It won't do you any good, you know. It didn't when you went there before. You're never going to find what you're looking for.'

Eve stared at the three pieces of her grandfather's work that Grace had laid out on the dining table. They were each so unique they might have been drawn by three different people.

'He was really talented wasn't he Gran?' she murmured, her eyes on the sketch of the oriental street scene. 'What a shame that wasn't as well recognised during his lifetime.'

'I wonder if it would have made a difference,' murmured Grace. Eve glanced at her. Grace's eyes were far away. She could have been speaking to herself. Eve didn't ask what she meant but she could guess what Grace was thinking.

'I wish I'd known him,' Eve said suddenly. 'And my real father too. I sometimes lie awake at night, wondering about them both.'

To her surprise, she felt Grace's arms slip around her shoulders. Grace pulled her into a stiff embrace.

'There's no point dwelling on these things, Eve.'

'But Gran...'

'Now I know that's why you've planned your travels. To look for your real father. But you know, you have to be realistic about it.'

Eve felt a prickle of irritation.

'Of course that isn't the reason Gran,' she said. 'How could I possibly hope to even start looking? I don't even know which town he lives in, whether he's alive even.'

'Well I'm relieved you're thinking that way. When you said you were going to Thailand again I automatically assumed...'

'No. I've come to terms with all that now, Gran. It's just that...' she looked into her grandmother's eyes. It was always hard to explain her feelings to Grace.

'Go on. What were you going to say?'

'It's just that I feel drawn to the place. How could I not be? Half of me belongs there after all. Just look at me, Gran; I'm half Asian and proud of that fact. But I only know it as a tourist. I'd like to go back, on my own this time, just for a few weeks, to be able to get to know it, without all the baggage I was carrying around before.'

'Baggage? Whatever does that mean?'

'You know. When I went there with Josh.'

She meant the ill-fated trip to Thailand she and Josh had made three years ago. It had been the beginning of the end for their relationship. It had seemed a good idea at the time. She'd had the long summer holiday from school and he'd been between consulting jobs.

They'd stayed for a few days with her mother and father in Singapore at the start of the trip in their penthouse flat in

Raffles place. The apartment felt crowded and the atmosphere a little tense.

One evening her father had taken Josh out for a drink at his club and Eve and her mother had stayed at home. Eve had seized the opportunity over dinner.

'Mum, you know partly why I'm going to Thailand don't you?' She'd seen her mother's shoulders tense at her words.

'I've got a fair idea Eve,' Louise had said, sipping her wine.

'Well, if you've guessed, would you please tell me at least where you met my real father? Which town? A starting point at least.'

Louise shook her head and reached for her cigarettes.

'It's painful to speak about Eve.'

'Why painful?'

'I can't tell you,' she said, fumbling with the lighter. 'I don't want to talk about it.'

'But why? Don't you think I've got a right to know?'

'Look, you've never asked before,' Louise said, the discomfort plain in her voice. 'Why now all of a sudden? Hasn't Jim been a good father to you?'

'Of course he has. It isn't that. I've just got this urge to find out about my real father. My flesh and blood. I can't get away from it, Mum. Can't you understand that?'

But Louise had stayed tight-lipped and evasive. Eve could tell she was getting irritated, by the spot of red that appeared on each cheek and the way she drew deeply on her cigarette. In the end she snapped.

'Look, Eve, if you must know, I don't want to remember it. It was just someone I met. A one-night stand to be absolutely blunt. The whole trip was a disaster. It's just a bad memory.'

With that she got up from the table and went out onto

the balcony, staring out across the restless city, in a cloud of cigarette smoke, lost in thought.

Eve and Josh had left the next day on the night train to Bangkok. They'd spent three weeks backpacking around Thailand, arguing about where to stay, what to do, where to eat, when to move on. Eve's naïve hope of finding out where her father lived, tracking him down and meeting him had been cruelly dashed. She couldn't raise her spirits or summon any enthusiasm for the trip. Nor could she forgive her mother either for her silence. Not for a long time.

More recently she'd softened, though, wondering if it was partly her own fault for springing the subject out of the blue on Louise like that. Perhaps if she'd mentioned it in advance, written her a letter beforehand, maybe? Perhaps Louise would have reacted differently then?

'Don't you remember Gran? That trip was a bit of a disaster.' she said now to Grace. 'But please don't worry about that. I'm over all that now. I realised back then that I'm never going to find my real father.'

Grace patted her arm, 'I know it's hard, but I'm glad you've come to terms with it I must say.'

Eve's eyes strayed back to the table. She picked up the drawing that looked like a map and frowned, reading the labels.

Her grandmother pursed her lips. 'I've no idea why they sent that one to me,' she said. 'They should have just binned it. it's just some old sketch map.'

'This must be from Burma,' said Eve, examining the lines depicting a prison camp. 'From his time as a prisoner.'

Grace nodded and let out a sigh.

'This is why Mum went to Burma wasn't it? Before I was born? To find out about Grandad's time as a prisoner there?'

'That was part of the reason, yes. But your mother was

very headstrong in those days, Eve. It all went very wrong for her out there. It very nearly ended in complete disaster.'

'Do you know what happened exactly? She's never really talked about it to me.'

Grace sat down heavily on a chair and put her head in her hands. Her shoulders drooped and she seemed to crumple. She suddenly looked every one of her eighty nine years.

'I don't remember the details,' she said in a vague voice. 'I'm not sure I ever knew them fully. All I know is that she had to leave Burma.'

'Did she get to see the camp where Grandad was?'

Grace shrugged and shook her head. 'I don't know, Eve. We didn't really talk about that when she came home. I think she wanted to spare me the details. And anyway, she had other things on her mind by then.'

Later, as Eve lay awake in the unfamiliar quiet of the countryside, listening to the patter of summer rain on the sloping roof above her bed, she thought about her grandfather's sketch map of the prisoner of war camp. She pictured him, skin and bone and dressed in rags, sketching out the rough lines with a lump of charcoal from the camp fire, then folding the paper over and over and slipping it into his shorts. Why had he done that? Why had he brought it all the way back to England and kept it for years? Eve knew very little about what had happened to the prisoners of the Japanese during the war but she could imagine it would have been risky to have carried something like that around right under the noses of the guards.

She thought about the cross he'd drawn on the map beside a tree in the graveyard, wondering what it might have represented. It didn't look like the type of cross that might mark out a grave.

She lay back on her pillow wide awake and stared into

the darkness. But gradually the germ of an idea formed in her mind. She sat up, wide awake, her brain suddenly alive with plans. Perhaps she could go there, find the camp if it still existed, and see the place for herself? It wouldn't take much organisation to add Myanmar to her itinerary. It must be much easier to travel there now it had opened up to the world. It had got to be less problematic than when her mother had gone there in the eighties. She could visit the place where her grandfather had suffered, see if the cemetery was still there. For a few minutes she let her mind run away with the idea. She lay back on the pillow, trying to imagine the journey, where the camp might be, what it might look like now.

But then her thoughts turned to Louise and she sighed deeply, wondering how her mother would react to the plan.

ABOUT THE AUTHOR

Ann Bennett was born in Pury End, a small village in Northamptonshire in the UK and now lives in Surrey.

Her first book, *Bamboo Heart: A Daughter's Quest*, was inspired by her father's experience as a prisoner of war on the Thai-Burma Railway. *Bamboo Island: The Planter's Wife*, *A Daughter's Promise*, *Bamboo Road: The Homecoming*, and *The Amulet* are also about WWII in South East Asia. Together with *The Tea Planter's Club*, they form the Echoes of Empire collection. She has also written *The Lake Pavilion,* set in British India in the 1930s, *The Lake Palace*, set in India during the Burma Campaign of WWII, *The Lake Pagoda,* and *The Lake Villa*, both set in Indochina during WWII. Ann's other books, *The Runaway Sisters*, bestselling *The Orphan House*, *The Child Without a Home* and *The Forgotten Children* are published by Bookouture.

Ann is married with three grown up sons and a granddaughter and works as a lawyer.

For more details please visit www.annbennettauthor.com

PRAISE FOR ANN BENNETT

'A vivid account of a brutal period and a searing exploration of trauma, memory and loss.' The Lady magazine (on *Bamboo Island: The Planter's Wife*)

'[Laura] represents for the author a whole generation of people whose parents refused to talk about the war leaving a gulf in knowledge and understanding. Bennett is primarily interested in how this generation reacts and changes their perspectives once they have a deeper feeling for what their parents suffered. The trilogy .... is the culmination of one such woman's journey of discovery to understand more about her father's past.'

Raelee Chapman, Singapore Review of Books (on *Bamboo Heart: A Daughter's Quest*), which won the Fiction Published in Asia award (AsianBooksBlog, 2015) and was shortlisted for Best Fiction Title (Singapore Book Awards, 2016). Learn more about the author at: www.annbennettauthor.com

ACKNOWLEDGMENTS

Special thanks go to my friend and writing buddy Siobhan Daiko for her constant support and encouragement over the past decade. To Rafa and Xavier at Cover Kitchen for their wonderful cover design; to my sisters Mary Clunes, Kathy Taylor, Liz Kulbicki and Dot Rood for reading and commenting on early drafts; and to everyone who's supported me down the years by reading my books.

OTHER BOOKS BY ANN BENNETT

Printed in Great Britain
by Amazon